THEODOR FONTANE was born in the Prussian province of Brandenburg in 1819. After qualifying as a pharmacist, he made his living as a writer. From 1855 to 1859, he lived in London and worked as a freelance journalist and press agent for the Prussian embassy. While working as a war correspondent during the Franco-Prussian war of 1870–71 he was taken prisoner, but released after two months. His first novel, *Before the Storm*, was published when he was 58 and was followed by sixteen further novels, of which *Effi Briest*, *No Way Back* and *On Tangled Paths* are all published in Penguin Classics. He died in 1898.

HUGH RORRISON and HELEN CHAMBERS have both published extensively on German literature, and translated together the Penguin Classics translation of Fontane's *Effi Briest*.

THEODOR FONTANE

No Way Back

Translated from the German by HUGH RORRISON *and* HELEN CHAMBERS
with an afterword by HELEN CHAMBERS

PENGUIN BOOKS

PENGUIN CLASSICS

Published by the Penguin Group
Penguin Books Ltd, 80 Strand, London WC2R 0RL, England
Penguin Group (USA) Inc., 375 Hudson Street, New York, New York 10014, USA
Penguin Group (Canada), 90 Eglinton Avenue East, Suite 700, Toronto, Ontario, Canada M4P 2Y3
(a division of Pearson Penguin Canada Inc.)
Penguin Ireland, 25 St Stephen's Green, Dublin 2, Ireland (a division of Penguin Books Ltd)
Penguin Group (Australia), 707 Collins Street, Melbourne, Victoria 3008, Australia
(a division of Pearson Australia Group Pty Ltd)
Penguin Books India Pvt Ltd, 11 Community Centre, Panchsheel Park, New Delhi – 110 017, India
Penguin Group (NZ), 67 Apollo Drive, Rosedale, Auckland 0632, New Zealand
(a division of Pearson New Zealand Ltd)
Penguin Books (South Africa) (Pty) Ltd, Block D, Rosebank Office Park,
181 Jan Smutts Avenue, Parktown North, Gauteng 2193, South Africa

Penguin Books Ltd, Registered Offices: 80 Strand, London WC2R 0RL, England

www.penguin.com

First published by Angel Books 2010
Published in Penguin Classics 2013
001

Translation copyright © Hugh Rorrison and Helen Chambers, 2010
Afterword copyright © Helen Chambers, 2010

ISBN: 978-0-141-39215-8

www.greenpenguin.co.uk

ALWAYS LEARNING

PEARSON

Contents

The Historical Background

THE POLITICAL SITUATION in the novel here translated as *No Way Back* is the product of a centuries-old chequered dynastic past. The novel is set in Schleswig-Holstein and Denmark in the late 1850s and early 1860s, a transitional period of government with King Frederick VII on the Danish throne and the status of the linked duchies of Schleswig and Holstein under pressure. Schleswig was originally a Danish and Holstein a German fief, united under the Danish Schauenburger house, and when that line died out they passed to Christian I, an Oldenburger, who in 1460, in order to retain the allegiance of the Schleswig-Holstein knights, famously promised that the two duchies would remain 'inseparable forever'. Over time the duchies passed to younger sons in the Danish royal line, with concomitant disputes about sovereignty, sometimes united, sometimes separated, and at times even with portions becoming independent. After the cession of Norway to Sweden in 1814, the Danish monarchy consisted of three principal parts, the kingdom of Denmark and the two duchies. Whereas Holstein was German-speaking and from 1815 also belonged to the German Confederation, Schleswig was divided into a Danish population primarily in the north and a German population in the south. As the nineteenth century wore on, the problems of succession, looming because Frederick VII was the last of the Oldenburg line, were exacerbated, and in 1848, the Year of Revolution in Europe, the Danish and German partisans sought opposing solutions. After the uprising in Schleswig-Holstein against Denmark was quelled and Prussian claims to the duchies temporarily abandoned after two years of war (1848–50), an uneasy peace followed, with agreement that the succession would pass to Christian of Glücksburg as ruler in the supranational state comprised of Denmark, Schleswig and Holstein. This solution was attacked by Danish sympathizers who wanted to cut Holstein loose, while German sympathizers supported the integration of the united duchies into the German Confederation. In the event, on his death in 1863 Frederick was succeeded by Christian IX, and the following year Bismarck would invade the duchies and defeat the Danes and Schleswig-Holstein would be ceded by Denmark to Prussia, with further Prussian victories over Austria and France resulting in the unification of Germany and the creation of the German Reich in 1871.

At the time when *No Way Back* is set, then, the Danish government is in an unsettled period, trying to maintain calm but at the same time bent on preventing German encroachment. Count Holk's position when he makes a plea for the Old Denmark shows his desire to maintain the status quo, with the preservation of the supranational state. His wife Christine inclines to the German side while somehow remaining true to Schleswig-Holstein. Both positions are, with hindsight, equally illusory, for within a very few years Prussian military might will have put paid to the old order. It has been suggested that when Fontane was writing the novel, between 1887 and 1890, he had his eye on parallels with contemporary German politics. Bismarck had recently been dismissed with the accession of young Wilhelm II, and so the account of the Danish Minister President Hall's dismissal and the sense that his loss will be felt is an allusion to public reactions to the political shift and the attendant uncertainties in 1890s Germany.

Fontane visited Denmark in September 1864 to see at first hand the theatres of battle and report on the Schleswig-Holstein war. The most immediate product was a 374-page documentary report on the conflict (1865), but he also accumulated material and inspiration for later poems and fiction. Although the Schleswig localities featured in *No Way Back*, Holkenäs and Arnewiek, like Kessin in *Effi Briest*, are fictitious, they are based on Fontane's knowledge of Southern Schleswig, and can be imagined to be situated in the area which includes Glücksburg and the Angeln peninsula in the northeastern corner of Schleswig-Holstein, close to the Danish border. Most of the Danish localities mentioned in the novel are real and their details largely authentic, only occasional place names being invented, such as Lille-Grimsby, which has the authentic ring of a Scandinavian settlement, partly a nod in the direction of England's Viking history. The topography of Copengagen as presented in *No Way Back* is generally accurate, although some details of the house in which Holk lodges are fictitious. The building at the location in question has more storeys than Fontane suggests; he appears to have reduced it to a more intimate and domestic scale.

It is still possible today to follow in Holk's footsteps, through Copenhagen, to the Hermitage and Deer Park at Klampenborg, to Hillerød and Frederiksborg Castle and Lake Arre. Fontane himself stayed on Kongens Nytorv, the great central square of the Danish capital, in the predecessor of the present Hotel d'Angleterre, where Vincent's restaurant was located. When Fontane visited the Renaissance castle of Frederiksborg in 1864, chosen by Frederick VII as his royal residence, only the outer façades had been restored after the fire on the night of 16 December 1859, which forms a centrepiece of the novel's action.

The principal characters of the novel, including the Princess, are all literary inventions. It is, however, easy to imagine the Princess's quarters in one of the four royal residences (called 'the Princesses' Palace' in the novel) that make up the Amalienborg Palace and stand imposingly around a spacious octagonal courtyard. The Princess herself is integrated plausibly into the royal family tree, as the King's aunt. The names of all the invented characters fit the geographical and historical context, with typical Schleswig and Danish ones like Petersen and Hansen, and others such as Schimmelmann, Bille and Moltke drawn from the Danish nobility, while Pentz is an old Mecklenburg family name. Historical personages like King Frederick VII and the Danish officers Tersling and du Plat feature in the margins. The portrayal of the Danish general de Meza, a revered national figure until his controversial dismissal in the conflict with Prussia in 1864, is based firmly on his real-life model in whom Fontane took considerable interest, as his diaries record.

Fontane's German readers in 1891 would of course have been more familiar with the historical and geographical background to a novel set only thirty years in the past than present-day readers across the globe, but previous knowledge of the milieu is never a prerequisite for enjoying the work of a great novelist. Fontane is no exception: he constantly creates associations with time and place which contribute unobtrusively to our understanding of the characters' lives, allowing us to follow developments from a position close to the centre of the action. The stone inscribed by Christian IV in 1628 to commemorate his unexplained exclusion from his wife's bedchamber prefigures Holk's predicament, while shifts in the narrative from the ordered and temperate milieu in Holkenäs to the pleasure-seeking and scandal-loving ambience in restaurant and palace in the Danish capital and on to the overheated intimacy of Frederiksborg mirror shifts in the plot which take the main character down a path he is ill-equipped to resist.

No Way Back

Five miles south of Glücksburg, on a dune that ran right down to the sea, stood Schloss Holkenäs, the family residence of Count Holk; to the occasional strangers who passed through the region, at this time still very much off the beaten track, it presented a remarkable sight. It was a building designed after Italian models, with just hint enough of classical Greece to allow the Count's brother-in-law, Baron Arne von Arnewiek, to speak of 'a latter-day temple at Paestum'. Quite ironically, of course. And yet with some justification. For what one saw from the sea was indeed an oblong formation of columns, behind which the lower part of the actual house with its living quarters and reception rooms was concealed, while the upper storey, which appeared to be set considerably further back, rose just over a man's height above the screen of columns which formed a portico on all four sides. It was this screen of columns that really gave the whole a Mediterranean feel; there were stone benches covered with rugs all round the portico, and there, day after day, the summer months were spent, except when it was preferred to climb up to the flat roof, which was less an actual roof than a broad terrace running round the whole upper storey. On this broad, flat roof-cum-terrace which rested on the columns of the ground floor stood potted cacti and aloes, and here, even on the hottest days, comparatively cool fresh air was to be enjoyed. If a breeze from the sea chanced to blow, it would catch the flag that hung limp on a flagstaff, making it swing back and forth with a heavy slap, adding a little to the slight movement of the air.

Schloss Holkenäs had not always stood on this dune. When seventeen years earlier the present Count married the beautiful Baroness Christine Arne, youngest sister of the neighbouring landowner Arne, he had moved into the modest quarters of the original old Schloss Holkenäs, which lay further inland in the large village of Holkeby, just opposite the fieldstone church which had neither choir nor tower. The old Schloss, like the church, dated back to the fourteenth century, and a new building had been planned by the Count's grandfather. But it took the present Count, who among an array of minor passions had a passion for building, to revive the project, and soon afterwards he built the much discussed and mocked, though admittedly also much admired castle on the dune, which was not only grander but above all more comfortable to live in. The Countess, however, had a persistent preference for the old Schloss, now reduced to the rank of bailiff's house, a preference so powerful that she never passed it without thinking with a touch of melancholy of the days spent there. For those had been her happiest times, the years when the two had always lived for love and had never known a difference of opinion. Here in the old Schloss opposite the church their three children had been born, and the death of the youngest, a boy who had been christened Estrid, had only brought the handsome youthful couple closer and increased their sense of belonging to one another.

All this had not entirely survived the move to the new Schloss, and the Countess, who had been educated by the Moravian Brethren and was of a sensitive disposition, had had a strong premonition of it, so strong she would have far preferred a reconstruction and extension of the old Schloss so that they could stay on there. The Count however was stubbornly enthusiastic at the prospect of his 'castle by the sea', and the very first time he discussed it with the Countess, recited the lines:

> 'Hast thou beheld the castle?
> The castle by the sea?
> Clouds of gold and crimson
> Glide over it silently …'

a quotation that produced quite the opposite effect on the person it was intended to win over, besides occasioning a certain derisive astonishment. For Holk was quite unliterary, and nobody knew this better than the Countess.

'Where did you pick that up, Helmuth?'

'At Arnewiek, where else? There's an engraving hanging on the wall at your brother's, and that was under it. And I have to say, Christine, I thought it was first-rate. A castle by the sea! I think it'll be splendid, a joy for us both.'

'If one is happy, one shouldn't wish to be happier still. And then, Helmuth, to choose *that* quotation of all things. You only know the first lines of the Uhland poem I imagine ... forgive me, that's who it's by, Uhland ... but it doesn't go on the way it begins, and there's so much sadness to come at the end:

> "The stormwinds and the waves
> In tranquil slumber slept;
> I heard within its chambers
> A funeral dirge, and wept ..."

You see, Helmuth, that's how it ends.'

'Excellent, Christine, I like that too,' Holk laughed. 'And by Uhland you say. Well, good for him. But you're not going to ask that I don't build my castle by the sea just because of a funeral dirge drifting from the chambers of a castle in a poem, even if it is by Uhland?'

'No Helmuth, I'm not asking that. But I have to confess I would rather stay down here in the old stone house with all its inconveniences and its ghost. I don't mind about the ghost, but I do believe in premonitions, even though the Moravians have no time for them, and they're probably right. But in spite of that, we all have our human weaknesses, and some things linger in the mind, so that try as we may, we can't shake them off.'

That was how the conversation had gone and it had never been referred to again, except for one occasion when both of them climbed up the dune (the sun had already set) to take a look at the new building that was going up. And when they reached the top Holk smiled and pointed to the clouds which at that moment stood 'gold and crimson' directly above them.

'I know what you're thinking,' said the Countess.

'And ...'

'I've had to ... I've put aside my other preference now. At the time, when you first talked about the new building, I was in low spirits, you know why. I couldn't forget the child, and I wanted to be close to the place where he lay.'

He kissed her hand and confessed that her words during that conversation really had made an impression on him. 'And now you're being so generous. And how beautiful you look in the golden sunset. I think, Christine, we'll be happy here. Is that your wish too?'

And she clung tenderly to his arm. But she said nothing.

That had been the year before the completion of the building, and soon afterwards, because the old Schloss in the village below was becoming less and less habitable, Holk had arranged with his brother-in-law to send Christine and the children to Arnewiek where they were to stay until Whitsun, by which time everything would be finished.

And so it had been.

And now Whitsun was approaching, and the day of the move into the new Schloss was upon them. The garden on the rear slope of the dune was only half-planted, and in general a good deal of work was still in progress. But one thing had been completed, the narrow colonnaded front facing the sea. Here shrubberies and round flower beds had been laid out, and further down, where the slope of the dune began, a stepped terrace descended to the beach and continued as a pier, built far out into the sea to serve as a landing-stage for the steamer that plied between Glücksburg and Copenhagen.

Christine was filled with admiration and delight far beyond her own expectations, and when, after walking round the house, she climbed up to the flat roof, the splendid panorama that spread before her dispelled all the worries and premonitions that had continued to assail her soul ever since she had reconciled herself to the new building the previous year; and she called to the children, still down by the terrace, to come up and share her delight. Holk could see how deeply she was moved and wanted to speak, to thank her. But she anticipated him.

'It will soon be a year, Helmuth, since we last stood here on the dune, and you asked me whether I wished to be happy here. I said nothing then …'

'And now?'

'Now I'll say yes.'

2

That was how the day the Countess moved into the new Schloss had ended. A few weeks later an old friend from her boarding school days at Gnadenfrei had arrived, Fräulein Julie von Dobschütz, a lady of slender means whose invitation had initially been intended for a short summer visit. But soon the wish arose to have the lady remain in the house as companion, friend and governess, a wish Holk shared, because at times he found Christine's loneliness depressing. And so Fräulein Dobschütz stayed and took over the instruction of Asta and Axel, the two children of the house. Asta continued to be entrusted to her; but when the doctoral student Strehlke joined the household the nature of Axel's lessons changed.

All that was seven years ago now, and the Count and Countess had grown accustomed to the house and really had experienced the 'days of happiness' that they had hoped for. The deep affection that had brought the couple together years before was still there, even if there were occasional differences of opinion, especially on matters of education and religion, but these were not such as might have seriously endangered the peace of the household. In recent times, to be sure, with the children growing up, there had been no lack of such disagreements, which was not surprising, given the difference in temperament between the Count and Countess. Holk, good and sound fellow that he was, was blessed with no more than average intelligence and fell well short of his wife, who was endowed with quite superior qualities. There was no doubt about that. But that didn't make it any less uncomfortable and oppressive for Holk, and no one understood this better than he did, for there were moments when he found Christine's virtues something of an incubus, and would have wished for a wife less excellent. In earlier days all this had been no more than an unspoken wish, scarcely acknowledged; but for some time now that wish had been growing articulate; it came to arguments, and if Julie von Dobschütz, who had a gift for diplomatic intervention, was mostly able to smooth over these differences with her deft touch, one thing never went away, and that was that Christine, who had had a presentiment of all this, kept recalling with a kind of melancholy the days in the old Schloss, where nothing like this had arisen, or at least far, far more rarely.

Now it was the end of September 1859 and the harvest was long in. The swallows that nested under the portico all the way round the house had left, a breeze was blowing and the flag up on the flat roof flapped languidly back and forth. They were sitting in the front portico, facing the sea, the grand dining room with its tall glass door standing open at their backs, while Fräulein Dobschütz prepared coffee. The Countess had sat down beside Fräulein Dobschütz but at a separate table, and was in conversation with Seminary Director Schwarzkoppen who had come over half an hour earlier with Baron Arne von Arnewiek to enjoy the fine day in the hospitality of the Holks' home. Arne himself was walking up and down the flag-stones with his brother-in-law Holk, stopping every now and then, arrested by the picture in front of him: boats were sailing out for the day's fishing, the sea was rippling gently, and the heavens hung blue above it. There was not a cloud in sight and all that was to be seen was the black smoke from a steamer trailing along the horizon.

'You did right, my friend, to move up here and build your temple on this spot. I was against it at the time, because the idea of moving out and changing house seemed somehow in bad taste, modern in a way that –'

'– only proletarians and civil servants went in for, that's what you said.'

'Yes, well, probably something like that. But since then I've been converted in a few matters, and this is one of them. Be that as it may, one thing I'm sure about, steadfast as I've remained in church and politics and indeed in agricultural questions – which are always the main thing, actually, for people of our sort – there's no denying it's charming up here, such a fresh, healthy breeze. You know, when you moved up here Holk, you added fifteen years to your life.'

And at that moment an old servant in gaiters, who had been taken over from the Count's father, served the coffee, and they each took a cup.

'Delicious,' said Arne, 'in fact a bit too good, especially for you, Holk; coffee like this will knock five years off the fifteen I just promised you, and homeopathy – philistine business but quite remarkable all the same, as you know it cuts out mocha and java – would probably deduct a few more. Apropos of homeopathy. Have you heard about the homeopathic vet we've had these last few weeks in Lille-Grimsby …?'

And walking slowly up and down, the two brothers-in-law carried on their conversation.

Meanwhile the Countess was expatiating on a very different topic in her discussion with Seminary Director Schwarzkoppen, who had left his parish in Wernigerode years before and ended up here in Schleswig-Holstein, where he had been appointed to the Arnewiek Seminary. He had the reputation and enjoyed the prestige of taking a positive church line; but more important for the Countess was that Schwarzkoppen was also an authority on schools and educational questions, which of late had become burning issues for her, for Asta was sixteen and Axel almost fifteen. Schwarzkoppen, now consulted yet again on this extremely delicate topic, answered with circumspection, and when the Countess noticed he was, perhaps in deference to Holk, not entirely inclined to take her side, she broke off the conversation, albeit reluctantly, and turned to another of her favourite plans, one she had already discussed with the Director on a number of occasions, the building of a family vault.

'So, where does the matter stand?' said Schwarzkoppen, who was glad to escape from the question of education.

'I haven't,' said Christine, 'been able to broach the subject, because I fear Holk is going to turn it down.'

'That's not good, my lady. Fear of that kind is always bad; it's meant to promote peace, but in fact it only serves to annoy and cause conflict. And there are no grounds for that. If you can't find better ways to persuade him, you must try through his special interests. As you have often assured me, he does have a passion for building.'

'Yes, that's true,' the Countess affirmed. 'The Schloss here is witness and proof of it, for it was really quite unnecessary; a conversion would have done just as well. But although he loves any kind of building, he has clear preferences, and he'll hardly applaud what I'm proposing. I'll wager he would rather build a hall to play badminton in or, to be up with today's fashion, for roller-skating, anything at all rather than something connected with the church. And a vault at that. He doesn't like to think about dying and he prefers to postpone what is so aptly and beautifully called "setting one's house in order".'

'I know,' said Schwarzkoppen. 'But you mustn't forget that all his most appealing qualities are connected with this weakness.'

'His appealing qualities,' she repeated, 'yes he has those, almost too many of them, if one can have too many appealing qualities. And truly he would be the ideal husband, if only he had some ideals. Forgive my play on words, but I can't help it, because that's exactly how it is, and I now have to say it again: he only thinks of the moment and never of what is to come. He avoids anything that could remind him of that. Since we buried our Estrid, he has never once been to his grave in the vault. So he doesn't know that the whole thing is in danger of collapse. But that's a fact and a new vault has to be built. I say has to be, and if it weren't that I prefer to avoid anything cutting or hurtful, I would tell him it doesn't matter in the slightest whether or not he takes the lead here, it's something *I* want …'

Schwarzkoppen was going to interrupt, but Christine paid no attention and repeating her last words, went on, '*I* want it; I should insist for my part on a future home that pleases me, and not one that is crumbling and derelict … But let us leave aside speculation about what I would or wouldn't say; at the moment I'm more interested in showing you a watercolour by Fräulein Dobschütz which illustrates my plan for the building; she has just produced it for me. I asked her to, of course; she draws very well. It's an open hall, Gothic, and the stones that form the floor also cover the vault. What I particularly want you to see (the little drawing doesn't show them very well) are the decorative paintings on the walls and ceiling. On the long wall there's a Dance of Death, perhaps modelled on the one in Lübeck, and on the ceiling vaults angels and palm leaves. The more beautiful the better. And if we can't have first-rate artists because our means don't stretch to that, then we'll have second- or third-rate ones; after all it's the thought that counts. Julie my dear, forgive me for troubling you. But could you bring us that sketch …'

Holk and Arne had meanwhile continued to walk round the portico and finally made for a gravel path which snaked down to the nearby terrace steps leading to the sea below. Just at this spot there was a little grove of cypresses and laurels with a marble bench in front of it, and here the two brothers-in-law sat down to smoke their cigars in peace, which the Countess never forbade when they were sitting under the portico, but never positively permitted either. The conversation of the two still revolved, strangely enough, around the wondrous vet, which might have been fairly inexplicable had Holk not had a second passion bedsides building – an enthusiasm for fine cattle. He was not a large-scale farmer like his brother-in-law Arne, in fact he made a point of *not* being one; but he was keen on his cattle, almost like a sportsman, and enjoyed having them admired and being able to tell of miraculous milk yields. For that reason the new vet was a really important person to Holk, and it was only his homeopathic methods of treatment that gave rise to some misgivings. But Arne cut these short. The most interesting part of the whole thing, he claimed, was precisely that the new vet not only produced effective cures, there were others who could do that, no, it was the *means* by which he did it. The whole story marked nothing more nor less than the final triumph of a new principle; for the triumph of homeopathy, about which there could no longer be any doubt, dated from the successful treatment of cattle. Up to then the old-style quacks had never tired of talking about the power of the imagination, meaning of course that homeopathic pills in themselves cured nothing; but your Schleswig cow was thankfully devoid of imagination, and if she recovered, it was from the treatment and had nothing to do with faith. Arne expatiated further on this, at the same time pointing out that in the case of the new vet's treatments – the man was from Saxony by the way – there were other things involved which had nothing directly to do with allopathy or homeopathy. Among these was absolute cleanliness bordering on sheer luxury, necessitating newly built cowsheds and in some circumstances even the installation of marble mangers and nickel-plated hay-racks. Holk listened to all this entranced, and felt such an urge to tell Christine about it that he put out his cigar and strode back up to the portico.

'I'm just hearing some interesting things Christine. Your brother is telling me about homeopathic treatments by a new vet from Saxony who studied in Leipzig. I stress Leipzig because it's the home of homeopathy. Truly miraculous treatments! ... Tell me Schwarzkoppen, what's *your* position on this? Homeopathy, it has something mysterious, mystical about it. Interesting in itself, and the mysticism makes it an ideal subject for Christine.'

Schwarzkoppen smiled. 'To my knowledge, homeopathy has no truck with anything mysterious or miraculous. It's all a matter of more or less, and whether you can get as far with a grain as with a hundredweight.'

'Of course,' said Holk. 'And then there's the saying "Similia similibus", which can be taken any way you like, and to many it means nothing at all, including no doubt our Enlightenment man and veterinary ace here. He administers homeopathic pills, but above all he's for cleanliness in the cowsheds, and marble mangers, and I dare say troughs have to be as clean as baptismal fonts.'

'Helmuth, I think you might choose your similes with a little more consideration for my sake, and not least in Schwarzkoppen's presence.'

'Granted. This by the way is all in the new miracle doctor's own words, as quoted by your brother, though it can't be denied that the good doctor himself might be well advised to avoid such analogies, being a convert. His name, you see, is Lissauer.'*

---

* Lissauer is taken by Holk to be a Jewish name. The suggestion is that the vet has converted to Christianity.

Schwarzkoppen and Christine exchanged glances.

'And of course if he comes out to the farm, I shall invite him to lunch down at the bailiff's house. Up here ...'

'We can do without him.'

'I know, and you needn't worry. But I respect him for having an independent mind and the courage to say what he thinks. The business about the marble mangers is pretty fair nonsense, just exaggeration that we have to make allowances for. But as for insisting on cleanliness, he's perfectly right. My cowsheds will have to go, the whole lot date from the end of last century, and I'm glad to have an excuse to get rid of the dead wood at last.'

The Countess remained silent and searched with her needle among the silk threads on the table in front of her.

The Count was annoyed at her silence. 'I thought you would at least tell me you approved.'

'It's farm business, and I thought we agreed I have nothing useful to say about that. If you think marble mangers and that kind of thing are necessary, then they will be found, if need be in Carrara.'

'What makes you speak with such bitterness again, Christine?'

'Forgive me Helmuth, it's not a good time. I was just discussing things much closer to my heart with Schwarzkoppen, building matters too as it happens, and you come wanting to build cowsheds, *cowsheds* ...'

'Of course. You always forget, Christine – even if you don't want to have any part in it, as you just said – you always forget that I'm a farmer first and foremost, and farm business is the proper concern of a farmer. It's the main thing.'

'No it is *not* the main thing.'

'What is then?'

'It's my misfortune and painful for me to have to keep spelling out the obvious to you.'

'Ah, I see. The church is to be extended, or we'll build a home for nuns, or an orphanage. And then a mausoleum, and then we'll buy up the entire works of Cornelius and have them painted on the walls as frescoes ...'

It was rare for the Count to resort to such speeches; but there

were a few topics which instantly prompted ill humour and irritation in him, making him forget the refined manners on which he
could otherwise pride himself. His brother-in-law knew this and
would intervene quickly to propel the conversation in another
direction, in which his constant good humour served him well.

'Dear sister, dear brother-in-law, I have to say to you both that
for my part I think you should do the one and not leave the other
undone. There you have the sum total of my wisdom, and peace to
boot. In addition to which, Holk, you don't know yet what this is
about.'

Holk laughed good-naturedly.

'You don't know,' Arne went on, 'nor do I, although I'm usually
a party to Christine's secrets. Of course, unless I'm very much
mistaken, we have the key here ...', and with that he picked up
the watercolour sketch that Fräulein Dobschütz had just brought
in. 'Charming, and by whose hand might this be, Gothic, angels,
palms? Well, you know what Goethe says – never dally under a palm
tree.[*] And all because of this unfortunate vet, a man in bucket-top
boots and to cap it all – with a Saxon accent. He really ought to speak
Plattdeutsch, in fact Mecklenburg dialect. That reminds me, have
you heard that there's a Low German school of writers in Kiel and
Rostock, or rather two, for whenever anything new happens, the
Germans always divide at once into two camps ... Scarcely has the
Low German school appeared when here comes our old friend *itio
in partes* again, the Mecklenburgers are on the march under their
man Fritz Reuter, and the Holsteiners under Klaus Groth. But
Klaus Groth is one up on them, because he's a poet and can be set to
music, and of course that's what everything depends on. In a year's
time, perhaps less, he'll be a permanent fixture on every piano. I've
already seen something of his lying on yours. Asta, you could sing
one of his songs.'

'I don't like things in Low German.'

'Well, sing something in High German, something sweet and
amusing of course.'

---

[*] Allusion to an entry in Ottilie's diary in Goethe's novel *Die Wahlverwandtschaften*
(*Elective Affinities*).

'I don't like amusing things.'

'Well, if it can't be amusing, sing something really sad. But then it has to be extremely sad if we're to have our money's worth. Something about a page who dies for Countess Asta, or a knight cut down by his rival in love and buried by the wayside. And his dog keeps watch by the knight's grave, and three ravens sit screeching in a black poplar and watch.'

Asta, who was always joking with her uncle, would have produced a rejoinder this time too if her attention at that moment had not been taken up in another quarter.

'There's Elisabeth,' she shouted excitedly, 'and old Petersen with her, and Schnuck too.'

And as she said this, they all stepped out from the portico into the front garden and joined Asta in waving to the others below.

3

Pastor Petersen and his granddaughter Elisabeth, perhaps dazzled by the sun, failed to notice the greeting addressed to them, but from the terrace and portico above they could be seen all the more clearly as they steadily approached from the beach. The old man, hat in hand, so that the wind was playing in his sparse but long white hair, was walking a few steps ahead, while Elisabeth bent to pick up small pieces of wood and bark lying among the seaweed and threw them into the sea for their wonderful black poodle Schnuck to fetch. Now she gave that up and contented herself with picking a few of the flowers growing among the marram grass. And thus strolling along, they eventually reached the pier, where they turned left to climb up the terrace steps.

'They're coming,' Asta burst out jubilantly again. 'And Elisabeth's bringing her grandfather with her.'

'Yes indeed,' said Baron Arne. 'Some might perhaps say her grandfather is bringing Elisabeth. But that's what you're like; youth is the main thing; when you're old you're just an appendage. To be young is to be selfish. Though actually it's no better later. My first thought when I saw the old man was: here comes our game of whist. Schwarzkoppen isn't in favour of card games, but he's not against them either, thank the Lord, and if he were a Catholic he would probably call them "venial sins". Which are the kind I like best. I admire that poodle too, what's his name again?'

'Schnuck,' said Asta.

'That's right, Schnuck; more a name for a character in a comedy really. He's already been up and down here three times. He's obviously immensely pleased. So tell me Asta, what's he so pleased about – seeing you, or about the tricks he's allowed to perform, or the sugar lump he gets for them?'

Two hours later it was quiet in the portico, evening had fallen and only on the horizon was there still a glint of red. They had all retired to the drawing room that lay directly behind the dining room and was the same size. It looked out on a carefully tended garden with hothouses, which opened into extensive parkland running down the slope beyond.

The drawing room was lavishly furnished but still had space enough to move freely in. Beside the grand piano, in the most sheltered corner, stood a large round table with a moderator lamp* on it. It was here that the Countess and her friend Fräulein Dobschütz, who was going to read for them, were sitting, while Asta and Elisabeth had sat down close by on two footstools, and were alternately chatting quietly and putting the dog through his tricks, to his evident delight. But in the end he tired of the effort, and unable to keep his balance any longer, struck the keys of the open piano with one of his paws.

'Aha, now he's playing too,' laughed Asta. 'I think, when he wants to, Schnuck plays better than me; he's so clever, and I don't think Aunt Julie will deny it. A bit earlier they wanted me to play or even sing, Uncle Arne was insisting, but I managed to get out of it. I quite enjoy playing, but I'm no good at all. Have you brought anything along Elisabeth? You always have something new, and you had a satchel under your arm when you arrived. Let's have a look.'

---

* A patent oil lamp invented in 1836.

The girls chatted on in this fashion, while in the corner of the room diagonally opposite, the four gentlemen sat playing whist, Arne as usual scolding old Petersen for playing as slowly as they used to at the Congress of Vienna back in 1815.

'Yes,' old Petersen laughed, 'the Congress of Vienna; playing slowly was the done thing then, it was regarded as distinguished and there's a story, I must tell it to you later, it's a little-known story, one of Thorvaldsen's I believe, and he had it from Wilhelm von Humboldt.'

'Alexander von Humboldt,' said Arne.

'No, I beg to differ Arne, from Wilhelm von Humboldt. Wilhelm was after all …'

'Have a care, Petersen …'

And the game went on without further interruption, and the girls lowered their voices, for Fräulein Dobschütz had begun to read. It was from a news broadsheet that the postman had delivered in the course of the afternoon, and she didn't read it out in full: the war in Italy was still rumbling on in the papers, and Fräulein Dobschütz contented herself at first with reading the headlines, in a questioning tone. 'Archduke Albrecht and Admiral Tegetthoff …' the Countess shook her head … 'March on Magenta … Bonnemain's Brigade of Cuirassiers.' More headshaking. 'There's a report from Charlottenburg on the condition of King Friedrich Wilhelm IV …'

'Yes,' the Countess interrupted, 'read *that* Dobschütz, my dear. I'm not interested in war stories, they're always the same, always somebody collapsing mortally wounded and saying long live something or other with their dying breath, something called Poland or France, or Schleswig-Holstein for that matter. But it's all the same really. This modern fetish of nationalism, it just isn't an idol I can worship. People's human concerns interest me more, and one of these, in my view at any rate, is religion. This unfortunate king in his palace at Charlottenburg … such a clever man, and now he's going out of his mind. Now that does interest me. Is it long?'

'A whole column.'

'That's rather a lot. But begin anyway, we can always stop.'

And Fräulein Dobschütz read on: '… All reports agree that the condition of the King is deteriorating; his concentration is failing,

and the periods when he can follow what people say are becoming
rarer all the time. Inevitably the invalid's condition is also beginning
to have an effect on affairs of State, and some previous assumptions can no longer be made. There is no overlooking the fact that a
regime change is being prepared, and that this will soon be revealed
in foreign policy. Relations with Russia and Austria have been
shattered, while a friendly relationship with the Western Powers
is constantly being fostered, above all with Britain. Everything
happening now is reminiscent of the period between 1806 and
1813, which saw a programme of rearmament and renewal of
our armed forces after the humiliation that had gone before. A
similar programme now constantly occupies the mind of the Prince
Regent, and once Prussia is militarily where the Prince Regent is
intent on taking her, we shall see what happens. And nowhere will
this be clearer than on the Schleswig-Holstein question.'

'That's enough,' said the Countess. 'I thought the article would
have news from the Court, anecdotes, titbits, which are generally
the main thing, but this is all just political speculation. I don't
believe in predictions, they mostly come from the people least
qualified to make them ... But what's that on the back, a picture of
a castle and towers ...'

Fräulein Dobschütz, who hadn't noticed it, turned the newspaper over and saw an almost full-page advertisement on the back
with a large wood engraving in the middle. She ran her eye over
it. Then she said, 'It's an advertisement for a boarding school in
Switzerland, on Lake Geneva, where else; the school is this small
building here; the big hotel in the foreground is just for show.'

'Read it. That's the kind of advertisement that interests me.'

'Beau Rivage Boarding School is now entering its twenty-fifth
year. In that time it has admitted young ladies from all over the
world, and by all accounts they cherish happy memories of us. This
we owe, apart from to the grace of God which there must always
be, to the unswerving principles on which we run our boarding
school. These are the principles of internationalism and confessional equality. The Head of the School is a Calvinist minister, but
he is entirely imbued with the spirit of tolerance, and leaves it to the
parents and guardians of the pupils entrusted to us whether or not

to permit them to take part in this religious instruction ...'

The Countess was visibly amused. Like most pious church-going people, she was inclined not only to doubt the devotional sincerity of others, but mostly also to see the funny side of it, so that announcements from the Catholic camp, and almost more so from the Calvinist, were always a source of pleasant entertainment for her, even when there was not, as was the case here, a blatantly commercial angle to provide amusement. She took the broadsheet herself to read the rest of the boarding school advertisement, but the servant, who had been observing the whist table for the last quarter of an hour awaiting the end of the rubber, now stepped forward and announced that tea was served.

'Excellent,' said Baron Arne. 'When you've won, a partridge, which is what I'm counting on next, is one of the healthiest dishes there is; otherwise of course it isn't.'

And with that he stood up and offered Fräulein von Dobschütz his arm, while Schwarzkoppen went on ahead with the Countess.

'Well then Petersen,' said the Count, 'we'll just have to make do with each other,' and as he walked past Asta and Elisabeth he said to them, 'Come, ladies ...'

But Asta just stroked his hand tenderly and said, 'No Papa, we're staying here, Mama said we can; we still have lots to tell each other.'

4

In the dining room the table had been laid, the double doors were open, and a blaze of light welcomed them as they entered. The Countess took her place between the two churchmen, while Fräulein von Dobschütz sat opposite with Holk and Arne. A moment later the tutor appeared with Axel.

The Countess turned to Schwarzkoppen, 'I've just been rather amused.'

'Aha ...' Holk interjected in a tone which, with a shade less mockery, might have been delightful, and Arne, all too acutely aware of the mockery (for Christine was never amused), laughed heartily to himself.

'I've just been rather amused,' the Countess repeated, somewhat nettled, and then went on, 'These Swiss boarding schools which blithely mix commerce and Calvinism really are in a class of their own. Being so worldly-wise was always the ugly side of Calvinism ...'

Schwarzkoppen, to whom this second remark too was addressed, inclined his head. But her brother said, 'That's news to me, Christine. Calvin, so far as I know, was obstinate and unbending, Knox was the same and Coligny wasn't altogether worldly-wise either, otherwise he might still be alive. And then there's La Rochelle. And the ten thousand who emigrated for the sake of their religion. It would be difficult for the Lutherans to match that, far less better it. I demand justice; Schwarzkoppen, you mustn't leave me in the lurch here against my sister. Nor you either Petersen.'

Holk, who was very fond of his brother-in-law, was hugely gratified to hear him speak in this vein. 'That's right, Alfred. We have to stand up for those who are absent.'

'Even if they were Prussians,' Arne added laughing. 'Which reminds me of that article Fräulein Dobschütz was reading out. What was that all about? It's a talent of mine to be able to win at whist and at the same time follow everything that's said or read in the room. I heard something about the Court at Charlottenburg and rearmament and 1813. Or have I got that wrong? I distinctly heard "1813" and "rearmament" too ...'

'Oh Dobschütz, my dear, tell him what it was,' said the Countess.

'It was exactly as the Baron supposes, and all in all the article seems to suggest that Denmark is finished if it refuses to negotiate on the language question.'

Holk laughed. 'Denmark finished! No Mr Prussian, things haven't gone that far yet, and in any case we still have the story of the stork and the fox. The fox in the fable can't get at the water because it's in a bottle, and today's fox – your Prussian – can't get at Denmark because it's all islands. Yes, water, thank the Lord. It's always the same story, some can do one thing, others another, and the Prussians may goosestep to perfection, but they still can't march over the Baltic, even if Klaus Groth does write, "the Baltic is nowt but a puddle.'''

Arne, who until late autumn regularly started his evening meal with a plate of sour milk, was sprinkling bread and sugar on the bowl in front of him. He took a first spoonful and said as he wiped his beard, 'On that, my dear fellow, we differ. On that point alone; fortunately, I may add. For a man can be at loggerheads with his sister, but not with his brother-in-law. I know Petersen agrees, he's seen more of life than we have ...'

Petersen nodded.

'You see Holk,' his brother-in-law went on, 'you mention the fox and the stork. Well, I've nothing against animal fables, on the contrary. For there's also the fable of the ostrich. My friend, you're simply burying your head in the sand and refusing to see the danger.'

Holk rocked from side to side and said, 'Oh, Alfred, who can see into the future? Not you and not me. But in the end, it's all about calculating probabilities, and any danger from Berlin or Potsdam is one of the least likely things in the world. The days when the Guards paraded in Potsdam are a thing of the past. Nothing against Old Fritz,[*] he has no greater admirer than me, but everything he achieved had the character of an adventure and that has proved fateful for his country.'

'So a country's fame, or even its greatness, is its doom.'

'Yes, it sounds odd, and yet my dear Arne ...'

Holk broke off, for they could hear Asta in the next room struggling to pick out the accompaniment to a song on the piano. But it quickly went quiet again, and Holk repeated, 'Yes Arne, that fame should be fateful sounds odd, but it often happens, and it's part of the scheme of things. It's possible that in the land of bog and sand that is Brandenburg, which the Semnoni and sundry other world-conquering redheads have trodden, some new world-conquering nation might have flourished; good, I'll grant you that, but for that to have happened, this land would have had to go through a normal, gradual process of development. And Frederick the Great cut that short. Prussia went to bed a small state and rose a great one. That

---

[*] Frederick II of Prussia (1712-86), Frederick the Great, affectionately known as Old Fritz.

was abnormal and only happened because it was stretched on the rack overnight, or more precisely for forty years.'

'Holk, these aren't your ideas,' said Christine.

'No, and they don't have to be, I've adopted them. So permit me to carry on with my borrowed ideas. All respect to the Great King, he was sui generis. But what we might call the posthumous Prussia, the Prussia that came after him, I really don't admire, always clinging to the coat-tails of another country, today Russia, tomorrow Austria. Everything it has achieved has been achieved under some double-headed eagle, not under its own eagle, either black or red. Well might its mockers call it the Prussian cuckoo. A state that is to survive and be more than a seven-day wonder must have natural frontiers and represent a nationality.'

'There are other kinds of mortar to bind a state together,' said Arne, and Schwarzkoppen and Christine looked at one another in agreement.

'Of course,' replied Holk. 'For example money. But who's laughing? Prussia and money!'

'No, *not* money, another small matter. And that small matter is nothing more or less than an idea, a belief. The Russians have the idea that they must possess Constantinople, and they will. History is rich in examples of this, and we see it in the Prussians too. It's unwise to scoff at it. Such ideas have a power of their own. Our stars are in our hearts, as it says somewhere, and what that inner voice speaks comes to be. In Prussia, which you don't think much of and haven't been able to stand since your youth, everything for the last century and a half has been preparation and development towards a great goal; it wasn't Old Fritz who was the fateful adventure, it was the age of weakness you spoke of, *that* was the interregnum. And that interregnum is now over. The newspaper article is right. The recruiting drum is moving quietly through the land, and in the end when it comes to the point, old Denmark will have to foot the bill. Petersen, a word from you please. People that reach your age have second sight and can foretell what's going to happen.'

The old man smiled to himself. 'I prefer to pass on that question. For what a man like me only acquires once he has eighty years behind him (and I still have to reach that), women have by nature, women are born seers. Our Countess most certainly is.'

'And I would like to answer that,' said Christine. 'What my dear Dobschütz read just now – at first I was just listening with half an ear, I wanted to hear about the royal couple, who are dear to my heart, and not about rearmament and the new age. But what the article said is right ...'

Arne blew his sister a kiss, while Holk, who already felt aspersions being cast in his direction, dug into a fieldfare.

'... The report in the Hamburg paper,' Christine went on, 'was obviously written by someone close to the new man in power who's familiar with his plans. And if they're not plans yet, then at least they're wishes. On the whole I have to agree with what Alfred has just said about the power of certain ideas. The world is ruled by such things, for better or for worse, depending on what the things are. And with the Prussians everything is rooted in –'

'– in duty,' interrupted Arne.

'Yes, in duty and in faith in God. And if that overstates the case, then it's at least in Luther's old catechism. For that they still do abide by. Thou shalt honour the Sabbath to keep it holy, thou shalt not commit adultery, thou shalt not covet thy neighbour's servant, nor his maidservant, nor his cattle nor anything that is his – yes, that's all still in force there –'

'And elsewhere it's disappeared off the face of the earth,' Holk laughed.

'No, Helmuth, not off the face of the earth, but from that little corner of the earth that is *our* corner. Not from our own dear Schleswig-Holstein, God in his mercy has not allowed it to sink so far, I mean the goings-on *over there*, where our masters reside, whom we are bound to obey, and whom I am indeed willing to obey, so long as right remains right. But that I should be happy about those goings-on, that you can't require of me, *that's* impossible. In Copenhagen ...'

'So it's that old *bête noire* of yours. What can you have against Copenhagen?'

'In Copenhagen everything is of *this* world, it's all pleasure, sensuality and intoxication, and that gives no strength. Strength is on the side of the sober, those who control themselves. Tell me, is there still a court over there, a kingdom? A kingdom, so long as it remains what it should be, has a compelling side, something the heart follows gladly, and for the love of which one sacrifices blood and fortune, life and limb. But a king whose main achievement is divorce, who is more interested in music halls and Danziger Goldwasser than running the country and upholding the law, *that* kind of king has no strength and *gives* no strength and will succumb to those who do have strength.'

'And we'll all become Prussians, and they'll stick a spiked helmet on a pole like the Reichsvogt's hat in Schiller's *William Tell*, and we'll kneel down and worship it.'

'God forbid. We're German, but not Prussian, that's how it should be. I'm a good Schleswig-Holsteiner, and I would invite the gentlemen to drink to that with me. You too, Helmuth, if your Copenhagen gentleman-in-waiting's key doesn't preclude it. And look, Schwarzkoppen, the moon is rising as if to put the seal of peace on all this. Yes, peace; that's the best thing. That's a belief I've held since childhood. My father used to say we're not just born under a particular star, but in the heavenly book where our names are written, there's always a special sign beside our names too: ivy, laurel or palm leaf ... Beside mine, I hope, is a palm leaf.'

Old Petersen took her hand and kissed it, 'Yes, Christine. Blessed are the peacemakers.'

It was spoken so calmly, without any intention of touching the depths of the Countess's heart. And yet that was what happened. She had almost boasted of her peace, or at least had uttered her firm hope for it, and at the very moment when old Petersen as good as assured her of that peace, she sensed that it was not hers. Despite having the best of husbands, who loved her and whom she loved in return, she did not have the peace she longed for. For all their love, his happy-go-lucky nature and her melancholy one were no longer properly in accord, and recent days, despite her best efforts, had shown this more than once and sadly, to a steadily growing degree. So old Petersen's well-meant words found no echo in anyone, each choosing to look straight ahead in silence, and Arne alone turned to look down the table through the tall, open glass door and out to a sea that lay in a shimmer of silver.

And at that moment of oppression and despondency Asta came in from the next room, went up to the table and whispered to her mother, 'Elisabeth would like to sing something. May she?'

'Certainly she may. But who will accompany her?'

'I will. It's very easy and we've just run through it. I think it'll be all right. And if I get stuck, it won't be the end of the world.'

And with that she went back to the piano, and the big central door was left open. The music was already opened, the lights were burning, and the two of them began. But what they had feared happened, voice and accompaniment were not together, and they had to laugh, half in fun, half from embarrassment. Then straight away they tried again and this time Elisabeth's still half-childlike voice rang bright and clear through both the rooms. Everyone listened in silence. The Countess especially seemed deeply moved, and when the last verse was sung she rose and walked over to the piano. There she picked up the open song sheet from the music-rest, and left the company without a further word. This struck no one as unusual, since all were well aware of her sensitive nature. Holk contented himself with asking Elisabeth who the words were by.

'Waiblinger, a poet I've never heard of before.'

'Nor have I,' said Holk. 'And what's the title?'

'"The Churchyard".'

'So that's why ...'

A quarter of an hour later the Arnewiek carriage drew up, and Arne insisted that Petersen and Elisabeth travel as far as the Holkeby vicarage with him—Schnuck would be able to make it trotting alongside. After some debate the offer was accepted. Arne took the front seat, and Elisabeth, because she liked to chat to the coachman, climbed up on to the box. And hardly was she up when she had him talking at length about his ailing wife and about the 'remedy of sympathy' that once again had done more good than the doctor, who only ever gave her some prescription or other, and never took a proper look to see where the problem was, or how her spleen was faring. For the root of the problem was in the spleen.

This conversation was only of brief duration, for in less than ten minutes they halted in front of the vicarage. Schnuck gave lively expression to his pleasure at being home, and Arne took his seat beside Schwarzkoppen. And now, after a few words of thanks and farewell had been exchanged, the two of them drove on to Arnewiek.

5

They drove between high embankments planted with bushes; the sea close by on the left could be heard but not seen as a low bank of dunes blocked the view. Both Arne and Schwarzkoppen had wrapped their legs in plaids and blankets, for after the fine, warm day it had become autumnally cool, cooler than usual for September. But that only made their conversation more animated, and of course it was about the evening just past.

'The little Petersen girl has a charming voice,' said Arne. 'I'd have preferred it though if she had sung "The Bridal Wreath"* rather than that melancholy song.'

'It was very beautiful.'

'Of course it was, and it didn't do either of us any harm to hear it. But my sister! You probably saw how she picked up the song sheet and left the room? I'll wager she learnt it off straight away, or else copied it out and stuck it into some album. For despite her thirty-seven years she's in some ways still quite the Gnadenfrei boarding-school girl, especially living the way she does here with Fräulein Dobschütz. Dobschütz is an excellent person, and I have the greatest possible respect for her knowledge and character; nevertheless, for my poor sister she's a misfortune. You're surprised, but that's how it is. Fräulein Dobschütz is far too clever and also much too good-hearted to stand between husband and wife of her own accord, or even out of vanity; but my sister forces her to take up a position she never would of her own volition. Christine always has to have someone to lament to, she's a pure soul, a latter-day figure

---

* From Weber's opera *Der Freischütz*.

out of Jean Paul who, if I may so put it, torments herself with all life's ills. There's only one thing that cheers her up, and that's false believers' little love stories. And the false believers include more or less anyone who isn't Lutheran of the old school or a Pietist or a Moravian. It's a wonder that she at least tolerates those three. And she's so strong-willed, so resistant to other views. I occasionally try to put in a good word and explain to her how she should be more accommodating and listen to her husband when he tells her some small thing from the real world, a joke, a pun, an anecdote.'

Schwarzkoppen nodded in agreement and then said, 'I said something similar to her myself today, and mentioned the Count's likeable sides.'

'A comment she'll have dismissed with disdain. I've had that experience. Always educational stuff or missionary reports from Greenland or Ceylon, always harmoniums, church candelabra, altar cloths with crosses. More than flesh and blood can stand. I'm telling you this fully and frankly because you're the only one who can help. You don't, I think, quite measure up to her standards, for one thing you don't, thank goodness, go in for "little flowers and angels" like the Pietists; but you do at least have the correct viewpoint. Your confessional temperature isn't high enough for her, but at least you have a confession she can accept, and because she can do that she not only listens to your advice, she also accepts it. And that's something.'

While Arne was chatting they had reached a point where the dunes opened up to reveal the sea. The breakers were now visible and further out the fishing boats, lying silent in the bright moonlight with their sails furled. On the horizon a rocket went up, and balls of light fell.

Arne had made the driver stop. 'Delightful, that's the steamer coming from Korsör. Perhaps the King is on board and is going to spend a few more weeks in Glücksburg. I've heard they've made another find in the bog, near Süderbrarup or somewhere, possibly a Viking ship or one of Canute the Great's pleasure yachts. I hope this particular cup will pass us by. For my part I prefer reading *David Copperfield* or *The Three Musketeers*. These bog finds, combs and pins, or a matted clump of something or other for Thomsen and Worsaae to dispute inconclusively, whether it's root fibres or a sea king's pigtail, they're of no interest to me – and royal breakfasts, where the liquor cabinet plays the leading role, unless it's the milliner Countess Danner, I actually find downright distasteful. I differ from my sister in almost everything, even when she's right but just makes too much fuss about being right, but on this point I have to agree with her. I don't understand why Holk doesn't drop that whole business over there, why to this day he enjoys prancing around in the Princesses' Palace dressed up as a gentleman-in-waiting. I'm prepared to overlook the fact that his Schleswig-Holstein heart doesn't forbid it, for as long as the King is alive, he's still our King and Duke. But I don't find it clever or wise. The Danner woman isn't a recipe for long life, for the King I mean, and it could all come to an end overnight. He suffers from apoplexy after all. And what then?'

'I don't think that's a question Holk thinks about. He lives for the moment and stands by the old adage *après moi le déluge*.'

'Very true. Lives for the moment. And that's one of the points my sister can't forgive him for, and here again I have to take her side. But that's enough of this; I've no desire to run through a list of my sister's virtues at the moment, what I'm more concerned about are *les défauts de ses vertus*, which we, my dear Schwarzkoppen, must fight together, otherwise we'll experience something very unpleasant. I'm sure of that, all I'm uncertain about is who will take the first fateful step. Because Holk adores her and because he's so chivalrous – he is modesty and compliance itself – he's got used to playing second fiddle to his wife. It's quite natural. First he was impressed by her beauty (she really was very beautiful, and still is, I may say), then he was impressed by her cleverness, or at least what he took for cleverness, then he was impressed, perhaps more than anything else, by her piety. But for some time and unfortunately to an increasing degree, he has been going through a change; he's impatient, ironic, makes insinuating comments, and just today I was struck again by the change in his tone. Do you remember when they were talking about the marble mangers? Now my sister as usual took what was meant more or less as a joke quite seriously, and her response was half-irritated and half-sentimental. Two or three years

ago Holk would have let that pass, but today his response was quite
caustic, and he told her mockingly that she was only ever happy
when she was talking about crypts and chapels, or having a half-
length angel painted.'

Schwarzkoppen had accompanied all this with only an occasional
'Very true', and there could be no doubt that he was in agreement.
But now Arne fell silent, because simply agreeing wasn't enough,
he would have liked to hear more from Schwarzkoppen. But the
latter showed no inclination to discuss the matter further: it was
too dangerous ground, and pointing over to Arnewiek, which just
at that moment hove into sight beyond a fjord that stretched far
inland, he said, 'How charming the town looks in the moonlight!
And see how the embankment over there just trims the roofs, and
then the gables between those poplars and willows! And there's St
Catherine's now! Just listen to how the sound of the bells carries
over to us. I bless the day that brought me here into your beautiful
land.'

'And we're grateful to you for that, Schwarzkoppen. Everyone
likes to hear his native land praised. But you're just being evasive.
I'm urgently requesting your support in this difficult matter, it's
much more difficult than you may suspect, and all you can do is
look at the embankment over there and tell me it trims off the roofs.
Quite right, it does. But I'm not going to let you off with that. With
the influence you have on my sister, you must take the opportunity
to approach her through the Bible and use half a dozen texts to make
her see that always claiming to be on the side of the angels doesn't
work, that genuine love has no time for covert arrogance that skulks
behind airs of humility, in other words that she has to change and
let her husband have his way more, instead of making his home life
a misery. Yes, and you can add, and this is hardly an exaggeration,
that he would probably have given up his Copenhagen post long ago
if he wasn't glad to escape now and again from the pressure that the
virtues of his wife, my dear revered sister, imposes on him.'

'Ah, my dear Baron,' and Schwarzkoppen did now speak, 'I'm
not trying to wriggle out of it, it's not that, it's not that I lack the
goodwill to back you up to the best of my ability, for I see the danger
just as you do. But goodwill isn't enough. If your good sister were a

Catholic countess instead of a Protestant one, and if I, instead of a seminar director in Arnewiek, were a Redemptorist or even a Jesuit priest, it would be a very simple matter. But that's not how matters stand. I have no authority. Our whole relationship is purely social, and if I were seen to be playing the soul doctor, the father confessor, then I would be an intruder, doing something I'm not entitled to do.'

'Intruder,' Arne laughed. 'You're not asking me to believe, Schwarzkoppen, that you're worried about Petersen, who at well-nigh eighty years has reached a point where all rivalry and taking offence cease.'

'It's not Petersen,' said Schwarzkoppen. 'He has indeed long since put the little vanities behind him, which are nowhere greater than among my pastoral brothers-in-arms, and he wouldn't begrudge me the role of converter and miracle-worker. But one mustn't always take advantage of what chance has to offer. There is so much here that speaks against it, makes it difficult and counsels caution.'

'So that's a refusal.'

'No, not a refusal. I'll do what's in my power, but it can only be very limited. For practical reasons for a start. I'm an official, and the journey to Holkenäs is scarcely a short one, so "taking the opportunity", as you put it, can't happen very often. But the chief difficulty remains with the Countess herself. I've seldom met a woman I esteem more highly. She combines all the superior qualities of a noble lady with the virtues of a Christian woman. At all times she wants the best, what duty requires, and to steer her views on duty in another direction is extraordinarily difficult. Our church, as you know, and as I have amply indicated, permits nothing beyond advice, encouragement, appeal. It all more or less comes down to textual exegesis, which opens the door wide to conflicts of opinion. And over and above that, the Countess is not only very well versed in the Scriptures, she also has all the strength of those who look neither left nor right, make no concessions and arm themselves with an implacable stubbornness which offers more protection than the flimsy armour of mild and conciliatory faith. Contradicting her will not work, far less any air of superiority.'

'That's true. But I can only repeat, it all has to seem to happen by chance.'

'All I can offer – if, as the half schoolmaster I now am, I may have recourse to a somewhat erudite turn of phrase – is a prophylactic procedure. Anticipation, precaution, prevention. I'll think of some stories, stories from my earlier life as a parson – you wouldn't believe the entanglements and upsets one sees! – and I'll try to ensure these stories quietly take effect. Your sister is imaginative and thoughtful in equal measure; and imagination will bring to life what she hears from me, and her thoughtfulness will force her to get to the bottom of the story and perhaps make her see things in a new way and ultimately bring about a change of heart. That's all I can promise. A very slow procedure, and perhaps the outcome won't be commensurate with the effort involved. But at least I'll not shirk my task, because I can see that something has to be done, within carefully defined boundaries.'

'Agreed, Schwarzkoppen; now I have your word. That's that. It's a good time too for what we propose. Holk is expecting to be summoned to join the Princess in Copenhagen in about four weeks, and then he'll be away until Christmas. In the meantime I shall often be over to keep an eye on the farm and the books, as I always do when Holk's in Copenhagen, and when I go, I shall regularly consult you and see if you can go with me. I would add that Christine is always in a gentle, almost tender mood when he's away, and the great love she used to have for him, and which she may at the moment devoutly wish she felt but actually doesn't, that love always revives again. In short, her state of mind in his absence is a fertile field in which every good seed germinates. All it needs is to make her see things from another angle, with a clearer view of both sides. If we succeed in that, then the game is won. Given the seriousness and application with which she approaches everything, once her mind is focused in the right direction she will reach the right outcome on her own.'

By this time they had reached the embankment on the other side of the bay which the highway followed for a short stretch. Down below lay the town, its centre dominated by St Catherine's church with the Seminary attached to it, and the road out by the ancient

castle on its eminence, Schloss Arne. As the carriage drove down
the sloping embankment into the town, Schwarzkoppen said, 'What
a strange game; here we are, like two conspirators hatching plans in
the night, plans which cast me in a role that should really fall to old
Petersen. And the more so since the Countess is a devoted admirer
of his, she just can't quite come to terms with the rationalist in him.
The rationalist! It's only a word, and in the cold light of day there's
nothing so bad about it, least of all nowadays. His life is now close
to the limit of our allotted span, and his eyes see more clearly than
ours, perhaps in all directions and in everything, but most certainly
in the things of this world.'

6

The fine autumn days seemed set to continue. The next morning too
was bright and sunny, and the couple took breakfast outdoors in the
front portico. Julie von Dobschütz with them. Asta was practising
in the next room, and Axel and his tutor were out shooting in the
dunes, taking advantage of the Michaelmas holiday. The Countess
had little time for this as a rule, or indeed for holidays in general;
holidays from school and from the town made sense, but out here,
in God's free nature, they were at the very least superfluous. The
Countess had long held by this principle, and she responded with
a superior smile whenever the Count defended the opposite view.
This year for once, though her views were unchanged, she made no
objection to the Michaelmas holiday because she had not yet given
up her plan to send both children to boarding school at the beginning of the winter term. So these few days mattered little. On the
question of schooling, the Count for his part continued to display
the limpness the Countess so often deplored: he wasn't actually
against sending the children to boarding school, but he wasn't for it
either. At any event he opined that there was no rush, to which the
Countess replied, with a degree of acerbity, that that was exactly
what she couldn't accept; it was not only time, it was high time;
Asta was sixteen, Axel would soon be fifteen, these were the years

when character was formed, crossroads reached, the path chosen, to left or to right. 'And whether to be black sheep or white,' the Count interjected mockingly, picking up the newspaper.

His recourse to mockery, which was meant to show the Countess that she was again taking it all far too seriously, only made her more earnest, and she went on, without regard for the presence of Julie von Dobschütz, who was in any case party to the situation, 'Please Helmuth! Is there any chance you might desist from joking about serious matters? I like to be amused ...'

'Pardon me, Christine, but that seems to be your watchword since yesterday.'

'I like to be amused,' she repeated, 'but there's a time and place for everything. I don't insist that you agree with me, but I would like you to have a firm opinion, you don't even need to have reasons. Just say that you find Herr Strehlke satisfactory, and that you would prefer Elisabeth Petersen to an entire boarding school for young ladies – I won't believe you in either case, but I will acquiesce and keep silent. Just refrain from calling that sort of thing education ...'

'Ah yes, my dear Christine, you're on your hobby-horse again I see, or on one of the many, and if you hadn't been born Baroness Arne, you'd have become a Basedow or a Pestalozzi and could take Schwarzkoppen's place as Seminary Director. Maybe even be his General Inspector. Education, education and more education. To be frank, I for my part don't believe all that kind of thing is important. Education! There too the best lies in predestination, grace. On this point, Lutheran as I am, I'm on Calvin's side. And if Calvin annoys you, another of your high-minded whims, then let me quote the old proverb, "As we are laid in the cradle, so too will we be laid to rest in the grave." Education makes little difference. And if we have to talk about education, then what matters is the education that home provides.' The Countess gave a slight shrug, but Holk ignored it and went on, 'Home sets the example, and the force of example is the only thing to which I attribute any educational effect. Example and of course love. And I love the children, which I trust you'll give me credit for, and I have a need to see them every day.'

'It's not about what *you* need, Helmuth, it's about what the children need. You only see them at breakfast, when you're reading the *Dagbladet*, and at tea, when you're reading the *Hamburger Nachrichten*, and if they speak, far less dare to ask you a question, you get cross. It's possible that having the children around gives you a certain comforting glow, but they're not very different from the sugar-bowl, which always has to stand to your right if you're to feel at ease. You say you need the children. Do you think that I don't need them, here in this loneliness and silence where all I have is my dear friend Dobschütz? But the happiness of my children means more to me than my own comfort, the demands of duty take no account of one's personal well-being.'

Holk ran his left hand over the tablecloth, while with his right he clicked the sugar-bowl open and shut three or four times, until the Countess, whom the sound made nervous, pushed the bowl aside, and he didn't resist. For he understood full well that bad habits like that are hard to bear. Furthermore, the trivial incident restored his good mood. 'Very well, Christine, why not discuss it with Schwarzkoppen and your brother, and of course with our good friend Fräulein Dobschütz. And then do what you all think fit. It really is pointless to feud about all this, and now that I think about it, I'm annoyed at every word I've replied to you. For actually,' and he took her hand and kissed it, 'actually it's just a little comedy you like to play, a charming little comedy. You want to make me believe, I don't really know why, that I have a say here at Holkenäs. Well Christine, you've not only a much stronger character than I have, you're much cleverer too: but I'm not so stupid that I don't know who rules the roost and who makes the decisions. And if I were to appear at the breakfast table one morning and you were to tell me, "I made up two parcels last night, and I sent one to Schnepfenthal and the other to Gnadenfrei, and in one of the parcels was Axel, and in the other was Asta", then you know beyond a shadow of doubt that I might be taken aback momentarily, but certainly wouldn't object, far less raise serious reproaches.'

The Countess smiled half in satisfaction, half in sorrow.

'There you are,' Holk went on, 'you admit that I'm right, and if you were to hesitate for another moment, I'd turn to our friend Julie for a ruling. Isn't it true, my dear Dobschütz, it's a foolish thing, actually an act of cruelty to talk about contradictions and indecision

in a man whose indecision never amounts to a hindrance because
his better half's certitudes render it totally without consequence.
But I see the *Dronning Maria* is just rounding Farö-Klint. Another
five minutes and she'll be here. I suggest we go down to the landing-
stage and pick up the post from Copenhagen.'

'No, let me,' cried Asta who, hearing the remark about the
arrival of the *Dronning Maria* in the next room, put an instant end
to her practice and banged the piano shut. 'No me, I'm quicker.'
And before anyone could answer yes or no, she was flying down
the terrace towards the pier and reached its end almost at the same
moment the ship tied up. The captain, who of course knew the
young comtesse,* saluted her in military fashion and then personally handed the newspapers and letters down from the bridge. A
moment later the ship pulled away again, heading for Glücksburg.
Asta raced back to the terrace, and by halfway up she was already
brandishing a letter in the air, easily recognizable to the Count and
Countess by its size and imposing seals as an official communication. And then almost immediately the young comtesse was back
in the portico laying the newspapers on the table and handing the
letter to her papa.

He ran his eye over the address and read, 'The Count Helmuth
Holk at Holkenäs, Vice-Provost of the Convent of St John in
Schleswig, gentleman-in-waiting to H.R.H. Princess Maria
Eleonora.'

'Only one person,' said the Countess, 'writes as punctiliously
and correctly as that. The letter must be from Pentz. I have to
laugh whenever I think of him, part Polonius and part Major-domo
Kalb.† Asta, you should still be practising; I think the *Dronning
Maria*'s arrival suited you very nicely.'

And Asta went back to the piano.

Holk had by now opened the letter, and without more ado began
to read it out, knowing he would give away no state secrets.

---

* A count's unmarried daughter.
† Vain, foolish courtier in Friedrich Schiller's *Kabale und Liebe (Intrigue and Love)*.

Copenhagen, Princesses' Palace
28th September 1859

Dear Holk,

First my baronial greeting. Following hard on its heels, my most humble request not to take it amiss that I must disrupt your domestic life at Schloss Holkenäs. Our old friend Thureson Bille, who was to take up his duties in the Princess's service on the first of October and alternate with Erichsen, has been laid low with measles for three weeks now, a children's ailment of which one might say in the present case (I quote Her Highness our Princess at this point) that it struck down the right man. We could of course call upon Baron Steen but, as chance has it, he has been in Sicily waiting for Etna to erupt for the last five weeks. Now that he can no longer rise to an eruptive life of his own, Steen has turned his attention to fire-spewing mountains. What must his past life seem like in comparison! I've known him now for thirty years. Despite all his efforts to be a Don Juan he was really only ever a Sir Andrew Aguecheek which, considering his aspirations, is more or less the most ridiculous thing he could be. But let us put that aside and address the main problem; Steen and Bille have let us down, so that just leaves *you*. The Princess wishes me to communicate her regrets to both you and the dear Countess, and she charges me to add that she will endeavour to make your time here as easy and agreeable as possible. And in this she will succeed. The King intends to spend late autumn in Glücksburg, with the Danner woman of course, and so you will find our Serenissima who, as you know, doesn't care to breathe the same air as the said Danner, in high good humour. The position of Hall, as ever the darling of the Princesses' Palace in political matters, has been shaken, but even that serves to improve the Princess's mood, for nobody expects the 'Farmers' Ministry', which is in immediate prospect, to last four weeks, and if Hall then takes office again (and they will beg him to), his position will be more secure than ever. For the rest, my dear Holk, and I am happy to be able to add this, there is no need for you to catch the first available steamer; the Princess herself asks me to tell you this, a very special mark of her favour, since punctuality in service is one thing on which she is normally strict and can in certain circumstances be very touchy. I'm going to stop here so as not to let any titbits of news out of the bag prematurely. The Princess tends to take it badly if one passes on gossip she might wish to tell herself. Just one little appetizer. Adda Nielsen is giving up the stage to become Countess Brede, having taken two weeks to make up her mind and decide whether she wouldn't be better to stick with her financially more advantageous position with Hoptrup, the wholesale merchant. But legitimacy has its charm, and to be a Countess! And Hoptrup, even if he were to become a widower (which is not, for the moment, a serious prospect) despite his millions won't ever be anything more than an Etatsrat.* And that, for the aspirations of a top tragedienne, is simply not enough. De Meza has been made an aide-de-camp, Thomsen and Worsaae are in dispute again, not surprisingly about a fossilized hollow tree trunk, which Worsaae says dates back to Ragnar Lodbrok, while Thomsen doesn't think that's enough and says it dates back to Noah. I'm for Noah; he conjures up more pleasant associations: ark, dove, rainbow, and above all the vine. Send me a note, or better still a telegram to let me know when we can expect you. *Tout à vous.*

Your Ebenezer Pentz

As soon as he had read the letter, Holk switched to a cheerful ebullient mood which the Countess was unable to share.

'Well, what do you say Christine? Pentz *from top to toe.*† Full of good humour, full of gossip, but fortunately also full of self-irony. Court life produces marvellous characters.'

'It certainly does. Especially over in dear old Copenhagen. Court life too remains resolutely true to form there.'

'And what form is that?'

'Ballrooms, music, fireworks. It's a town for ships' captains who are on the high seas for six months and come back intent on

* Title conferred by the Danish king on distinguished individuals, especially senior government officials and university professors.

† Fontane's English words and phrases, as passing foreign expressions, are given in italics throughout.

wasting all they've saved, and catching up on all they've missed.
Copenhagen is nothing but taverns and palaces of pleasure.'

Holk laughed. 'The Thorvaldsen Museum, Nordic antiquities
and the Olaf Cross, and also the Church of Our Lady with Christ
and The Twelve Apostles … you mean that too?'

'Really Holk, what a question! Plenty more could be added to
your list and I'm not blind to all the beautiful things to be found
over there. It's actually a fine nation, very clever people, very
gifted, with many talents. And as surely as they have the virtues
that commerce with the world brings, they have its darker sides
too. They're all hedonists; they've never really had to suffer and
struggle, and wealth and good fortune have fallen into their lap.
They've been spared the rod and that's what gives them this tone,
this propensity to pleasure, and the Court not only goes right along
with it, it gives the lead, instead of recognizing that those who
would rule must start by ruling themselves. But they don't see it
that way in Copenhagen, not your Princess, and least of all the good
Baron Pentz who, I imagine, views the Tivoli Theatre as a corner-
stone of society. And he writes like that too. I really can't bear that
tone, I have to say, it's a tone that to my way of thinking, and I could
almost say in my experience too, goes before a catastrophe.'

Holk was of a different opinion. 'Believe me Christine, however
much royal and non-royal entertaining goes on over there, it's not
Belshazzar's feast, not by a long chalk, and the writing is far from
being on the wall just yet for my friends in Copenhagen … but what
am I to do about this summons from the Princess?'

'Obey and accept, of course. You're in her service, and as long
as you consider it right to remain in that service, then you're bound
by certain duties which you must fulfil. And in the present case, the
sooner the better. At least that's how I see it. I wouldn't believe the
business about your own free time and that there's no rush, or at
least I wouldn't take it seriously. I've always avoided anything to do
with the Court and have a horror of princesses, old and young alike;
but I understand enough about Court life and its rules to know that
you can never overdo the compliments and that blithely accepting
any concession is always the wrong thing to do. And then, Holk, if
you did stay on here a while, it would just mean uneasy days for you

and me, for us all. So if you want my advice, leave tomorrow.'

'You're right; that would be best, don't think about it too long. But you must accompany me, Christine. Widow Hansen has an entire house over there, so there's ample space, and she's the best landlady you can imagine. And as for people you know, you'll find Fräulein Schimmelmann, and dear old Brockdorff's sister-in-law and Helene Moltke. I mention these three because I know you like them. And of course there are churches in Copenhagen too, and Melbye is your favourite painter and all your life you've held old Grundtvig in high regard.'

The Countess smiled, then she said: 'Yes Helmuth, now you're your old self again. It's barely an hour since we were talking about the children and where to place them, and already you've forgotten all about it. One of us has to be here to see that what needs to be done is done, and done properly. I would like to know what actually goes through your mind. All the corn drops out of your memory and only the chaff is left. I'm sorry, but I can't spare you these bitter words. If my brother Alfred died today, or perhaps somebody closer to you, and you'd just planned a partridge shoot, you'd forget to go to the funeral.'

Holk bit his lip. 'I can't seem to get you into a friendly mood, or to stop your constant brooding and taking life too seriously. And I ask myself, is it my fault or yours?'

These words were not without effect on Christine. She took his hand and said, 'Guilt is everywhere, and perhaps mine is the greater. You're easy-going, fickle and indecisive, and I incline to melancholy and take life too seriously, even where taking it lightly would be the better option. It wasn't a good day for you when your choice fell on me, and I wish you had a wife who knew how to laugh more. I do try now and then, and I give myself a pat on the back for having tried, but it doesn't really work. I'm serious by nature, it's true, and perhaps sentimental too. Forget what I just said; it was hard and unjust, and I got carried away. It's true, I often accuse you and I won't deny it, but you must allow me to say that I blame myself for it.'

At this moment Asta emerged from the drawing room with a broad-brimmed Heligoland hat over her left arm.

'Where are you going?'

'To Elisabeth's. I want to take back the music case she left here yesterday.'

'Ah, good,' said Holk, 'I'll go with you part of the way.' And Asta, who could clearly see that a serious conversation had taken place, first greeted Fräulein Dobschütz and then kissed her mother on the forehead. And straight after that she took her father's hand and the two went down through the portico to the garden side of the house.

When they had left, Fräulein Dobschütz said, 'I rather think, Christine, that you would have liked to keep the music case here for a few days. I saw yesterday evening what an impression that song made on you.'

'Not the music, just the words. And in the first flush of enthusiasm yesterday I copied them out. Please, Julie my dear, fetch them from my desk. I would like you to read the whole thing to me again, or at least the first verse.'

'I know that one by heart,' said Fräulein Dobschütz.

'Maybe I do too. But I would like to hear it all the same; recite it for me, and take your time.'

And with that Fräulein Dobschütz began to speak slowly and quietly,

> 'The best in life is peace,
> Of Earth's enjoyments all;
> What lasts from that great feast?
> What never turns to gall?
> The rose that blooms soon fades,
> For all that Springtime laves,
> Pity him who hates,
> And almost more, who loves.'

The Countess laid aside her work, and a tear fell on her hand. Then she said, 'A wonderful verse. And I don't know which are the more beautiful, the two lines at the beginning or the two at the end.'

'I think they belong together,' said her friend, 'and each pair of lines is made more beautiful by the other. "Pity him who hates, and almost more, who loves." Yes, Christine, that's true. But precisely because it's so true ...'

'The other pair of lines, with which the verse begins, is even truer: "*The best in life is peace ...*".'

7

While Christine was having this conversation with Fräulein Dobschütz, Holk and Asta walked down from the portico, only parting a hundred paces further on when they reached the grassed-over roundel below, where cricket was played when visitors came;[*] Holk turned to speak to a gardener who was busy outside a greenhouse, Asta continued on her way along the carefully tended park drive. This descended gradually and finally turned sharp left into a wide avenue of chestnuts that was already on the flat and reached as far as the village of Holkeby. There were chestnuts lying everywhere, bursting out of their shells as they fell on the road in front of Asta. She bent down to pick up every single one; but when the vicarage, which was built into the churchyard wall, came into view, she threw them away again and quickened her step as she approached the house. It still had a knocker from times gone by, but this seemed about to fail in its duty, for nobody came. Only when she had knocked again several times was the door opened, and by Pastor Petersen himself, who had clearly been disturbed. But when he recognized Asta the displeasure clouding his brow soon disappeared and he took her hand and led her into his study, the door to which he had left open. The windows looked on to the churchyard with its slight rise, so that the gravestones seemed to look over each other's shoulders. Between them stood ash and weeping willow, and the scent of mignonette drifted in from outside, although it was late in the year.

'Do sit down, Asta,' said Petersen. 'I'd just nodded off. At my advanced years sleep is no respecter of the clock; at night it refuses

---

[*] The anglophilia widespread in northern Europe in the middle of the nineteenth century left its mark in various ways in various places.

to come, then by day it takes you by surprise. Elisabeth is over at the Schünemanns', taking the poor lady a few grapes we cut this morning; I fear she has not long left. But she'll be back soon; Hanna is helping in the fields. And now you'll drink a glass of malmsey with me. That's a ladies' wine.'

And with that he pushed the open bible to the right, a box of antiquities (for like most Schleswig pastors he was a collector) to the far left, and set two wineglasses on his desk.

'Let's drink a toast. But to what? To a happy Christmas of course.'

'Oh, that's still too far ahead.'

'For you it is. But I count time differently … and may Father Christmas bring you all you wish.'

Their glasses clinked, and at that moment Elisabeth came in and said, 'I'm going to join you, even though I don't know who you're drinking to.'

And now the two young girls exchanged greetings, and Asta gave Elisabeth back the music case and passed on her mother's thanks for the beautiful song she had sung the night before.

This was casually done for, as she passed on her mother's message, Asta's eyes were already fixed on the many numbered items, small and large, that filled the archaeological box. One thing she saw seemed to be gold wire, gold wire twisted into a great spiral.

'Why is this gold?' Asta asked. 'It looks like a sofa spring.'

The old man was amused at that, and told her it was something better: a piece of jewellery, a sort of bracelet a Comtesse Asta of the day would have worn two thousand years ago.

Asta liked this and nodded, and Elisabeth, who knew more than she cared to about these things, for she was virtually the curator of the collection, added, 'And if they find your little horseshoe brooch two thousand years from now I can assure you speculations will be made and conclusions drawn … but come on, Asta, we don't want to disturb Grandfather in his study any longer.'

And with that she took Asta's arm and went through the hall to a door leading directly out to the churchyard. Only a few steps more and they came to a broad path running crosswise between the graves to the old fieldstone church, an early Gothic building with no tower that could have passed for a barn but for the tall lancet windows with the thick covering of small-leaved ivy that climbed up to the roof. The bell hung under a few protective boards on one gable of the church, while a low brick house with small windows, each with two iron bars, was built on to the other. The heads of a few of the gravestones, which here beside the church were particularly numerous, lay close up against the crypt, for that is what the building was, and Asta climbed on to one of these gravestones and peered curiously through the little iron-barred windows. In doing so she rested her hand on a loose stone and it moved, displacing another half-stone that was already loose too, and this toppled and fell with a clatter down into the crypt.

Asta started and jumped down from the gravestone she had been standing on. Elisabeth also got a fright, and only when they had both escaped from that uncanny place and straight afterwards were out of the churchyard too did they find their tongues again. Outside, along the churchyard wall lay great piles of sawn boards and beams, which was little wonder, for parallel to the wall, separated only by a broad track, there was a large wood and timber yard overgrown with short grass, where logs from Norway were constantly being sawn up. A tree trunk that had been roughly trimmed with an axe was lying on two tall wooden trestles, and just then a couple of carpenters, one on top and the other below, were sawing along the trunk with a cross-cut saw that was growing shinier as they worked. The two girls watched intently, and the proximity of people together with the lively tenor of their work had a soothing effect after the horror that had so recently gripped them at the sight of the crumbling crypt.

It was a most welcoming spot; the nettles, otherwise rampant all round, were trodden flat here, and so the two friends sat, comfortable and contented, on the stacked-up boards, with beams as a footstool and the churchyard wall as a backrest.

'You know,' said Asta, 'Mama is quite right, not wanting to have anything to do with the crypt and being afraid to go into it. It's as if every stone is loose and it's all just waiting to collapse. And yet she does go there twice a year to lay a wreath on the coffin; on his birthday and on the day he died.'

'Can you still remember your brother Estrid?'

'Of course I can. I was seven at the time.'

'And is it true that he wasn't only called Estrid but Adam as well?'

'Yes. Mama actually wanted him to have Helmuth as his second name like his father, Estrid Helmuth—Aunt Dobschütz has often told me about it; but Papa insisted on Adam, because he had heard that children called that don't die, and then Mama said (I have all this from Aunt Julie) that's all heathen superstition and it will come back to punish you, for God doesn't like being told what to do, and it's blasphemous and reprehensible to try to tie his hands.'

'I can imagine your mother saying that. And it did come back to punish them. But I still think, Asta, that your mother is too strict about these things, and Grandfather who loves her so, and who married her—which the Arnewiek pastor at the time was deeply offended at—and for whom his "dear Christine" as he still calls her is his favourite person in all the world, and he's still on familiar terms with your papa from the old days too ... he also says she's too set in her ways and too hard on other people ...'

'Yes, everybody says that, your grandfather says it, Director Schwarzkoppen says it, and Uncle Arne says it. And Axel and I hear them, even if we aren't supposed to, and we think our own thoughts about it all ...'

'And who comes out best in your thoughts?'

'Mama, every time.'

'That really surprises me. I thought you were your father's pride and joy. That you loved him most.'

'Oh of course I love him; he's so kind and he grants our every wish. But Mama always thinks what's best for us, that's why she's so strict. All out of love.'

'I haven't always heard you speak like that of her, Asta. It's hardly a week since you were complaining bitterly and saying it was almost impossible to live with your mama, that she said no to everything, that everything was so serious, as if life and salvation depended on it ...'

'Yes, I probably did say that. But who doesn't complain some-times! And then it's often so quiet here, and you begin to feel sad, and wish things were different … You see, this is what I think, Mama can often be depressing, but she looks after us, and with Papa every moment is fun, but all in all he isn't really concerned for us. He's always somewhere else in his thoughts and Mama is always with us. If it was left to Papa, everything would tick along quietly until one day somebody came and wanted to have me. Comtesse Holk, red blond hair, sound in limb, with some capital – I think that's all he has in mind, and he's convinced it's for the best. But the idea that I might have a soul doesn't occur to him, maybe he doesn't even believe it.'

'The things you say. Surely he believes you have a soul?'

'Maybe. I don't know. And that's the difference from Mama. She does believe it, and she wants me to learn, to achieve a firm faith, "an anchor in the storms of life" as she puts it and I would be quite happy if it wasn't for parting from you. I'll never find a friend like you again anywhere in the whole world.'

'But you don't mean to go away, Asta? What for? Isn't Fräulein Dobschütz a clever woman, and good and kind as well? You can chatter on so well in French that it's fun to hear, and Strehlke has won two prizes, one in Copenhagen for his work on shore vegetation in Northern Schleswig and one in Kiel for work on jellyfish and starfish. And he's good at geography, I know for a fact: the other day he could name the King of Naples's country castle, so that even your uncle Arne congratulated him. What else do you want to learn? I'll be hurt if you want to learn so much more than me, and then when you come back, there'll be nothing between us any more. And I want us to be together, for I love you so much. And if she does send you away, your mama will certainly want to place you in a big Swiss boarding school.'

'No, a small Moravian boarding school.'

'Well, that I can live with, Asta. I know the Moravians, they're good people.'

'That's what I think. Mama went to a Moravian boarding school too.'

'So it's been decided?'

'As good as. Papa has given in. In addition to which he leaves for Copenhagen and the Princess tomorrow, which nobody expected, and Mama will probably take the opportunity to get everything moving along the right lines. I would think in two weeks or even sooner ...'

'Oh Asta, if it wasn't for Grandpa, I'd ask your mama to send me too. What am I going to do here when you're gone?'

'It'll be all right, Elisabeth, it has to be. It'll be hard for me as well. And Mama will be alone too with nobody around except Fräulein Dobschütz, but she's *still* sending us away. For Axel's going too. What she said to me last night is right: life isn't just fun and pleasure; we're here to do our duty. And she begged me always to remember that our happiness and eternal life depend on that.'

'That's all very true, but it doesn't help me.' And Elisabeth had to blink back tears as she said this. 'I can't walk up and down the beach all day long searching for amber and write up catalogues and number the pieces. And think of it, winter, when everything is buried in snow and the crows are sitting on the crosses and then at midday the bells strike twelve ...'

And at that moment the noonday bell Elisabeth had just mentioned struck. Both girls started. But then they laughed again and stood up, for it was high time to go.

'When are you coming again?'

'Tomorrow.'

With that they parted, and straight afterwards as Asta passed the spot where the bell hung, it was just striking the twelfth stroke and the sexton's son who had been ringing it touched his cap and disappeared behind the graves.

8

When he had parted from Asta at the cricket pitch Holk, seeing his gardener hard at work in front of the nearest greenhouse, had gone over to him. After a word of greeting, he tore two pages from his notebook and jotted down a few lines for telegrams to Pentz and Widow Hansen announcing his arrival in Copenhagen the following evening. 'Ohlsen my man, these telegrams have to be taken to

Glücksburg, or Arnewiek for that matter, it's all one to me where you hand them in. Take the shooting-brake.'

The gardener, a surly fellow like most of his calling, was visibly irked so Holk added, 'Sorry to interrupt your work Ohlsen; but I need Philip for packing and your wife's brother, who's showing well, doesn't quite know the ropes yet and so I can't rely on him.'

The gardener was placated and said that if it was all the same to the Count he'd rather go to Glücksburg; his wife had the itches again, most likely her gall-bladder, she was so irritable, so he wanted to see Dr Eschke for a prescription when he was there.

'That's fine,' said Holk. 'And while you're at it, make sure the ship will definitely call here tomorrow morning; it's been known to sail on by, and enquire if the King is there already, in Glücksburg I mean, and how long he's likely to stay.'

With that the Count started back for the Schloss, where Philip was in his dressing-room and had not only brought out the trunks but had already begun packing them.

'Very good, Philip; I see the Countess has told you that I have to go away. Now you know what I need; but not too much, the more you take the more you miss. Isn't that true? If the trunk's full, you expect everything to be there, just like home. One thing you mustn't forget, the fur boots and the galoshes. You stumble around in them like an elephant, but the heart stays safe and warm, and that's always the main thing. Wouldn't you say?'

Philip was in agreement, whereupon the Count, visibly at ease, sat down at his desk and wrote some letters, one of them to his brother-in-law Arne, while the old servant went on packing the trunks.

'Which books do you wish me to pack, Sir?'

'None. The ones we have here aren't right for Copenhagen. Or let's take a few volumes of Walter Scott; you never know, and he's right for all occasions.'

At noon—Asta was still down in the village—Baron Arne came over from Arnewiek, and as they were sitting chatting in the portico with the ladies Holk, laughing, handed him the letter that he had written that morning. 'There you are Alfred; but read it when you get home, that'll be time enough, and in any case you know what's in it. It's the same old story. As so often before, I entrust Schloss Holkenäs and the farm to your care, and I appoint you major-domo for the duration of my absence. Be advisor to your sister, discuss with her' (this he said *sotto voce*) 'the building of a new chapel and crypt or whatever it is she wants, and draw up plans for the cowsheds. Start with the one for the *shorthorns*. Consult the homeo-pathic vet you recently told me such marvellous things about, and then send the plans over to Copenhagen. Pentz has some idea about these things and Bille, who's so widely travelled, even more so, and his measles' (and with that he turned back to the ladies) 'surely can't last for ever. Once his spots have gone – I have to laugh when I think of him moulting – I shall look him up and show him the plans. Invalids are always happy to hear something other than the clink of the medicine spoon and the tap of the doctor's stick.'

Holk continued to speak in this tone, which left no one in any doubt that he was in fact delighted to be able to leave Holkenäs behind for three months. It almost hurt the Countess to hear it, and she would have said as much had she not caught a similar senti-ment in herself. As with many married couples, so it was with the Holks. When they were apart physically they were closest in spirit, and not only did their mutual needling and differences of opinion cease, they rediscovered their love from times past and wrote one another tender letters. No one knew this better than Holk's brother-in-law over in Arnewiek. So Arne regaled them once more with some reflections on the topic and made a few jokes about it. But it wasn't such a good idea: pertinent as his comments were, nothing was further from his sister's wishes than to hear these things spoken of. Perhaps it was this turn in the conversation that caused Holk, observing his wife's slight displeasure, to invite Julie von Dobschütz to join him for a walk in the park, since he still had 'one or two things to discuss with her'.

When they had gone Christine said to her brother with whom she had remained behind alone, 'You didn't have to say that Alfred, not in front of him. As you well know, he already has a tendency to take serious things lightly, and if you lead him on, then he'll feel free to go even further and end up playing the freethinker.'

Arne smiled.

'You smile. But you're wrong. I didn't say *being* a freethinker. He's incapable of *being* a freethinker, he has neither the talent nor the character for that. And there's the problem. I could live with an atheist, at least I consider it possible, and more than that, it could be a challenge for me to have serious arguments with him. But with Helmuth I couldn't. Serious argument! He doesn't know the meaning of the words. To *me* you can very well say all these things, but they just confuse him and reinforce everything that is weak and vain in him.'

Arne contented himself with throwing a few crumbs to the chaffinches that had ventured in under the portico during this conversation; but he remained silent.

'Why do you say nothing? Am I being too churchy for you again? I haven't said a word about the church. Or am I being too severe?'

Arne nodded.

'Too severe. Strange. You really don't understand me any more, Alfred, and if that's a reproach, and I think it is, then I have to return that reproach. I don't understand *you* any more. You know how close I am to you in my heart, how thankful I've been to you since I was a child, and I still have that feeling of gratitude. But one thing I have to say: it's *you* who have changed in your views and principles, not me. One day I'm too moralistic for you, the next I'm too strict in my faith, on the third I'm too Prussian and on the fourth not Danish enough. I can get nothing right. And yet all that I am, Alfred, or at least most of what I am, I am because of you. You pointed me in this direction. You were already thirty when I was left with you after our parents died, and I was brought up according to *your* views, not those of our parents; you chose the Moravian boarding school for me, you introduced me to the Reckes and the Reusses and all the other devout families, and now that I've become what you then intended, you're not pleased. And why not? Because in the meantime you've gone over to the other side. At thirty you were ultra-aristocratic, or as good as, but now at almost sixty, you suddenly see the world through liberal spectacles. I'm prepared to respect that. But can you really reproach me for standing where you once stood and where you yourself placed me?'

Arne took his sister's hand tenderly. 'Ah Christine, you can stand where you like. I no longer have the courage to reject people's viewpoints. That's one thing I've learnt in my second thirty years. It's not the viewpoint that matters; it's the way it's represented. And I have to tell you, you tend to overdo it, you go too far in a good cause.'

'Is it possible to go too far in a good cause?'

'Of course it is. Every form of excess is bad. Since the first time I heard the expression "moderation in all things" I've been most profoundly impressed by the fact that the Ancients prized nothing more highly than that.'

Holk and Fräulein Dobschütz returned from their walk at that moment, and Asta came up the beach terrace from the other side and at once ran up to Arne whose favourite she was, and who was her best listener at all times. With her mother she was mostly reserved; but when Uncle Alfred was there, she poured out everything that was on her mind.

'This morning I was sitting at Pastor Petersen's desk, and on the right lay the bible and on the left a wooden box of antiquities, and there wasn't an inch of space left to show me what was in all the other cardboard boxes. Mostly it was stones. But in the end, once he had pushed the bible aside ...'

'You did have room,' laughed the Countess. 'Dear old Petersen, he always pushes the bible aside and he's always at his stones, indeed he has a tendency to offer stones instead of bread.'

Arne was about to object; but remembering the conversation he and his sister had just had, swiftly changed his mind and was relieved when Asta went on, 'And then out in the churchyard Elisabeth and I stood at her mother's grave and that's when I saw that Elisabeth's real name is Elisabeth Kruse, and it was only her mother who was a Petersen and we shouldn't really be calling her Elisabeth Petersen. But, as she told me, she never knew her father, and when they spoke about her mother in the village, everyone called her old Petersen's daughter, and that's why she's called Elisabeth Petersen and she thinks that's perfectly all right.

'And then,' Asta went on, 'we went further up the churchyard path to the church and climbed on one of the sloping headstones and were just about to look through the barred window into our crypt when a stone fell in with a clatter, and I felt as if I had killed someone. Well, I can't tell you what a fright it gave me. I don't ever want to go in there, and when I die, you all have to promise me that I'll have the sky above my grave.'

The Countess's gaze fell on the Count who was visibly moved and nodded amiably to his wife. 'That's going to change, Christine. I've discussed it with Alfred already, and with Fräulein Dobschütz just now too. There will be an open courtyard with Gothic arches surrounding the burial site, and you'll decide yourself what else is needed.'

While the Count and Countess continued to talk for a short while, Arne spoke with Asta and then, as the conversation became general once more, he changed the subject to other matters, which was easily done since Ohlsen the gardener had just come back from Glücksburg with the news that the King would arrive next day, and Countess Danner too, and he intended to stay a month and excavate a Hun grave on Brarup Moor. And he had bought a ticket for the Kirkegard Line, and the steamer would tie up at the landing-stage around ten in the morning. It would be the line's best ship, the *King Christian* with Captain Brödstedt on the bridge.

Before Ohlsen had finished his report, Axel arrived with his tutor and produced the partridges he had shot from his game-bag.

'Just what I need, Axel,' said Holk, that will make a nice breakfast en route. You're going to be a real huntsman in the Holk tradition after all, and I must confess, that's what would please me most. Studying is for others.'

And as he spoke Holk's gaze fell involuntarily on poor Strehlke, who, while his pupil was shooting partridge, had contented himself with collecting a dozen fieldfare from the snares.

9

The *King Christian* was as good as its word: it hove into sight promptly at ten o'clock and tied up ten minutes later at the landing-stage. The Count was already there, Axel and Asta sitting on his trunks beside him, the boy with his shotgun over his shoulder. It was time now to say goodbye to the children, and afterwards Holk quickly climbed on board with two of the crew walking ahead carrying his luggage. A moment later Captain Brödstedt shouted orders down to the engine room to get under way, the helmsman let the wheel run through his hands, and with a few heavy strokes (it was still a paddle-steamer) the ship pulled away from the landing-stage on an easterly course out to the open sea. Holk had meantime gone up to the Captain and was looking down from the bridge at the pier where the two children were still waving energetically; Axel even fired a salute with his gun. Up above, the Countess and Fräulein Dobschütz stood on the top step of the terrace until, after staying briefly at this level, they went back up to the portico to be able to follow the ship more easily. At the same time they looked down to the pier along which brother and sister, plainly in lively conversation, were now returning together. Only when they reached the beach did they part; Axel turned into the dunes to hunt seagulls, while Asta climbed up the terrace.

At the top she pushed a footstool alongside her mother's seat, took her hand and tried to amuse her. 'It was Captain Brödstedt in command of the ship, a fine-looking man, and Philip told me he's supposed to have a very pretty wife, and they say he carried her off from the Bornholm lighthouse. It's really a pity one can't marry a man like Captain Brödstedt just because of class prejudice.'

'My goodness Asta, whatever put that into your head?'

'It's only natural, Mama. One has eyes in one's head and hears all kinds of things and can draw a few conclusions. Take for example the good Seminar Director, who married a titled lady; of course he's a widower now. You'll surely admit Mama, Schwarzkoppen is no Brödstedt, not by a long chalk. Well, Schwarzkoppen might just pass, but Herr Strehlke ...'

The two ladies laughed, and since her mama said nothing, Fräulein Dobschütz said, 'Asta, you're like a young foal, and I'm afraid you're missing your lessons. The things you say, as if there were any difference socially between a man like Brödstedt and a man like Strehlke.'

'Of course there's a difference. Not for me that is, definitely not, I can assure you. But for others there's a difference. Just look around. I've never heard of a steamer captain marrying a countess, of course I haven't; but would you like me to count on my ten fingers all the private tutors and doctoral students who ...'

'Asta, it would be best if we could dispense with these comparisons.'

'That's fine,' Asta laughed. 'But to be a lighthouse-keeper's daughter, and carried off from the lighthouse by a man like Captain Brödstedt – it's a lovely story, a real-life fairytale. And I love everything to do with fairytales, they're my passion, and I love the story of the Brave Little Tin Soldier much, much more than the whole of the Seven Years' War!' And with that she stood up from her footstool and left the two ladies alone to go and sit at the piano in the next room. Presently a Chopin étude could be heard, halting to be sure and full of mistakes.

'How did Asta come to make a remark like that? Is it just high spirits, or something else? What's taking her mind down such strange paths?'

'Nothing that need worry you,' said Fräulein Dobschütz. 'If there was, she'd keep quiet about it. I spend more time with her than you and I can vouch for her good sense. Asta has a lively mind and a lively imagination ...'

'Which is always a danger ...'

'Yes. But often a blessing too. A lively imagination hides the ugly sides of life behind pictures, it's like a shield, a protective screen.'

The Countess was silent, gazing ahead, and when she looked out to sea a little while later, all she could see of the steamer was its smoke becoming ever fainter, like a brushstroke along the horizon. She seemed preoccupied with all kinds of thoughts, and when her friend cast a fleeting sidelong glance at her she saw there was a tear in her eye.

'What is it Christine?' she said.

'Nothing.'

'You seem so moved ...'

'It's nothing,' the Countess repeated. 'Or at least nothing I can put my finger on. But a nameless fear is tormenting me, and if I didn't abhor fortune-telling and dream-interpretation from the bottom of my soul because to me they're godless and a cause of sorrow, then I'd have to tell you about a dream I had last night. And it wasn't even a terrible dream, just sad and melancholy. There was a funeral procession, just you and me and Holk in the distance. And suddenly I was walking in a wedding procession, and then it was a funeral procession again. I can't get this dream out of my mind. And the strange thing is, as long as it lasted I wasn't afraid, and only when I woke up did the fear set in. And that's why what Asta said worries me. Even yesterday it would just have amused me, for I know the child and I know that she's just as you say she is … and to be frank, this trip worries me too. Look, now the last smoke-trail has disappeared …'

'But Christine, you must put it behind you; it's just like worrying that you're going to fall off a chair, or the ceiling is going to come down. Ceilings do fall down, and houses too, and ships are wrecked between Glücksburg and Copenhagen, but only once in a hundred years, thank goodness …'

'But then somebody suffers, and who's to say who that person will be. But it's not that, Julie … I'm not thinking about an accident on the voyage … The things that worry me are quite different. As you know, I was looking forward to these quiet days which were also going to be busy days, but since this morning I'm not looking forward to them any more.'

'Have you changed your mind about the children?'

'No. We discussed that some time ago and it still stands, just with Axel it's still not clear where he's to go. But that won't be hard to settle. No Julie, what's been on my mind since this morning is simply this: I shouldn't have let Holk go, or at least not on his own. I've always been uneasy and mistrustful about this strange position of his, and if he had to go again this time, because it would have caused offence not to, I should have gone with him …'

Fräulein Dobschütz, surprised, struggled to suppress a smile.

'Jealous?' and as she asked this question she took the Countess's hand and felt that it was trembling. 'You say nothing. So I'm right, you really are jealous, otherwise you would say something or laugh at the suggestion. One never ceases to be amazed, even at what is in one's best friend's heart.'

There was a pause, painful for both of them, especially for Julie von Dobschütz, who had prompted all this quite involuntarily. Yes, embarrassment on both sides, that much was certain, embarrassment that could be overcome only if the conversation were continued as it had begun, with complete frankness.

'Will you allow me to say something?'

The Countess nodded.

'Well, Christine, I've been in many houses and I've seen things that I'd rather not have seen. Stately homes often leave much to be desired. But on the other hand, if ever I saw a house that could be relied upon, it's yours. You're an angel, like all beautiful women when they're not just beautiful but good as well, which is rare. I personally have never known anyone who was better than you. But right after you comes your husband. He's a model in everything we're talking about here. And if I had to show a foreigner what a German house and German manners are, I would bring him straight here to Holkenäs.'

The Countess's brow cleared.

'Yes Christine, all things considered you're a very privileged woman. Holk is sincere and reliable, and even if every third woman in Copenhagen were Potiphar's wife in person, you could still be sure of him. And finally, Christine, if in spite of all that you were still to be in doubt …'

'What then?'

'Then you would have to suppress that doubt, and persuade yourself wisely and lovingly that it wasn't so. Steadfast faith is a joy that improves and restores, while ugly suspicion ruins everything.'

'Oh my dear Julie, you can only say that because, for all your familiarity with our house and our life here, you don't really know (and you just said so yourself) what is in my heart. You know everything and then again you don't. I think only the couples involved know what marriages are like, and sometimes even they don't know. An outsider sees every little annoyance and hears every argument; for, strange to say, married couples don't conceal much of their feuding and arguing from the world, indeed, sometimes it seems as if it's intended for other people to hear, and as if the most violent things are said for others' benefit. But that gives a false impression,

for as long as there's still some love left in it, a marriage always has
another side too. You see, Julie, when I want to talk to Holk about
something and look for him in his study and see that he's doing
accounts or writing, I take a book and sit opposite him and say,
"Don't let me disturb you, Holk, I'll wait." And then, while I'm
reading or just pretending to, I often look up over my book and take
pleasure in his dear, good face, and feel I would like to fly to him and
say, "Holk, my dear." You see, Julie, that happens too; but nobody
sees or hears it.'

'Oh Christine, to hear that from your own lips is a greater
pleasure than I can say. I've sometimes feared for the two of you and
your happiness. But if that's how it is ...'

'That is indeed how it is, Julie, sometimes in spite of myself. But
precisely because that's how it is, you're wrong in your advice that
one should always believe the best, sometimes even turn a blind eye.
It doesn't work like that when you love somebody. And then, my
dear Julie, you're wrong too, or at least half wrong, in what you say
about Holk. He is good and faithful, the best husband in the world,
that's true, but he's also weak and vain, and Copenhagen is not the
place to make a weak character firm. You see, Julie, you act as his
advocate, and you do so with total conviction, but you also speak
of possibilities, and it is precisely these that are preying on my
mind ...'

Fräulein Dobschütz was about to reassure her further, but Philip
came in and handed over a letter which a messenger had just
brought from Arnewiek. The Countess first took it to be from her
brother but after a glance at the address she saw that it was from
Schwarzkoppen. And then she read:

My dear lady, since the day before yesterday I have gone more
fully into the question we discussed then, and have also reviewed
the list of educational institutions that might be considered
for Axel. Some of the best are too strict, not only in the matter
of discipline but also in that of religion, and so my assumption would be that the College at Bunzlau corresponds most
closely to your stated requirements. I know the headmaster and
would consider it an honour if you were to permit me to write

a few words of introduction to him. In addition, Gnadenfrei is relatively close, so that brother and sister could see each other frequently and could travel back together for the summer holidays.

I remain, my esteemed Countess, your most devoted servant,

Schwarzkoppen

'Well Julie, things are falling into place very nicely. In this question I shall rely entirely on our friend over there, and Holk left me a free hand. How nice that we now have something to do. We'll write down today what each of the children requires, it'll be a whole array of things. And then there's the journey, and of course you must accompany us. I'm really looking forward with all my heart to seeing my beloved Gnadenfrei again, and you will be too. And then when I think of how my brother, oh how long ago it is, came to bring me home and Holk was with him ... It was almost like the lighthouse that Captain Brödstedt carried off the young woman of Bornholm from. And it certainly was a lighthouse, both for you and for me, a light for life and, I hope, until death.'

10

The steamer crossing was smooth, and it was not yet nine in the evening when the *King Christian* turned between Nyholm and Tolboden into Copenhagen harbour. Holk stood on deck, enjoying the splendid sight; the stars sparkled above in almost wintry clarity, while below the shimmering expanse of water reflected both these and the shore lights. Shore porters and commission agents pressed forward, coachmen held their whips raised and waited for a signal from a fare, but Holk, who preferred to walk the few hundred paces to Dronningens Tværgade, refused all services, merely instructing the ship's steward to have his luggage delivered as soon as possible to Widow Hansen's house. Then, after a friendly farewell from the Captain, he walked along the quay, first to St Anne's Place and from there round a short bend to Dronningens Tværgade,

where Widow Hansen's two-storey house stood immediately on
the left. When he caught sight of his lodging after a few minutes
from the other side of the street, he looked it over and was pleased
at the clean and welcoming impression it all made. The first floor
where his two rooms were located was already lit up and the sash
windows had been opened a little to let in fresh air. 'I'll wager
there's a fire burning in the grate. An ideal landlady.' With these
thoughts he went across the street to the house and rapped firmly
with the knocker, not too loud and not too quietly. The door was
opened instantly and Widow Hansen herself, almost fifty but still an
attractive woman, greeted the Count with a degree of warmth and
expressed her pleasure at seeing him once again that year, for she
had expected him some time after New Year at the earliest. 'That
Baron Bille, and he's no child, had to catch measles of all things: but
that's life, one man's loss is another man's gain.'

With these words, the landlady had stepped back into the hall
and gone ahead with a lamp to show the Count up. And he duly
followed. At the foot of the stairs, however, he stopped for a
moment; he could hardly have done otherwise, given the sight that
met him. The half of the narrow hall towards the back was pitch
dark; however, right at the end, where a door stood open, presumably leading into the kitchen, a shaft of light fell into the dark hall,
and in that light a young woman stood, perhaps in order to see him,
more probably in order to be seen. Holk was taken aback and said,
'Your daughter I assume? I've already heard about her, I'm told she
isn't accompanying her husband on this occasion.' Widow Hansen
acknowledged Holk's question only briefly, presumably because she
had no desire to diminish the effect of the tableau with a lengthy
explanation.

Upstairs in his rooms, which were carpeted with heavy rugs and
amply but not excessively appointed with vases and other pieces of
Chinese and Japanese porcelain, everything was just as Holk had
surmised: the lamps were lit, the fire was duly burning in the grate,
and there was fruit on the sofa-table, probably more to enhance the
welcoming still-life effect than to be eaten. Beside the fruit-bowl lay
cards from Baron Pentz and Baron Erichsen who had both called
an hour earlier, enquiring after the Count. 'They said they would

come back.'

At that moment voices were heard down in the vestibule. 'That will be my things,' said Holk, expecting to see the young woman who was still on his mind come in with two shore porters carrying his trunks. But it was not the young woman, nor was it his luggage, it was the two barons who appeared, and Holk now exchanged greetings with them, heartily and jovially with Pentz, courteously and with a degree of reserve with Erichsen. Widow Hansen made to withdraw, asking only what the Count might require for the evening. Holk was about to reply but Pentz intervened, 'Dear Frau Hansen, Count Holk has no further wishes for today, apart from the wish to accompany us to Vincent's. You must resign yourselves, you and your good daughter, to our commandeering him at the very first opportunity. Which reminds me, is there any news of Captain Hansen yet, that happiest and most enviable, but at the same time most negligent of husbands? If I had a wife like his, I'd have looked for a different occupation, one that kept me at home twenty-four hours a day; ship's captain at any rate would have been the last thing.'

Widow Hansen was visibly amused but she chose to adopt a rather serious demeanour and said with matronly dignity, 'Oh Sir, someone waiting for their husband has no eyes for others. My dear departed was also a ship's captain. And I always thought only of him ...'

Pentz laughed. 'Well Frau Hansen, one has to believe the things women tell one, there's no other way. And I shall endeavour to do that.'

And with that he took Holk by the arm and led him off to Vincent's restaurant for their evening meal together with the obligatory causerie. Baron Erichsen followed with an expression on his face that seemed disapproving of the preceding pleasantries with the widow, despite the fact that he was familiar enough with Pentz's small talk.

Widow Hansen had already lifted the shade off one of the two lamps and lit the way downstairs until the three gentlemen had left the house.

Pentz and Erichsen were opposites, which didn't prevent them from being on fairly good terms. Indeed everyone was on good terms with Pentz, because not only did he subscribe wholeheartedly to the Dutch proverb 'Be surprised, but never annoyed', he even went somewhat beyond this dictum. For nothing surprised him any more: surprise itself was excessive for him. His motto was *ride si sapis*, and he saw the funny side of everything. To Pontius Pilate's question 'What is truth?' he offered the widest possible latitude in life, politics and the church, and to get hot under the collar about questions of morality – in discussion of which he regularly cited the Greeks, Egyptians, Indians and Circassians as representatives of *every* school of thought in life and love – was simply proof to him of abysmal ignorance and extreme unfamiliarity with the 'ever-changing forms of human socialization', as he liked to put it, waving his small gold spectacles in the air as he did so. On these occasions there was always an artful, superior smile in his little eyes. He was in his sixties, unmarried and of course a gourmet; the Princess appreciated him because he never bored her and could apparently carry out the duties of his office, which were not always straightforward, with supreme ease and yet always with great exactitude. This meant that other things could be overlooked, in particular that despite all his merits he cut a comic figure in all aspects of his physical appearance. As long as he was at table all was well; but when he stood up, the places in which nature had on the one hand endowed him with too much and on the other with too little were revealed. In the pedestal area he left much to be desired, or as the Princess put it, 'she had never seen anyone walk less on stilts than Baron Pentz.' Since she used this expression only when something morally very 'unstilted' had cropped up in his conversation, she had the double pleasure of ridiculing him and delighting him in a single word. He was very nimble and might have seemed destined for eternal life had it not been for his ample girth, short neck and ruddy complexion, three things that betrayed an apoplectic constitution.

Erichsen could be seen as the counterpart of Pentz; if the latter was apoplectic the former was a born hectic. He came from a family with a history of consumption, which, because it was very rich, had supplied churchyards in health resorts everywhere with monuments in marble, syenite and bronze. The symbols of immortality on these monuments were always the same: in Nice, San Remo, Funchal and Cairo, and more prosaically in Görbersdorf too, the butterfly soared heavenwards, as if it were the Erichsen coat of arms. Our present gentleman-in-waiting, who had been in the Princess's service for about ten years, had bluffed his way through the whole course, completing it more successfully than others who bore his name. From his fortieth year he had settled down and was in a position to opt for a quiet life, which he did, to the extent of scarcely ever leaving Copenhagen again. He had had enough of travel, and days of fasting prescribed on medical grounds had left him with an aversion to all forms of excess, which he eschewed in his present life at court. Accustomed to living off milk, chicken breast and Kränchen water from Bad Ems, his only function at banquets and celebrations was, as Pentz said, to warn with his long, exclamation-mark of a frame against anything that might recall the cult of Bacchus. 'Erichsen the Conscience' was one of the many nicknames Pentz had given him.

From Widow Hansen's house in Dronningens Tværgade to Vincent's restaurant on Kongens Nytorv was only five minutes' walk. Pentz instructed Erichsen to go on ahead and reconnoitre, because 'as a six-footer he would have a better view of the seating situation at Vincent's.' And there was good reason for this cautious instruction, jokingly as it was given, for when Pentz and Holk entered the establishment a minute after Erichsen, it seemed impossible to find a free table. But finally they did spot a good corner which not only had a few comfortable seats but also enabled them to observe the rest of the company in comfort.

'I think we'll begin with a medium Rüdesheimer Riesling. Doctor Grämig recently told me, the most amusing man in the world by the way, that it's remarkable I'm still free of gout, because not only my lifestyle, but more especially my station in life, gives me a historical entitlement to it. He may be right of course, but it just makes me more determined to utilize what gout-free time I have left. Erichsen, what can I order for you? Bilin or Seltzer or Pyrmont mineral water …'

A waiter came and a short while later they drank to each other from fine cut glass goblets, for Erichsen too had taken the

Rüdesheimer, after having first made sure that he had a carafe of water.

'Old Denmark,' said Pentz, to which Holk, clinking glasses a second time, replied, 'Of course, Pentz, to Old Denmark. And the older the better. For the thing that might separate us – God grant that the day may be far away – is the new Denmark. The old one, I'm all for it, I'll drink to that. Frederick VII, and our Princess . . . But tell me Pentz, what has got into my good Copenhageners, above all in a convivial wine lodge like this? Just look at those people over there, all steamed up, snatching the papers out of each other's hands. And isn't that Lieutenant-Colonel Faaborg – yes, that's who it is, I must pay my respects to him later – he's as red as a turkey-cock, and waving a newspaper in its holder in the air like a dragoon's sabre. Who's that he's belabouring with his opinion?'

'Poor Thott.'

'Poor? How's that?

'As far as I know, it's because people suspect Thott of being involved in the conspiracy too.'

'What conspiracy?'

'Dear me, Holk, you're at least a generation behind the times. Of course if you packed yesterday and travelled today you're half-excused. We've had a conspiracy of a sort here: they say Hall's head will have to roll.'

'And you call that a conspiracy. Now I remember, you wrote to me about it … I ask you, let dear old Hall's head roll. He won't be overly keen to bring an out-of-joint Denmark – not that I believe that any more – back into joint. Hamlet didn't want to in his day. Nor will Hall.'

'He doesn't want to either, you're right about that. But our Princess wants him to, and that's what counts. The less she trusts the King, all because of her aversion to the Danner woman, the more she trusts Hall; only Hall can save us, and for that reason he must remain in office. And there are many who think like the Princess – I would beg of you, on no account reveal your contrary views in her presence. And that's why you see Faaborg brandishing his newspaper-holder like a gladiator.'

Erichsen had also been following the animated scene opposite. 'A stroke of luck that de Meza is sitting at the next table,' he said, 'he'll bring them to order.'

'Oh come on, Erichsen, bring them to order! As if Faaborg, who is Danish through and through, will allow himself to be called to order once his dander is up and he gets into his stride. And by de Meza if you please.'

'De Meza is his superior officer.'

'Well, it depends on what you mean by superior. He's his superior officer when he's inspecting the brigade, but he's not here at Vincent's or anywhere else, especially when it's a matter of politics, Danish politics, of which de Meza understands nothing, at least not in Faaborg's eyes. To him de Meza is a foreigner, and there's some truth in that. De Meza's father was a Portuguese Jew, all Portuguese are Jews really, and he came to Copenhagen, which Holk may not know, as a ship's doctor years and years ago. And even if it weren't fully authenticated – you can look it up in any book, and de Meza himself makes no secret of it – his ancestry is written all over his face. And especially in that Portuguese complexion of his.'

Erichsen took some pleasure in this, and nodded in agreement.

'As if it were just his southern complexion,' Pentz went on, 'but he's altogether a man of the South, not to say the Levant, and a barometer and a windsock I'd say are the two things he can least do without. He constantly feels the cold, and what other people call fresh air is an icy draught, a chill wind or a hurricane to him. I'd like to know what our Valdemar the Conqueror, the king who spent at least fifty-three weeks of the year at sea, would have made of de Meza.'

Thus far Erichsen had followed in full agreement, but the last points were rather injudiciously chosen and applied to the tall, thin, ailing old gentleman-in-waiting much more than to de Meza.

He was a man who seldom spoke as a rule, but now he was nettled and broke in: 'I don't understand you, Pentz. Next thing you'll be telling us a man must live entirely without wool to be considered a soldier at all. I know de Meza wears flannel because he's always cold, but his chilly condition didn't prevent him from distinguishing himself at Fredericia in '49 and then winning the day at Idstedt the following year. Personally I have no doubt that

Napoleon kept an eye on the thermometer just like other people; in Russia of course it wasn't necessary. Incidentally I now see that over there in the officers' corner they've gone back to reading the papers, and left the arguing to us. Shall we go over and pay our compliments to de Meza?'

'I think not,' said Holk. 'He might ask about this or that, questions that just today I'd not be inclined to answer. I'm not worried about de Meza who respects all opinions, but about the other gentlemen, among whom there are some hotheads, if my admittedly shaky personal knowledge serves. For example Lieutenant-Colonel Tersling there on the left by the window, if I'm seeing right. And I'm thinking about the Princess too: a political lady, who gets everything reported back. I'm already on tenterhooks about the cross-examination I'll be subjected to tomorrow or in the next few days.'

Pentz laughed. 'Holk, dear fellow, you know what women are like I hope …'

Erichsen narrowed a roguish eye, because he knew that Pentz, though he thought he knew, certainly did *not*.

'… women, I say. And if not women, then at least princesses, and if not all princesses then at least *our* Princess. You're quite right, she's a political lady and you mustn't approach her with a Schleswig-Holstein programme. There's no change there, but things haven't got any worse, because despite all the politicking, she remains, as ever, *ancien régime*.'

'I'll grant you that. But what am I personally supposed to gain from it?'

'Everything. And I'm surprised to have to enlighten you on this. *Ancien régime*: what does it mean? The people of the *ancien régime* were political too, but they did everything out of sentiment, certainly the women did, and perhaps that was the right thing to do. At any rate it was the more entertaining thing to do. And there you have the word on which it all turns. For entertainment which in politics at least invariably means *chronique scandaleuse*, occupied centre-stage back then, and that's still the case as far as our Princess is concerned, so if you're afraid of a political cross-examination, all you have to do is mention Berling, or the Danner woman, or

von Blixen-Fineke, or just hint at the shepherdesses and satyrs in
the kind of theatricals they put on at Skodsborg, or in good Frau
Rasmussen's villa, and that'll be the end of any political conversation and you'll be off the hook. Am I right Erichsen?'

Erichsen confirmed this.

'Yes gentlemen,' laughed Holk, 'I can see all that, but unfortunately I don't see that it helps me particularly. It's just replacing
one difficulty with another. What's supposed to protect me from
political discussion is almost a bigger problem than political discussion itself. For me at least. You forget that I'm not privy to all this;
my knowledge of Copenhagen life, despite occasional sojourns here,
is really quite superficial, just what I glean from the *Dagbladet* or the
Flyveposten. And now I'm suddenly supposed to talk about Danner
and Berling or Danner and Blixen-Fineke; but what do I know
about them? Nothing, nothing at all; nothing but what I've picked
up in the latest satirical magazines, and the Princess knows all that,
for she reads them and all the newspapers far into the night. All I
have is Widow Hansen, and as a source of information she's surely
not enough.'

'Quite wrong Holk. You haven't grasped the point about Widow
Hansen and her daughter. They're an encyclopedia of all the
Copenhagen gossip. Where they get it from is their own sweet
secret. Something like Dionysius's Ear,* some say, others speak of
underground passages, others of a Hansen telescope that brings
things hidden from normal mortals out of their place of concealment. Some speak of the chief of police. For me that's the most
obvious assumption. But whatever the explanation, one thing is
certain, both women, or ladies if you like, for their rank is hard to
pin down, know everything, and if you take up your duties every
morning fully briefed by Frau Hansen, then I'll guarantee you'll be
safe from all awkward political discussions. The Hansens, especially
the younger one, know more about Countess Danner than Danner
herself. For in this interesting field police officers have, so to speak,
the gift of divination, or poetry, and where no evidence exists, some
will be invented.'

---

* A limestone cave in Syracuse whose fine acoustics allegedly allowed the tyrant
Dionysius I (405–367 BC) to overhear what political prisoners were saying.

'Now I'm getting to know the good Frau Hansen from a completely new side. I had assumed utter respectability ...'

'That's there too, in a certain sense ... If there's no plaintiff, there's no judge ...'

'Under these circumstances, I shall have to proceed with particular caution ...'

'I would counsel against that, if I may. The disadvantages are glaringly obvious, and the advantages are more than questionable. In that house you can hide nothing, even if your character permitted it; the Hansens will read everything out of your very soul, and the best I can suggest is for you to be free and frank and talk a lot. Talking a lot is a good thing anyway, and on occasion it's the ultimate diplomatic stroke; for then details are very hard to verify, or even better, they cancel one another out.'

Erichsen smiled.

'You're smiling Erichsen, and it suits you. But it also reminds me – for a smile, because its intention generally remains indefinite, can always criticize in many directions – that it's time to release our friend Holk; it's already a quarter past eleven, and the Hansens are respectable folk who don't like to be awake as the witching hour approaches, or at least not visibly so with a lamp lit in the hall. At the other table over there I see they've all left. You can wait outside by the Guard House while I settle the bill.'

Holk and Erichsen strolled up and down outside. When Pentz had rejoined them they walked towards Dronningens Tværgade, where they took their leave opposite Frau Hansen's house. The house stood in darkness, with only the moon, when the clouds revealed it, looking in at the panes of the top-storey windows. Holk lifted the knocker, but before he could let it fall, the door opened and the young Frau Hansen received him. She wore a skirt and jacket of the same simple, light material, but all cleverly calculated for effect. In her hand she held a hanging lamp of the kind featured in pictures of Antiquity. All in all a curious combination of Froufrou* and Lady Macbeth. Holk, in some confusion, struggled for a form of address; but the young Frau Hansen was quicker and

---

* Title-role in a popular drawing-room comedy by Henri Meilhac and Ludovic Halévy.

said, half-closing her eyes ostensibly from fatigue, that her mother begged to be excused since, robust as she was, she needed to be asleep before midnight. Holk then expressed his regret at having chatted for so long and added an urgent plea, should it happen again, not to wait up for him. But the young woman, without quite saying it outright, seemed to indicate that they would not willingly abdicate the right to wait up for their house guest on all occasions. At the same time she went on ahead with slow tread, bearing her lamp, until she reached the foot of the stairs, where she stood aside and, resting her left arm on the banister, raised her right arm to light the Count to his rooms. As she did so, her wide sleeve fell back, baring her beautiful arm. Holk, when he reached the upper floor, bade her goodnight again and, as the young woman slowly and silently withdrew, watched the dwindling play of light and shadow in the hall and on the staircase. He stood and listened for a few more moments with his door half-open, and only when it had gone quite dark down below did he close it.

'A beautiful person. But uncanny. I daren't mention her at all in my letter to Christine, or she'll reply sounding the alarm and parading all the dubious females from the Old and New Testaments before me.'

11

Despite his fatigue from the journey, Holk had dwelt longer on the image of the young Frau Hansen before falling asleep than on politics or the Princess. Next morning, however, it had all evaporated, and if he did still recall the apparition with the lamp, it was with a smile. He tried to remember which goddess or lover was usually depicted on classical frescoes searching with a lamp, but he couldn't think of one and eventually gave up the attempt. Then he tugged the bell-pull and opened the window for a breath of fresh air and to look down at the street before breakfast appeared. There were only a few passers-by on Dronningens Tværgade at this relatively early hour, but they all without exception bore themselves well and were fresh and radiant, and he could understand the pride that made the Danes see themselves as the Parisians of the North, differing from their models only by being superior to them. At that moment the window curtains bulged and when he looked round, he saw that Widow Hansen had come in with the breakfast tray. They exchanged greetings and after the usual enquiry about how the Count had slept and what he had dreamt, 'for the first dream always comes true', Frau Hansen spread the tablecloth and arranged the breakfast table with all the things that moments before had stood on the tray. Holk surveyed the magnificent spread and said, 'Nowhere is a man better looked after than at Frau Hansen's; everything smiles at you, everything so spick and span, above all Frau Hansen herself. And tea from Chinese porcelain! One can't fail to notice that the dear departed sailed the China run, and so does your son-in-law, as Baron Pentz told me last night, and he's called Hansen too; the same name, the same title, so that one could readily confuse mother and daughter.'

'Oh Sir,' said Widow Hansen, 'who could confuse us? An old woman like me who's has such a long, hard life …'

'Come now.'

'… and Brigitte who'll only turn thirty tomorrow! But my dear Count, you mustn't give me away – that I told you tomorrow's Brigitte's birthday.'

'Give you away? I ask you, Frau Hansen … but you look as if you're about to rush off, standing there; it makes me nervous. I tell you what, you must sit down and talk to me, provided I'm not inter-rupting the housework or anything more important.'

Frau Hansen pretended to hesitate.

'Yes indeed, and let this be the first visit of many that you will be kind enough to make on a regular basis; I've so many questions to ask you. Please, here on this chair, I can see you best there, and seeing tells at least half as much as hearing. My hearing used to be very good, but it's been letting me down now and then recently; the first sign of age.'

'Who could believe that, Sir. I think you only hear what you want to hear, and see what you want to see.'

'I see and hear nothing, Frau Hansen, and what I do see I forget again. Not everything of course. Last night I saw your daughter, Brigitte you said her name was, a wonderful name to add to all her other charms. Now she's a person one couldn't forget. You can be proud to have such a beautiful daughter and I can't understand her husband, calmly leaving his wife behind and sailing back and forth between Singapore and Shanghai. At least I assume he does, for they more or less all ply that route. Yes, Frau Hansen, in my view a man would take a beautiful woman like that along with him from the North Pole to the South Pole, if not out of love, then out of fear and jealousy. For my part, and as I well know, I always say you mustn't expect more of youth than it can deliver. Isn't that so? I think we're agreed on this point, you think so too. So why doesn't he take her with him? Why does he expose her to danger? And himself too, himself even more.'

'Oh, that's a long story Sir ...'

'So much the better. A love story can never be too long, and it is a love story, I take it.'

'I'm not sure I would call it that; there's something of the kind in it, but it's not a proper love story, not really ... it's just that it could have turned into one.'

'Now you're really whetting my curiosity ... excellent tea, incidentally; one can see he was a China hand, and my pleasure would be even greater if you would permit me to pour some of your own tea for you.'

With that he stood up and took a cup inscribed in gold 'To the Happy Couple' from an étagère by the window. 'To the Happy Couple,' Holk repeated. 'Who does it mean? Perhaps you, my dear Frau Hansen; you're laughing ... but one is never too old to make a sensible move, and the most sensible thing a widow can do is –'

'Stay a widow.'

'Well, so be it, if you say so. But the story, the story. Captain Hansen, your son-in-law, will no doubt be a handsome man, captains are always handsome, and Frau Brigitte no doubt married him for love.'

'That she did, at least she never told me different, except once. But that was later, and I'm talking about the early days now when they'd just married. They were very much in love and she was always on board with him wherever the voyage took them, even to places where there was yellow fever, and whenever they were back here in Copenhagen ... she had a place of her own then, for my dear old Hansen, the Count must certainly remember him from Glücksburg, was still alive at the time ... well, what I was going to say was, always when they were back after a long, long trip, all she wanted was to be off again straight away, because she didn't like the people here, or so she always said, and to be out in the wide world was best.'

'But that's wonderful. Did she have so little vanity? Had she no desire at all to be flattered and flirted with? For there would have been no lack of that. As I'll wager the Copenhageners will have started showing her from the day she was confirmed.'

'Indeed they did. But Brigitte was always indifferent to that kind of attention and remained that way when she was married too. There were just a few times when she rebelled. And that's how things stayed until '54; I know the exact date because it was the year the English fleet called here on its way to Russia. And that same summer we had a very young officer from the Life Guards in Copenhagen who was constantly in and out of the Rasmussen house—Countess Danner's I mean, but that's what we always call her—he ran up such debts that there was nothing for it but to resign his commission. But because he was so clever and knew about everybody, for he was on familiar terms with all the rich houses, especially the women, Baron Scheele, who was a Minister at the time, said he wanted to take the lieutenant on in the Ministry of the Interior. And he did, and there he's working still and has become very distinguished already. But back then he was a bit of a rogue, and handsome with it, and when Brigitte saw him—it was just at the time when news came through of that bombardment up North, I forget the name of it now I'm afraid—she said to me, "*He's* the man for me." And she showed it soon enough. And that autumn when Hansen had to sail to China again, she told him outright she wasn't going with him and she told him why. Or maybe other people told him. To cut a long story short, when the day came for the ship to sail, Hansen turned very serious, refused to stand for any nonsense, and said, "Brigitte, you're coming with me now ..." And if he had taken her along for love before, he now took her, just as you said yourself, Count, as a precaution or out of jealousy.'

'And did it help? Did the trip cure her of her love? Her love for the man at the Ministry, I mean?'

'Yes, it did, although with Brigitte you can never be quite sure. She says plenty, but she also keeps plenty to herself. And it's all one really, for we did end up with the main thing.'

'And the main thing was what?'

'That my son-in-law has regained his trust in Brigitte, absolutely. Hansen you see is a very good man, and he's calm and reasonable again, and back on the old China run.'

'I can truly say I'm pleased to hear it. But we mustn't forget or omit anything, and what you were actually going to tell me I think, dear Frau Hansen, was how it came about that your son-in-law recovered from his jealousy …'

'Yes, and I always say man proposes and God disposes, and when danger is greatest, then help is closest. For I do worry, I have to say; a mother always worries about her child and it doesn't matter whether she's married or not; yes, I worried about Brigitte for I did think, this will end in divorce, for she's very strong-willed, stubborn you might even say, and she's very excitable, for all she sometimes seems so sleepy and quiet …'

'Yes, indeed,' Holk laughed, 'it's always the same, still waters run deep.'

'So I worried. But it all turned out quite differently, and that happened just at the time when Brigitte was more or less forced to sail with him. It was like this. On that trip Hansen had to take a cargo to Bangkok on the way back, a great city in Siam that I myself visited with my husband many years ago. And when Hansen arrived there and had been moored for a day or two in front of the Imperial Palace, for they have an Emperor in Siam, a Minister came on board and invited Hansen and his wife to a grand Court banquet. The Emperor must have seen her. And Brigitte sat at his side and spoke English to him, and the Emperor kept looking at her. And when they had risen from the table, he was still very gracious and attentive and never took his eyes off her, and when they were taking their leave, he said to Hansen he would very much like the

Captain's wife to come to the palace again next day so that his loyal subjects, but above all his wives (of whom there were very many) could see the beautiful *German lady* again face to face. This further honour, which might be treachery, gave Hansen a moment's fright, for all round the palace there were heads stuck on spikes, the way we spike pineapples; but Brigitte, who had heard the conversation, bowed to the Emperor and said with a fitting demeanour, for she has something assured and refined about her, that she would come at the appointed hour.'

'Daring, very daring.'

'And she really did go back, and took her place on a dais erected in front of the palace gate in the shade of the portal, and on this throne, after the Emperor had first put a string of pearls around her neck, she sat with a peacock feather fan. It was a magnificent neck-lace, I've heard. And then everyone who was anyone in Bangkok processed past her, followed by the general populace, all bowing, with the women at the tail-end, and when the last one had passed, Brigitte rose and went to the Emperor to lay before him the fan and pearl necklace, which she thought she had just been lent for the ceremony. And the Emperor did take both back, but then gave her the necklace and said that she was to wear it in his eternal memory. And straight afterwards, led by the Ministers between two ranks of Life Guards, she returned to the landing-stage, from which Hansen had witnessed the whole event.'

'And then?'

'And from that day on a great change of attitude could be observed in her, and the following winter when she was back here and the man for whose sake she had almost lost her happiness tried to court her again, she rejected his attentions, as far as I could see, with cold indifference. Hansen boarded ship again six months later, and Brigitte declared that, provided he had nothing against it, she would prefer to stay at home—because the idea of living among sailors again, and perhaps sleeping in harbour inns, where all you heard was Negro music and everything smelt of gin, seemed rather strange to her now that she had received such a mark of favour from an emperor—and Hansen not only agreed, he was quite delighted she no longer wished to come on the voyage, not this one and none that might follow. For there was no trace of jealousy in him any longer. He could see what Brigitte was like now, and his only worry was that it had been too much and that the Emperor of Siam had gone to her head more than was good for her.'

Holk was in some doubt whether to believe the tale or to take it as a cock and bull story and at the same time a brazen test of his credulity. After all Pentz's hints the previous evening, the latter was the more likely. And yet it might be true. Hadn't stranger things happened? And so, to justify himself with a touch of irony in his own eyes at least, he asked where the white elephants had been.

'They were probably in the elephant shed,' said Frau Hansen with a mischievous laugh.

'And what about the pearl necklace, my dear Frau Hansen, you must show me *that*.'

'If only that were possible ...'

'Were possible? Why wouldn't it be?'

'Because when Brigitte got back on board, the necklace was suddenly missing; she must have lost it or left it at the palace in the excitement.'

'Well, I would have enquired immediately.'

'So would I. But Brigitte's a strange one, and when Hansen tried to insist, as I later heard, she just said that was vulgar and contrary to court etiquette.'

'Yes,' said Holk, who was beginning to see things more clearly, 'that's right. And one must respect such sentiments.'

12

Finishing her story, which when it came to the lost pearl necklace had begun to sound something of a fairytale even to the credulous Holk, Frau Hansen stood up 'so as not to disturb him further' and Holk made no attempt to detain her. Not that his patience was exhausted, quite the contrary, he liked listening to gossip like this, and the suspect semi-obscurity in which it was all shrouded only increased his interest. No, it was simply a glance at the console clock that led him to desist from enjoying more of Widow Hansen's artful storytelling; he was expected at eleven at the Princess's, less than an hour hence, and first a short letter had to be written to his wife reporting his safe arrival. Haste was indicated in the circumstances, and at five to eleven he climbed into a cab to take him to the Princesses' Palace only two minutes away.

The Princess's apartments were on the first floor. Holk in the uniform of a gentleman-in-waiting, in which he rather fancied himself, climbed the staircase and entered the antechamber, and from there passed into a comfortable sitting room richly wood-panelled and carpeted but otherwise, apart from a desk, sparsely furnished; here the Princess was accustomed to receive visitors and give audiences. The footman promised to announce him immediately. Holk stepped up to one of the windows directly opposite the door through which the Princess was to be expected, and looked down on the square and the street beyond. The square was dead and lifeless; distinguished but boring, and there was nothing to be seen but fallen leaves being swept over the stones by a moderate wind. A feeling of desolation and abandonment came over Holk, and he turned back into the room to look at the only two portraits that adorned the smooth stucco walls. One of them, above an uphol-stered sofa, was a picture of King Christian VII of blessed memory, the Princess's uncle, and the other, above the writing-desk, was a portrait of another close relative, the Landgrave of Thuringia, also deceased. Its gilt frame had dusty crêpe over it, and the dust made it look less like crêpe than a spider's web. The Landgrave had a good, courageous but average sort of face, and Holk was involuntarily moved to wonder what ideas for bettering the welfare of his people the deceased might have had in his time. All that could be discerned with certainty was a keen eye for the daughters of the land.

Before Holk had concluded these reflections, a small door opened in the right-hand corner of the rear wall and the Princess entered, dressed comfortably and almost casually, at any rate with a complete indifference to elegance, just as one would have expected, judging by the furnishings of her room. Holk went towards his royal mistress to kiss her hand which was clad in a long silk glove, and then led her, following her eye, to the dark, slightly sagging sofa.

'Sit down, my dear Holk. This fauteuil will not meet with your approval, but the high armchair over there ...'

Holk drew up the chair, and the Princess, visibly delighted at the sight of this handsome man, went on when he was seated, with great bonhomie, like a good old friend, 'What fresh colour you bring with you, dear Holk. All I have around me here are town faces; can you imagine Pentz as a *gentleman farmer*? Or Erichsen as a hop-grower? You're laughing, and I know what you're thinking ... a pole to train the hops up ... yes, he's tall enough for that. Town faces, as I said. So it's a pleasure to see your good Schleswig colouring, red and white, like the State colours. And how is your dear wife, the Countess? I know she doesn't particularly care for us, but we like her all the more, and that she will have to endure.'

Holk bowed.

'And what do you say to the uproar we have here? A regular assault on poor Hall, who is the cleverest, in fact the best of them all and whom I am almost willing to forgive for standing by the milliner Countess, for whom, incidentally, if *I* had ever been asked to decide, I would have assembled a fitting coat-of-arms consisting of a milliner's block and crinoline, perhaps with the motto "Breadth not depth". I shall never be reconciled to this error of taste of my nephew's, even if I am only his half-aunt; the Countess, despite her forty years, is still not quite old enough for me to view her as an archaeological specimen, which is how my nephew views pretty well everything, or–which comes to much the same thing–as a recently excavated national antiquity. But why am I surprised? George II–my grandfather used to tell me about him when I was young–was also much given to the phrase *fair, fat and forty*. So why not my nephew the King too? Incidentally, have you read yesterday's parliamentary report yet? A really scandalous, spiteful episode. At the head of it, naturally, that Thompsen-Oldensworth fellow, a half-compatriot of yours, to my mind an insufferable tub-thumper and windbag with his mixture of advocate's smartness and petty bourgeois Holsteinism.'

Holk was embarrassed to find the conversation with the Princess instantly turning to politics and something of his embarrassment must have shown in his face, as the Princess went on, 'But enough of these wretched politics, I don't wish to cause you embarrassment, especially when you've just arrived, for I'm well aware you're a heretical Schleswig-Holsteiner, one of those no headway can be made with, who are always furthest from us when we think we've made peace with them. Don't say anything, don't speak of your loyalty, I know you have as much of that as is possible for you, but when it comes down to it, the old stumbling-block is always there, and that dreadful "Undivided we shall remain",* that eternal quotation, that incomparable commonplace, will always be the last word.'

Holk smiled.

'And this is of course the heart of the matter. Where does Schleswig belong? *Your* Schleswig, my dear Holk. That is the question. Hall had the courage to answer the question as befits a Dane, and because he wants to do it wisely and not rattle his sabre straight away, we have this assault on him by friend and foe alike. And that's the worst of it. It neither surprises nor alarms me that your Thompsen has gone on the attack; but that our good, loyal Danes, who are of one mind with Hall, with the King, and with myself, but unfortunately have a wild streak – that our good loyal Danes I say, like the students and professors who only ever want their own programme, are about to depose the best man, the only one who has any idea of politics and knows how to bide his time, which is the first law in politics – that does infuriate me.'

Before she had finished her sentence, Baron Pentz was announced … 'He's most welcome,' the Princess called … and the very moment that Pentz walked through the portière screening the double doors, there appeared from the other side of the room, quite close to the small door by which the Princess had entered, a young blonde lady with a fine figure and beautiful complexion, but with features otherwise not at all regular, who walked over to the Princess while Pentz stopped halfway and repeated his bow.

'*Soyez le bienvenu,*' said the Princess with a slight wave of her hand. 'You come at a good time Pentz, for you have put an end to a political lecture, a task for which no one is better fitted than you. For as soon as I set eyes on you, the world is transformed into a

---

* Motto of the Schleswig-Holsteiners since the fifteenth century.

world of peace, and if just now I had been speaking of Henri IV and Ravaillac,[*] then on your arrival I would have switched to Henri IV and his *poule au pot*.[†] Quite a difference.'

'And a most pleasant one, Ma'am. I'm delighted to find myself installed, with no effort on my part, as the bearer and bringer of all things idyllic. But ...' And his eye flitted back and forth between Holk and the young blonde ... 'even in Arcadia custom, it is said, prescribed that introductions should be made. I don't know whether I should exercise my prerogative in this function ...'

'Or cede it to Her Royal Highness,' laughed the Princess. 'I think, my dear Pentz, that right and duty are on your side, but I am disinclined to deny myself the pleasure of personally introducing to one another two persons so dear to me: Count Holk – Fräulein Ebba von Rosenberg.'

Both bowed to one another, Holk somewhat stiffly and with mixed feelings, the young lady with ease and with an expression of self-sufficiency tinged with humour. The Princess however, paying scant attention to the introduction, turned back at once to Pentz and said, 'That's that out of the way, and the ceremonial has been observed according to your remit. But you don't expect me to believe, Pentz, that you appear here simply to be ceremonially present at the act of introduction that has just taken place, or to perform it yourself. You have something else in mind, and I hereby grant you permission to speak to your original intent. When one reads as many parliamentary reports as I do, one ends up a virtuoso exponent of parliamentary phraseology oneself.'

'I come, Your Highness, to make humble report of a great military banquet being held this afternoon in Klampenborg ...'

'To what purpose? Or in whose honour?'

'In honour of General de Meza, who arrived here yesterday morning from Jutland.'

'De Meza. I see, very good. But my dear Pentz, frankly speaking, what are we to do in this matter? It is impossible for me to preside over a celebration in an officers' mess and drink toasts to de Meza.'

---

[*] Assassinated King Henri IV of France in 1610.
[†] King Henri IV reputedly voiced his intention to ensure that every peasant would have a chicken for his cooking-pot.

'I wonder if this might not just be possible. Your Royal Highness has done more surprising things before now. And doing them is what has won you the people's affection.'

'Ah, the people. Not an easy subject. You know my views on so-called popularity. My nephew the King is popular; but I have no desire to be the ideal of our blue-jackets, or even of our market women. No, Pentz, popularity, we'll have none of it! Since you mention Klampenborg and the sun is shining and the afternoon is free, perhaps we could ride out there, not for the banquet, but in spite of it; we've been stuck here now for a whole week without a proper breath of fresh air, and my dear Rosenberg would have chlorosis by now if she didn't have so much iron in her blood.'

The young lady's face brightened visibly at the prospect of escaping for a whole afternoon from the dull monotony of the Princesses' Palace, and Pentz, who as an incipient asthmatic was always in favour of fresh air, despite assurances from the experts that sea-breezes made his condition worse, concurred with alacrity too and enquired at what time Her Royal Highness would require the carriage.

'Let us say half past two, but no later. It takes an hour and a quarter, and by five it's beginning to get dark. And if we are in Klampenborg, we must take a walk as far as the Hermitage, if only to introduce my darlings personally to my dear Ebba. Who these darlings are will not, for the moment, be divulged. I hope Count Holk will sacrifice the time for his old friend and join the party, even though his duties only begin tomorrow.'

'And does Her Royal Highness require further companions?'

'Just Countess Schimmelmann and Erichsen. Two carriages. And I will arrange the seating. *Au revoir*, my dear Holk. And if you're keeping up an intensive correspondence as usual ...'

He smiled.

'Ah, I see, you've already written. So I'm too late with my greetings to the Countess. Rosenberg dear, your arm.'

And as she walked slowly towards the small door that led to her personal sitting room, the two gentlemen-in-waiting stood respectfully bowing.

13

The carriages drove up promptly at half past two with their hoods folded back; the Countess Schimmelmann took her place beside the Princess with Holk facing them. In the rear of the second carriage sat Fräulein von Rosenberg with Pentz and Erichsen facing her, their backs to the driver.

Countess Schimmelmann, a lady of forty, was rather reminiscent of Erichsen; like him she was tall and gaunt, and she displayed a similar earnestness; but whereas Erichsen's earnestness was only a touch solemn, the Countess's was distinctly morose. She had been a court beauty in her time, and occasional flashes of her black eyes bore witness to this; but everything else had faded into sallowness and migraine. There were stories of an unhappy love. General demeanour: court of Philip II of Spain, so that one automatically looked for her ruff. Otherwise the Countess was benign, of strong character and had the positive distinction in court circles of having no truck with tittle-tattle or malicious gossip. She told people the truth to their faces, and when she could not, she remained silent. She was not loved, but she was highly respected and deservedly so.

In the first carriage as long as they were in town not a word was spoken; Holk and Countess Schimmelmann sat upright opposite one another, while the Princess leaned back in the seat. They drove along Bredgade and Ny-Østergade, first towards the suburb of Østerbrö, and once past that in the direction of the shore road that skirted the sound. Holk was delighted with the picture that presented itself: immediately to the left was a row of pretty country houses with gardens that were now autumnal but still full of flowers, and out to the right, almost unruffled, the wide stretch of water with the Swedish coast on the far side and in between, sailing boats and steamers heading for Klampenborg and Skodsborg and up as far as Elsinore.

Holk would have devoted himself more fully to the view if life on the highway they were travelling along had not kept distracting him from the landscape. Vehicles of every conceivable kind not only came towards them, they also overtook the Princess, who disliked excessive speed when she was out for a drive. This meant that there were constant meetings and moments of recognition. 'That was Marstrand,' said the Princess. 'And if I saw right, it was Worsaae beside him. He never misses anything. What can he want at a dinner for de Meza? It's supposed to be a celebration for him, not an archaeological dig. He's still alive and isn't even the right size to fit a Hun grave.' The Princess was about to expatiate further on this topic, but didn't because at that moment several officers had approached very close to the carriage and were beginning to escort the Princess to right and left. Among them was Lieutenant-Colonel Tersling, our friend from Vincent's restaurant, a tall handsome man of distinctly military bearing. He found himself the recipient of an especially amicable greeting from the Princess, and he in turn enquired after her health.

'I am very well, especially well on a day like today. For I hear that you and the other gentlemen are having a celebration for de Meza. That is what tempted me out, I want to be there.'

Tersling smiled in embarrassment, and the Princess, who was enjoying this, delayed a little before adding: 'Yes, I want to be there; but have no fear, my dear Tersling, only on the periphery. When you toast the King or the guest of honour, I shall be enjoying a walk with my dear Countess here and Ebba Rosenberg, whom you must have seen in the second carriage, in our Klampenborg Deer Park, and I shall be pleased if the acclaim from good Danish throats reaches us there. And I would ask you to give de Meza my greetings, and tell him that I'm still living at the same place. It's of course never easy to get generals to court, and if they aspire to rival Beethoven and compose symphonies into the bargain, there's no chance; and by the by, if he were to hear from you that I still honour the memory of Idstedt, he may consider it worthwhile to remember me. But now I don't wish to keep you tied to the door of my carriage any longer.'

Tersling kissed the Princess's hand and sped away to make up the lost time; while the Princess, turning to Holk, went on: 'A fine-looking man, our Tersling; there was a time when he partnered princesses in the ballroom and was a cavalier *comme il faut*, the sharpest tongue, the keenest blade, you may perhaps remember the duel he fought before '48 with Captain Dahlberg? On that occasion Dahlberg escaped with a graze on his neck, but he's lain buried outside Fredericia for a long time now. Do forgive me, my dear Schimmelmann, for bringing this up in your presence; it has just occurred to me that you were the cause of that duel. I must confess, I would like to know more about it. But not today, these are women's matters.'

Holk moved to assure the Princess of his discretion, saying that he didn't even hear things that were not directly addressed to him; but the Princess kept to her word and said, 'No, none of it today, let's postpone it! And besides, my dear Holk, discretion is a large and difficult subject. I have been observing these things for fifty-five years now, for I was initiated at the age of fifteen.'

'But Your Royal Highness surely believes that in her company discretion is guaranteed.'

'No, thank goodness I do not,' replied the Princess. 'And I mean that more seriously than you can imagine. Discretion *à tout prix* does occur, but it's in its unconditional form that it's so terrible, it should never be unconditional. Human beings, in particular human beings at court, must develop the totally reliable ability to distinguish what can be said from what cannot; and those who do not have the ability to differentiate and always stay silent – they're not only boring, but dangerous too. There's something inhuman in that, for the most human faculty we have is language, and we have it in order to speak … I know that I make copious use of it myself, but I'm not ashamed of that, on the contrary, it gives me pleasure.'

In the second carriage there had been similar meetings and greetings; but the main topic of conversation was Holk, and this offered Pentz the chance to elicit from Fräulein von Rosenberg how she had found Holk at the audience in the morning. Erichsen did not participate in the questions and answers, but listened intently, for he enjoyed this kind of chit-chat, perhaps the more so for realizing that he himself was incapable of it.

'He's a Schleswig-Holsteiner,' said Ebba. 'Germans aren't courtiers …'

Pentz laughed. 'Now one can really see, milady, that Denmark is not privileged to have borne you. The Schleswig-Holsteiners not courtiers! The Rantzaus, the Bernstorffs, the Moltkes –'

'– were Ministers, not courtiers.'

'But that's almost the same thing.'

'Not at all, my dear Baron. I read a lot of history, even if it's only in French novels, but that has to suffice for a court lady, and I make so bold as to maintain that there's a contradiction between Minister and courtier. At least if each of them is truly worthy of the name. The Germans have a certain brutal talent for governing – please allow me that harsh adjective, for I can't stand the Germans – but precisely because they know how to govern, they're poor courtiers. Governing is a crude business. Ask Erichsen if I'm right …'

The latter nodded gravely, and Fräulein Ebba, pointing this out with a laugh, continued, 'and that more or less all applies to the Count. It might perhaps be possible to make a Minister of him –'

'My goodness …'

'– but to be cavalier to a Princess, for that he lacks absolutely everything. He stands there with a solemn expression like a high priest and never knows when to laugh. And that's very important. Our esteemed Princess, as I think we agree, has certain little weaknesses, among them the wish to play the part of a lady of wit from the last century. So she has a predilection for superannuated anecdotes and quotations, which she requires one not merely to understand, but to smile at approvingly too. This ABC of court behaviour is a closed book to the Count, however.'

'And this was written all over the poor Count's face for you to read during a ten-minute audience?'

'I'm not sure I can accept that expression, for the main thing is that during the whole time there was nothing at all written on his face. And that's the worst of it. For example, the Princess talked about Henri IV and referred to the "chicken in the pot", which it really isn't correct to mention nowadays. But precisely because that chicken is currently in such jeopardy, a courtier is doubly obliged to smile, not stand like a dummy leaving a Princess in the lurch when she's looking for applause.'

A look of quiet satisfaction spread over Erichsen's earnest visage.

'And then the Princess graciously spoke of chlorosis, or rather of the fact that I must risk suffering from it. Now I ask you Baron, at the mention of chlorosis you have to smile, it's simply traditional, and if the Princess has the grace to add something about "iron in the blood" which indicates that she has read Darwin or some other illustrious scientist, then the amused smile must be joined by a smile of admiration too, and if none of that happens and the gentleman-in-waiting just stands there unresponsively, as if the town crier had just announced it was ten o'clock, then I have to deny that gentleman-in-waiting any claim to be a courtier.'

It was almost four when they halted in Klampenborg. Holk assisted the Princess, and after the question of where to take coffee had been resolved in favour of the Hermitage, they quickly set out for the great hunting lodge which stood at the northern end of the Deer Park. The way there led first past a large Klampenborg hotel, and in front of it on a strip of lawn that lay between the path and the beach, a canvas marquee had been erected, a hundred paces long and closed on three sides. The open side happened to face the path on which the Princess was now approaching. The banquet itself had not yet begun, but numerous officers belonging to a wide variety of units in the Copenhagen garrison had already gathered; the glittering uniforms of the Horse Guards and the Household Hussars were everywhere to be seen, and more colourful even than the brightly coloured uniforms were the flags and pennants flying from the top of the marquee. When the Princess was within a hundred paces she turned sharply to the left on to a gravel path, because she had no wish to intrude on the festivities that were clearly about to commence; but she had already been recognized and de Meza, who had been alerted to her approach, hastened across the lawn to greet her most respectfully.

'My dear General,' she said, 'this was not our intention. It is just striking four, and already I can see the column of soup-bearers from the hotel starting to move. And I have no wish to be responsible for cold soup. Least of all on an October day when the breeze is fresh. General de Meza only enjoys that in exceptional circumstances, when bivouacking in the field with his men.'

She said all this with a certain princessly grace, whereupon she dismissed the general, who was not insensitive to her tone, amid renewed indications of her favour. From the marquee a volley of jubilant acclamations was already ringing out, and the music struck up the national anthem 'King Christian stood by the lofty mast', until it turned into 'The Brave Soldier'.*

By now the Princess and her suite had reached the Deer Park, whose southernmost tip abutted the highway just past Klampenborg. Here she gave Erichsen her arm. Then Fräulein Schimmelmann followed with Pentz, and further behind, Holk with Ebba, Holk evidently embarrassed as to how to open the conversation. For it had not escaped him that during the audience with the Princess that morning Ebba had been observing him with a slight air of mockery and superiority; during the trip in the afternoon however, an opportunity to make some kind of contact had not yet arisen.

Finally he began with: 'We're going to have a wonderful sunset. And there is no more beautiful spot for it than this. This splendid Plaine!† It's seven years now since I was last in Klampenborg, and I've never been at the Hermitage.'

'Were you frightened by the name?'

'No. For by inclination and lifestyle I am more or less a hermit, and if it weren't for the Princess occasionally summoning me into the world, I might call myself the hermit of Holkenäs. Sky and sea and an isolated castle on the dunes.'

'On the dunes?' Fräulein Ebba repeated. 'And an isolated castle. How enviable and romantic. Like a ballad, with a touch of "The King of Thule". Though the King of Thule if I remember aright was unmarried.'

'I can't say I know,' said Holk whose embarrassment had melted away at her tone. 'I really don't know. That's a question for a doctoral student. Was he unmarried? He says, as I remember, he's leaving everything to his heirs, which would seem to indicate a family. Of course it could have been a secondary line. All the same I should think he was married and possessed of a clever wife, who

---

* 'Den Tapren Landsoldat', popular patriotic Danish song composed in 1848 when troops were mobilized for the First Schleswig War.

† The extensive grassland surrounding the Hermitage, the grand hunting lodge in the middle of the Deer Park.

perhaps, or should we say very probably, was wont to smile at the old fellow, and inclined to indulge his youthful dalliance with the goblet.'

'That's good, I like that,' said Fräulein Ebba, with a glint of high spirits in her eye. 'How strange. Until now the ballad seemed as rounded and complete as possible to me: the king dead, the goblet drunk, and the kingdom (always the least important thing from the point of view of the ballad) willingly handed down, divided among all. But if we believe in the presence of a queen, and now that I think about it, I'm entirely on your side, then the whole thing only really begins with the old man's death, and "The King of Thule" is, at the very least, unfinished and in need of continuation. And why not? In the end a page will turn up somewhere who has hitherto been wasting away, but has now regained some colour, or, to finish with a quotation from our gracious Princess, some "iron in the blood".'

'Ah, my dear lady,' said Holk, 'you mock Romanticism and forget that there's a romantic episode bound up with your own name, worthy of a ballad of its own.'

'My name?' the Fräulein laughed, 'associated with a romantic episode? To do with Ebba? Now that I would like to hear, that would be a thing; for in the end all ballads come down to Ebba. Ebba is Eva, or Eve, as you're aware, and it's well known that there's no romance without the apple. But I see you're shaking your head, and you don't mean Ebba or Eve but Rosenberg.'

'I certainly do mean Rosenberg, my dear Fräulein. Genealogy happens to be a little hobby of mine, and my great uncle's second wife was a Rosenberg; so I'm initiated in the legends of your family tree. All the Rosenbergs, at least all those who call themselves Rosenberg-Gruszczyński – on the Lipiński side it's different – stem from a brother of Archbishop Adalbert of Prague, who was snatched from the pulpit and killed by pagan Prussians on the so-called Amber Coast. That pulpit still exists, even if it's battered and broken in pieces, and is my family's sacred relic ...'

'Which it's my misfortune never to have heard of,' said Fräulein Ebba, in feigned, or perhaps even genuine earnest.

'From which I would conclude that you belong to the Lipiński branch of the family.'

'Not that either, unfortunately. Of course, if I'm permitted to translate Lipiński into Lipesohn, if that distinguished family would permit me to make so bold, then perhaps from that form of the name it would be possible to establish a bridge to my family. I am in fact a Rosenberg–Meyer, or more precisely a Meyer–Rosenberg, granddaughter of Meyer-Rosenberg, King Gustav III's favourite court Jew, and a well-known figure in Swedish history.'

Holk gave a slight start; Fräulein Ebba, however, with deliberate calmness went on, 'Granddaughter of Meyer-Rosenberg on whom King Gustav later bestowed the title of Baron Rosenberg, Baron Rosenberg von Filehne, after the Prussian-Polish place we originate from. It was the seat of our family for several centuries. And now, since you have an interest in genealogical anecdotes, let me add briefly that the investiture was not before time, for three days later the chivalrous and for our house unforgotten King was shot dead by a Lieutenant Anckarström. Also an incident for a ballad, just like the murdered archbishop, although with only the remotest connection to my family. But you mustn't give me up because of that. The grass has grown over all that long since, and my father married a Wrangel, and in Paris no less, which is where I was born too, in the days of the July Revolution to be precise. There are people who say you can see it in my face. Well anyway, you can work out my age from that.'

Holk was a dyed-in-the-wool aristocrat who never hesitated to equate the divine world order intimately with the continued existence of his family, and who normally never spoke of such things because he held them too sacred. In this matter he was all for reintroducing every possible medieval stricture, and the more stringently his family's noble lineage were to be tested, the happier he would have been, for his name would have emerged at the end shining all the more brightly. His easy, agreeable manners, so acceptable to the middle-class world too, were merely the result of his certitude in this highly important particular. But he was as critical of all other family trees, not excluding the princely houses, as he was certain about his own, which was why it was possible to speak freely with him about these matters, but only if the Holks were left out of the discussion. And so it was that today too he not only recovered quickly from the initial shock that the Swedish name of Rosenberg with its uncanny *epitheton ornans* had given him, but also found it highly piquant to hear this question, which in the majority of cases could not be treated lightly enough, being handled with real lightness by such a manifestly clever person.

14

The path they had to take ran along the eastern edge of the Deer Park, for the most part under tall plane trees whose trailing branches, many still emblazoned with yellow foliage, so obscured the view that only on emerging from the avenue of planes could one see the Hermitage standing in the middle of extensive sunlit meadowland. This meant little to the two leading couples who were long familiar with the scene, but Holk and Ebba, seeing this sight for the first time, stopped involuntarily, almost bedazzled as they gazed at the great hunting lodge, encircled by all the charms of isolation, rising some distance away into the clear autumn sky. No smoke rose, and only the sun lay on the wide Plaine, still covered with thick fresh grass, while above hundreds of gulls floated in the steel-blue sky, heading in long lines from the sound to their familiar destination, Lake Fure which lay further inland.

'Your Schloss on the dunes can't be more isolated,' said Ebba as they turned on to a narrow path that led almost in a straight line across the meadow to the Hermitage.

'No, neither more isolated nor more beautiful. But beautiful as this is, I still wouldn't wish to exchange mine for it. I find the silence surrounding this place oppressive. In Holkenäs there's always a slight swell and a breeze wafts up from the sea and ruffles the tree-tops in the park. Here not a blade of grass stirs, and every word we speak sounds as if the world might overhear it.'

'Luckily no harm can come of that,' laughed Ebba, 'for I can't imagine a conversation more suited than this for public consumption.'

Holk was disconcerted by this response, and was on the point of expressing mild displeasure; but before he could answer, they reached the broad steps of the stairway leading up to the hunting lodge. In front of them stood an old forester who also did service as castellan, and the Princess now approached this person, who had respectfully doffed his cap, to give him his orders. These were initially to the effect that coffee was to be served in the large central salon. She announced this in a loud voice so that everyone could hear. Then she took the forester aside for a moment to make a further arrangement, concluding, 'and no later than five. It's already evening then before you know it, and we need good light.'

The old man bowed, and the Princess then stepped straight into the lodge and, leaning on Countess Schimmelmann, climbed up to the first floor.

Here, in the central salon, busy hands had already placed high-backed chairs round a long oak table and opened the balcony windows that faced east and west opposite one another, so that the whole splendour of the landscape could be admired as if through two large picture frames. Of course the meadowland immediately surrounding the lodge on all sides was too close to be seen, but everything in the distance was clear and sharp, and while far to the left the tops of a swathe of trees flashed in the setting sun, to the right the shimmering blue surface of the sea was in view. Holk and Ebba wanted to stand up to enjoy the picture more fully, first from one window and then another; the Princess however would have none of it, she knew about landscape and could assure them that the picture was at its most beautiful just as it was from where they sat. In any case the coffee (the castellan's wife had just appeared carrying a tray set with the finest Meissen service) also deserved respect, and as for the momentarily invisible splendour of the grassy Plaine, it would come into its own again in a little while. Everything in its proper time. 'And now my dear Schimmelmann, please do the honours. I have to admit, I'm longing for refreshment; short as the way was, it was long enough. For me at least.'

The Princess seemed in the best of spirits, which among other things manifested itself in even greater loquacity. She joked about this and sought indemnity with Pentz who had not, she said, spoken a word all day. 'Indemnity,' she went on, 'that's another word from the timeless vocabulary of parliament. But, parliamentary or not, I have a valid claim to the thing itself, to remission of guilt, since there is nowhere, and that includes my beloved Frederiksborg, where I have such a compulsion to gossip as in this place. There used to be times when I was here almost daily, spending hours enjoying the magnificent views of the sea and the forest. Of course if I were to say that this pleasure was what is generally known as "happiness", it wouldn't be accurate. What I found here was always a refreshing sense of peace, which is less than joy but also much more. The best in life is peace.'

Holk pricked up his ears. He felt he had heard those same words only a very short time ago. But where? And then, thinking and searching, he found them, and the evening at Holkenäs and the image of Elisabeth Petersen suddenly came back to him; he could hear the song again and her clear voice. That wasn't even a week ago, and already it sounded to him as if it were far, far away.

The Princess must have noticed that Holk's attention had wandered, so she dropped her general reflections and went on, 'You will hardly guess, my dear Holk, what stretch of coast that is, looking in at our window from over there.'

'Sweden, I thought.'

'No, not really. It's Hveen, the little island where our Tycho de Brahe built his astronomical tower, his "Star Castle", as the world chose to call it … yes the Brahes, I always think of them with affection and love, for my own personal reasons. It's exactly forty-five years now since Ebba Brahe,[*] an admired Court beauty at the time, was my lady-in-waiting, and also my friend, which meant more to me. For we always need a friend, at all times,' and the Princess reached out her hand to Countess Schimmelmann, 'especially when we're young and in our first year of marriage. Pentz is smiling of course; he has never known the first year of marriage.'

The Baron bowed and seemed about to express not only approbation but a certain amused satisfaction with this state of affairs; the Princess however intervened and said: 'But it was Ebba Brahe I wanted to talk about. Some names are blessed, and I have always

---

[*] The name also of a mistress of the greatest of Swedish kings, Gustavus Adolphus.

been fortunate with the Ebbas of this world. As if it were yesterday,
I can see before me the day when, from this very spot, I pointed
across to Hveen and said to Ebba Brahe, "Now, Ebba, wouldn't
you like to make an exchange? Don't you have a longing for your
ancestors' castle over there?" But she wouldn't hear of an exchange,
and I can still hear her enchanting voice as she said, "I prefer the
view from the Hermitage to Hveen to the view from Hveen to
the Hermitage", and then she began to joke, to insist that she was
completely earthly, far too much so to feel any enthusiasm for the
Star Castle. Of all the planets, she was interested only in the earth,
and the sole purpose of the others was its nocturnal illumination ...
Oh she was charming, beguiling, everybody's darling – I'd almost
be inclined to say more of an Ebba than a Brahe, while our new
Ebba ...'

The Princess hesitated ...

'... is more of a Rosenberg than an Ebba,' Ebba interjected,
bowing quite unembarrassed to the Princess.

This self-mockery was greeted with immense amusement, which
even the two nodding mandarins of the company, Erichsen and
Schimmelmann, joined in, for everyone was only too familiar with
Fräulein Ebba's family tree and fully understood the meaning of
her words. Not least the Princess herself, who was on the point
of turning to Ebba with particular warmth when the old forester
appeared in the doorway, and his appearance was the prearranged
signal to the Princess. And shortly afterwards they all proceeded
from the salon out on to a projecting balcony, from which there
was a magnificent view of the vast sweep of forest that closed the
overall picture to the west. The meadowland in between was vast,
but at a few places stands of trees jutted well out into the meadow,
and from these herds of deer emerged on to the Plaine in tens and
twenties and started to advance at a playful tempo, neither fast nor
slow, towards the Hermitage. Ebba was transported with delight,
but before she could give voice to this she saw that in the background the whole wide arc of the forest seemed to be coming alive,
and in exactly the same way as the single groups of deer had come
out of the projecting trees, many hundreds of deer now advanced
out of the depths of the forest and, reluctant to miss the imminent

march-past, started at a lively trot, at first out of step and almost in wild confusion, until, as they came closer, they formed into orderly groups and progressed in detachments past the Hermitage. Finally, when the last ones had passed, they broke up again all over the meadowland, and only then was a full view of them possible. All sizes and colours were to order, and if Ebba had already admired the black stags, she was even more enthusiastic about the white ones that were present in relatively large numbers among the deer population as a whole. But as usual this mood of Ebba's was very quick to pass, and she went on to quote all kinds of verses from Danish and German folksongs, assuring the company that, as far as ballads were concerned, the white hart still played the leading role, with the exception of the 'white hind' of course, which was even more important. Pentz for his part was unwilling to accept this and asserted emphatically that 'The Princess and the Page' held pride of place and always would, a remark with which the Princess concurred, though not without a touch of melancholy. 'I accept what Pentz says, and shouldn't like to hear him contradicted. We poor princesses don't have much to start with, and we have been as good as excluded from the world of reality; if our place in ballads and fairytales is taken away too, then I don't know what's left for us.' No one spoke, because they felt all too keenly how right this was, and it was left to Ebba to kiss her benefactress's hand and say, 'Most gracious Princess, there is, thank goodness, a great deal left still, you can still be a place of refuge, and make others happy, and laugh at prejudice.' It was obvious that these words comforted the Princess, perhaps because she discerned that, even if they came from Ebba, they were more than just empty phrases; but she still shook her head and said, 'My dear Ebba, that too will soon be a fairytale.'

While they were speaking, the carriages that they had really intended to walk down towards had drawn right up to the steps, and when the Princess noticed at the same time that dusk and with it the cool of the evening was drawing in more and more, she declared that she wished to abandon the rest of their walk and set out straight away on the return journey. 'But we will arrange ourselves differently, and I shall dispense with the escort of my cavaliers.'

This coincided with everyone's wishes. The Princess took her seat with Countess Schimmelmann at her side and Fräulein Ebba opposite; Pentz and Holk and Erichsen followed in the second carriage. When they passed through Klampenborg the officers' marquee was already closed with tarpaulins at the front, and only a narrow gap cast a strip of light on the dark foreground. Snatches of a speech that was just being delivered drifted across to them on the evening breeze, then that too ceased and only shouts of acclamation rang out into the night.

15

The trip back passed without further incident, but not of course without malicious gossip, of which Ebba could never have too much. The story about the various branches of Rosenbergs was the most fruitful topic imaginable for her. 'The poor Count,' she said, 'There's no getting away from it, he has to get right to the bottom of everything, well, he's a German, and when it comes to genealogical questions he just can't stop boring away and scrutinizing every detail. He picks up every name, and if I had had the misfortune to be christened Cordelia, I'd wager anything he'd have asked me about old King Lear.' The Princess gave Ebba an affectionate pat on the hand, more in encouragement than in reprimand, so she went on, 'He has something of the museum catalogue about him, complete with historical annotations, and I can still see his face, when Your Royal Highness mentioned Tycho de Brahe and pointed across to the island of Hveen; he was all agog, visibly itching for a discussion of cosmological systems. That would have been just the thing for him, back to Ptolemy. Thank goodness there was an interruption, for I have to confess, I find astronomy even worse then genealogy.'

The following day too was passed in similar prattle, which didn't however prevent Holk from receiving the most amiable reception from the ladies, so amiable that it both flattered him and left him in the best of moods.

Still in this mood he returned to the comforts of the Hansen apartment, and sitting at breakfast the next day, he once again became aware of the stimulating tingle of court life in Copenhagen. How dull the days back home were in comparison, and when he realized that in ten minutes or so he had to sit down at his desk and report his impressions back to Holkenäs, he almost took fright because he sensed how difficult it was going to be to strike the right tone. And yet the tone was more important than the content, for Christine was good at reading between the lines.

He was still thinking it over when there was a knock. 'Come in.' And Captain Hansen's wife entered, not the mother this time, but Brigitte the daughter. He had scarcely seen her since the evening he arrived, but he had been unable to get her picture out of his mind, not even during his conversations with Ebba. Brigitte's appearance at this moment displayed a certain muted *grandezza*, composed of a feeling of superiority that stemmed from her sense of her power and beauty and at the same time one of inferiority that derived from her modest station in life, modest at least so long as the Count was the tenant in her house. With no more than a brief good morning, she proceeded, erect and almost statuesque, straight to the table where she began to clear away the breakfast service, still holding in her left hand, concealing her bosom, the large tray she had brought for the purpose. Holk for his part had by now stood up from his seat at the window and moved towards her, holding out his hand in amicable greeting.

'Welcome, dear Frau Hansen, and if your time permits ...', and with that he indicated a chair with a courteous wave of the hand, while he himself returned to his seat at the window. The young woman however stood where she was, continuing to hold the Japanese tray in front of her like a shield and looking steadily at the Count, all without the slightest sign of embarrassment, evidently expecting him to say something more. He could not fail to notice how calculated everything in her pose was, especially the way she was dressed. She was wearing the same day dress she had worn on the first evening, wide and comfortable, no cuffs, no collar, for the simple reason that anything of that kind would have diminished the effect of her person. For her neck was a thing of special beauty, and had, as it were, a complexion of its own. The same calculation was evident in every detail. Her loose bodice, its belt of the same material left unfastened, seemed devoid of cut or shape, but only so as to display her own shape the more clearly. In overall appearance she was to perfection the picture of a Dutch beauty, and Holk's eye was drawn involuntarily to her temples in search of the traditional gold hair ornaments.

'You prefer,' he carried on when she continued to return his gaze steadily, 'you prefer not to sit down, and to stand there in full figure knowing perfectly well, my beautiful Frau Brigitte, what you're doing. In fact if I had been the Emperor of Siam when you made that trip from Shanghai to Bangkok – which your mother told me of yesterday – then the business with the throne in front of the palace would have been arranged quite differently, and instead of being seated, which never shows to advantage, you would have stood beside the throne and just rested your arm on its white ivory. And then it would have been obvious which was the winner, the ivory or the arm of the beautiful Frau Hansen.'

'Ah,' said Brigitte, adeptly feigning embarrassment, 'Mother always talks about that as if it were something special. But it was only a game.'

'Yes, Frau Brigitte, a game, since it happened in Siam, but we're not in Siam now. And we have much the same in good old Copenhagen, namely an eye for beauty. And the person who has it most and, because of his exalted position, to greatest effect … but there's no need to name names Frau Hansen, and I can only admire your good spouse, whom I have heard so well spoken of …'

'Ach Hansen. Yes. Well, he knows his Brigitte,' she said, lowering her eyes modestly.

'He knows you, my dear Frau Hansen, and he knows that he can have absolute faith in you. And I might add that I know it too. Because if beauty on the one hand is a danger, it's equally a shield,' and at that his eye moved to her tray. 'One look at your white forehead is enough to tell me that you're not subject to the weaknesses of your sex …'

Frau Brigitte was uncertain how to respond to these pronouncements; but suddenly noticing the hint of a wink in Holk's eye, she realized that Pentz or Erichsen, perhaps both, must have been talking, so that she abandoned her pose of high respectability and met his smile with a smile of complicity, resting her left elbow, as on the very first evening, on the tall mantelpiece so that her wide sleeve fell back.

That would certainly have been the appropriate moment for the conversation to take an intimate turn; Holk however elected, albeit with a touch of jocular irony, to go on playing the moral guardian meantime and said, 'Yes, my dear Frau Hansen, I repeat, not subject to the weaknesses of your sex. We'll leave it at that. And yet I should still like to offer a word of warning. To live in a city where the kings have a keen eye for beauty, as I have already permitted myself to hint, is always dangerous. It may be possible to resist the love of the mighty of the earth, but not their power ... And as for Countess Danner, with whom we must continue to reckon for the present, she won't last for ever ...'

'Yes, she will.'

'Well then, perhaps her royal admirer's fancy will fade ...'

'No, that won't happen either, Sir. For Danner has a particular charm – one occasionally hears about that.'

'And may I hear what?'

'No. My mother is always saying, "Listen Brigitte, you don't know when to hold your tongue", but that business with the Danner woman is just too much.'

'Well in that case, I'll have to ask Baron Pentz.'

'Yes, he knows, he can tell you ... Some say she has the apple of beauty, Danner I mean; but it isn't her main charm, only her lesser one ...'

'I can well believe it. But anyway, to tell the truth, I could never understand what this apple is supposed to mean. It's only ever half made sense to me. I can see cherries might mean something, but an apple ...'

'Well I don't know, Sir,' said Brigitte, smoothing her bodice to give her figure its proper line, 'I don't know if you're right about that ...' And having once trodden the slippery slope she seemed fully inclined to pursue the subject. But before she could do so she heard a muffled 'Brigitte!' from the staircase.

'That's mother,' she said, annoyed, putting the crockery on the tray. Then, with a dignified bow as if they had been discussing matters of church and state, she left the room.

As soon as Brigitte had closed the door, Holk began pacing up and down, the prey to very mixed feelings. He was not insensitive to the beauty and coquetry of this captivating person who seemed made to cause all kinds of confusion; but her willingness to flirt so openly significantly diminished the danger. All sorts of conflicting emotions struggled within him until in the end his better nature triumphed and gave him the strength to view his recent experiences with detached humour. And with that he was in the mood to write to Holkenäs and follow up his first note, in which he had merely reported his arrival, with a longer letter. He had a moment of alarm again at the thought of how much there was to report, for a passion for letter-writing was one of the things he lacked. In the end however, he seated himself at the roll-top desk, took out a sheet of paper and wrote.

Copenhagen, 3rd October 1859
Dronningens Tværgade 4

My dear Christine,
You will have received the few lines with which I reported my safe arrival; it is now time for a further sign of life from me and, as I am happily in a position to tell you, a sign of my well-being. Let me start with what is closest to hand, my accommodation with Widow Hansen. Everything is just as it was before, only more elegant and one can clearly see how her circumstances have improved. Perhaps it is all due to the fact that she now has her daughter living with her, also a Captain Hansen's wife (who used to accompany her husband on his voyages to China). This must mean that she has greater resources at her disposal. Captain Hansen's wife is a beautiful woman, so beautiful that she was presented to the Emperor of Siam, and on the occasion was accorded a Siamese Court ovation. She has an air of statuesque repose, red blond hair (not too much, but very skilfully arranged) and naturally the complexion that usually goes with it. I would call her Rubensesque, were it not that Rubens's figures are made

of coarser stuff. But enough of Captain Hansen's wife. You will laugh, and rightly so, at the apparent interest my comparison with Rubens suggests. And surpassing Rubens too! On the very first evening I was at Vincent's on Kongens Nytorv, having been picked up and taken along by Pentz and Erichsen. Saw many people I knew – including de Meza who had come over from Jutland – but spoke to no one, the reason being that there was a great political commotion going on. Hall is to be thrown out and Rotwitt installed in his place. Just an interim ministry of course, if it actually gets off the ground, which is still in question. Read the reports in the *Dagbladet*, they are more detailed and less partisan than those in the *Flyveposten*. The next morning I was at the Princess's to present myself. She behaved to me exactly as before; she knows my deviant political standpoint, but she forgives me for being more for the old Denmark than the new. She is assured of my loyalty, and doubly and triply of my devotion to her person. That allows her to overlook a great deal, at least as long as the King is alive and there can be no question of serious political crisis. So we are in the agreeable position of being able to meet on a completely peaceful footing.

Around the Princess nothing has changed, almost too little. Everything is cosy and comfortable, but at the same time grey and dusty; the Princess has no eye for this and Pentz, who could perhaps bring about change, considers it politic to let things carry on quietly as they are. Countess Schimmelmann is dignified and benign as ever, as to character a treasure, but a little dispiriting. The place of Countess Frijs, the Princess's favourite for the last ten years, has been taken by a certain Fräulein von Rosenberg. Her mother was a Wrangel. These Rosenbergs originate from Filehne, a small town in West Prussia, and they were only elevated to the Baronetcy under Gustav III, and are related neither to the Bohemian nor to the Silesian Rosenbergs. The Fräulein herself – only the eldest son inherits the title of Baron – is clever and witty and is in control of the Princess, insofar as princesses are controllable. She has undoubtedly, and for that we must be grateful, dispelled the aura of boredom that used to dominate the little ancillary court in the Princess's palace. Yesterday, when I was on duty, I saw clear evidence of the change, as I did to an even greater degree the day before when we went on an excursion to Klampenborg and the Hermitage. It was a wonderful day and when something like two thousand deer paraded past us in squadrons at sunset, my heart pounded with delight and I wished that you and the children were with me to witness it – it's a spectacle I've often heard about but never seen. I am longing to hear from you all. What have you decided in the matter of boarding schools? I was happy to leave you a free hand in full confidence, though I hope you will do nothing hasty. Sending children out into the world has its advantages, that is not in dispute, but what the family has to offer, the parental home, remains best. And when a hand like yours rules the home, then this is doubly true. My greetings to Fräulein Dobschütz and Alfred when he comes over from Arnewiek, which I hope he does often; for I know you love him, and I know too how richly he deserves that love. When Asta visits the Petersens, ask her to take my greetings to the old man and to give the very kindest regards to him and his granddaughter. Strehlke shouldn't torture Axel with mathematics and algebra, he should be building his character. Unfortunately he himself doesn't have any, good chap though he otherwise is. But then, who does? Not everyone has turned out as well as you; you have what most people lack; but unless I'm much mistaken, you too are occasionally filled with a secret wish to have a little less of what most distinguishes you. Am I wrong in this? Let me hear soon from yourself and the children, good news if possible.

Your
Helmuth H.

He laid down his pen and ran his eye again over what he had written. Partly with satisfaction. But when near the end he read the words 'what the family has to offer, the parental home, remains best …', and then 'when a hand like yours rules the home …', he felt momentarily touched by tender emotion, for which he could barely account or suggest a cause. If he could have done so, he would have known that his good angel was warning him.

16

Holk posted the letter himself, then he went to see Pentz who had invited him to his rooms for breakfast. None of the Ministers was there, not even Hall, despite his having accepted the invitation, but various members of Parliament and military men were. General Bülow, Colonel du Plat, Lieutenant-Colonel Tersling, Captain Lundbye, Worsaae of course, who as freethinker and raconteur had to be there. Tersling was in good form, as was Worsaae, which their altercations made abundantly clear; but amusing as their clashes were, Holk found them only moderately entertaining, partly because, not being a Copenhagener, he often missed the point, partly because he had nagging questions and no proper chance to ask them, with the two combative humorists' unremitting verbal cut and thrust. For Pentz was all ears, listening as they needled one another. Breakfast, like all good breakfasts, lasted until the evening. When it was all over some of the younger members went on to Tivoli for the last act of an operetta; Holk however, unused to city life and ever concerned in almost philistine fashion about his health, accompanied Bülow and du Plat as far as the War Ministry and then returned to his lodgings. The elder Frau Hansen received him as attentively and politely as ever, asked if he would like anything, and brought tea. Her conversation was brief, and all she said today had an emotional tinge: how her daughter Brigitte was not entirely well, and when she thought that the poor young woman, for she really was still young, and her husband already away seven months and not likely to return for a long time yet, yes, when she thought about it all, and that Brigitte could become seriously ill and pass away, she would rather die herself. 'And what, in the end, is the point of it all, Sir, if you're fifty and a widow too,' and she dried a tear, 'what kind of life is left? The sooner it comes, the better. Poverty isn't the worst thing, loneliness is worse, being lonely all the time and no love ...' Holk, amused at this sentimentality, of course concurred with it all. 'Yes indeed, dear Frau Hansen, you've hit the nail on the head there, it's just as you say. But you mustn't take it so seriously. A little love is still to be found.'

She looked at him sideways, gratified by his understanding.

Next day Holk was on duty again, not that it amounted to much at the Princess's court. At almost seventy—as a child of the previous century—she always retired late, rose even later, and never appeared in her reception rooms before noon; so that the gentlemen-in-waiting on duty had nothing to do until then except wait in the antechamber. That was when newspapers were read and letters written and when, long before the Princess was in evidence, the manservant brought a well-served breakfast; then Pentz would withdraw into a window bay, half-filled by a small horseshoe divan, and there Holk or Erichsen would join him. That was the form today too, and when they had sipped their sherry and Pentz had commented very favourably on the sardines, Holk said, 'Yes, they're excellent. But today Pentz, I'd like, if possible, to hear something from you on other topics besides cuisine and breakfast. Yesterday I had a couple of questions ready for you, but those two fighting cocks took up your whole attention. Worsaae, I must say, was very entertaining. So I had to say to myself, a brilliant host like you has to play host and nothing else; he has no time for private conversations in a secluded corner.'

'Good of you to say so, my dear Holk. I really rather neglected you, and instead of reproach, you heap praise on my hospitality. And I must confess that if I did miss a private conversation with you yesterday, and indeed, if I heard right, "a private conversation in a secluded corner", then I must curse all the hostly virtues you were kind enough to ascribe to me. "In a secluded corner"—that smacks of something out of the ordinary.'

'I'm in some doubt about that myself. At first sight at any rate, it's something quite ordinary and touches on a subject we discussed on our first evening. But when I consider how everything about the matter is veiled in such mystery, it ceases to be trivial and common-place. In short, I don't know myself how things stand, except that I'm curious, so tell me now, what's the story with those two women, mother and daughter?'

Either Pentz really didn't understand or he was pretending not to, so Holk went on, 'I mean of course the two Hansens. In fact, quite apart from what you've already told me, I should know as much as you about them; for both women are Schleswigers by extraction, born in Husum I believe, and they later moved to Glücksburg, and as you know, the last time I was here on duty I lodged with the mother. But I can't have paid much attention, or else the daughter who's there now has changed the atmosphere in the household. The sum total is, I can't decide what to make of it. Sometimes I feel I'm right in my assumption that it's all cunning play-acting, but then I see those superior airs and graces again, and even though I'm well aware anyone can put on airs and graces, I keep finding myself back on uncertain ground. For example there's a marvellous story about the Emperor of Siam, complete with fairytale court compliments and gifts, even a splendid string of pearls. Is that the truth, or fabrication? Perhaps it's delusions of grandeur. The daughter is certainly a very beautiful creature, and if a person occasionally enjoys great triumphs because of her beauty, which I don't doubt was the case, and then has go back to sitting quietly brooding and waiting, well then, in her solitude she's likely to embroider her triumphs somewhat, and that's when we get an Emperor of Siam from who knows where with his string of pearls and his elephants.'

Pentz smiled to himself but remained silent, for he saw clearly that Holk had not yet said all he wanted to. The latter then carried on, 'So it could all be the product of a fevered imagination, a hallucination. But then I think of the occasional giggles and saucy looks, and at the same time I recall your words on that very first night at Vincent's, when you used the expression "the forces of order", and I must confess it all seems a little like some uncanny fairytale – and if it were only a fairytale, but the fear and anxiety are real. For, my dear Pentz, what's meant by the forces of order? "The forces of order" in plain terms means the police, whose most skilful and dedicated practitioners are sometimes members of secret political lodges. And that's enough to cause me some apprehension. Is there really a connection between the daughter and a police inspector, or even between the Chief of Police himself and the mother – that kind of thing happens, and police chiefs can have unpredictable tastes – if so, where I'm lodging with this Hansen brood is little more than a low dive. The gilt furniture and Turkish carpets and the fact that mother and daughter make tea that could come straight from the kingdom of heaven, far less Siam, all this is no comfort at all. I had the impression that the Princess, when she heard Frau Hansen's name, looked somewhat askance. In short, what's the truth of the matter? Give me a straight answer now.'

Pentz, gently clinking sherry-glasses, laughed heartily, then said, 'Let me tell you something Holk, you're head over heels in love with this beautiful creature and because you're afraid of her, or don't trust yourself, which comes to the same thing – you want me to come up with some terrible story as a safety manual to pull out at any moment and use to shield yourself from the beautiful Frau Hansen. With the best will in the world, I can't oblige with said horror story. And if you think about it, how could I, when it was at my recommendation that you first took lodgings with Frau Hansen two years ago, how could I have dared to place you, Count Holk, gentleman-in-waiting to our Princess, in a *chambre garnie* which, in your bright-eyed innocence, from all the riches of your native tongue you have chosen to dignify with the word "dive" …'

'You've no call to be offended, Pentz. Especially since you and your hints are really to blame for my suspicions. What made you speak of "the forces of law and order"?'

'Because that's how it is. Why shouldn't I speak of the forces of law and order? Why shouldn't a member of the force find the beautiful Frau Brigitte just as attractive as you do? Maybe he's a cousin of hers, or of the elder Frau Hansen, whom, incidentally, I trust even less than the younger one …'

Holk nodded in agreement.

'In addition to which, there's no need to puzzle over this or most other things. It's all so very Copenhagen, it's always been like that here; three hundred years ago we had the Dyveke affair, mother and daughter, and it doesn't make a deal of difference whether it's Hansen or Dyveke.* You'll be aware, incidentally, that Dyveke isn't a name, just an *epitheton ornans*. And it was a clever choice too. "Little Turtle Dove", the Little Turtle Dove from Amsterdam – can you imagine anything more innocent?'

Holk had to concur; Pentz, however, who was a walking ency-

---

* The low-born and politically troublesome Dutch mistress of the sixteenth-century Danish King Christian II.

clopedia of the capital's *chronique scandaleuse,* and especially of the love stories of kings old and new, was not displeased to be able to expatiate on a topic which he had at his fingertips. 'There's something quite odd about this Dyveke story. You know she's supposed to have been poisoned with red cherries. Be that as it may, the story was half-forgotten, or as good as forgotten, people had stopped puzzling over Dyveke, they were more interested in other less remote figures, when all of a sudden the good Rasmussen, milliner of this city, was freshly minted as a bright new Danish countess. And can you believe it, Holk, from that day on all that old stuff was revived, and every lass in Denmark with a pair of rosy cheeks who's as pretty as your Frau Brigitte with her languid boudoir eyes wants to be another Dyveke, complete with title and beach villa, and they sit with their hands in their lap and preen themselves and wait. And they're all thinking, if it's not the King, our revered sailor-king Frederick VII, that comes along – for the Danner woman knows how to hold on to him, that much they can see, and she must have a magic charm which the rest of humanity hasn't yet discovered – if, as I say, it's not the King that comes along, then someone else will, Holk or Pentz; you must forgive me the liberty of naming myself alongside you. No Holk, it's not a low dive. The beautiful *capitana,* whose husband, incidentally, I don't envy – they say by the way he's always on the rum – is no worse than the rest, just a touch more dangerous since she's more beautiful with her red blond hair and that jacket that doesn't do up. I trust, my dear Holk, that I don't need to appeal to your chivalry to persuade you to steer well clear of the poor creature ...'

'Go ahead, mock me, Pentz. But you're barking up the wrong tree, you forget that I'm forty-five.'

'And I, my dear Holk, am sixty-five. And if I base my calculations on that, you're still in a risky position, and the beautiful Brigitte too, for that matter.'

He clearly intended to carry on in the same vein, but at that moment the manservant emerged from the Princess's rooms and announced that Her Royal Highness wished to speak with the gentlemen.

Pentz and Holk went in. The Princess was holding a newspaper in her hand and was evidently not merely irritated, but in a thoroughly bad mood. She tossed the paper aside, and what followed, instead of her usual gracious words of welcome, was the bare question, 'Have you seen this yourselves, gentlemen?'

Holk, who as a semi-stranger was under no particular obligation to read the press, remained calm; Pentz however was covered in embarrassment, the more so since lately he had often been caught committing such sins of omission. His manifest embarrassment instantly restored the Princess's good humour. 'Now my dear Pentz, don't be too alarmed, and to reassure you, let me say that in the course of long years and that's what we have to think in terms of – I have always far, far preferred a man of truffles and game pie like yourself to a man of politics and daily newspaper gossip or even newspaper malice. For that's what we're dealing with here. They're blaming it on a trading firm, a trading firm on Kokkegarde no less, but it doesn't take much local knowledge and insight to guess the individuals responsible for staging this scandal.'

The expression of embarrassment vanished from Pentz's face, to be replaced by curiosity. 'Presumably aspersions on the Countess ...'

'Oh no,' and the Princess laughed heartily, 'in the first place there are no aspersions on the Countess, and if you were a model gentleman-in-waiting, which thank goodness you aren't, then you would have a modicum more respect for my well-known feelings about the Countess. But you are what you are, Baron, and the prospect of breakfast, if you haven't had it yet, has made you forget that lampoons on Countess Danner would be more likely to put me in a good mood than a bad one. Yes, my dear Pentz, you slipped up there, or perhaps gave yourself away, and if we lived in other times, I would proceed forthwith to the King and urge him to start Struensee proceedings against you for illicit relations with the milliner Countess.* Just imagine if your head were to roll! But I don't propose to take my threat that far and merely condemn you to read the article, here, *this* one; Ebba has underscored every line in

---

* Johann Struensee, a court favourite of King Christian VII, was executed in 1772, accused of the paternity of Queen Matilda's daughter.

red, she likes that kind of thing, and then you may wonder how far
down the road to the regime of the gutter we've gone in Denmark,
unfortunately – naturally we should be reluctant to admit it in front
of Holk, for it leaves us exposed, grist to his Schleswig-Holstein
mill. But what's the use, the article is already in print, and if he
doesn't read it here, he'll read it in his lodgings, or Captain Hansen's
wife may even read it out to him. People with their own claim to
an "article", or something of the sort, are always the most avid for
anything sensational.'

Holk had a sinking feeling because he read from this final remark
a further serious question mark against the Hansens' good name;
there was no time however to dwell on this sentiment, for Pentz
already had the paper in his hand and, adjusting his pince-nez, he
began, 'For sale – Hereditary Prince Ferdinand's promissory notes!'

'Now Pentz, you've stopped already, you're pulling out your
handkerchief, you presumably wish to polish your glasses to make
sure you've read correctly. But you have read correctly. So do
continue.'

'... Various promissory notes signed by His Royal Highness
Prince Ferdinand, crossed with "on my royal honour" and endorsed
by Herr Plöther, his Private Secretary, are up for sale at prices that
collectors of sundry curiosities will put on papers of such importance, but not below fifty per cent of face value. Interested parties are
invited to contact the office at 143 Kokkegarde.'

Pentz laid down the paper; that was the end of the article.

'Now gentlemen, what do you say about this business; I have
to say I haven't seen the like in my seventy years. You're silent and
Holk is presumably thinking, you've made your bed, now you must
lie on it; people who put their signature to promissory notes and
cross them "on my royal honour" must honour those notes, and
if they don't, they have to accept being put in the stocks, as in this
case at 143 Kokkegarde. That's presumably Holk's view, and he's
certainly right, that's how the matter stands. Anyway the Prince
is of supreme indifference to me, and the more he ruins himself,
the more he plays into the hands of the man who is destined to

succeed to this country* in the place of the so-called Hereditary Prince. But I can't fully indulge my egotistical pleasure at seeing my political plans advanced, when so much else and so much that is in the end more important is being lost in the process ... No bird soils its own nest and there is a community of interest that has to recognize the Kingdom as such, otherwise the Kingdom is doomed. I might have felt piqued by the *Dagbladet*, and I confess that my first reaction was in that direction. But what does a newspaper signify? Nothing at all. I feel piqued at the King, who has lost all sense of the common good. All he thinks about is that Danner woman and excavating massive graves, on the face of it two very different matters, though it's quite possible that future interpretations may bring them together in some strange kind of unity. Above all else, he's thinking: *après nous le déluge*. And that is unfortunate. I hate moral sermons and simplistic fiddle-faddle about virtue, but on the other hand one thing remains hard and fast, no good can come of lax principles – and principles are more important than facts. I say this to you, Pentz. It's different for Holk, he's a German, even if he were to waver (Fräulein Rosenberg tells me wondrous tales of Frau Brigitte Hansen), he has his wife Christine at home. And I would have to be much mistaken about her if her powers didn't reach from Holkenäs to Copenhagen. And now gentlemen, *au revoir*.'

17

Holk had no time to reflect on what he had just heard, for the day was packed full with visits and generally rather unsettled. At twelve, two of the Princess's *petites-nièces*, still half children but both pretty as pictures, arrived to take their great-aunt to visit a historical exhibition, organized by Professors Marstrand and Melbye, that had been opened on 1st October in some of the side rooms of the Museum. The whole town was talking about this exhibition, and as usual politics paled into insignificance beside it, despite these being

---

* Prince Christian of Sonderburg-Glücksburg, later Christian IX (reigned 1863–1906).

days when not only a ministry but almost the monarchy itself was being called into question. But what did that amount to compared to a city's pursuit of pleasure? This was after all Copenhagen, and this time the pleasure principle could shelter behind lofty phrases in the guise of patriotism. For here was something that had never been seen before, a Danish *national* exhibition, for which everything in the way of historical portraiture that was to be found anywhere in town and country had been studiously assembled. It began with three-quarter portraits of Christian II and his consort Isabella and ended with three life-size portraits of the present ruler, His Majesty King Frederick VII. There was even a discreetly placed portrait of Countess Danner. Among these were endless battles on land and sea, battles against the Lübeckers, the storming of Visby, the bombardment of Copenhagen, generals in red tunics every-where, and even more naval heroes from at least three centuries, and naturally also portraits of Thorvaldsen and Oehlenschläger and ugly old Grundtvig.* The Princess displayed only moderate interest, since most of what she saw had come from the numerous royal castles scattered across Zealand and was well known to her; the young great-nieces however seemed bowled over, asking all kinds of questions, and for a moment they really did give the impression of being filled with admiration for every old admiral – one of the most famous ones had a patch over one eye. But in the long run it could escape no one, neither the Princess nor her entourage, that all this interest in admirals was just pretence and play-acting, and that the young princesses were only truly enraptured by portraits, whether of men or women, that were linked to some romantic and mysterious love story.

'Strange,' Pentz remarked to Ebba, pointing to the elder of the two princesses, who seemed unable to drag herself away from the portrait of Struensee.

'No,' Ebba laughed. 'Not strange. Not at all. Or do you think young princesses should be interested in old Grundtvig or even in Bishop Monrad? Bishops are of no great importance when you're fourteen.'

---

* All great patriotic figures of the nineteenth century – respectively sculptor, poet and theologian-historian.

'But the Struensee business?'
'Of course.'

In the afternoon the Princess went for an outing in the surrounding countryside, something which did not happen often, and in the evening, which was rarer still, she even appeared at the theatre, with Fräulein Schimmelmann and Ebba behind her in her box, and behind them Pentz and Holk.

It was Shakespeare's *Henry IV Part 2*, and after the third act which was followed by a lengthy interval, they took tea, using the opportunity as usual to set about criticizing the play, for the Princess still held to the literary manners of the previous century. She was highly amused that not only could they not agree on a verdict, but that each had a favourite and a *bête noire*, not only among the actors but also among Shakespeare's characters. The Princess herself, who always had to be different, was most taken by the two country Justices and declared she had had this taste in younger years too; a perfect embodiment of philistinism had always caused her immense delight, not only on the stage. Such Justices of the Peace were also to be found in the upper reaches of politics, and in every Ministry – yes, in fact she couldn't even quite exclude her friend Hall – every synod moreover could boast at least half a dozen Shallows and Silences. Nobody chose Falstaff, possibly because he wasn't very well acted, whereas Holk was taken by Ensign Pistol and Pentz was for Doll Tearsheet. But he refrained from mentioning her full name, always simply calling her 'Dolly'. The Princess could allow him, as she said, this small gaffe, and indeed she had words verging on recognition for him for at least being honest and consistent; in fact, this was his wisest move, and any other opinion on his part would only have aroused her suspicion. Ebba made an effort to match the Princess's bantering tone, but failed entirely and lapsed in the end into a fit of nervous twitching and trembling which progressively worsened. Holk, seeing this, tried to steer the conversation in a different direction, but he made little headway and was heartily relieved when the action resumed on the stage. But they did not stay much longer, scarcely till the end of the next act. Then the carriage was ordered and Pentz and Holk, after they had been graciously dismissed by the Princess, strolled by a roundabout route towards Vincent's restaurant for an hour's chat over Swedish punch.

On the way Holk said, 'Tell me, Pentz, what was all that with Rosenberg? She was on the brink of hysterics. Embarrassing, quite extraordinary.'

'Embarrassing, yes, but not in the least extraordinary.'

'How so?'

Pentz laughed. 'My dear Holk, I can see your knowledge of the female of the species is lamentable.'

'I make no claims to the contrary, since I hate boasting, particularly on this subject. But in Rosenberg's case I thought I had grasped the picture. To my mind she is a free spirit and an audacious one, and I would seriously contend that anyone who can juggle questions of faith and morality as she can is pretty well obliged to delight in Falstaff's Doll, or at the least not to be offended by her.'

'Yes, that's what you think, Holk. But that's exactly why I say you know nothing about women. If you did, you'd know that it's precisely the ones who have this and that on their slate who find nothing more wounding than grossly, or even slightly distorted images of themselves. They learn to live with their own image, even if they entertain the occasional doubt about their moral physiognomy; but if a second image chances to crop up that reflects their doubtful aspects back with interest, that puts an end to any complacency. In other words, such dubious ladies are inclined to let the little bit of Eve that they represent pass, but not a jot more; more is simply inadmissible, and if they do encounter it nevertheless, it reduces them to fits of tears.'

Holk stopped short, then he said, 'Is *that* how it is? Aren't you saying more there than you can justify? For one thing, I really can't accept that when she brought Fräulein Rosenberg to court, the Princess made a choice that—irrespective of all other reservations—should have been ruled out from the outset because of Countess Danner, who's a constant target for her moral barbs.'

'And yet that's how it is. There is nothing for me to withdraw. Ebba wants a future, that's certain, and only one thing is more certain—she has a past.'

'Are you able to talk about that?'

'Yes, I'm in the happy position of not having to hold anything back, certainly not in the case of Fräulein Ebba. Someone who practises so little restraint herself has lost any claim to restraint from others and someone who constantly scorns discretion, and what have I not had to put up with from the lips of that fire-cracker, has no claim to discretion from anyone else.'

'And what was it then?' Holk interrupted, growing more curious by the minute.

'Nothing, if you like, or at least not much. The same old story. She was a lady-in-waiting to Queen Josephina over in Stockholm. The Leuchtenbergs, as you know, are all very charming. Well, it was about a year ago now, or a bit longer, that people began to wonder about the affection and the little attentions that the Queen's youngest son was suddenly –'

'The Duke of Jämtland …'

'That's the one … that the Queen's youngest son was suddenly displaying to his mother. The astonishment didn't last too long, however. You know the little boats that travel back and forth between the love-islands on Lake Mälar, well, since the Stockholm gondoliers are just as easy to bribe as the Venetian ones, the motives for the Prince's attentions very soon became public knowledge; they were, in a word, Fräulein Ebba. Then there was a scene, of course. In spite of everything the Queen, who was just as taken with the Fräulein as our Princess, wouldn't hear of dismissal or even disfavour, and backed down only with great reluctance to pressure from the Court. The person most opposed to her was the King,* who could see it all quite clearly …'

'And that's the reason she's so passionately anti-Bernadotte,' said Holk, who suddenly remembered some comments the Fräulein had made on the way to the Hermitage. 'That's the reason for her fervent enthusiasm for the House of Vasa.'

'The House of Vasa,' Pentz laughed. 'Yes, that's a favourite expression of hers now. And yet, believe me, there have been hours and days when Fräulein Rosenberg would have given the entire

---

* The exemplary Oscar I, second ruler (1844–59) of the Swedish royal dynasty founded by his father the former French general Jean-Baptiste Bernadotte.

House of Vasa, including the great Gustavus Adolphus, for the ring finger of the youngest Bernadotte. That may still be the case, perhaps her bridges to Sweden are not all burnt yet, at least until quite recently they were still corresponding. It's only since this autumn that everything has gone quiet and, as far as I know, no more letters are coming. Presumably there's something else in the offing. For Ebba always has several irons in the fire.'

'And does the Princess know about this?'

'As far as her Swedish past is concerned, certainly everything, perhaps more than everything. Sometimes it's a good idea to add a little extra that's sheer invention. That gives added piquancy. In love stories there can be no half-measures, and if merciless reality happens to snip the thread prematurely, then artifice must spin it further. That's what every reader demands in a novel, and so does our Princess.'

At this point in their chat the two broke off because they had reached Vincent's, and when they left the restaurant again an hour later, it was in the company of others, so that the conversation could not be resumed.

Widow Hansen proved rather monosyllabic when Holk stepped into the vestibule, and she restricted herself to handing over a telegram that had arrived in the course of the afternoon. It consisted of a few words in which Christine, with a brevity that would have done credit to any businessman, communicated only three things to Holk: thanks for his note, satisfaction that he was well, and the prospect of a longer letter at a later date. Holk glanced at the telegram, and then, declining to be accompanied, bade Widow Hansen good night and went straight upstairs to his rooms where the lamp was already lit. It could not be said that Christine's words were of immediate concern to him, he was thinking more about Pentz than the telegram, and anticipating further information about Ebba with more curiosity than the prospective letter from Christine. Before he fell asleep these thoughts too vanished, for he suddenly thought he could distinctly hear muted giggles, punctuated by the sharp, penetrating clink of fine glassware. Was it from the house next door, or was it directly below him? It was not an agreeable feeling, the

more so because he could not avoid recognizing that there was jealousy in play, jealousy of the 'forces of law and order'. These words
in themselves however also contained the cure, and as he muttered
them to himself, his good mood returned and soon afterwards so
too did sleep.

Next morning the younger Frau Hansen appeared with breakfast,
and as Holk looked her up and down, he was almost ashamed at the
thoughts with which he had fallen asleep the night before. Brigitte
looked bright as day, her complexion and eyes clear, suffused with a
serene feminine beauty, almost an innocence. And as usual she was
silent; only as she made to leave did she turn back to say, 'We trust
the Count wasn't disturbed. Mother and I didn't shut an eye until
after twelve. There are some very strange people next door, noisy
far into the night and you can hear every word through the walls.
And if only that were all ...' The Count assured her he had heard
nothing, and when Brigitte had gone he was once more completely
under her influence. 'I don't trust her, at least scarcely more than I
do her mother, in fact all I know is she's very pretty. What does it
really mean after all, that conversation I had with her yesterday or
the day before? You can have conversations like that with any young
woman, or at least with plenty of them. In fact she said nothing that
anyone else couldn't equally well have said; looks are always unreli-
able. Sometimes it seems to me that everything Pentz trots out is
just stuff and nonsense. The business with Ebba will probably turn
out to be something quite different too.'

An hour later the postman came with the letter that had been
announced in the telegram. Holk was pleased because he was genuinely keen to be extricated from all the unedifying thoughts that
these women, Ebba included, had stirred up in him. And a letter
from Christine was ideal for that purpose. It came from a trust-
worthy heart, and he breathed a sigh of relief when he had opened
the envelope and taken out the letter. But he was heading for a
disappointment; the letter was so cold and sober that all he was left
with was one uncomfortable feeling in place of another.

'I had intended, dear Holk,' Christine announced, 'to write you
a longer letter, but Alfred, whom you installed as your alter ego for

the duration of your absence, has just come over from Arnewiek, and so it now falls to me to submit my report to your stand-in. Schwarzkoppen is here too of course, which is most welcome for me but also time-consuming, so I must keep it short and console you, as regards more comprehensive information, with a promise for a future occasion. Your eagerness to hear from me will not be all that great, for I know you are always quite taken up by your immediate surroundings. And when you are surrounded by persons as beautiful as Captain Hansen's wife and as piquant as Fräulein Ebba, who unfortunately did not quite measure up to your genealogical expectations, you will not be overly curious about reports from sleepy Holkenäs where it's an event if the black hen hatches seven chicks. I am hoping finally to conclude with Schwarzkoppen the matter that you are aware of. I shall write to you about it when definite decisions, for which I have your authority, have been made. Our health is good. The day before yesterday old Petersen collapsed. It was quite serious and we thought the end was near; but he has made a complete recovery and visited me this morning as bright and jovial as ever. He wants to excavate behind the farmyard between the little pond and the old poplar meadow with all the crows' nests, and he is confident of finding something, urns or stone tombs or both. I gave him permission at once and Alfred, your regent, will I think concur, as will you. My dear Dobschütz has been coughing again, but Ems Spring Water and whey have worked absolute wonders as usual. Axel is bright as a button due to the fact that Strehlke thinks more about hunting than grammar. I shall let that pass for the moment, but it must change. Asta spends half-days at a time down with Elisabeth. Both children love one another dearly, which makes me infinitely happy. For bonds of the heart cultivated from youth are truly the most beautiful thing that life has to offer. I know, thank goodness, that you are at one with me on this. Yours as ever, Christine.'

Holk laid down the letter. 'What's that all supposed to mean? I expect tender words and find needling remarks. That they're couched in formalities just makes it worse. "Alfred, your regent" and before that, "as beautiful as Captain Hansen's wife, and as piquant as Fräulein Ebba", that's bad enough in itself. But her final reflection is just the limit, "bonds of the heart cultivated from youth are the most beautiful thing." Bitter honey, that's what it's like. And on top of that the prospect of boarding school and educational questions to come. Perhaps that's just the point that explains it all, and she's taking a harsh, mocking tone to intimidate me and gain a freer hand. But there's really no need to resort to that sort of thing. She always gets what she wants. I would prefer to have the children around me; when they're gone, all I have left is a dauntingly perfect wife who depresses me. She knows it too, and sometimes I think she's frightened herself by her own perfection. If the children have to go away, and I've given in to that, then I don't care in the least whether it's to Gnadau or Gnadenberg or Gnadenfrei, it's bound to involve a bit of Gnade, the quality of Grace. With Asta that's fair enough, why not? But Axel? Well, him too, as far as I'm concerned; he's a Holk, and if he does receive the full Moravian treatment and goes and serves a term as a missionary in Greenland, he'll soon recover.'

18

There was a change in the weather and several rainy days followed. The Princess stayed in her rooms and apart from fleeting encounters, Holk saw her only in the evenings when tea was taken after a game of whist. Nothing changed in these social contacts, least of all between Holk and Ebba. She grew saucier and more audacious with each passing day, and when she realized that Pentz must have been gossiping about what happened in Stockholm, she alluded to it herself and talked about love affairs, particularly love affairs at Court, as if they were not merely permissible but virtually obligatory. 'Life comes in so many forms,' she said, 'One may be Countess Aurora Schimmelmann or one may be Ebba Rosenberg; each can be justified, but one mustn't try to be both at once.' Holk, somewhat astonished, looked at her half in amusement and half in alarm. Ebba, however, went on, 'There are many standards for judging people and one of the best and surest is their attitude to love affairs. There are those who come out in goose pimples as soon as they hear of some assignation or *billet doux*, but personally, I feel quite free from this weakness. What would life be without love affairs? Dull, dismal, boring. But to watch, to feel, to understand as something builds from the most fleeting encounters and glances to end up stronger than death – oh, there's only one thing better than watching, and that's experiencing it. I feel sorry for people who can't appreciate this, or fail to commit themselves openly and joyfully if they do. Anyone who has the courage of their convictions will always find sympathetic hearts, and it's enough after all if there's only one.' Not an evening passed without remarks like this being dropped, and Holk endeavoured for a while to fend them off, but with less and less success. With every passing day it became clearer to him how accurate and apposite Pentz's words about the power of so-called piquant relationships had been, the kind women often deemed it better to play up than down. Yes, Pentz was right, and it was with quite oddly mixed feelings of satisfaction, irritation and fear that he realized with increasing clarity that Fräulein Ebba was toying with him. The Princess saw this too, of course, and decided to speak to Ebba about it.

'Ebba,' she said, 'Holk has been with us now for two weeks, and I should like to hear what you think of him. I trust your perception …'

'His politics?'

'Ah, you minx, you know I don't care about politics: if I did he wouldn't be in my service. I mean his character and, I'm tempted to add, his heart.'

'I think he has a good heart, but a weak one.'

The Princess laughed. 'That's certainly true, that he has. But this isn't getting us anywhere. So tell me something about his character. Character is more important than the heart. A person can be weak at heart, but at the same time a strong character, because he has principles. And that strong character can be the saving of him.'

'In that case Holk is lost,' laughed Ebba. 'For I think his character is even weaker than his heart; his character is what's really weak about him. And the worst of it is, he doesn't even know it. Because he looks like a man, he thinks that's what he is. But all he is is a handsome fellow, which generally amounts to no man at all. All in all he hasn't had the proper schooling to be able to develop his modest talents along the lines that suit him. He should have been a collector or an antiquarian or the manager of a home for fallen women, or even just a pomologist.'

'Well, well,' said the Princess, 'that's a great deal all at once. But tell me more.'

'He's vague and half-hearted, and that half-heartedness will get him into trouble one day. He behaves as if he were a Schleswig-Holsteiner, and yet remains in the service of a princess who is most definitely Danish; he's a walking genealogical handbook and can reel off all the Rosenbergs at the drop of a hat, apart from the Filehne branch, and yet he has pretensions to liberalism and enlightenment. I haven't known him long enough to pick up all his half-measures, but I'm sure they're there in every field. For example, I don't doubt for a minute that he sits in his village church every Sunday and wakes from his doze with a start each time the articles of faith are read out; but I doubt if he knows what's in them, and if he does, he doesn't believe them. But he'll spring to his feet just the same, perhaps precisely because he doesn't.'

'Ebba, you go too far.'

'Oh, by no means. In fact I can put my finger on a much more important example of his half-heartedness. He's a moral fellow, indeed you might almost say he's a paragon of virtue, but he's not entirely averse to being a man of the world, and that's the worst part of his half-heartedness, worse than his half-hearted attitude to the so-called big questions, which mostly aren't big at all.'

'Only too true. But now, my dear Ebba, I have you just where I want you, and where I'm going to keep you. He's not entirely averse to being a man of the world, you say. There, unfortunately, you've hit the nail on the head; I see it more clearly every day. But because he has this weakness we must smooth the path for him, not to attack but to retreat. You mustn't tease him as you're doing at the moment, perpetually flickering in front of him like a will o' the wisp. He's already quite dazzled enough. As long as he's here you must hide your light under a bushel. I know it's asking a great deal, for when somebody has a light, they like to keep it shining; but you must make this sacrifice for me, and if it's difficult for you, you can console yourself with the thought that he won't be here for ever. At New Year he's going home, and then when we have our old trio around us you can do what you like, marry Pentz or have a fling with Erichsen or even with Bille – his measles must come to an end some time; I shan't mind. Perhaps you might supplant the Countess, Danner I mean, not Countess Holk, that might be best of all.'

Ebba shook her head. 'That can't be done, if I took Danner's place I should no longer be my gracious Princess's devoted and grateful servant.'

'Oh Ebba, don't say things like that, you don't deceive me. You're grateful to me when it suits you, that's all. And I don't ever do anything in the expectation of gratitude. The most thankless thing one can do, because it's the least clever, is to expect thanks. But think about the matter of Holk.'

'Forgive me Ma'am, but what is there to think about? For as long as I've been able to think, it's been "a girl has to look after herself" and that's as it ought to be; we have to know how to do that. And if somebody can't, then it's because they don't want to. So there it is, we have to look after ourselves. But what's a young girl beside a grown man and count of forty-five, who any day now may be presenting a grandchild at the font? If anybody has to look after themselves then it's a count who's been married, for seventeen years I believe, and has an excellent and able wife, and a very pretty one at that, as Pentz assured me only today.'

'It's precisely because of this woman that I'm pressing you ...'

'Well, Ma'am, if it is your Royal Highness's command, then I'll endeavour to obey. But am I the right person to be instructing? No I'm not, not at all. Holk is. *He's* the one who owes his wife fidelity, not me, and if he can't keep to it, that's his concern, not mine. Am I to be my brother's keeper?'

'Ah, you're right of course,' said the Princess, running her hand over Ebba's wavy blond hair. 'But be that as it may, you know people are watching us because we're also watching them, and I wouldn't like us to show the King and his Countess any sign of weakness ...'

The day after this conversation Holk was off duty, and he planned
to deal with a variety of letters that were outstanding. In front of
him lay his entire correspondence of the last two weeks, including
letters from the Countess. He ran his eye over these, which didn't
take long since there were only a few, the last item being a new telegram in which she excused herself for not having written for four
days. That was all; it didn't amount to much nor did it say much.
This annoyed him, because he had been shrewdly avoiding the
question of who was actually guilty in all this. He told himself, and
he was entitled to, that it had all been very different before. Earlier,
during his last stay in Copenhagen, the letters they had exchanged
had been true love letters in which, regardless of all their disagreements, the great affection they had cherished for each other in the
early years had repeatedly found fresh expression. But this time
there was no tenderness, everything was frosty, and when she tried
to make a joke, there was a tart, mocking edge to it which dispelled
any pleasure. Yes, that was it, unfortunately, and yet he had to
write. But what to say? He was casting around, thinking, when Frau
Hansen came in and handed him some letters that the postman had
just brought. Two of them were postmarked Copenhagen, the third
was in Christine's hand, but it wasn't the usual format and instead
of Glücksburg it was postmarked Hamburg. Holk was surprised for
a moment, but he had guessed what it meant before he opened it.
'Of course, Christine is doing her round of boarding schools.' That
was indeed the case, and what she wrote was the following:

Streit's Hotel, Hamburg
14th October, 1859

Dear Holk,
You will have received my telegram with my apologies for my
silence of several days. Now you can see from the postmark the
reason for this silence: I was busy with preparations for the trip
which, despite the help of my good Dobschütz, and despite my
having reduced everything to the bare necessities, took all my
strength. We travelled to Schleswig by carriage, from there by
train, and since midday today we have been at Streit's Hotel
which holds so many agreeable memories for both of us. If such

memories still mean something to you! I have taken rooms on the second floor with a view of the Inner Alster with its pavilion and bridges, and when dusk fell I lay down in the bay window to let the beautiful picture take effect as it used to. Only Asta was with me, Axel had gone into town; he wanted to go with Strehlke, who has accompanied us this far, to Uhlenhorst, and then to Rainville's, and then from there to Ottensen to see Meta Klopstock's grave. I was glad to agree, because I know the deep and lasting effect such moments have on people's lives. And now would be a good time for me to inform you of the decisions I have taken, after further exhaustive consultation, with regard to the children. Alfred agreed too, even though he disputes the importance of the matter. Asta, of course, goes to Gnadenfrei. That no other solution was appropriate you will yourself have come to accept. I spent happy years there, I don't say my happiest (you know which were my happiest), and I wish my child the same enviable lot, the same harmonious youth. To come to Axel, on Schwarzkoppen's advice I have decided on the Bunzlau Pedagogium. It has the best reputation, and for strict principles is the equal of the Thuringian educational institutions, though it relaxes its strictness where principles are not involved. Strehlke, who first wanted to move to Malchin, will now become vicar with his brother in Mölln; in the long holidays he has had to promise me to stay with us and look after Axel. He is a good person and would be excellent if he had spent the years before completing his studies in Berlin at Halle rather than Jena. One can never quite extirpate the effect of Jena and its influence. With regard to the children, I can't think of anything to add to this. Perhaps there's one thing; that their delight when it was certain they were leaving the parental home came as a painful surprise to me. It is not, it seems to me, just the appeal of the new that is coming out here, the desire for a change that is always innate in youth – or at least not this alone. But if it isn't this, what is it? Have we perhaps fallen short somewhere in our love? Or have the children been longing to escape from the conflicts of opinion they've all too often witnessed? Oh my dear Holk, I would dearly have loved to avoid those conflicts, but I could not manage to, and so I chose what I considered the lesser evil. I may have forfeited much by this, but I did what my conscience dictated, and I live in the conviction that you are prepared to make this concession to me. My trip will not keep me away from home for more than five or six days, and I hope to be back around the twentieth in Holkenäs, where the good Dobschütz is in charge for the duration. Communicate my devoted thanks to the Princess for her being as gracious as to remember me, and give my regards to Pentz and to Fräulein von Rosenberg, even if I have to say that I do not warm to her. I do not care for these freethinking airs. I long for the New Year when I hope to see you here again, perhaps by New Year's Eve. Let this time in Copenhagen be your last stay in the capital, at least in your present office. Why these obligations when one might be free?

With all my love
Your Christine

When he had read the letter, Holk succumbed to a certain sentimentality. There was so much love in it that he could feel the old times and the old happiness rising up again. She was after all the best. What was the beautiful Brigitte in comparison? Yes, or even Ebba alongside her? Ebba was a rocket to be admired with an astonished 'ah' as long as it was rising, but it was soon over, just fireworks, nothing but artifice; Christine in contrast was the simple light of day. And absorbed by these feelings, he ran his eye over the letter once more. And then it all disappeared again, the friendly impressions went and what he heard now was, in the main at least, the self-righteous tone. And so his reflections of a hundred times before came back: 'Oh these virtuous women; always on their high horse, and always on a crusade for truthfulness. That may be how they feel in their hearts. But without intending to deceive anyone, they deceive themselves, and only one thing is certain: the horror of their perfection.'

19

Four weeks had passed and it was mid-November. Holk had adapted completely to Copenhagen, was party to all the gossip in the city, great and small, and was occasionally thinking, not without a sinking feeling, that the monotonous life of Holkenäs was once again in prospect in six more weeks. The letters coming from there were not of a kind to make him feel otherwise; Christine, now back from her boarding school trip, was writing more regularly and was even refraining from gloomy comment, but a certain sobriety remained and above all the doctrinaire tone that was now normal for her. And it was precisely this tone, with its note of infallibility, that Holk revolted against again and again, deep down. Christine was so sure about everything; but what was truly definite? Nothing, nothing at all, and every conversation with the Princess or even with Ebba was calculated only to strengthen him in this view. Everything was a temporary accommodation, everything was a majority decision; morality, dogma, taste, everything was in flux, and only for Christine was every question solved, only Christine knew so definitely that the doctrine of predestination was false and to be rejected, and that the Calvinist form of Communion was an 'affront'; she knew with equal certainty which books were to be read or not read, which persons and principles were to be sought out or not sought out, and above all she knew how questions of education were to be handled. Heavens, how clever the woman was! And if she ever actually admitted to not knowing something, she accompanied this concession with an expression that made it clear one didn't need to know that kind of thing.

Holk's reflections would run along these lines when he looked out of his window in the morning on to Dronningens Tværgade which, quiet as it was, nevertheless was alive with traffic compared to the lonely farm road that led down from Schloss Holkenäs to Holkeby village. And as he sat there thinking and musing, there would be a knock at the door and Widow Hansen or even the beautiful Brigitte would enter to clear the breakfast table, and if it was the garrulous widow, he was all ears for everything she said, and if it was the taciturn Brigitte he was all eyes, completely absorbed by the picture she presented. There was something about their presence, in spite of the fact that both women, and particularly Brigitte, were not in the least interesting in themselves, which continued to arouse our friend Holk, even if the Hansen question was now quite clear to him, and there was no longer the slightest suggestion of any mystery. The Emperor of Siam had become ever more uncertain, the 'forces of order' by contrast ever more certain; everything was exactly as Pentz had said, for appearances were preserved, as were the little attentions which they both contrived to match skilfully to Holk's taste, and thus it came about that he would anticipate his morning encounters with mother and daughter with a kind of gratification, especially since he felt that these encounters had ceased to be in any way dangerous for him. Was he aware of where this sense that all danger had ceased actually came from? Perhaps he personally was not, but others saw all too distinctly that it was Ebba.

Meanwhile in politics everything was moving along nicely. A further onslaught was not planned until the beginning of December, and the Princess's view was that on this occasion it would actually be politic to yield to it; the moment Hall went, the country would realize what it had had in him. Her court naturally took this view too, and Holk was busy writing to Christine in these terms, expounding Hall's significance as a statesman to her, when Pentz came in.

'Well Pentz, to what do I owe the honour this early in the morning?'

'Important news.'

'Louis Napoleon dead?'

'More important.'

'Then the Tivoli Theatre must have burnt down or Madame Nielsen has a catarrhal infection.'

'Somewhere in between: we're going to Frederiksborg[*] tomorrow.'

'We? Who's we?'

'Well, the Princess and everyone belonging to her.'

'Tomorrow?'

---

[*] Danish royal castle, situated north of Copenhagen outside the town of Hillerød; frequent residence of Frederick VII.

'Yes. The Princess isn't for half-measures, and when she decides on something, plan and execution must coincide if possible. I confess that I would rather have stayed here. You don't know Frederiksborg yet, because as a Danish gentleman-in-waiting, you have addressed the task of *not* knowing Danish castles with remarkable assiduity. And since you don't yet know Frederiksborg, you'll be able to stand three days there, or even three weeks, studying all sorts of bric-à-brac and pictures of men in wigs, and stones with runes. For there's a great deal of that kind of thing to see: Thyra Danebod's ivory comb, a hairpiece *à la chinoise* belonging to Gorm the Old, and an oddly shaped molar about which scholars are in dispute as to whether it's one of King Harald Bluetooth's or from a boar of the alluvial period. I'm personally for the former. For what's a boar supposed to mean? A boar isn't worth mentioning, for the simple reason that the main thing is always the historical note in the catalogue, and while there's generally not much to say about a boar, there's always a great deal to be said about a half-legendary sea king. I'm pretty sure you're interested in that sort of thing and as a genealogist you'll be able to determine Harald Bluetooth's degree of kinship with Ragnar Lodbrok, or perhaps even with Rolf Krake. So you're catered for Holk, whatever happens. But as for me, I'm more for Lucile Grahn* and Vincent's, and if all else fails, even a common or garden harlequinade.'

'I can believe it,' laughed Holk.

'Yes, you can laugh, Holk. But we'll talk again. I said something about three weeks just a moment ago; well, three weeks would be all right, but six, or more accurately nearly seven – for the Princess doesn't give away a single hour, and she has no faith in the New Year if she hasn't rung out the old in Frederiksborg – seven weeks, I tell you, that's presumably too much even for you, though Pastor Schleppegrell is certainly a character and Doctor Bie his brother-in-law an amusing fellow. Don't misunderstand me, I know full well what a character's worth in certain circumstances, and more so an amusing fellow; but for seven weeks it's all a bit meagre. And if it isn't snowing it's raining, and failing rain and snow there'll be a

---

* The odd one out in this list of historical figures: a famous ballerina and early friend of Baroness Danner.

storm. In my time I've heard plenty of weather-vanes creaking and gutters and lightning-conductors rattling, but such a clattering din as you can hear at Frederiksborg has its equal nowhere in the world. And if we're in luck, there'll be a ghost too, and if it isn't a dead princess, then it'll be a living chambermaid or a lady-in-waiting with piercing, water-blue eyes ...'

'Oh Pentz, you can't open your mouth without having a dig at the poor Fräulein. For by that living lady-in-waiting with piercing blue eyes you mean Rosenberg of course. If you weren't sixty-five, and I didn't know you had other divinities to worship, I'd truly believe you were in love with Ebba.'

'That I leave to others.'

'Erichsen?'

'Of course, Erichsen.' And he laughed heartily.

The following day two carriages drew up in front of the Princesses' Palace exactly at noon, the servants having departed an hour earlier together with the luggage, taking the Elsinore train. Seating arrangements in the two carriages were as on the way back from the Hermitage; the Princess sat with Fräulein Schimmelmann and Ebba in the first carriage, in the second the three gentlemen. It was a sunless day and towering masses of grey cloud drifted across the sky. But these cloud-masses gave the landscape a tone that only enhanced its appeal, and as they drove along the shore of Lake Fure, which was about halfway, Ebba stood up; she could not get her fill of the steely, gently rippling surface as the seagulls swooped over it, almost touching the water. The shore was lined with dense reeds growing far out into the lake, broken only now and then by willows whose leafless twigs trailed low over the water, while on the other side of the lake there was a dark stretch of forest with a church tower rising above it. All was sunk in deep silence, disturbed only when an occasional shot rang out in the woods or the rattle of a passing train could be heard a thousand paces off. Ebba was making this trip for the first time. 'I don't know the South,' she said, 'but it can't be more beautiful than this. Everything seems so mysterious, as if each foot of earth hides a story or a secret. It's just like a place of sacrifice from the past, or perhaps even the present, with the clouds, those grotesque shapes drifting overhead – as if they knew all about it.'

The Princess laughed. 'To have such a romantic young lady about me! Who would have thought it; my dear Rosenberg with intimations of Ossian! Or to risk a pun, Ebba in pursuit of the Edda.'

Ebba smiled, as she could well have seemed a little strange to herself in this romantic role; but the Princess went on, 'And all this at the sight of Lake Fure which is really only a lake like a hundred others; think what's in store for us once we reach Frederiksborg, with Lake Esrom to the right and Lake Arre to the left, the great Lake Arre which is directly connected to the Kattegat Strait and the sea. And it never freezes, except for the narrows and the bays. But why am I talking of lakes, the main thing is the castle itself, my dear old Frederiksborg with its gables and towers and its hundred curiosities on every base and capital. And where other castles make do with a simple downpipe, in Frederiksborg the gutter juts out ten feet, and a basilisk with three iron bars in its gaping jaws sits at its outflow, and the water rushes through the bars on to the castle yard below. And if the weather changes and the full moon stands bright and gleaming above it and everything is so eerily silent and the assembled infernal creatures stare out from every nook and cranny, as if they were biding their time, then the effect can certainly be spine-chilling, but that's just what I like so much about the castle.'

'I thought Frederiksborg was one of the "good castles", a castle free of ghosts and spirits, because it has been free of blood and murder, and perhaps even of serious guilt and sin.'

'No, there you're hoping for more than my beautiful Frederiksborg can offer. It may be free of blood and murder. But free of guilt and sin! My dear Ebba, what could survive for two hundred years without guilt and sin! Nothing occurs to me that would prompt a shudder or lament, but there won't have been any shortage of guilt and sin …'

'If I may I would almost like to contradict that, Ma'am,' said Fräulein Schimmelmann. 'I think Ebba is right when she speaks of a "good castle". Our dear old Frederiksborg is after all just a museum, and museums are, I think, the most innocent –'

'– things of all,' laughed the Princess. 'Yes, they do say that, and it's probably the general rule. But there are always exceptions. Altars, sacristies, graves and of course museums too – everything can be desecrated, everything has suffered its own sacrileges. And that still leaves the question of *what* a museum holds and exhibits. They often have curious things in them, things that I wouldn't care to call innocent. Or at least they're sad and gloomy enough. When I was a young princess I was once in London and saw the axe they used to execute Anne Boleyn. That was in a museum too, the Tower of London, naturally, but that doesn't make much difference, a museum's a museum. Anyway, we don't want to spoil our most beautiful castle for Ebba, our most beautiful castle and my favourite as well, for over many years I've always passed happy days in it. And haunted and spine-chilling or not, you at least, my dear Ebba, will be safe inside, because I've decided to accommodate you in the tower.'

'In the tower?'

'In the tower, quite right, but not one with snakes. Because your Swedish maid will be living below you and Holk above. That should put your mind at rest. And every morning when you stand at the tower window, you'll have the most beautiful view of the lake and the town and the castle courtyard and all that surrounds it, and if my wishes come true, you will pass many happy hours in your cell in the tower … And I already know what I am going to give you for Yuletide.'

As they continued speaking in this vein they passed far beyond the north-eastern corner of Lake Fure, and driving along the almost straight highway, with its rowan trees standing here and there still with clusters of red berries, they gradually approached their destination. What came into view first was not the castle itself, of course, but the little town of Hillerød lying before it, and when they drew close, already driving between the little town's mills and barns, there was a flurry of snow. But a breeze came up suddenly, blowing away the snowflakes, and when the Princess's carriage drove on to the market square in Hillerød, the heavens suddenly cleared and a patch of blue sky became visible, and beneath it a fading sunset.

In the midst of this sunset stood Schloss Frederiksborg, its many tall towers silently mirrored like a fairytale castle in the small lake that lay in front of it, entirely filling the narrow space between the little town and the castle. Behind the castle lay the park which ran right down to the lake with occasional screening trees to left and right, magnificent planes whose leaves, shaken off by the autumn wind, floated in large numbers on the still surface of the lake. By now the second carriage had also drawn up. Holk, since anything was supposed to be allowed when driving in the country, had been astute enough to choose the seat beside the coachman, and he now jumped down and went over to the door of the Princess's carriage to tell her what a rustic idyll this market square was, and how beautiful the view of the Schloss, words which visibly warmed the Princess's heart and would have been sure of a gracious reply had not another gentleman emerged from a house next to the square and gone up to her carriage at the same moment. This other person was Pastor Schleppegrell of Hillerød, an impressive fifty-year-old, whose impressiveness was substantially enhanced by his long cassock. He kissed the Princess's hand, more out of chivalry than devotion, and assured his patroness of his pleasure at seeing her again.

'You know that you're indispensable,' said the Princess, 'I only stopped on this dreadful, windswept market place – just feel this wind blowing from all four corners as usual – to make certain you would come to see me, this evening in point of fact … But I'm forgetting to introduce you gentlemen: Pastor Schleppegrell, Count Holk …'

Both bowed.

'And please, my dear Pastor, be forbearing and of good cheer. Incidentally Count Holk is a genealogist, so something of a historian, and as such, excellent questioner that he is, he will afford the opportunity for learned conversation. For one is at one's best in conversation when one is being asked questions one is able to answer. That I myself am inquisitive you already know: I wouldn't put my penchant for questioning any higher than that. And bring your dear wife with you. In Hillerød and Frederiksborg the tea only tastes good when it is served by my old friend from the vicarage. Yes, Ebba, that's the fact of the matter, you have to accept it and you mustn't be jealous. But I see I'm committing another sin of omission: Pastor Schleppegrell, Fräulein Ebba von Rosenberg.'

The Pastor greeted Fräulein Ebba and promised not only to come but also to bring his wife, whereupon the journey proceeded from the market place to the castle, after Holk, obeying a request from the Princess, had taken the back seat in her carriage for the short distance remaining. Here, sitting beside Ebba and opposite Fräulein Schimmelmann, he felt sufficiently emboldened to attempt conversation.

'There is something imposing in Pastor Schleppegrell's appearance, but he has an amiability that tones that down again, I have seen few men so relaxed and assured when speaking to a Princess. Is he a Democrat? Or a Dissenter General?'

'No,' laughed the Princess. 'Schleppegrell is no Dissenter General, though he is of course the brother of a real general, General Schleppegrell who fell at Idstedt. Perhaps at the right moment. For then de Meza took over command.'

'Aha,' said Holk, 'that's the reason.'

'No, my dear Holk, *that's* not the reason either; unfortunately I have to contradict you once more. There's quite another reason for what you call his "assurance". He came to Court at the age of twenty as a tutor, a tutor in religion to various young princesses in fact, the rest you can imagine. He has seen too many young princesses to be impressed by old ones. And furthermore, we owe a great debt of gratitude to him for his wise restraint, for there were three occasions when, if he had so wished, he might now be a member of the family. Schleppegrell was always very sensible. Not that I'd reproach the princesses at that time. He was a very handsome man, and a good Christian who was able to say no. Resist that who can.'

Holk was amused, as was Ebba, and a fleeting smile ran over even Fräulein Schimmelmann's features. They could see that the Princess was in the best of humours, and took it as a good sign for the days ahead. And as they continued to chat, the carriage drove over some narrow bridges into the castle courtyard and immediately drew up in front of the portal of Frederiksborg.

20

Servants with lanterns were already waiting and they moved forward when the Princess started to ascend the broad staircase that divided into twin flights at the first landing. She was on the way to her modest suite of rooms in the central block of the castle, which was flanked by two towers. The towers stood at the two acute angles formed by the protruding wings, which were in turn connected by a colonnade.

At the first landing, on a small rococo settee placed there, she sat down for a moment, asthmatic as she was, dismissing the gentlemen and ladies in her retinue with instructions to make themselves as comfortable as possible in their tower rooms. Tea, she added, turning to Holk, would be taken at seven as usual. Pastor Schleppegrell and his wife would be arriving a little earlier to bring her the news from Hillerød, and she was greatly looking forward to this: the things that went on in small towns were quite the most interesting of all, they were a joy to laugh at. And when one grows old, laughing at one's dear fellow creatures is just about the best pleasure to be had. After these gracious words they parted, and half an hour later anyone crossing the castle courtyard could see clearly which rooms the new arrivals had taken. On the first floor where the Princess herself occupied the *corps de logis*, only two tall Gothic windows were faintly lit, while both the towers that flanked it were ablaze with light from top to bottom. In the main everything was in accordance with the Princess's original dispositions: the maidservants downstairs; the two ladies-in-waiting on the first floor; above Fräulein Schimmelmann, Pentz and Erichsen, and above Ebba, Holk.

Seven o'clock was approaching; and the castle clock struck half past six as Pastor and Frau Schleppegrell, preceded by a maid with a lantern, crossed the castle courtyard from the direction of Hillerød. Soon afterwards Holk too readied himself. Downstairs in the hallway of the right-hand tower where he was quartered, Holk met Karin, Ebba's maid – in fact almost her friend – from Stockholm, and she informed him that her mistress was already with the Princess. The way which he still had to cover, passing half the frontage of the main building, was quite short, and on reaching the top of the stairs a minute later, Holk entered the lofty first-floor hall which served as the reception and drawing room whenever the Princess was in residence at Frederiksborg. Towards the courtyard, and also at the rear facing the park, the hall had only a narrow frontage: in spite of this it was still a large room, compensating in depth for what it lacked in breadth. In the middle of one of the long walls there was a tall Renaissance fireplace and over it a larger-than-life-size portrait of King Christian IV, who had been very fond of this hall in his day and, just like the Princess now, had preferred it to all the other rooms in the castle. To the left beside the fireplace stood baskets filled partly with great logs, partly with pine cones and juniper branches, while on the right, as well as a stout poker, lay a few pine-wood torches, whose purpose was to light the guests through the dark corridors late in the evening when they dispersed. Everything about the decor of the hall was still half medieval like the hall itself, above whose wood panelling, apart from the portrait of King Christian over the fireplace, large pictures, dark with age, could be made out. At the very back of the room there was a serving table; the usual high-backed chairs were missing and in their stead a number of modern armchairs were grouped around the fireplace.

Holk strode towards the Princess, bowed, and told her how beautiful he found the hall, that it must be a wonderful place to celebrate Yuletide festivals, everything was there, not just large pine-wood torches, but pine-cones and juniper too. The Princess replied the she fully intended to have such a festivity: Christmas day in Frederiksborg was the best day of the year, and after she had said a few words more and announced a kind of early Yuletide celebration for the next day, she invited Pastor Schleppegrell's wife to come and sit by her side. The Pastor's wife was a plump little woman with red cheeks and black hair pinned up on her head, quite remarkably unprepossessing in a general way, not that this bothered her one whit, because she was one of the happy few who never gave a thought to herself, least of all to her appearance. Ebba had sensed this immediately and developed a liking for her.

'Isn't it difficult for you, dear Frau Schleppegrell,' she said, turning to the Pastor's wife, 'to spend a whole evening away from your children?'

'I have none,' the latter replied, laughing so heartily as she did so that the Princess asked what was happening. This occasioned general amusement, and in the end Schleppegrell too had to join in, despite feeling slightly discomfited since the joke was primarily on him. Noticing this, Holk felt it incumbent on him to change the subject, and enquired casually, or so it seemed, about the portrait above the fireplace. 'I can see it's King Christian (is one nowhere safe from the man?) so there's no question of any special interest. But I would be interested to know who it's by. I would suspect a Spaniard, if I could think of any Spanish painter we've ever had in Copenhagen.'

Schleppegrell was about to explain, but Ebba cut him short: 'Well, if we're going to discuss art and pictures, it simply won't do to start with a picture of King Christian, even if it really were by a Spaniard, which I doubt, just like Count Holk, with whom I'm often in agreement, at least in matters of art. So let's forget the ubiquitous King. For my part, I would rather hear,' and she pointed to the wall opposite, 'who those two there are? The old fellow with the goatee and the distinguished lady with the white hood?'

'The man with the goatee is Admiral Herluf Trolle, the selfsame that King Frederick II, by purchase or exchange, acquired this house from, and then christened it Frederiksborg after himself. Not a stone of the old castle was left standing, and nothing was kept, apart from the pictures here to right and left, glorifying the great sea victory at Öland under Admiral Herluf Trolle, along with the portraits hanging between them of Herluf Trolle himself and Brigitte Gøye, his beloved wife, who was almost more celebrated than her spouse on account of her devout Protestantism.'

'Which can surprise no one, if she really was as devout as all that,' Pentz said with conviction. 'For sure as I am that actresses and princes' mistresses have the greatest popular appeal, the paragons of piety are hard on their heels, and sometimes even a step ahead.'

'Yes, sometimes,' Ebba laughed. 'Sometimes, but not often. And now Pastor Schleppegrell, what's all this about Herluf Trolle and his battle on the high seas? I rather fear it was fought against my beloved compatriots the Swedes. To judge by the costumes though, it was in pre-Rosenberg times, so I don't feel my patriotism too directly challenged. And as for naval battles! The thing about naval battles is that friend and foe always drown in equal numbers and it's all so discreetly shrouded in gun smoke that the few bodies more or less that might signify victory or defeat can never really be determined. Especially here, where quite apart from the gun smoke, age has darkened the paint over the past three hundred years.'

'And yet,' said Holk, 'everything still seems fairly recognizable to me, and if we give it a little help … we need a light for that, but where can we find one?'

'Oh, here,' said the Princess, pointing to where the pine-wood torches lay. 'They'll give off some smoke, but that'll only add to the illusion, and if I tell myself our pastor and cicerone is perhaps having one of his good days, then we'll all have the chance to relive the battle. So, Schleppegrell, to work and do your best, we owe that to a historian of Holk's calibre. And perhaps we can even convert him from Schleswig-Holsteinism to Denmarkism.'

Everyone agreed, Pentz gently tapping two fingers in applause while Schleppegrell, who was a keen amateur picture curator, took one of the large pine-wood torches and, after kindling it, shone it over the left half of the picture, dimly but garishly illuminating countless ships' sails, flags and pennants and gilded figureheads, while white crested waves too could be made out, but no trace of a battle or gun smoke.

'But that can't possibly be a battle,' said Ebba.

'No, but it's the preliminaries. The battle is yet to come; the battle's on the other side, just to the right of Brigitte Gøye.'

'Ah,' said Ebba. 'I see; a battle scene in two parts, before and after. Now I'm all ears, and eyes too. And each time your torch passes the ship with Herluf Trolle on the bridge, I would ask you to grant him (or me, actually) a quarter of a minute, so that I can pay my respects and memorize his features, even in the heat of battle.'

'You won't be able to, Ebba,' said the Princess. 'Herluf Trolle is engulfed in gunsmoke, apart from having been swallowed up by the darkening varnish, so you'll have to content yourself with the actual portrait … But now, Schleppegrell, you may begin and please do strike a balance, not so short that it's worth nothing at all, and not so long that it makes us exchange anxious glances. Holk is a connoisseur, but not the kind to intimidate a storyteller thank goodness – he knows that art is difficult.'

And at these gracious words Schleppegrell had stepped forward into the circle gathered round the fireplace, and he said, 'My Gracious Princess commands and I obey. What we see here, or perhaps don't see,' and he pointed to the second half of the large picture on the wall, which the reflection of the flames didn't reach, 'what we see here is the decisive moment when the *Immaculate* goes up in smoke.'

'The *Immaculate*?'

'Yes, the *Immaculate*. That was the flagship of the Swedish navy, which just at that time, in spite of their mad king (for these were the days of King Eric XIV) was at the height of its power. And against the Swedes and their fleet, which was very powerful and outclassed them, and also had other big ships besides the *Immaculate*, against this Swedish fleet our men, as I say, set sail, and the man in command of them was our great Herluf Trolle. And when they emerged from Køge Bay into the open sea, they sailed due east towards Bornholm, where Herluf Trolle suspected the Swedish fleet to be lying. But it was no longer at Bornholm, it was standing off Stralsund under Admiral Jakob Bagge. And hardly had Jakob Bagge heard that the Danes were looking for him when he left his anchorage off Stralsund and sailed northeast to meet the enemy. And just short of Öland the two fleets met, and that was the beginning of a three-day battle the like of which the Baltic had never seen. And on the third day it looked as if victory would fall to the Swedes. Then Herluf Trolle, whose own ship had taken a severe pounding, called for Vice-Admiral Otto Rud, and gave him orders to board the *Immaculate*, whatever the cost. And Rud was only too happy to turn towards the enemy. But hardly had his ship, which was only small, cast its grappling irons when Admiral Jakob Bagge hoisted all sail on the *Immaculate* in order to drag the little Danish ship that had attached itself to him into the midst of the Swedish fleet. This was a bad moment for Otto Rud. But he didn't call off the attack on the boarding bridge, and when a fair number of our men had got over, one of them fired an incendiary shot into the armoury, and when the fire it caused spread to the powder magazine, the *Immaculate* blew up with friend and foe, and Claus Flemming took command of the Swedes and led what was left of the fleet back to Stockholm.'

A short pause ensued, then Holk said, 'The real hero of this story seems to me to be Otto Rud. However I won't argue; Herluf Trolle presumably did his bit too, so all I'd still like to ask is, what became of him and how did he end?'

'In a manner befitting him. He died a year later of a wound sustained in a naval encounter off the coast of Pomerania. The wound wasn't mortal in itself. But it was that remarkable war when everyone who sustained any wound, serious or minor, died of it. At least that's what the history books say.'

Pentz spoke of 'poisoned bullets', but Ebba dismissed this (Sweden is not a land of poisoners) and said she would prefer, after all these heroics, to hear something of Brigitte Gøye, after all Pastor Schleppegrell had already said that she was almost more celebrated than her husband the naval hero. 'I don't see why we should always be concerned with the men, or even their battles, the history of women is usually far more interesting. And perhaps in this case too. What was the story about this Brigitte?'

'She was very beautiful ...'

'That seems to go with the name,' said Ebba, looking over at Holk. 'But beauty doesn't matter much when you're dead ...'

'And precisely because of that beauty,' Schleppegrell went on undaunted, 'she became the pillar of the new doctrine, so that there are those who say that without Brigitte Gøye Denmark would have languished in darkest Popery.'

'Dreadful ... And why didn't it?'

'It was the time of the religious wars and the people had already adopted the new doctrine, but the Danish aristocracy and the senior churchmen opposed them, above all Joachim Rönnow, Bishop of Roeskilde, who wanted to trample out the flame and drive the lower and poorer Lutheran clergy, who had already established them-selves, out of the country. That was when Brigitte Gøye confronted the Bishop and pleaded for the persecuted Lutherans to be allowed to stay, and because the Bishop was touched by her beauty he countermanded the order, and he was so moved in heart and soul that he asked Mogen Gøye, Brigitte's father, for her hand and wanted to make her his wife.'

'Not possible,' said the Princess. 'A Catholic bishop!'

Schleppegrell smiled. 'Maybe this was the one practice from the new doctrine that he wanted to adopt. Just like the situation over in England. Be that as it may, we have reports which deal with the courtship of the beautiful damsel so exhaustively that it might already have been the nuptials themselves.'

'And did nothing come of it?'

'No. It fell through, and in the end she took Herluf Trolle.'

'She did the right thing. Isn't that so Ebba?'

'Perhaps, Your Highness, but perhaps not. I'm not really in favour of bishops; but if they are exceptional bishops like this one in Roeskilde, I'm not sure whether they might not rank above naval heroes. A bishop who wants to marry, setting aside how impressive that fact alone is, somehow has something conciliatory about him too, which to my mind almost amounts to a resolution of the entire church conflict.'

The Pastor's little wife was delighted at this and went over to Ebba to whisper a little declaration of affection in her ear. But before she could do so, the scene changed, and tables set for supper were carried in through a low side-door far in the background, and when these were quickly followed by double candelabras with a generous array of lights, the second half of the hall that had hitherto lain in complete darkness was lit up, greatly to the advantage not only of the entire room, but above all of the large wall painting and also the portraits set into the wall between its two parts.

It was Pentz who noticed this first. 'See how Brigitte Gøye is smiling, Holk. There is always something special about a Brigitte, even a devout one.'

Holk laughed. The days when such a remark might have embarrassed him were past.

21

It was past eleven when they broke up, but Holk still insisted on accompanying the Schleppegrells part of their way. His offer was of course gratefully accepted, and it was only when they had reached the point where their way curved round the tip of the lake that Holk took his leave, having previously, much to her astonishment, relinquished the accompaniment of Ebba to Erichsen.

From the tip of the lake back to the castle courtyard was not far, but far enough to give a semblance of justification to Holk's astonishment when on climbing the stairs into his tower he found Erichsen and Ebba still in lively conversation outside the latter's door. But his astonishment was short-lived, for it was abundantly clear that the lady had only kept the poor Baron talking out of a desire to show Holk somehow, on his return, that she was not accustomed to being neglected for anybody, least of all these small-town Schleppegrells. 'Ah it's you again,' she said, turning to greet the Count with a courteous smile as he tried to go past her and Erichsen. 'Ah yes, these Schleppegrells ... and him especially! In his youth, the Princess assured me, he made his conquests with his Apostle's head; now in his old age it's Herluf Trolle. I must admit I can't see that as progress.'

And with that she bowed and withdrew into her room, where Karin was already awaiting her mistress.

Now it was morning; the light shone in at the window as brightly as a November morning can, but for hours on end the night just past had been a very stormy one. A southeaster had caught the lightning-conductor running up the tower and worked it loose in places, shaking it back and forth and rattling it fiercely; what had disturbed Holk most, however, was that the moon, despite the storm, had shone straight into his alcove which was recessed deep into the wall. Holk could have blocked out this uncanny gaze by drawing the curtain, but he objected to that even more; he wanted at least to see *who* was standing out there, robbing him of his sleep. Only towards morning did he fall asleep and even then he was restless with all manner of anxious dreams. He had been blown up on the *Immaculate*—Admiral Jakob Bagge was on board too—and when he clung to a piece of mast to save himself, Ebba had surfaced like a mermaid from the other side and dragged him off it and back into the waves. At that point he woke up. He thought about the dream and said, 'She'd be capable of it.'

He was fully in the mood to pursue this thought, but any lingering on it was ruled out, for just then an old gardener, whose duty it was to service both towers in the morning when the Princess was in residence, came in with breakfast and, as he set the table, excused himself for being so late. Fräulein von Rosenberg had already complained, quite rightly. But things would change; just at the moment nothing was in proper order. As he spoke he handed over the newspapers which had come for Holk, along with a letter.

Holk took the letter and noticed that there was no postmark. 'No, there isn't one,' the gardener confirmed. 'It didn't come by post; Pastor Schleppegrell had it handed in. And one for Fräulein Ebba.' And with that the old man left the room.

'Aha, from Pastor Schleppegrell,' said Holk, when he was alone. 'I'm glad to see it, I wonder what he has to say.'

But his curiosity could not have been very great, for he put the letter aside for a fair while until he had finished breakfast, which he visibly relished, and then he picked it up again and sat down in a rocking chair by his desk, a chair that didn't quite match the rest of the furnishings in the tower room. Only there did he break the seal. And then he read:

My Lord,
The interest that you were kind enough to show in my friend Herluf Trolle yesterday emboldens me to send you a passage from a ballad concerning that self-same friend which I translated from the Old Danish years ago. It is hardly necessary to crave your indulgence, for when we read with love, we make allowances.—At about eleven my wife and I intend to call upon you and Fräulein von Rosenberg, whom I have also informed, to take a walk together in the park. Perhaps in the direction of Fredensborg. We shall scarcely manage a third of the way of course, but it is this first third that is specially beautiful, and at

this time of the year perhaps more beautiful than at any other.
By twelve we shall be back to appear punctually for our gracious
Princess and partake of her festive lunch. For a small festivity is
what it will certainly be.

Your most obliging servant
Arvid Schleppegrell

Enclosed with the letter was a sheet of pink paper with verses
written in a female hand. 'Ah, presumably the handwriting of my
little friend the Pastor's wife. She seems to be one of those amiable
people who know how to make themselves useful with small services on all occasions, for I can't imagine that she could herself have
a personal passion for Herluf Trolle. Be that as it may, first let me
see what Pastor Schleppegrell has christened his piece.' And with
that Holk picked up the pink paper again and scanned the title. It
read: 'How Herluf Trolle was buried.' 'That's good, one knows
what to expect.' And with that he pushed the rocking chair close to
the window and read:

> A rider had ridden ahead with the news.
> > Into the courtyard they stepped,
> Brigitta stood at the castle doors,
> > The women around her wept.

'Aha, that must be Brigitte Gøye, the pious spouse we heard
about yesterday: pious and beautiful and a danger to the Bishop of
Roeskilde. But let's see what else Schleppegrell and his ballad have
to report about her.'

> At the doors she stood, and greeted all,
> > Upright and unbroken.
> The first of those that bore the pall
> > Stepped up, and thus he has spoken:

> 'You know the news we sent ahead,
> > The news of this dreadful thing,
> His soul is free, the rest is here,
> > You know who it is we bring.

'At sea he fought, by Pudagla-Golm,
    He saved us though hard-pressed,
And fell. Now Mistress of Herlufsholm,
    Say, where shall we lay him to rest?

'Shall we lay him in the Totensaal
    Of Torslund or Olaf's Church?
Or shall we lay him in Gjeddesdal
    Under the weeping birch?

'Shall we lay him in a chapel crypt
    In Hleidra? Ringsted? Roeskilde?
My Lady, tell us where to lay him,
    Each would give him shelter.

'Whatever was asked he gave each church,
    Altar or tower or bell,
And each that hears of his approach
    Will ring a joyful knell.

'Every church invites him in
    To rest in its columns' shade ...'
Brigitta now addressed her men:
    '*Here* he shall be laid.

'This church here he did not build –
    For centuries it's stood –
But I was Herluf Trolle's bride,
    Here at the altar we stood.

'Let him come to this spot once more,
    To this altar and this stone,
And nothing shall be spoken here
    But: Lord, thy will be done.

'Tomorrow, though, ere day has dawned,
   From his churches all around,
Across the sea, across the land,
   All the bells shall sound.

'When all the air is rent to heaven,
   As if with battle's holler,
Then into the crypt of Herlufsholm
   We'll lower Herluf Trolle.'

Holk slipped the sheet into the letter again and the letter back into the envelope and repeated quietly to himself: 'Then into the crypt of Herlufsholm we'll lower Herluf Trolle ...' Hm, I like it, I like it very much. It hasn't any real content and it's just a situation, not a poem, but no matter. It has the tone, and just as the palette makes the picture, as my brother-in-law often assures me, the tone makes the poem. And Alfred is probably right as usual. I'll copy it out today and send it to Christine. Or better still, I'll send off the pink sheet to her. Coming from a pastor's house will be a special recommendation for the poem. But of course I shall have to ask the little lady beforehand to write her name and above all her station in life beneath it, otherwise the whole thing could go wrong. Pink paper is suspect enough, and the stiff laundry list handwriting, yes, who's to say where that might come from; ladies-in-waiting often have quite peculiar handwriting.'

He broke off these reflections because looking at the clock he saw it was already approaching eleven. He would have to hurry if he was to be dressed and in marching order by the time the Schleppegrells arrived. And what would the paths be like underfoot? Shortly before midnight rain had fallen, and even if the southeaster had dried up a good deal already, he knew from Holkenäs that park paths are mostly soft going after rain. He chose the appropriate clothing and was hardly finished dressing when the Schleppegrells crossed the courtyard. He called down not to trouble to climb the stairs, he would fetch Fräulein Ebba and be with them straight away. And so it was, and in less than five minutes they had passed from the great front portal through the entire depth of the castle and stepped out into the park through an equally grand portal at the back. Here they also met Erichsen, who was just returning from an hour and a half's walk for his health but instantly declared himself ready to participate in the new excursion. They welcomed this and marvelled at it. Erichsen offered Ebba his arm and Holk followed with the Pastor's little wife, while Schleppegrell took the lead. As when they first met on the market square in Hillerød, his coat-like, unwaisted cassock hung from shoulder to ankle, and he wore a floppy hat and carried an oak stick, which he brandished expansively in all directions except when he elected to twirl it in the air and catch it again.

Holk, much as he would have preferred to be at Ebba's side, was the soul of courtesy to the Pastor's wife, asking her to tell her husband, in case he personally failed to do so, how pleased he had been by the missive; and he was scarcely less indebted to her, for he felt sure the fair copy was by her hand.

'Yes,' she said. 'Each has to help the other, that's really the best thing about marriage. Helping and supporting each other, and above all being considerate and developing a sense of the other's rights. For what are these rights? In point of fact they change constantly. But readiness to yield to a good person is always right.'

Holk was silent. The little woman carried on in this vein, without the least idea of the images she was conjuring up or the thoughts she had aroused in him. The sun which had shone so brightly in the early morning was gone again, the wind had turned once more, and the sky was clad in a fine grey; but this particular light made the clumps of trees that were dotted over the broad park meadow stand out wonderfully with all the more clarity. The air was at once soft and refreshing, and on the slope of a terrace sheltered from the wind all sorts of flowerbeds with late asters could be seen; but wherever there were dips in the meadow ponds came into view, small and large, with kiosks and pavilions on their banks and all kinds of leafless twigs hanging down in front of their fantastic roofs. Indeed, everything was bare. Only the plane trees held on to their foliage; but every strong gust that blew lifted batches of the large, yellowing leaves and strewed them over path and meadow. At a short distance from the castle there was a broad moat, crossed by a number of birchwood bridges of various styles but just at the point where Schleppegrell, ahead of the others, reached the moat, there was no bridge; instead there was a ferry with a rope stretched from one side to the other along which the flat-bottomed boat could be drawn with ease. Once on the other side it was only a short walk to an artificial hill from which, Schleppegrell assured them, there was a virtually open view of Schloss Fredensborg to the north and of Schloss Frederiksborg to the south. This was the spot they wanted to reach. But in view of the limited time available that goal soon had to be abandoned and a shorter way back chosen.

All this time Holk had not moved from the Pastor's wife's side, but when they had crossed on the ferry a second time and reached the other bank again, they exchanged ladies, and while Erichsen offered his arm to the Pastor's wife, Holk and Ebba, who until then had scarcely had time to exchange greetings, followed at a constantly increasing distance.

'I thought I was becoming a sacrifice to your latest fancy,' said Ebba. 'A dangerous pair, these Schleppegrells: yesterday *him*, today *her*.'

'Ah, dear lady, nothing could be more flattering for me than to find myself cast in the role of Don Juan like this.'

'And for the sake of a Zerline like that! More like Zerline's great aunt actually. What did she talk to you about? As far as I could see, she was talking nineteen to the dozen …'

'Well, all sorts of things; Hillerød and life there in winter, and that the town is split between the Assembly Rooms and the officers' mess. You might almost think you were in Germany. Charming little lady incidentally, full of common sense, and yet so simple and so limited that I find it hard to imagine how the Pastor manages with her, still less how the Princess can spend hours chatting to her.'

Ebba laughed. 'You really are out of touch! It's clear you're only in contact with princesses once in a blue moon. Believe me, nothing is so trivial that it wouldn't interest a princess. As for gossip, the more the merrier. Tom Jensen went to the Indies and married a black woman, and the daughters are all black and the sons all white; Brodersen the chemist has poisoned his wife, with nicotine they say; Holmsen the assistant gamekeeper fell into a lime-pit last night climbing out of his sweetheart's window – I can assure you that kind of thing interests our Princess more than the whole Schleswig-Holstein question, despite the fact that some claim she's its heart and soul.'

'Ah Ebba, you're just saying that because you love to mock and take things to extremes.'

'I'll accept that, because I'd rather be like that than the opposite. Very good, I have a mocking and malicious tongue, and whatever else you care to say; but I don't retract a jot of what I just said about princesses. And the cleverer and wittier persons in high places are, the keener their sense of the ridiculous and their eye for it, and the sooner they are to find boring people just as agreeable and entertaining as interesting ones.'

'How can *you* of all people say that! Aren't you walking proof of the contrary? What won you your place in the Princess's heart? Simply the fact that you're clever and astute, have original ideas and know how to talk and, in a word, are more interesting than Fräulein Schimmelmann.'

'No, it's simply because I'm different from Schimmelmann, who is just as necessary to the Princess as I am, or Erichsen, or Pentz, or even perhaps ...

'... as Holk.'

'That's not what I was going to say, but let's drop the subject and take a rest – even if we're so far behind the others, a little moment at this delightful spot, from which we have such a good view of the rear of the castle. See how the main roof and, to left and right, the pointed tower roofs stand out so wonderfully from one another, even though they're all the same shade of grey.'

'Yes,' said Holk. 'Everything does stand out wonderfully. It's the light that does it, but castles shouldn't be built with special lighting effects in mind. I think the two brick towers we're staying in, with their magnificent red, should have been built higher, before the slate or shingle peaks begin. As it is, it looks as if you could step out of the lowest lancet window on to the main roof and go for a walk along the gutter.'

Ebba nodded, perhaps because she was indifferent to the conclusion of this discussion of buildings and illumination, and the two of them then quickly hurried on their way, since they thought they could see that the Pastor was stopping to wait for them. As they approached, however, they saw that it was something else, and that Schleppegrell, pressing as the time was, was bent on drawing attention to an especially noteworthy sight. This was no more nor less than a giant, partly hollowed stone lying by the wayside, with the words 'Christian IV, 1628' chiselled into the shallow depression. Holk voiced the opinion as they came up to it that it was presumably one of the king's favourite seats and resting-places, to which Schleppegrell rejoined, 'Yes, so it was indeed; a resting-place. But not a regular one, only once, and thereby hangs a little tale ...'

'Tell us!' everyone cried. The Pastor however took out his silver pocket-watch from which a large clock key dangled on a rather worn green cord, and pointed at the face which was already showing ten to twelve. 'We must hurry, or we'll be late. I'll tell it at lunch, that's assuming it's fit for table, which I rather doubt.'

'A pastor can say anything,' said Ebba, 'especially in the presence of a princess. For princesses are law unto themselves, and if they let it pass, it's good and fit. And as for ours! She won't say no, that I guarantee.'

And they hastened towards the castle at a more rapid pace.

22

They were back at the castle shortly before twelve, just in time to appear punctually in the Princess's apartment. Pentz and Schimmelmann, who were on duty, received the invited guests, and after the Princess, who came in soon afterwards, had addressed a word of greeting to each of them, they left the drawing room and reception room and went down a corridor richly decorated with caryatids, which appeared to date from a later period, into the great Herluf Trolle Hall where the evening before they had first viewed the large-scale pictures as best they could by the light of the log fire and pine torches and listened to Schleppegrell's account of them. Yes, it was the same hall; but there was a difference from yesterday, for bright daylight now streamed in (midday had brought the sun out again), giving everything a more cheerful feel, an impression enhanced by the grand table with its almost fantastical decoration of flowers and Old Nordic drinking vessels. There were decorations everywhere, even the walls were decorated. Where the high wood panelling touched the wide baroque picture frames, bunches of mistletoe and rowan-berries hung from garlands of oak leaves, while a screen of cypresses and young fir trees was placed right across the hall, separating the dark space at the rear from the festively adorned area in front. It was all intended, so much was apparent, to have the effect of Christmas, or as the Princess had put it, at least a prelude to the Yule Festival. Oranges in almost excessive profusion hung from the branches of the fir trees, and little wax Christmas angels waved their flags, while all over the gleaming white tablecloth lay holly branches with their red berries.

And now with a graceful wave of her hand, the Princess invited the guests to be seated. For several minutes they were silent or restricted themselves to talking in whispers; however, by the time the first glass of Cyprus wine had been emptied, the light-hearted mood that distinguished this small circle had returned. At the invitation of the Princess, each first reported experiences of the previous night's storm, and all agreed that the beautiful castle in which, unfortunately, all the windows rattled and one lived in constant fear of being snatched up and blown away by a nor'wester, was more a summer palace than a winter one. 'Yes,' said the Princess, 'that is unfortunately the case. I can't exonerate my dear Frederiksborg from that; and the worst of it is that I can't do anything about it, I just have to leave everything as it is.' And then she recounted, with her characteristic joviality, how she had years ago submitted a formal request for 'doors and windows that close,' and it was rejected out of hand by the administrative or buildings authority concerned on the grounds that the fitness of the palace for habitation, or at least the proper functioning of the fireplaces, was intimately bound up with the continued existence of draughty windows; airtight windows would have meant fireplaces that didn't draw. 'And now that I know this, I have accepted my fate: indeed, after everything I heard on that occasion, I have to be grateful when good draughts from doors and windows continue to save us from blocked flues and all the dangers that could entail. Frankly, I sometimes fear that something of the kind could still happen. The chimneys in the castle are no doubt in a pretty poor state, and particularly in this one here I suspect there might well be a layer of soot that goes back to King Christian's time.'

After the mention of King Christian's name it was more or less inevitable that the conversation would turn to the Frederiksborg days of this favourite Danish king, about whom Schleppegrell, even more inevitably, produced an instant wealth of local anecdotes. After a time, however, Holk interrupted and said, 'We've had a quarter of an hour of anecdotes about King Christian already, and we still haven't heard the story of the stone out there with his name and the year 1628. What's that about? In the park you promised ...'

Schleppegrell shook his head doubtfully, then began to speak. 'It was indeed my intention to talk about that. But there isn't much to tell, and I expect you'll be disappointed. The story goes that it's the stone where Christian IV, when he began directing the great reconstruction of the Schloss after he came to the throne, gathered the workers round him on the first Saturday and paid them their week's wages in person.'

'That's all?'

'Yes,' said Schleppegrell.

Ebba however wouldn't hear of it. 'No, Pastor Schleppegrell, you don't get off so easily; what you say just can't be the whole story. You're forgetting that to get out of a tight corner or pull the wool over people's eyes, one must have a good memory. It isn't two hours since we heard from your own mouth that you would only tell us about the stone if the Princess gave her blessing. Now you can't possibly have believed that the Princess might forbid you to report a Saturday wage payment.'

The Princess was thoroughly enjoying Schleppegrell's embarrassment, and Ebba, unwilling to relinquish her advantage, went on, 'You see, you can only get out of your dreadful situation if you take the bull by the horns and come clean and tell us the whole story just as it really happened.'

Schleppegrell, who had tied his napkin across his chest in the old-fashioned manner, undid the knot mechanically, laid the napkin aside and said, 'Very well, if you insist: there is another version, and it's said to be the more accurate one. The King was out walking in the castle garden with Christine Munk, who was his wife, and then again wasn't, something that has unfortunately occurred more than once in our history, and with the two of them were Prince Ullrich and Princess Fritz-Anna, and when they reached this stone they sat down to have a chat. And the King was gracious and charming as never before. But Christine Munk, for reasons that to this minute no one knows or can even guess at (or perhaps she had none) remained silent and sat looking so sour-faced and ill-tempered that she caused an extremely awkward situation. And the worst part of it was that Christine's ill-humour still wasn't over when evening came and the King went to retire to the bedchamber. He found the door locked and bolted and had to sleep elsewhere. And since such a thing had never happened to the King before, because Christine was not only one of the most good-humoured but also one of the tenderest of women, the King decided to mark the day of this remarkable aberration for all eternity, and had his name and the year inscribed on the stone where the mysterious strife had begun.'

'Well,' said the Princess, 'that's certainly a little more embarrassing, but still not remotely enough to make me the ogre of prudery that my dear Schleppegrell seems to have painted me this morning. And by the way, apropos of prudery! Something I found just yesterday in a French book: "Prudery, when one is no longer young and beautiful, is nothing but a scarecrow left standing after the harvest." Not bad: the French understand these things. But, not to forget our topic, as far as the story of King Christian and his "exclusion" is concerned, I could wish that all the stories about our kings and princes, which just at the moment tend to the opposite extreme, might be as harmless, and Count Holk will surely concur with me in this wish. Tell me, Count, what do you think of the story?'

'To tell the truth Ma'am, I find the story too trivial, altogether too minor a matter.'

'Too minor a matter,' repeated Ebba. 'I'd wish to contradict that. The business about paying wages on a Saturday was indeed a minor matter, but not *this*. When a woman persists in being sour-faced it's never a minor matter, and when her bad mood runs to locking her husband out of the bedroom (I'm sorry to have to touch on this point but history demands the truth be told, not covered up), then it's absolutely not minor. I call upon my Princess as my witness and take refuge in her protection. But that's how gentlemen are today; King Christian has the event set in stone as something remarkable with a message for times far in the future, and Count Holk finds it "too minor a matter, too trivial".'

Holk found himself cornered, and, noticing that the Princess was evidently in the mood to take Ebba's side, he shilly-shallied somewhat and, alternately striking a serious and then an ironic note, attempted to reason that in such a matter it was absolutely necessary to distinguish between a private and a historical point of view; from a private point of view being 'excluded' like that was deeply saddening and almost tragic, but to shut out a king went entirely beyond the pale and should not happen, and if history were nonetheless to record such an event, it would have relinquished both its authority and its dignity, and that, for better or worse, was what he had had to call 'trivial'.

'He's extricated himself nicely,' said the Princess. 'Now Ebba, would you dispute that?'

'Yes Ma'am, I would indeed, and if perhaps as a German Fräulein I could not, as a pure Scandinavian woman I certainly can.'

Everybody was amused.

'As a pure Scandinavian woman,' Ebba repeated, 'naturally on my mother's side, which is always the decisive one; for fathers never count for much. And now to our proposition. What Count Holk said there ... well yes, from his Schleswig-Holstein point of view he may be right with his predilection for grandeur. For his protest against what is trivial naturally means that he favours the grand style. But what is meant by "grand style"? Grand style means simply bypassing everything that actually interests people. Christine Munk interests us, and her ill-humour interests us too, and what followed her ill-humour on that memorable evening is something that interests us a great deal more ...'

'And what interests us most of all is Fräulein Ebba when she's in high spirits …'

'Which are perhaps not as marked as usual at this moment. In so far as I can be serious, that's what I'm being now. At any rate I insist with all conceivable seriousness and honesty that I'm prepared to put to the vote, in any girls' boarding school, that Henry VIII with his six wives sweeps all before him as far as the grand style is concerned, and not because of a few beheadings, those crop up elsewhere too, but because of the sensitive little matters that preceded those beheadings. And after Henry VIII comes Mary Stuart, and after her comes France with its "teeming visions",[*] from Agnes Sorel to Mesdames de Pompadour and Dubarry, and Germany only comes a long way after that. And Prussia brings up the rear. Prussia has a major deficit in this field, and that a few women writers of genius have penned some half dozen amorous adventures to add to the Frederick the Great story is not unconnected with this; they quite rightly felt that something of the sort is simply a sine qua non.'

Pentz nodded in agreement, while Holk shook his head indecisively.

'You evidently have doubts, Count, above all doubts about my conviction. But it is as I say. Grand style! Pah! Of course I know people are supposed to be virtuous, but they aren't, and once we accept that, things in general look better than when we just make a pretence of morality. Loose living ruins morals, but parading false virtue ruins the whole person.'

And as she said that, a wax angel fell from one of the little fir trees standing round the table just where Pentz was sitting. He picked it up and said, 'A fallen angel; we're seeing a sign or a miracle. But for whom?'

'Not me,' laughed Ebba.

'No,' Pentz affirmed, and the tone in which it was said caused Ebba to blush. But before she could punish the miscreant, what sounded like the patter of feet came from behind the screen of firs and cypresses. At the same time instructions were given, albeit in a muted voice, and children's voices struck up a song. Some verses

---

[*] Goethe, *Faust* I, line 520.

composed by Schleppegrell for this pre-Christmas celebration rang
through the hall.

> Autumn's not quite fled
> When Ruprecht* comes instead;
> Soon Winter will set in,
> And as the snows begin,
> Bells jingle on the sled.
>
> And all that did appear
> In colours, far and near,
> Is white, branch, roof and tower; –
> Before the year's last hour
> Its finest feast is here.
>
> Day of our Lord, still far
> From all of us you are,
> But angels, flags and firs
> Announce that day to us,
> And we can see the star.

23

The little pre-Christmas party which had ended with a fireside
chat (the theologian and historian Grundtvig was the main topic
of conversation) lasted until darkness was falling, and it was past
six when it broke up, shortly after the Princess had withdrawn
to her rooms. Holk again accompanied the Schleppegrells, this
time right into the town, and he had to agree to visit the vicarage
and inspect Schleppegrell's collections in situ as soon as he had
some free time before he returned to his tower room where in the

---

* Knecht (Servant) Ruprecht, helper to St Nicholas. Ruprecht traditionally accom-
panies St Nicholas on the night of 5th December when he visits children's homes to
check on their behaviour throughout the year. Good children will receive gifts, but
Ruprecht's whip awaits the naughty ones.

course of the evening he wrote letters, to Asta, to Axel, to Fräulein Dobschütz. On the previous day, just before the Princess's court left for Frederiksborg, a few lines had arrived from the last-named, informing the Count that Christine was unable to write because she was ill. It couldn't be said that this information made much impression on him. He knew his wife's love of the truth, but observed nonetheless, 'She'll be in an ill-humour and she chooses to call it illness. Anyone can always claim to be ill; it has the advantage of justifying their every mood.'

The next morning again brought a clear and cloudless day; no wind blew, and Holk, who had to report for duty at noon, sat by the window looking towards the Hillerød church tower whose weather-vane glinted in the sun; the houses lay in silence, the roofs bright and shining, and had it not been for the smoke rising from the tall chimney pots one might have thought the town enchanted. Not a person in sight. 'Living in such silence,' he said to himself, 'what bliss!' and then he realized that there was the same silence in Holkenäs and added, 'Yes, the same silence, but not the same peace. How enviable this pastor is! He has his congregation, his stone graves, and his bog finds, not to mention Herluf Trolle, and he just lets the outside world go its own way. Hillerød is his world. Yet who knows what goes on inside him. He seems so placid and serene, so wholly at peace, but is he really? If it's true that three princesses fell for him one after the other, or perhaps all at once, then it seems to me that this idyll, as the outcome of all that, is a somewhat questionable kind of happiness. To marry a princess is of course still more questionable, but if in one's wisdom one chooses not to, and all that one has in return for one's wisdom is small-town life here in Hillerød, then surely some kind of longing must remain. A splendid woman, this plump, spherical little pastor's wife, but not the woman to make a man like Schleppegrell forget his past. Everyone has his vanity when all's said and done, and pastors, they say, not least.'

He mused thus for a while longer, running over all the images and experiences again that the previous day had brought, besides the little party at the Princess's: the walk up to Fredensborg, the flat-bottomed ferry with its rope stretched across to pull you over the moat to the other bank, the wonderful view of the rear of the castle with its steep roof and its towers, and finally the hollow stone and the conversation with Ebba. 'Ebba is too unkind when she's talking about the Princess, and that's one more proof that wit and gratitude don't mix. If she has something piquant on the tip of her tongue it has to come out, and propriety can go hang. The Stockholm story … I won't go into that, just leave it be, although there too she clearly should have reason for gratitude; but the Princess spoils her with everything she says and does, and Ebba just takes it not only as if it were natural, but as if she were superior to the Princess. And that isn't the case, the Princess just has a plainer way of expressing herself. Yesterday how good her comments were on old Grundtvig, drawn from the fullness of her experience, which reminds me that this could provide a good postscript for my letter to Fräulein Dobschütz. It has turned out a trifle thin.'

And as he said this he sat down at the desk to the right of the window and wrote on the page that remained blank: 'A little postscript, my dear Dobschütz. One of the topics of conversation at the Princess's yesterday was Grundtvig. Schleppegrell was inclined to make him halfway a saint, in which Pentz and Fräulein Rosenberg supported him, ironically of course. The Princess, however, took the matter quite seriously, almost as seriously as Schleppegrell, and said, "Grundtvig is an important man, and very much on the way to becoming the pride of Denmark, or one of them. But he does have one flaw, he always has to be a little bit out of the ordinary, to be different from the rest of humanity, even the Danes, and though they do say he holds Denmark in such esteem that he seriously believes the Good Lord speaks Danish, I'm sure that if the day came when this was established as fact, he'd insist that the Good Lord speaks Prussian and he'd prove it too. Grundtvig can't bear to be in agreement with anyone." This, my dear Dobschütz, will give you a clear idea of the tone and tenor of the table-talk and evening conversations here, and I thought I should add this little story to my letter, knowing Christine's interest in clerical anecdotes and theological arguments, and the question of what language God speaks in private perhaps falls into that category. Again my best wishes. I shall write to Christine tomorrow, but only a few lines.'

He had just finished putting this letter to Fräulein Dobschütz and then the two others to Asta and Axel into envelopes when there was a knock on the door. 'Come in.' There was another knock, so Holk stood up to see who it was. Outside stood Karin, looking straight ahead, too embarrassed to meet his eye, though embarrassment was the least of her propensities. She handed over some newspapers and letters to Holk. The postman had been very pressed for time and had delivered them downstairs to Fräulein Ebba's rooms. She was to give him Fräulein Ebba's regards and tell him that her mistress was intending to take a walk to the 'stone' in the park with Baron Pentz – the Count would know which stone. Holk smiled, excused himself and went back to his seat to see what the latest post had brought. He pushed the newspapers, which with the current lull in politics promised little, to one side and examined the handwriting on the letters that had come. They were all easy to recognize; this one was from old Petersen, that one from his gardener, and here was his brother-in-law Arne's hand, the postmark 'Arnewiek' serving as confirmation.

'Alfred? What can he want? He normally interprets his powers as major-domo widely enough not to disturb me with too many queries. It's my great good fortune that he proceeds in this way and generally, that he is as he is. I've no desire to concern myself here with the price of wool or how much fatstock is to be shipped to England. That's his affair, or else Christine's, and in any case both understand the business much better than I do; the Arnes were always leading farmers, which is not something I can say about the Holks; for my part I have always just muddled through. So what does he want? But why do I bother to speculate?' And with that he took the letter and cut it open with a little ivory knife, proceeding slowly, for he had a premonition that the letter was not going to make very pleasant reading.

And then he read:

Dear Holk, I make it a principle, as you know, to refrain from molesting you with business matters from Holkenäs during your time in Copenhagen. Neither has it ever been necessary until now, since your obliging nature makes it easy to manage your affairs in your place; you not only have a happy gift of always agreeing with what others do, you also have the even happier one, when that is not the case, of calling it evens. But to come straight to the point, I am not writing to you today about pressing farm business, far less do I intend to come back to my cherished plans with which you are familiar–a change from Oldenburg cows to Shorthorns (dairy farming has had its day) and Southdown sheep in place of the Rambouillet Merinos. What sense does wool production make for us now? It's a branch that has long been superseded, it may be suitable for the Lüneburg Heath, but not for us. The London cattle market is the *only* one there can be any question of for our produce. *Meat, meat*! But enough of this. I am writing to you about more important matters, namely Christine. Christine, as Fräulein Dobschütz will have told you, is not well, it's serious or not serious depending on how you choose to look at it. She doesn't need to be sent to Karlsbad or Nice, but she is sick just the same, sick at heart. And for that, my dear Holk, you are to blame. What kind of letters have you been writing for the past six weeks, or I might say, not writing? I don't understand you, and if, from the very start of our friend- ship, I have always reproached you with knowing nothing about women, it was in fun, but it isn't now, I have to say there's no joking when I tell you now in all seriousness that you really don't understand women, least of all your own wife, my dear Christine. I scarcely dare call her *our* dear Christine in view of the attitude you have been displaying. I can see you becoming impatient and taking the line that I am to blame, being the prime cause and instigator of all the strange behaviour that you have been indulging in with as much virtuosity as consistency since your departure from Holkenäs. And if you choose to see me and the previous advice I have given you entirely in that light, then I cannot deny that you have a certain right to do so. Yes, it is true that I have more than once advised you to take the path that you have now elected to follow. But my dear brother-in-law, do I have to say to you, *est modus in rebus*. Do I have to remind you that *moderation* is the decisive factor in all we do, and that the wisest counsel, bear with me if I seem to include my own in that, becomes its own opposite when the person who follows it gets the balance wrong and ends up badly overdoing it? And that's what you have been and still are doing. I have pleaded with you to be on your guard against Christine's stubbornness and the desire to take control that lurks behind that religious commitment of hers and constantly draws new strength from it, and I have advised you to resist it energetically, and I have also advised you on occasion to try a little jealousy and make your wife, my dear sister, realize that even the securest possessions can be put at risk, and that the best man can also have his hour of weakness. Yes, my dear Holk, I have spoken to you along these lines, not lightly, but, if you will permit the expression, with pedagogical intent, and I have no regrets and no need to retract any of what I said. But what have you actually done in putting these, to my mind correct, suggestions into practice? A little dig that might once have been perfectly harmless has become quite wounding, pinpricks have become poisoned darts, and, worst of all, where for a time there was restraint on your part, so that she should have recognized what an effort and struggle that was costing you, now a certain coldness has set in and a not entirely happy, indeed rather forced attempt to conceal that coldness behind gossip from town and court. I have read your letters – there were not many of them, and not one could be criticized for excessive length – and half of these few dwelt on the fairytale beauty of the, to say the least, rather strange Frau Brigitte Hansen and the other half on the witticisms of the equally rather strange Fräulein Ebba von Rosenberg. In all this long time you have not had as much as twenty lines for your wife or your children, always just questions, and questions where one sensed no particular desire for an answer. I think, my dear Holk, that it should suffice to have made all this clear to you. You are too fair-minded to close your ears to the validity of these charges and too kind and noble of heart, if you admit the justice of the charges, not to take immediate steps to remedy the matter. The hour when that letter arrives at Holkenäs will also be the hour when Christine is cured; permit me to hope that it is not far away. As always

Your faithful and devoted brother-in-law
Alfred Arne

The content of this letter hit Holk so hard that he did not read the others. Petersen had perhaps written something similar. In addition it was time for him to appear at the Princess's, and he was afraid he would be unable to conceal his agitation from her. And he would in fact have been unable to do so if everything had been normal when he appeared, and the Princess had been her usual alert self. This was not, however, the case, because the Princess had meanwhile received a letter which entirely preoccupied her and left her unable to concern herself with Holk's bemusement.

24

The letter delivered to the Princess was from Baron Blixen-Fineke, one of the royal gentlemen-in-waiting. It read:

> Your Royal Highness, Your devoted servant begs in all haste to inform you that His Majesty the King, who returns later today to Copenhagen from Glücksburg, is considering spending the next few weeks in Schloss Frederiksborg, probably until the New Year, in any event he proposes to celebrate Christmas there. Only a few persons from his inner circle will accompany him: Colonel du Plat perhaps, Captain Westergaard and Captain Lundbye for certain. I felt called upon to inform Your Royal Highness about this decision of His Majesty's.
>
> Your Royal Highness's most devoted servant
Blixen-Fineke

The first thought on reading these lines had been to quit the field instantly, before the King's arrival, possibly to return to Copenhagen before the next twenty-four hours were over. Once the King was in residence, such a retreat, if not impossible, would be very much more awkward, because, given the good personal relations between nephew and aunt, it would be all too obvious that the Princess simply wanted to avoid finding herself under the same roof as the detested Countess Danner. So a swift decision was essential,

'To leave or not to leave,' that was the question that preoccupied the circle gathered around the Princess, above all Ebba for whom the prospect of a quick return to the capital gave rise to more hopes than fears. For finely attuned as her feeling for nature was, and much as she liked Schleppegrell, despite occasional little revolts against him and his eternal harping on old times, all in all she far preferred the capital where the latest news was available six hours earlier and there was always a box at the theatre in the evening. The grand hall at Frederiksborg was a splendid example of its kind, it was true, and when light and shade played on the walls and ceiling it had a romantic charm as well as a slight *frisson* all of its own; but it simply wasn't possible to gaze for six hours on end from dusk to bedtime at Herluf Trolle and maintain the same level of interest, far less at the great sea battle and the *Immaculate* being blown to smithereens.

Yes, if it had been left to Ebba, the decision to return would have been quickly taken; the Princess however, who out of superstition alone was unwilling to leave the place she had been accustomed for decades to regard as her home for Christmas, was caught in a certain indecision, quite contrary to her usual character, and she was pleased when Holk remarked, 'If you will permit my asking Your Highness, is it at all certain that the Countess will accompany the King? His Majesty is, to my knowledge, full of consideration for Your Royal Highness, and not only does he know your feelings, he also respects them. He doesn't allow this to deter him in his affection, nor can he, if the popular view that Danner has cast a spell and bewitched him is correct; but he can persist in his affection and still leave the Countess over in Skodsborg and visit her daily, which may suit him better than having her here with him from morning to night. For the time for constantly gazing at her with the eyes of love, if there ever was such a time – must certainly be *tempi passati* by now.'

'Who knows,' laughed the Princess. 'You seem to see bewitchment, my dear Holk, as something like an intermittent fever, and believe there are days of remission. I can't see that myself. A proper spell doesn't come and go, it's uninterrupted. Now my dear Ebba, pass me Blixen-Fineke's letter again, I want to read exactly what he says. He is a man of carefully chosen words.'

Ebba brought the letter, and the Princess read, '"Only a few persons from his inner circle will accompany him: Colonel du Plat perhaps, Captain Westergaard and Captain Lundbye for certain ..." Holk is right; Blixen-Fineke knows too well how matters stand between us for him not to give me at least a hint. The Countess is *not* coming, and I get on rather well with my nephew. He is a good-hearted soul, kind, the best in the world. At any rate we need give no thought today to leaving. In all probability Berling will write too and he will express himself less diplomatically than Fineke.'

The next day a note from the gentleman-in-waiting Berling did come, first confirming the imminent arrival of the King, but at the same time bringing full reassurance with regard to the Danner question. The Countess would again, at her own request, take up residence in Skodsborg and receive the King's visits there. With that, the state of uncertainty they had been in for a day was quite lifted, and it was definite that they were staying. But even if the opposite had been decided, the execution of that decision would have met with an insurmountable obstacle: the Princess fell ill. The nature of the illness remained undiagnosed, but whatever it was (ultimately there was talk of an incipient but benign nervous fever), Doctor Bie from Hillerød called three times daily and regularly partook of the lunch served for the members of the court, and usually of the other meals served during the day as well. Doctor Bie was the brother of Pastor Schleppegrell's wife with whom he shared the small stature, the embonpoint and the clever, kindly eyes, as well as being well liked by the Princess. He carried a bamboo cane with a gold knob and had gold spectacles which he regularly removed when he wanted to look at something, he counted out loud like a piano teacher marking the beat when he took his patient's pulse, and he liked to chat about Iceland and Greenland where he had spent fourteen years as a ship's doctor. He was generally most ill-disposed towards the capital-dwellers. 'In Copenhagen it has become the custom to laugh at the Icelanders; but I would just mention Are Marson who discovered America five hundred years before Columbus, and Erik the Red and Ulf the Cross-eyed and his entire tribe, heroes and wise men all – they were all Icelanders and I greatly regret that Her Royal Highness has never visited the island. It is a quite special feeling to eat an egg that was boiled in a geyser, perhaps at the very moment when two fire-spewing peaks were lighting up the scene. It is an arrogant Copenhagen fantasy that the Icelanders read our papers twelve months too late, always the exact issue from the previous year; the Icelanders write their own newspapers, and they can do so very well, for every third day an English or American ship arrives, and when a district administrator or even simply a magistrate is elected in Reykjavik, it's just as interesting as when a new mayor is elected in Copenhagen. Ah, Your Royal Highness, I'm almost inclined to say there's no difference at all between a village and a capital city; there are people living everywhere, hating and loving each other, and whether a soprano holds a trill for a full minute or a fiddler plays "The Brave Soldier" makes no great difference, at least not to me.' With observations like this Doctor Bie was always certain of the Princess's most amused approval, and when Pentz and Ebba asked whether Her Royal Highness might not send for her personal physician, Doctor Wilkins, saying he was never called upon to do anything and ought to be reminded once in a while that he wasn't paid his stipend for an absolute sinecure, the Princess demurred and said, 'No, I'm not dying yet. And if I were, Doctor Wilkins, who reads everything but knows nothing, would be unable to postpone the end. Everything that anyone can do for me Doctor Bie is doing, and when I've listened to him for half an hour and sat beside him in his reindeer sled hearing his stories, or even eaten red fruit jelly with him in Missionary Dahlström's house, on every such occasion I've experienced what is known as the healing presence of a doctor; *medico praesente* as they say. No, Bie must stay. And what would his sister say to such an insult, the Pastor's good little wife, who thinks him as famous as Boerhaave[*] and quite genuinely believes a letter could be sent from the North or South Pole addressed "To Doctor Bie, Europe" and it would be delivered to him here.'

The Princess's illness, for all it posed no danger, dragged on.

---

[*] Herman Boerhaave, professor of medicine and botany at Leiden University, one of the most eminent doctors of eighteenth-century Europe.

The King had meanwhile arrived and moved into the left wing with his immediate entourage, and limited himself, as far as the Princess was concerned, to sending every day to find out about her state of health. Otherwise his presence was scarcely noticeable, partly because he was frequently absent in Skodsborg, and partly because of the life he led. He was a true lover of open-air pastimes. If he wasn't riding to hounds he was stalking, and if he wasn't digging out badgers he was digging for stone graves and bog relics, or on occasion he even went as far afield as Vinderød and Arresødal, where his boats were moored, for some sailing on the great Lake Arre.

Holk, who knew the adjutants Captain Westergaard and Captain Lundbye well from Schleswig and Flensburg where they had briefly been garrisoned, made an effort to renew the acquaintance and he succeeded, which resulted in a few pleasant hours' chatting; but once he was alone again and his thoughts turned to Holkenäs, a feeling of serious embarrassment and worry came over him. Things couldn't go on like this. Correspondence between him and Christine had broken down completely; and the letters from Petersen and Arne were still to be dealt with too. The latter at least had to be answered (a week had already passed since it was received) if he wasn't going to ruin his relationship with his long-standing best friend and adviser, and perhaps only too often his advocate in his little wrangles with Christine in earlier times.

It was his day off, bright and clear, and Doctor Bie on his way from the Princess had called on him and put him in a good humour with some Hillerød town gossip and some doctor's anecdotes. He had no wish to let this good humour pass unutilized. With letters the right mood was half the battle. And what was it all about after all? Christine was less amusing than was desirable in a woman and had more principles than were necessary; it was the old story, denied by nobody, and scarcely by Christine herself. He debated this aloud with himself for a while in these terms, and when he had eventually convinced himself that, all things considered, the story had been blown up out of all proportion because in fact there was no evidence, he finally sat down at his desk and wrote:

Dear Arne,

My warm thanks for your kind letter of the 23rd, the warmer because after so many proofs of your feelings of friendship for me, I know very well that you're only doing what you take to be your duty in stressing your reservations about my behaviour and failings so firmly. But my dear Arne, let me ask you this: was there any call of duty here in the first place? Have you not, in taking the role of Christine's advocate in this instance (previously you have been mine), put me in the wrong in order to make your client right in a way that has no basis in fact? All the material for the case against me is taken from my own letters. Well, these letters are over in Holkenäs and I no longer have every detail present in my mind, but reviewing their content from memory, I can find nothing to justify my incrimination. There are the Hansens and there is Fräulein von Rosenberg, and in describing her I may have 'over-egged the pudding' as the English saying has it; but this might have been interpreted as innocent frankness, or as a tendency to let what is ludicrous expose its own folly. I remember in one of my letters describing the beautiful *capitana* having a sort of fairytale audience with the Emperor of Siam, and in another mentioning the racy and certainly rather freethinking Fräulein von Rosenberg as an 'amanuensis of David Strauss,'* and I ask you, my dear Arne, do these remarks really justify Christine's being upset, not to mention the reproaches in your letters? I've just spoken of my innocent frankness, for which I might be given some credit, but against that I must concede – and this is really the only thing I can admit to – that the proper tone has in fact deserted me in my correspondence with Christine. From the moment one feels under suspicion, it becomes difficult to strike the right tone and attitude, and it is all the more difficult because *no* degree of innocence exists that would make one immune once and for all from reservations and little self-reproaches once the seed of doubt has been sown. What does not come over us, what does not creep up on us? All kinds of things. But even Martin Luther

---

* Nineteenth-century theologian who rejected supranaturalism and challenged the historical accuracy of the Gospels.

once said, as I know from all the religious tracts that were forever being delivered to the house, "We cannot prevent evil birds from flying over us; we can only prevent them from building nests on our heads." Yes, my dear Arne, there's no way round it, with all the many virtues Christine can boast of, there is one she does *not* have, and that is humility, and having been nourished and brought up with the idea of a special infallible faith from which she constantly expects salvation and illumination, it never occurs to her that, like other people, she too might err. She has sent Asta to Gnadenfrei and Axel to Bunzlau, and these actions exclude all weakness and error, error which others who go off to Copenhagen instead of the Moravians are automatically prone to. And now that I have conducted my defence and in the end, more than I like, have exchanged the role of defendant for that of plaintiff, I take my leave and place my case in your hands, secure in the belief that your astuteness and above all the love you bear me and Christine in equal measure will bring everything to a good end. And with that God bless. As ever,

> Your devoted friend
> Holk

But when he had laid down his pen he took the sheet of paper and went over to the window to read it through again line by line. He found a number things to criticize and when dissatisfied with this or that muttered, 'almost as doctrinaire as Christine'; but he was pleased with 'special infallible faith', and even more with the part about forfeited frankness, forfeited because '*no* degree of innocence exists that would make one immune once and for all from reservations and little self-reproaches once the seed of doubt has been sown.'

His eye rested on the letter as if spellbound until finally his satisfaction dissolved and all that he could see looking back at him was a confession of his own guilt.

25

The fine days which, in defiance of its reputation, had lasted almost right through November, ended with the turn of the month and violent storms set in from the northwest, only interrupted now and then by showers of rain which, however, often gave way after only a few hours to a new nor'wester. This change in the weather naturally changed life in the castle; the walks, which not infrequently had extended as far as Fredensborg, and to Lillerød in the south, all ceased, and in place of the semi-official gatherings in the great Herluf Trolle Hall there were smaller evening get-togethers alternating between 'over here' and 'over there', in other words between the two towers, taking place in the rooms of each lady-in-waiting in turn. The Princess herself had wished it so, and Fräulein Schimmelmann, stiff and ceremonious as she might otherwise be, was a most charming hostess, so that her evenings could rival Ebba's. The composition of the company was always the same: the Princess's retinue, then the two Schleppegrells, and both the King's adjutants, of whom Lundbye posed as courtier and man-of-the-world while Westergaard affected to be a liberal, slight social nuances which made their company all the more stimulating. They saw one another daily, the left- and the right-hand towers providing the only change, and as the constitution of the company remained constant, so too did the forms of entertainment, limited to reading comedies, declamations or, on a good night, performing *tableaux vivants*. Now and again, largely for the sake of Pentz and Fräulein Schimmelmann, they enjoyed a game of whist which, after supper, would give way to a little harmless gambling. Ebba always won, because she was, so she claimed, 'unlucky in love'. The company were amused to the point of exuberance, and while they understandably complained about the perpetual storms and rain, and even more about the Princess's illness which refused to go away, they also freely confessed that they owed all this enjoyment to that ostensible misfortune.

Things went on like this until the second Sunday of Advent; then the weather turned again, and the onset of a keen nor'easter was quickly followed by bitter cold, which on the very first night covered all the ponds and puddles with ice, and by the following day the little castle lake too. After the castle lake it was the turn of the wide park moat that formed the connection with the Lakes Esrøm and Arre to east and west, and when, after a further week, the news came that these great lakes themselves were covered in thick ice, as least round the edges – and after Doctor Bie had sworn that an excursion when the weather was bright was just the thing to clear up the Princess's condition, which had been brought on by 'Schloss malaria' as he was pleased to call it – a sleigh ride and skating party to Lake Arre was fixed for the following day.

When it came, it was suddenly sunnier and crisper than all those that had preceded it, and shortly before two the party met at the spot we are now familiar with, where the rope ferry lay frozen in the ice. Those who had opted to meet there were in the first instance the Princess herself with Holk and Ebba, then Schleppegrell and the two adjutants. Pentz was absent because of his age and the Pastor's wife because of her corpulence, while Erichsen and Fräulein Schimmelmann were reluctant to expose themselves to the rather keen northeast wind that was blowing. But those four, too, had been unwilling to forego at least a measure of participation, and had climbed into a closed carriage to go on ahead and wait for the more weather-proof half of the company in the little inn close by the confluence of the park moat and Lake Arre.

Beside the ferry, which had been converted by servants sent on ahead into a reception and accommodation marquee, stood an elegant chair-sledge, and when the Princess had been installed and insulated from the cold with all manner of furs, the only question that remained for the skaters was, first, who should take the lead, and secondly, who was to have the honour of guiding the Princess's sledge over the ice. It was quickly decided that Schleppegrell, with his local knowledge, should lead the party, but Holk should steer the Princess's sledge, while Fräulein Ebba should fall in close behind, with an officer holding each hand. In that order they then set off, and since they were all very accomplished skaters, besides which the costume of each was well-chosen and becoming, they were a joy to watch, shooting in line over the smooth surface of the ice. Most imposing of all to behold was Schleppegrell, who today looked more like a heathen Wotan than a Christian apostle; the wind blew his coat collar high over the brim of his hat as he thrust his metal-tipped pole more and more vigorously into the ice to increase his speed. The Princess was delighted, as she told Holk, with the fantastic sight of her 'pathfinder' racing ahead before her; but the sense of beauty she possessed in large measure, though having little sense of order and elegance, would have been more gratified still if she had looked back occasionally at the spectacle of the three following behind. Ebba, in high-laced skating boots with her skirts tucked up, wore a tam o'shanter with its ribbons fluttering in the wind, and she gave her hand now to the partner on her right, now to the other on her left, as if dancing on ice, and despite swerving far out to each side she raced ahead faster and faster. The distance to be covered was nearly five miles; but less than half an hour brought the sight of the inn on a rise, with pale smoke ascending, and behind it the vast expanse of Lake Arre, glinting and sparkling as far as the ice reached and then the bluish shimmer where the lake, still free of ice, stretched towards the sea.

Schleppegrell, when he had their goal in sight, brandished his skating-pole in triumph and, seeming to accelerate his already cracking pace even more, was at the inn in a trice, where Pentz, Fräulein Schimmelmann and the Pastor's little wife were already standing on the steps that led down to the lake waving their handkerchiefs as the party arrived. Only Erichsen, as it later turned out, had stayed in the restaurant clutching a box of liquorice pastilles. Holk, with one hand on the back of the sledge, doffed his hat with the other, and the next moment halted at a little jetty whose duckboards continued up to the inn. Pentz, who had meanwhile come down, offered the Princess his arm to escort her up the dune, while Schleppegrell and the two captains followed; only Holk and Ebba were left standing by the jetty, looking first at those going on ahead and then at one another. In Holk's glance there was something like jealousy, and when Ebba's eyes seemed to respond with a half-mocking 'A man has to find his own luck,' he grabbed her hand fiercely and pointed far out to the west where the sun was setting. She nodded almost recklessly in acquiescence, and next they were flying, as if the astonishment of those on shore only spurred them

on, towards the spot where, glinting with ice, the channel with its
bank receding further and further was lost in the vast expanse of
Lake Arre. They were coming closer and closer to danger, and now
it seemed as if the pair really intended to skate over the last few
hundred paces of the broad belt of ice and into the open water of
the lake; their eyes sought each other and seemed to ask, 'Shall we?'
And the answer was at least not entirely negative. But at the very
moment when they were about to pass through the row of low pines
marking the final safety barrier, Holk swerved abruptly to the right
and pulled Ebba round with him.

'This is the borderline, Ebba. Are we going to cross it?' Ebba
stabbed her skate into the ice and said, 'Anyone who *thinks* of going
back *wants* to go back. And I'm content with that. Anyhow, Erichsen
and Fräulein Schimmelmann will be expecting us – the Princess
perhaps not.'

26

An hour after sunset when Holk and Ebba, as Pentz put it, had
'returned safe and sound from their Arctic expedition', they set
out back to Frederiksborg, amply provided with rugs in a covered
charabanc that had room for all of them. On the way home the
'romantic escapade' was, despite the presence of the fugitive pair,
by far the favourite topic, and the tone of the conversation left no
doubt that it was regarded as comparatively harmless, an audacious prank that had got out of hand; Ebba had led poor Holk
on, and he had been forced to give in willy-nilly. This was the
majority view and only the Princess, contrary to her usual practice,
could not bring herself to share their light-hearted tone, prefer-
ring to remain silent. This, though no one else noticed, struck the
two adjutants, whom the Princess's silence may have reminded of
some earlier half-anxious, half-disapproving remarks of hers. 'Ebba
enjoys flirting with danger', that was how the conversation in the
inn had begun, 'and she's able to do it because she has a cunning
knack of slipping her head out of the noose. She's probably wearing

a life-belt under her fur jacket, just in case. But not everyone is as cunning and far-sighted, least of all our good Holk.' This had all been said half-jokingly at the coffee table, while Holk and Ebba were still out on the ice; but behind the joking there had clearly been a serious note.

By about six they were back at the castle, and promptly taking leave of the Princess who still liked to spend her evenings alone, they split up but with the words, 'Auf Wiedersehen, till this evening.'

'Which tower?' asked the two captains, who had missed the previous evenings because of duties.

'Ebba's tower this time, and no later than eight. Latecomers pay a forfeit.'

'What?'

'We'll think of something.'

And with that, once Schleppegrell had promised to bring along his brother-in-law Doctor Bie, they all retired to their rooms.

The Schleppegrells and Bie, who had furthest to come, were naturally the most punctual and the first to arrive in the lower hall of the tower, powdered with small snowflakes for in the meantime it had begun to snow gently. From there a spiral staircase led first to Ebba's room and then on up to Holk's. What there was above on the third and fourth floors none of the tower's occupants had yet bothered to find out, not even Karin, whose only concern, now that it had turned cold, was somewhere warm to sit, first for her own sake and then for that of a young gardener's lad with whom she had struck up a close relationship in her first twenty-four hours at Frederiksborg. She had considerable experience in such matters, and warmth, as she well knew, was propitious for love. Today too she had been at pains to make things particularly cosy, and as the guests from Hillerød felt the homely welcome created by the temperature in the hall, Doctor Bie patted Karin's hand and said, 'Just as it should be, Karin. You Swedish girls know how it's done. But how do you manage to keep it so warm here in the hall? It's enough to make a fellow sit down on the stairs and spend the evening with you.'

Schleppegrell, who was only too familiar with his brother-in-law's ship's doctor's ways, gave him a look that suggested toning down his familiarity; Karin however, who liked to be on good terms with everyone, not least superannuated ship's doctors, pointed to a part of the wall behind the staircase which seemed to be positively glowing in the middle. And on closer inspection our friend Bie could see that also built into the wall there was an imposing stove whose front, of course, opened on to Karin's room, while the back, which consisted of unadorned bricks and a large iron plate, heated the whole lower hall and half the stairwell. 'Excellent,' said Bie, 'excellent. I shall mention this to the steward and recommend that they do this in other parts of the Castle. An iron stove with double heating so to speak, hall and chamber at once. Over at Fräulein Schimmelmann's, who of course has no Karin to look after her, it's always bitterly cold; you freeze to the marrow, as does Fräulein Schimmelmann herself. And then one is supposed to do something for her permanent catarrh, not to mention her freezing hands and red nose. It's fortunate that Countess Danner isn't here. She of course has her personal physician, and more natural warmth, one mustn't forget. Otherwise she wouldn't be the woman she is.'

Schleppegrell was visibly in disagreement with everything his brother-in-law suggested in the way of building improvements as the three of them climbed the stairs: 'I'm totally against it, Bie. Leave the towers exactly as they are.'

'Oh dear,' laughed Bie, 'you've got a touch of the historical reservations again. In a tower where people have been freezing for two hundred years, the freezing must go on. And you call that respect for tradition, and pastors may even have a grander word for it. I for my part, I like to sit in the warmth.'

'Yes,' said Schleppegrell, 'that's the privilege of all Polar travellers. The nearer they get to the North Pole, the closer they huddle up to the stove. And the steward you say, you intend going and suggesting this innovation to him. Well, if you do, I'll come too, and if you put in a request for a double stove, and a half-iron one at that, *I* shall request that this one is ripped out of the wall. It's utter folly. What with all the fir cones and pine-wood and resin, and the floorboards and panelling as worm-eaten as tinder.'

With these words they reached the top of the stairs and entered

Ebba's room where festive preparations were everywhere in evidence: the lamps and lights were lit, and the table, already set, had been pushed as far as possible into the deep window recess. Everything was well-arranged and spacious. But before ten minutes had passed the whole room was buzzing confusion, and the floor cleared again only when most people were seated at two card tables that had been swiftly installed, Schimmelmann with Pentz and Lundbye on the left, and the Pastor's wife with Erichsen and Westergaard on the right. Holk and Bie, who would gladly have joined in and elevated the dummy whist into proper whist, had to forego the game because Schleppegrell, who couldn't be left alone, refused on principle to touch a card. That of course also left Ebba; but she, as hostess, had to devote at least a moment or two to each guest, and although the tables had been set in advance there was still much to do, and there were endless instructions to be given to Karin and the gardener who had been recruited to assist.

Holk and Bie, once they had accepted their exclusion, had withdrawn into a corner formed by a pillar that stood proud of the wall close to the alcove niche. They were very soon engaged in an intimate conversation which the ever-curious Holk managed to steer to the subject of Iceland.

'Do you know, Doctor Bie, I really envy you your spell as a ship's doctor up there, not because of the scurvy or the amputations that are involved, so they tell me, but because of the ethnographic ...'

Bie, who had been simply a better class of wound dresser, and had probably never heard the word 'ethnographic', or at any rate had never given any thought to what it might mean, was somewhat startled, and would have been entirely incapable of responding on the spot; but Holk, completely wrapped up in his train of questioning, failed to notice and went on: 'Now if Iceland were just any old place and really no concern of ours, we could refrain from showing any interest; but the Icelanders are our half-brothers no less, and every Sunday they pray for King Frederick, just as we do, perhaps even more so. For they are serious and devout men. And then when I think of how we just live for the day here, and don't know anything about things we really should know about, then I feel ashamed and reproach myself. Petersen, my old pastor over there, has said to me a hundred times: Where, for example, would the entire Germanic-Scandinavian literature be if we hadn't had Snorri Sturluson, the pride of the Icelanders? What would have become of the Edda and much else besides? Nothing at all. And now I ask you, Doctor Bie, in your Iceland days did you come across any of this as something that everyone still knows and loves and sings and recites, the girls and women at their spinning wheels, the men when they set out to hunt seal?'

Schleppegrell, who had also been listening to all these questions, was covered in embarrassment for his brother-in-law; Bie himself had regained his composure in the meantime and said good-naturedly, 'Yes, well actually my brother-in-law Schleppegrell, who wasn't there, is much better informed about all that; people who weren't there always know everything best. All I know about the Icelanders is that their beds could be better, despite having eider ducks more or less on the doorstep. And the down is really very good and warm to lie in, and, if the truth be told, that's the main thing up there. But bed linen, that's their weak point. We could overlook the fact that the threads of yarn sometimes lie side by side like bits of string, but what in England they call *cleanliness* is in short supply. You can see all too clearly that there's more ice than water up there, and that the washerwomen are happy when they can get their hands back into their fur gloves. It's not a land of cleanliness, I give you that. But their salmon is *comme il faut*. And the drinks! There are those who think they have nothing but infusions of Icelandic moss; well, there's that too, but I can assure you, Count, that nowhere in the world did I find better whisky, not in Copenhagen and not in London, not even in Glasgow where the finest comes from.'

The Iceland discussion continued for a while longer, and Schleppegrell, who at first could only look on in embarrassment, began to enjoy seeing Holk's relentless questions in pursuit of 'higher things' deftly evaded by Bie. Joining them from time to time, Ebba laughed when she found the conversation still where it had been before, and quickly turned back to the card tables, where she would pick up dummy cards and lay them on the table for the benefit of the Pastor's wife and then Fräulein Schimmelmann, until Pentz, who was constantly losing, protested. Nothing could have pleased Ebba more and, abandoning her role at the tables, she busied herself at the fireplace, tipping coals and adding juniper branches to the dying fire, just a little at a time, for the abundance of lights that were burning were already enough to ward off the cold which reigned outside. Besides, the frost that had lasted all day had relented considerably since the first snowflakes had begun to fall, though the wind had freshened, as they could hear each time Karin, serving skilfully and with a smile, appeared at the door with an endless flow of trays.

Now it was ten, the game over and the players had stopped, and while they moved the card tables aside to make room, a dining table set on only three sides – for no one wanted to sit with their back to the fire – was placed across the room. Fräulein Schimmelmann had the place of honour at the middle of the table, with Holk and Pentz beside her; then to right and left came the four other gentlemen, while the Pastor's wife and Ebba sat at the two short sides where they were best able to keep the table under review, and when necessary see to the service. And if everyone had previously been in good spirits, these now became even better, which was due not least to Doctor Bie's varied repertoire of dinner-table accomplishments. For he was not only a raconteur and toastmaster, he was above all a virtuoso laugher, capable of applauding other people's stories as well as his own with veritable gales of uncritical laughter, carrying everyone along with him, including those who had no idea what they were laughing at. Even Fräulein Schimmelmann, as everyone was pleased to see, was quite unmistakably enjoying herself, though that didn't mean that there was not a marked increase in the merriment round the table when, as always, she withdrew at eleven. Another factor contributing to this increase was the Swedish punch which, unusually, was today served in a large silver punchbowl. Everyone sang its praises, especially Bie, who after his fifth glass, which he had reached comparatively swiftly, rose and with the gracious permission of the ladies proposed a toast. 'Yes, ladies, a toast. But to whom? Naturally our charming hostess, in whom our Swedish brother folk – a maritime people like ourselves, a people of the sea – so to speak find their highest expression. From the sea, as we all know, beauty is born, but from the North Sea, Nordic courage too, Swedish courage. I was not witness to this afternoon's feat of such Nordic courage, but I heard about it. And to glide along at death's edge, one false step and the deep has us forever, that is life's supreme challenge. And the life in question is the life of the Nordic lands. Where the ice begins, the heart's flame burns brightest. To the Nordic lands and to their beautiful, their intrepid daughter!'

The glasses all clinked as one, and the 'Lake Arre Escapade,' which had already been the subject of much banter earlier in the day, was so again. Pentz, who trusted neither Ebba nor Holk, was pleased to indulge in another series of jibes and enjoyed himself elaborating what would have become of them if an ice floe with a single fir tree had broken away beneath them and carried them out to sea. Perhaps they would have fetched up in Thule. Or perhaps not, and they would have had nothing on their ice floe but a little Christmas tree with neither nuts nor marzipan. Holk would then have killed himself and offered his heart's blood, perforce in emulation of the celebrated pelican. Things like that used to happen in the old days.

'In the old days,' laughed Ebba. 'Yes, what didn't happen in the old days! I won't presume to draw historical parallels, that I leave to others, and certainly not ones from ancient history; but one need only know a little about the Trojan War to have a healthy respect for the old days and people's courage then, greater respect than for the Scandinavian courage Doctor Bie spoke so eloquently about – and in such flattering terms for me personally.'

Westergaard and Lundbye hastened to insist that things never changed in respect of the most important point, namely the heroic courage of passion, and they would personally guarantee that love still produced the same miracles as in the past.

The company at once split into two camps, those who were of the same mind (among them, beaming, the Pastor's little wife) and those in categorical opposition, foremost of these, naturally, Ebba. 'The same miracles,' she repeated. 'That's impossible, for those miracles were the product of something the world has lost, the product of a great, sublime disregard for danger. I choose these words because I prefer to avoid the word "passion" which somebody just mentioned; disregard for danger is something we can talk about, indeed one need not even blush to do so. And now I ask you, the Herr Capitanos to the fore, which of you would like to set off a Trojan War for Helen's sake? Who would kill Agamemnon for Clytemnestra's sake?'

'We would – we would.' And Pentz, brandishing a four-tined fork, even added, 'I am Aegisthus.'

Everyone laughed, but Ebba, in increasingly high spirits, continued, 'No gentlemen, the statement stands, disregard for danger has departed this world. Of course, it has to be conceded (and it's up to you to exploit this against me) that isolated instances of cowardice are also to be found in antiquity. I remember in the dim and distant, for I was still in a gauze party frock, seeing Racine's *Phèdre* with the celebrated Rachel in the title role; she was on her way from St Petersburg and took in our little Stockholm with a passing visit. Now the said Phèdre loves her stepson, a total stranger so to speak, with absolutely no right to invoke any blood relationship, and this stepson refuses to say yes, rejecting the love of a beautiful queen. Perhaps the first instance of decadence, the first premonition of effete modernity.'

'Not at all,' insisted Lundbye. 'Not of modernity that is. Modernity condemns such weakness outright', and Pentz for his part added, 'Pity we don't have a Phèdre to hand to put an instant end to this controversy; perhaps one could contact Skodsborg where ...' But at this point he broke off abruptly, having noticed the two officers fixing him with a sharp stare, making it clear that in their presence he must not mock the name Danner, which was on the tip of his tongue.

At this point dinner broke up and everyone prepared to depart. Holk, as the only other inhabitant of Ebba's tower, felt half-obliged to accompany the guests down to Karin's room in the hall which served as a cloakroom. Here he stayed until all had departed. Then he took his leave of Karin, suggesting she open doors and windows, since she had overdone it with the stove, and quickly made his way back upstairs.

Ebba was standing there in her open door, lights were still burning on the table, and Holk may have wondered, seeing her like this, whether she had just been watching the guests' departure over the banister or had been waiting for his return. 'Good night,' she said, and seemed, with a mock-serious bow, about to withdraw from the threshold into her room. But Holk seized her hand and said, 'No, Ebba – you must listen to me.' And stepping into the room with her, he looked at her passionately, covered in confusion.

She, however, neatly disengaged herself and, picking up on the conversation of a few minutes earlier, said, 'Well, Holk, what part for you now? Paris or Aegisthus? You heard Pentz volunteering.'

She laughed.

Her amusement, however, only increased his confusion, and for a while she revelled in this until in the end, half-pityingly, she remarked, 'Holk, you're almost more German than the Germans ... It went on for ten years at the gates of Troy. That seems to be your ideal.'

27

An hour had passed when there was a knock at the door. Holk started. Ebba however, by her very nature less afraid of discovery than of the ridicule of any pretence of concealment, swiftly went and opened the door.

Karin was standing there.

'What is it, Karin?'

'There's something wrong. My room's full of smoke and it's lucky a piece of soot fell down the chimney and woke me. I've thrown open the door and window to create a draught, but it's not helping, it's as if it's coming out of the walls and floorboards.'

'What can it be?' asked Ebba, whose first assumption was that curiosity had brought Karin upstairs. 'The wind is blowing against the chimney. I'll take a look, but first I'll throw a blanket round me and fetch a light. You must have groped your way up in the dark.' With that she stepped back and let the door click back into place. It was scarcely half a minute before she was back again with a light in her hand, leading the way with Karin following. Karin had not exaggerated; the staircase was already filled with smoke and fumes, and before the two were halfway down, it became almost impossible to breathe. 'We must get through quickly,' said Karin and dashed across the hallway, where little flames were already rising through the floorboards, to the outside door which was fortunately unlocked. Immediately afterwards shouts of 'Fire!' rang out across the courtyard. Ebba was about to follow and flee to safety like Karin. But the next moment she remembered Holk, and instantly deciding not to leave him in the lurch, she dashed upstairs and back into her room again. In vain, he was no longer there. 'The fool, he wants to save my reputation, or maybe his own too, and he's going to kill himself, and me with him.' And as she said this she ran quickly up the second flight of stairs to look for him in his own room. He was standing there in the doorway. From the courtyard Karin could be heard shouting 'Fire!' and other voices were now joining in. 'Quick Holk, or we're dead. Karin has saved herself, let's try to do the same.' And without waiting for a yes or a no she grabbed his arm and dragged him back down both flights of stairs after her. But quickly as all this happened, the catastrophe unfolding below was even quicker, and what might have been possible one or two minutes before no longer was. 'We're lost,' and Ebba seemed about to collapse on the stairs. But Holk picked up the half-conscious woman and with the strength that desperation gives, carried her back up the spiral staircase from floor to floor until he eventually stood with her under the tower roof which was braced with beams and struts. An open skylight gave just enough light for him to get his bearings in the confusion and, threading his way through the beams towards the skylight, he stepped out, pulling Ebba into the open air after him. Here they were for the moment in safety, and if the pitch of the near-vertical castle roof had been just slightly less, this temporary refuge would have meant they were completely safe; but being so steep, the roof prevented any proper movement along it, so they had little to show for all their efforts, except for the handhold provided by the lightning-conductor and a wide gutter that they could wedge their feet against. And it was a stroke of luck that the prevailing wind was blowing the smoke in the opposite direction.

Yes, a stroke of luck, but only a temporary relief. What good would it do if those below failed to see them or if the wind shifted and set the roof they were leaning against on fire?

'Do you want to give it a try?' said Holk, pointing to the lightning-conductor, by means of which, with the necessary determination, it would still have been possible to climb down. But Ebba, whose strength was exhausted, shook her head. 'Then let's see if we can slide along the roof to the next mansard window and climb in,' and leaning back carefully they eased themselves along the steeply sloping roof with their feet wedged against the gutter. All went well for nearly ten paces; but before they were halfway to the mansard Ebba said, 'It's no good, I can't move.' Holk was going to shout and wave his handkerchief, but he soon saw that it would be pointless, because for safety's sake he had to keep leaning back, so that it was impossible for anyone to see him from the courtyard. This meant that Karin was their only hope, assuming that she would not only scan the building for them herself, but would direct others to scan the tower roof for them as well. And that is in fact what happened, and how they finally came to be rescued from their terrifying predicament. Perhaps a quarter of an hour had passed when they noticed that a number of people had gone round the end of the lake, and almost at the same moment they also heard shouts from the Hillerød bank which had a better view. They couldn't make out the words, though the jubilant tone of the shouts left them in no doubt that their rescue was now certain. Before long they heard the sound of hammers and axes, and then various heads came into view looking at them through the hole that had been opened in the roof. The right spot had of course been missed, but that was easily remedied, and only a short while later strong arms were reaching out for them and pulling first Ebba and then Holk up into the castle loft, and from there the pair were carried in triumph down the stairs and out into the courtyard. The first person to approach them here was the King.

Only at midnight, an hour before the fire broke out, had he returned to Frederiksborg from Skodsborg, and ahead of all others it was he who had directed the rescue work and contributed to saving his beloved antique treasures with more good fortune and success than anyone else. What they managed to save was due to him personally. The two adjutants were at his side.

'Well, well, it's Holk,' said the King when he recognized the Count. 'A knight in shining armour with his lady. I shall be lavish in his praise over in Skodsborg.' And casually uttered as they were, these words, despite the seriousness of the situation, had a touch of mockery.

Westergaard and Lundbye attended to Ebba. 'Where is the Princess?' she asked.

'At the station,' was the answer; 'They're putting on a special train for her. The ground here, she says, is burning under her feet.'

It was an unintentional pun and no one took it as such. Only Ebba, who even at a time like this still had an ear for a pointed remark, was able to hear something quite unintended in it, and she said, 'Well, the ground under her feet! The Princess is hardly entitled to say that … but Holk and I are.'

28

Ebba keenly desired to take the special train too and wanted to go to the station, but her condition was so weak that both Holk and the two young adjutants urged her to give up the idea. She did then acquiesce and allowed herself to be taken over to the left wing of the castle which the fire had spared. Here the Schloss church was serving as a temporary shelter; the lights were burning on the altar, while all around it the wives and children of the castle staff and servants sat or had camped down, the children covered with all manner of clothing, including old Mass vestments that they had found in the sacristy, remnants of its days as a Catholic chapel. For Ebba nothing was left; all that could be found were a couple of cushions to protect her at least from the bitter cold of the floor. But that was too little, and when Holk had searched in vain for something better in the castellan's house nearby, he suggested, with Ebba beginning to shiver more and more violently, that they try to reach the station after all, an idea that had previously been rejected in view of her exhaustion. An old servant from the castle was ready to show them the quickest way, so they set out and heard the station clock strike six just as they arrived. The Princess had left more than an hour earlier, and the next train expected from Elsinore was not due for thirty minutes. At the station itself, all was confusion and there was no room left in the small waiting-room, it was full to bursting with young and old from Hillerød, all wanting to get to Copenhagen as fast as possible to spread the news of the terrible events that had taken place, the most sensational of which were, happily, mostly invented. In one tower, it was confidently reported, everybody had burnt to death, three persons from the Court and a gardener. As Ebba, who could only stay on her feet with difficulty, listened to all this, her situation would scarcely have been better than in the freezing church had not one of the station staff shown some understanding and opened up the separate saloon reserved for the King and Court for Holk and Ebba. Here not only was it warm and spacious, they also found Pentz and Erichsen, who had stayed behind in order to report to the Princess on the fate of the missing persons. This had been her last instruction when she had already boarded the train with Fräulein Schimmelmann. The two gentlemen-in-waiting, who had not been unconcerned, greeted Holk and Ebba with genuine warmth; a warmth, however, which was hugely exceeded straight afterwards when Karin burst in, having until then been sitting huddled in a corner of the adjacent waiting-room. 'Never mind, child,' Ebba tried to joke. 'It wasn't so bad, was it? A little too hot at first and then a little too cold.' But Karin, willing as she usually was to laugh, this time refused to take up Ebba's joking tone, continuing to sob and weep and kiss her mistress's hands. Pentz, as was to be expected, asked all sorts of questions, but before Holk, to whom they were in the main addressed, could answer, a locomotive whistle in the distance announced the arrival of the train expected from Elsinore. Another minute and it rolled to a stop, and in spite of the shortage of carriages a separate compartment was found for Ebba, in which she could lie down covered by plaid rugs and coats. Karin sat down beside her, while the three gentlemen climbed into the next compartment.

At eight they stopped at Copenhagen Station, carriages were ordered, and when these arrived Pentz drove with Ebba and Karin to the Princesses' Palace, while Erichsen and Holk repaired to their private lodgings. Holk knocked. The beautiful Brigitte appeared before him and said, 'Thank goodness, Count, you're back,' but her relief was visibly tinged with disappointment, which could hardly be otherwise, for immediately after the arrival of the special train rumours had begun to circulate about the terrible end of Count Holk and Fräulein von Rosenberg, as sensational a piece of news as mother and daughter could have wished for. And now the Count *was* still alive and the Fräulein too, possibly, or actually quite certainly. You couldn't rely on anything any more, and it was always the most interesting things that let you down. Brigitte however recovered herself and repeated, 'Thank goodness, Count. We've been so afraid for you … and for the beautiful Swedish lady too …'

And as she said these words her eyes never left Holk, for her intuition, which was quite phenomenally developed in this specific area, enabled her to see the entire event, especially in its intimate aspects, as clearly as if she had been present.

'Yes, my beautiful Frau Brigitte,' said Holk, who had either really heard only what sounded like sympathy, or had chosen to hear only that, 'yes, my beautiful Frau Hansen, it was a bad time, you wouldn't have wished it on your worst enemy, far less on yourself and …'

'… so beautiful a lady.'

'Well yes, if you wish. Fräulein Ebba isn't as beautiful as you always seem to assume, at least not as beautiful by far as some whom I don't care to name. But we'll discuss that and decide the matter another time. For now I'm tired out, my dear Frau Hansen, and I want to catch up on the sleep I've lost. Please turn everyone away, even Baron Pentz, if he should call. But knock at twelve, please. And bring breakfast promptly afterwards.'

Holk slept soundly, and only when he heard knocking did he get up and dress in all haste. He still felt tense, with the result that everything that had happened passed hazily before his mind's eye, and only when he had opened the window and looked down into the street did he recognize in all clarity what lay behind him. And now Brigitte appeared with his breakfast and waited for Holk to start the

conversation, purposely not only arranging the service very slowly
but also, which she did not normally do, even resorting to direct
questions. This time, however, Holk remained aloof, giving the
briefest of answers and indicating with his entire demeanour that
he would prefer to be alone, which not only astonished the beautiful
Frau Hansen in the extreme but also lowered the Swedish lady, who
must naturally be to blame, even further in her estimation. None of
this escaped Holk; but because he was shrewd enough not to wish
to offend the beautiful Brigitte he asked her to forgive his absent-
mindedness and to bear in mind that he was still feeling the effects
of all the terrible things he had experienced.

'Yes,' said Frau Hansen, 'terrible; it must have been really terrible
and over and above that the responsibility, and being there to help
and not being able to. And in full view of everyone, and perhaps in
a very thin dress … if it was a dress.'

She said all this with the straightest of faces and in a tone of such
touching concern that when she left the room Holk was in some
doubt as to whether he should regard it all as malicious, perfidious
play-acting. Perhaps there was also a touch of real sympathy; it
is said that sort of person always has a kind streak. However, he
was not in a position to pursue this, and hardly was he alone again
when the images and imaginings that Brigitte's appearance had
only interrupted resumed their assault again. It was not yet a full
day since they had set out on the excursion to the little inn on Lake
Arre, and how much had happened since then! First, skating right
up to the edge of the cracked and crumbling ice with Ebba, and
then the trip back and the teasing and Ebba's high spirits at table
… and then Karin coming and the flames bursting out of the walls
and floorboards, and finally, stepping out on to the castle roof with
death and destruction below, and how stepping out like that had
meant rescue for them.

'Yes, rescue,' he said to himself. 'Everything hangs by a thread;
that's how it was this time and that's how it always is. What saved
us? That on the very first day we took a walk by the ponds and
pavilions, as far as the ferry in the park, that the sun was shining
on that day and my eye fell on the brightly illuminated castle, and
because it was all so bright and clear I could see quite distinctly how

the foot of the tower roof joined the foot of the castle roof. Yes, that's what saved us. Pure chance, if such a thing as chance exists. But there's really no such thing as chance, this was intended to be, a higher hand decreed it. And I must hold on to that, and it will be my support for what I intend to do. When we find ourselves in difficulty and doubt, we wait for a sign, and from that we can determine what is the right way. And now I've had such a sign; a higher hand has led us out of danger. If the path my heart has been following all this time had been a false path, I would have been punished, both myself and Ebba, and we would have collapsed unconscious and suffocated and would not have saved ourselves or escaped into the fresh air and freedom. And Christine herself, if I've understood those last lines of hers correctly, Christine herself seems to have felt that it's best so. The good days shall not be forgotten, no, no, and grateful memory shall remove all bitterness from separation; but separation itself is necessary, and is, I think I can add, our duty, because inside we have become strangers to each other. Ah, all these harsh words. I long for a different life, for days that don't begin with tracts and end with more; I don't want a harmonium in the house, but harmony, the cheerful accord of souls, air, light, freedom. That is what I want, and have wanted from the first day I arrived here. And now I've had a sign that I may have it.'

He broke off but only for a few moments, then he was back where he had left off. All his ideas were going round in circles, and the aim remained the same: to placate an inner voice that refused to be silenced. For while he thought he had proved everything to himself, in the innermost recesses of his heart he was filled with the conviction that his proofs did not stand up, and if he could have stood outside himself and listened to his inner discussion, he would have noticed that there were two words he was strenuously avoiding: God and Heaven. He made no appeal to either, because he felt vaguely, but quite certainly, that he was not fighting a good fight and should not abuse the name of his God by bringing it into play. Yes, he would have seen all that if he had been able to observe himself like an outsider; but it was not given to him to do this, and so he drifted along with a flow of false proofs, clinging to dreams, lulling his conscience and giving himself one good testimonial after another. And why not? He was so easy to live with, that he was correct in saying, you only had to know how to; but Christine didn't know, and didn't want to know, yes, he was the victim of her Christian clichés, that was clear to him, or should at least be clear to him, and he was increasingly filled with the desire to bring his good, his just cause to a conclusion as swiftly as possible, and judgement and calm consideration finally deserted him altogether. He wanted to go to Ebba that very hour, then he wanted to present himself with her to the Princess and confess all and beg first for her pardon, then for her assent. Also to tell her that Christine herself had already written to him in these terms or had at least hinted at them and that there would be no question of opposition from Holkenäs, the separation was as good as achieved, it only remained to be formalized, and he would ask the Princess to approve what he proposed and regard his relationship with Ebba as a provisional betrothal.

He felt a sense of relief once he had formulated this plan; Ebba would hear of it this very hour; he could see no obstacles, or at least leapt over them all in his thoughts.

The clock on the town hall tower struck two as he set out for the Palace. He was held up twice or three times because he ran into acquaintances who had heard of the danger from which he had miraculously escaped; he stopped to talk to them, but each time broke off quickly, excusing himself on the pretext of 'duties' at the Princess's.

Ebba was living in the palace itself, above the Princess's apartments. Holk rang the bell; no one came. Finally Karin appeared. But what she had to say offered small satisfaction to Holk in his present frame of mind in which everything pressed for instant settlement. All he heard was that the lady, after several hours in a fever, had just fallen asleep and was not to be wakened. 'In that case I shall call again. And don't forget, Karin, to tell your mistress that I called and asked after her.' Karin promised to do that and smiled. She had no inkling of what was happening in Holk's heart and mind, all she saw in him was the ardent lover thirsting for fresh embraces.

Holk walked slowly down the stairs, and only after passing along the long corridor on to which the Princess's apartments opened did it occur to him that he had neglected the very things that in the line of duty should have been his prime concern. But were they his prime concern? Certainly not. For him in his present mood, the state of the Princess's health was a matter of some indifference; for him, all she was there for was to give her blessing and make him and Ebba happy. Suddenly (for he was convinced that Ebba thought the same), he was possessed with the desire to receive the Princess's assent that very day. And so it was that he stepped into an ante-room and learned from the chambermaid on duty that Her Royal Highness was confined to bed. One more irritation. If the Princess was confined to bed, then naturally there could be no question of that decision, which in his mind would inevitably amount to her approval. How tiresome; nothing was going according to his wishes. Pentz and Erichsen were in the next room, but he didn't want to see them and swiftly departed, first to take a walk to the citadel and finally to stroll for an hour on Ostergade. At five he was back on the upper floor of the Palace enquiring a second time after Ebba. 'The doctor has been,' he was told, 'and has prescribed two things; medicine and a night nurse. For the Fräulein has a high fever again, which is small wonder after the ordeal she has been through and everything else …' The last words Karin added *sotto voce* and seem-ingly casually, because she didn't want to miss the chance of letting Holk guess what she was thinking.

Holk saw his patience put to a severe test. He had hoped to see his fate decided within a single hour and now obstacle upon obstacle. Ebba sick, the Princess sick. About Ebba he was certain in his own mind, so with Ebba, it was all right; but the Princess! He didn't know how to put in the hours, hours that could turn into days, and when he swiftly reviewed what generally passed for amusements in the fun-loving and diversion-filled city of Copenhagen, he was alarmed at how alien these all seemed to him. The Alhambra and the Tivoli, the Harlequin and Columbine ballet, the Thorvaldsen Museum and Klampenborg, everything, including the beautiful Brigitte, had lost its charm for him, all in equal measure. The very thought of Pentz filled him with horror. That would be the last straw; he would rather put up with Erichsen's platitudes and Fräulein Schimmelmann's starchiness than Pentz's puns and *bons mots*.

The night passed with a feeling of pressure in his head and little sleep, for which excitement and a cold may have been equally responsible, and he was glad when the morning sun reddened the roofs opposite. Breakfast came and the newspapers, with detailed descriptions of the fire at Schloss Frederiksborg. Reading them all he cheered up, and as long as he was reading almost forgot what was tormenting him. The actual course of events was very much embellished in his favour; he had, so it was said in two almost identical accounts, been about to climb down the lightning-conductor and then, once he was down, summon help for the unfortunate Fräulein; but when he reached the level of the fire in the burning tower, the iron rod was already virtually red-hot and so further descent was ruled out, and with a combination of great fortitude, strength and skill he had climbed back up. He read this and said to himself that he must be the hero of the hour after all. The hero! But how unheroic he was feeling. He felt that his nerves were threatening collapse, and that if he didn't manage this very day to conclude the matter he had yesterday tried in vain to direct into the proper channels he would fall ill or become mentally deranged. It could not be assumed that Ebba would have recovered; but the Princess would have, and that was in fact more important. What she had gone through since the day before yesterday was after all relatively trivial, and if, as was very probable, she was out of bed again, she would certainly hear him and decide his fate. 'And to decide my fate can only mean to decide in my favour, for she is kind-hearted and not hidebound in her views.'

Yes, that was how it was to be, and at ten o'clock he was back in the Palace again where, to his infinite joy, he heard that the Princess had spent a tolerably good night. Through the same chambermaid he had already spoken to the previous day, he enquired whether Her Royal Highness might require his presence. And soon afterwards he entered her rooms, for she had sent word that she wished to see him urgently.

The room was the one where he had had his first audience with the Princess after his arrival. The same large picture of King Christian VII still hung there, and directly opposite, the deceased Landgrave, the crêpe over the frame even greyer and dustier than before. On the sofa under the picture of the King sat the old lady, shrunken and bent, not much of a princess and no trace of the *esprit fort* at all. It was evident that – even if her actual ailment was as good as cured – she had still not remotely recovered from the shock and agitation of the last hours at Frederiksborg. All vigour was drained, her eye dull and tired.

'It was a bad night, my dear Holk. You can see I'm still suffering from the after-effects of it all. And yet what does it amount to compared to what *you* had to go through. And Ebba along with you. A miracle that you were rescued; and all because of your own presence of mind, so they tell me. I wanted to see you and take the opportunity to express to you how great my gratitude is. Such things remain unforgotten. And above all by Ebba herself. She can never forget this and will feel indebted to you, I'm sure of it, for the rest of her life.'

These words could not have been more happily chosen for Holk and for everything that trembled on the tip of his tongue, and for an instant he was really on the point of going up to the Princess and, repeating and interpreting her words, pouring out his heart and informing her of his plans. But for all that the content of her words seemed to encourage him, the Princess's demeanour and the tone in which her words were spoken did not. It all sounded little short of lifeless, and greatly as Holk in his soul longed for certainty and closure, he felt quite distinctly that this would not be the best possible moment, but on the contrary the worst possible one for his confession. Of the freethinker who always had a heart for or at the least an interest in escapades and *mésalliances*, divorces and marital strife, not the slightest trace was to be seen in the old lady sitting bowed with age under the solemn royal portrait, and what instead could be read in her sunken visage proclaimed only one thing, that as a rule nothing much came of daring antics and extravagances, and keeping one's word and obeying the law were alone to be recommended, but that above all a proper marriage (not an enforced one) was the only safe haven. Holk would have liked to decode the signs quite differently, but it wasn't possible, indeed it was so totally out of the question that, instead of making any confessions, he confined himself to requesting several days' leave. In doing so he had no clear plan in mind, and he would have been unable to answer any questions in that regard; the Princess, however, who from the outset had been animated only by the desire to withdraw as soon as possible into her private sitting room, refrained from any inquisitive questions and granted his request.

And then just a gracious nod of the head, and the audience, if it could be called that, was at an end.

29

When Holk requested leave, only one thing was clear to him, that something had to happen. Now he *was* on leave, and the question that immediately arose was '*What* happens now?' To talk it over with Ebba, for all he was certain of her agreement, make arrangements with her for the future together – that would have been the most natural thing to do; but Ebba was ill, and Karin's reply each time he called remained the same: her mistress could see no one. So he faced a period of real trial, days with nothing to do but wait. And in his troubled frame of mind, nothing could be worse. In the end he decided to accept the situation, cut himself off and see no one; read the papers, write letters. But to whom? He soon saw that there was no one he could write to. Petersen, Arne, the children – all were out of the question. Fräulein Dobschütz even more so. That left only Christine herself. He stood up from his writing-desk at which he had sat brooding for a while, and paced up and down. 'Christine. Yes, that would be the best. She is going to have to know some time and the sooner the better ... But write to her? Must I really write, as if I hadn't the courage to face her? I do have the courage, for I have a perfect right to do what I'm proposing. People don't live together in order to be of two minds all the time and go their separate ways. Christine has frozen me out of her life. Yes, that's the word, and this growing frostiness is worse than arguing and lost tempers. A woman has to have warmth, temperament, a bit of life, and sensual responses. What am I supposed to do with an iceberg? Even if the ice is of the purest; it's precisely the purest that's the coldest, and I've no desire to freeze to death. Yes, that's it, that's a good subject to start with, that'll be my approach, face to face; I'll not write to her, I'll tell her to her face. Her own letter has given me a golden opportunity. And once I'm free again and back here ... Oh how I long for life, warmth, joy. I've been spending my days as if shades from the underworld were gliding along by my side. The good Fräulein Dobschütz was one of these shades too. I'm not old enough to do without flesh and blood.'

At that he rang. Widow Hansen came in.

'My dear Frau Hansen, I'm going across to Holkenäs for a day ...'

'Aha, for the Christmas presents. Her ladyship will be pleased, since she is so alone now that the children are gone too, as his lordship was good enough to tell me.'

'Yes, to Holkenäs,' said Holk. 'Do you know when the steamers sail? To Glücksburg and Flensburg, I mean. It would suit me best if it was still possible today at noon, or perhaps this evening. Then I would be there in good time tomorrow. Perhaps, dear Frau Hansen, you could send someone down to the harbour to ask. The messenger must be one we can rely on, for I want to be certain.'

Frau Hansen said she would go herself, and within an hour she was back from her errand, bringing the news that there were no more sailings that day, but the *Holger Danske* would sail the next day towards evening and would be at Holkenäs at ten in the morning.

'That's the day after tomorrow. What's today's date?'

'The twenty-first, it's the shortest –'

Holk thanked her for her trouble, and in his heart was glad that the ship would not be tying up at the jetty at Holkenäs on Christmas Eve.

On the twenty-third the coast of Angeln hove into sight, and by ten they could see Schloss Holkenäs on its dune from the deck. Its lines were obscured, for there was a light mist drifting, and for a moment it even began to snow. But the dance of the snowflakes soon ceased, and the mist too had as good as disappeared when the ship's bell began to ring and the stately steamer berthed. Holk crossed the small gangway that they had pushed out on to the jetty from the deck, then the steward passed his luggage down after him and in less than five minutes the *Holger Danske* was steaming on towards Glücksburg. Holk looked after the ship for a while, then he tossed his coat between his two suitcases, for it would only have hampered the climb up the terrace, and began to walk along the path. Every now and then he stopped and looked up at Holkenäs. The mist had lifted momentarily, and now it lay before him quite clear, yet dull and deserted, and the thin column of smoke rising made it seem as if only a half-life was to be found up there. The shrubs clustered in front of the portico were bare and leafless, apart from a few small cypresses, and the portico itself turned out to be boarded up and hung with mats to protect the rooms behind as far as possible against the northeast wind. Everything silent and melancholy, yet a sort of peace, like the afterglow of an earlier happiness, lay over it, and now he was coming to disturb that. He was suddenly stricken by fear of what he was about to do; doubts surfaced, and his conscience, try as he might to suppress it, refused to be silent. But whatever was to happen, it was too late for him to go back. It had to be. How Ebba would have laughed at him and turned on her heel if he had said on his return to Copenhagen, 'I meant to, but I couldn't do it.' And so he set off again, at last slowly climbing the terrace. When he reached the top, he called to an ancient servant who chanced to be passing. The man had been living for years in a grace and favour cottage nearby and Holk asked him, 'Is the Countess at home?' 'Certainly, Sir,' said the old man, almost in shock, 'upstairs in her bedroom. I shall go ahead and announce your lordship's arrival to her ladyship.' – 'No, there's no need,' said Holk, 'I shall go myself.' With that he continued, walking down one side and then round the rear façade of the Schloss which looked inland, down the slope to the park and gardens.

Here everything seemed warmer and more lived in, and Holk, after taking a moment to look round, climbed the three marble steps that led between two columns to the door of the garden room. Now he entered the drawing room itself, and there, despite the children's not being at home, all the Christmas preparations seemed to be underway. On the corner table with the Turkish cover, where Christine had formerly sat at her needlework with Fräulein

Dobschütz and Asta, stood a Christmas crib with numerous figures, still well preserved though it had been in use for years, while in the corner diagonally opposite a Christmas tree stood, still undecorated, but very tall, so that the top almost reached the ceiling. Someone must have been working there moments before, yet there was no one in sight. Had everyone fled at his arrival? But before he could answer his own question, he saw that he was mistaken, at least as far as general flight was concerned; for from the dark corner created in the background by the Christmas tree, a lady in black emerged. It was Fräulein Dobschütz, carrying in her hand a bowl of gold and silver nuts with which she must just have begun to decorate the tree. She started when she recognized the Count. 'What has happened? Shall I call Christine?'

'No, my dear Dobschütz,' said Holk. 'Let us leave Christine for a little longer. What she has to hear she will hear soon enough. I'm earlier than expected and would rather have chosen a different day from today. But I shall not stay long.'

Fräulein Dobschütz knew how matters stood and how many sobering and hurtful events had accumulated in the last few weeks; but what she had just heard from Holk himself was surely more than that, went further. What was meant by these words which said nothing and everything? And there he was standing in front of her with a half-defiant and yet also abashed expression, as if he was coming to accuse himself as well as others.

'I had better go and tell Christine that you're here.'

He nodded, as if to say, we can do it that way, it doesn't matter whether it's now or in a quarter of an hour.

And with that he walked over to the crib, took a number of the figures in his hand and looked round to see whether the Fräulein had left the room or not.

Yes, she had gone. And now he let his gaze wander, running his eyes half-indifferently over things large and small, looking out at the paths in the park too, where a few hens were taking a stroll as there was no one there to prevent them. Only then did he step back over to the grand piano which stood open, the instrument at which Elisabeth Petersen and Asta had so often sat playing duets or singing their songs, one of them on the last day before his departure or the day before that. And suddenly it was as if he could hear it again, but far, far away.

He was standing there dreaming, what he had actually come for half-forgotten, when he thought he heard the door opening. He turned and saw that Christine had entered the room. She stopped, and had taken Fräulein Dobschütz's hand as if for support. Holk went up to her. 'Good day, Christine. You see me earlier than I expected.'

'Yes,' she said, 'earlier.' And she gave him her hand and waited to see what he would do. That would be a sign for her of how matters stood, for she knew that, for all his weaknesses, he was honest and could not dissemble.

Holk held her hand in his and would have looked her in the eye. But he could not bear the steady gaze that met his, and so he looked aside, not wishing to cast his eyes down, and when she persisted in her silence he said, 'Shall we sit down, Christine?'

They both went over to the corner table. Fräulein Dobschütz followed but remained standing, while the Countess sat down, with Holk opposite after he had pushed up an armchair. The Christmas crib stood between them and their questioning gaze met over it.

'Leave us, my dear Julie,' said the Countess after a pause. 'It will be better if we're alone. I think Holk has something to say to me.'

Fräulein Dobschütz hesitated, not because she wanted to witness the painful scene which was obviously coming, but out of love for Christine, who might, she feared, require her assistance. In the end however she left the room.

Holk, for his part, at first seemed to disprove his wife's words that 'he had something to say to her'; he remained silent, playing with the Christ child that, without realizing what he was doing, he had taken from the arms of the Virgin Mary.

Christine, looking at him, almost felt pity for him. 'I'll make it easy for you Holk,' she said. 'What you can't bring yourself to say, *I'm* going to say. We were expecting you on New Year's Eve or New Year's Day, and now you have come at Christmas. I don't think that you came for the crib, nor for that Christ child you're playing with either. What you have on your mind is something very different from the Christ child, and the only question that remains is the name of your new happiness, whether it's Brigitte or Ebba. Actually it doesn't matter. You have come to take up what I suggested as a last, extreme option, and to tell me "that it's how I wanted it." And if that's what you want to say, then say it; you have the right to. Yes, it's how I wanted it, because I am not for half-measures. You can add one more selfish trait to the many that characterize me, the inability to share. I want a whole man and a whole heart, and I don't wish to be someone's summer wife while another plays the winter wife and they alternate. So out with it, you have come to talk to me about a separation.'

That the Countess was unable to control her heart was not good. Perhaps with a milder form of words she might have changed his mind, suggestible as he was, and made him realize his error. For the voice of right and conscience never ceased to speak in him, and all that was lacking was the strength to help this voice to triumph. If Christine had succeeded in increasing that strength, it would still have been possible for him to turn back, even now; but her tone was wrong and it reawakened everything that had irritated him for oh so long, and that, since he had met Ebba, had made him so ready to grant himself absolution.

And so, when Christine ceased speaking, he threw the Christ child back into the crib, careless of where the little doll fell, and said: 'You want to make it easy for me, those were, I think, your words. Well, you have not fallen short in your good will, I have to grant you that. Always the same superior tone. Let me just say, I was devastated just now, when I saw you walk in, leaning upon the good Dobschütz as you came towards me. But not any longer. Of the things that offer comfort and solace, that take the burden from our shoulders or strew flowers in our path, you have nothing. Of light and sun you have nothing. You lack everything feminine, you are harsh and sullen ...'

'And self-righteous ...'

'And self-righteous. And above all so certain in your beliefs, and in everything you say and do, that for a while one begins to believe it oneself, and believes and believes until one day the scales fall from one's eyes and one is outraged at having mistaken the view on to a narrow plank fence with a shroud over it not ten paces away for a view into God's beautiful world. Yes Christine, for there is such a thing as God's beautiful world, light and wide, and that is the world I want to live in, a world which isn't paradise, but is at least a reflection of it, and in that light and cheerful world I want to hear the nightingales sing instead of seeing a golden eagle, or a condor for that matter, soaring up to heaven in eternal solemnity.'

'Holk, let's leave it at that, I don't want to ban you from your paradise any longer, for what you call "at least a reflection" is just talk; you want to have your real paradise on earth, and in it, as you so quaintly put it, you want to hear the nightingales sing. But sooner or later they will fall silent and all you will hear will be the sound of one single bird, not one that brings you joy, but one that grows more and more quiet and painful, and by that time you will be looking back on an unhappy life. I won't mention the children, I don't care to bring them into a conversation like this; a man who has no ear for the voice of his wife, a wife who had a claim to his love because her whole life revolved round her love for him – to that man the very names of his children will mean nothing. I am going. My brother will manage my affairs from Arnewiek, not in any spirit of resistance or protest against what you intend to do, God forbid, only to put in order what has to be put in order, first and foremost whether the children are to be yours or mine. You will,' and she smiled bitterly, 'as I know you, create no problems in that regard; there was a time when the children meant something to you, but that's a long time ago now. Times change, and what once was a joy to you has become a burden. I shall do what I can to relieve your future household of difficulties, including the difficulties of being a stepmother ... and now goodbye, and may you not be too severely punished for this hour.'

So saying she had risen from her seat and, having no wish to avoid him, she walked close by him towards the door. Of the weakness she had shown when she entered, nothing remained in her entire bearing; the outrage that filled her heart had given her strength for anything.

Holk too rose to his feet. A world of conflicting emotions stirred in his soul, but what predominated, after hearing it all yet again, was a feeling of bitter weariness. He paced up and down for a while, and only then did he walk over to the verandah door and look out again at the path in the park, strewn with leaves and pine cones, as it sloped gently downwards and finally turned left to Holkeby. The sky had clouded over again, and less than a minute passed before there was a violent snowstorm, dancing and swirling until the wind suddenly abated and left the snowflakes drifting down, thick and heavy.

Holk could see only a few paces ahead, but thickly as the snow was falling, it still allowed him to make out the outlines of two women as they now came from the right side of the castle, turned into the path through the park and walked down towards Holkeby.

It was the Countess and Fräulein Dobschütz.

No one accompanied them.

30

Holk was shaken at the sight of Christine walking down the path through the park and quickly disappearing in the dancing snow-flakes, but only in his heart, not in his decision, not in what he planned to do. The happiness of days past lay behind him, that was certain, 'my fault perhaps,' he added, 'but certainly hers too. She wanted it like this, she goaded and tormented me, first with her superiority and then with her jealousy, and in the end she cried out, "Go!" to me. And she would make no concessions; on the contrary, she outdid herself and instead of just her usual superciliousness she even went as far as to adopt an air of pity, and with that, off she went … I may have wronged her, in these last weeks certainly, but she began it, she grew away from me, more and more, and this is how it's to end. Yes, the end of the song, but not of life. No, on the contrary, it's to be the beginning of something else, something better and more joyful, and if I bring bitterness from what lies behind me into the new life, that bitterness mustn't taint the joy forever. How I long for a laughing face! Oh this eternal *mater dolorosa* with the sword in her heart while in reality it was only pinpricks. It was hard to take, really, and at all events I was tired of it.'

The old servant, who in the meantime had brought the luggage up from the landing-stage, now entered the room and asked whether the Count required breakfast. 'No, Dooren, not now; I'll ring.' And when he was alone again he was faced by the question of what to do next. 'Should I stay and cut up a stick of wax and add a dozen lights to this Christmas tree, which I disturbed Fräulein Dobschütz decorating, then light them tomorrow evening, and present myself with the gift of happiness? Can't be done. And I can't stay either just to play the genial and generous lord of the manor up here and in the village, put a silver taler in the maids' apples and ask Michael about his Annemarie or Annemarie about her Michael and whether the wedding is to be at Easter or Whitsun. If I were inclined to do all that, it would take another whole day, or rather two, for here they don't exchange gifts until the morning. Two days, it can't be done, what would I do here? That's a small eternity, and I'm not in the mood to inspect the books or talk about rapeseed and rye. And go to Petersen's? He would appeal to my conscience, which would achieve nothing. And then Christine is presumably still there. She'll have stayed down in the village and sent a messenger to Arnewiek, and Alfred will come to fetch her. I have no desire to be present, or even in the vicinity, when that happens. No, it would be better to go over to Flensburg, maybe there's still a boat for Copenhagen today. And even if there isn't, I can't stay *here*; I have to get away.'

And he tugged the bell-pull. 'Tell Johann to harness the horses. The little trap and the ponies. I'm going to Flensburg.'

It was striking three when Holk drove into Flensburg, and soon afterwards he drew up in front of Hillmann's where he regularly lodged on his frequent stays in the town. The landlord was rather surprised to see him, until he learned that the Count, whose position at the Princess's court he knew about, had only been to Holkenäs for a brief period of leave.

'When's the next boat to Copenhagen, my dear Hillmann?'

Hillmann fetched the timetable with the departures and arrivals of the steamers meticulously entered and ran his finger along the times. 'Here we are, it's due to be Iversen's boat, and it would normally leave tomorrow. But there's no sailing on the twenty-fourth; it's an old tradition, and Iversen, who lives with his daughter and already has grandchildren, he won't be breaking with tradition; he prefers to spend Christmas Eve under the Christmas tree rather than on deck. He's a good captain otherwise, one of the old school who have worked their way up from the bottom. So he'll sail on the twenty-fifth, first day of the holidays, seven in the evening.'

'And that gets in when?'

'That gets into Copenhagen on the second day of the holidays in the morning. That's to say at nine, or maybe an hour later.'

Holk was not exactly delighted at all this, and only when he thought back to Holkenäs was he actually very glad to be able to spend so long, more than two days, in Flensburg. He took a room on the second floor that looked on to the square in front of the town hall, and after a decent late lunch–for he had eaten next to nothing since the previous evening–he left the inn to take a long walk round Flensburg Bay. It was dusk; but before long the stars came out in their wintry splendour and were reflected in the wide expanse of water. Holk could feel the pressure which weighed on him diminishing by the minute, and if his state of mind remained somewhat short of equanimity, the remnants of unease had more to do with the future than the past, and in the main took the form of a certain excited anticipation. He imagined all manner of heart-warming scenes that were to come, by May at the latest. By then everything would surely be in order; the wedding arranged, and he could see himself in the Hillerød church overflowing with people, Schleppegrell delivering the wedding oration; the good pastor's wife deeply moved by her husband's eloquence, and Doctor Bie delighted that with the aid of a beautiful Swedish woman a Schleswig-Holstein heart had been conquered for Denmark; the Princess seated in state in the little Court gallery, beside her Fräulein Schimmelmann and behind them Pentz and Erichsen. And then they would take their leave of Hillerød and the assembled guests to travel by special train to Copenhagen and on to Korsør and Kiel on the same evening, first stop Hamburg. Then Dresden and Munich and on to Lake Garda, with an excursion to Mantua where, curiously, they wished to visit the moat where Hofer* had been shot,

---

* Andreas Hofer, Tyrolean patriot executed by Napoleon in 1810.

and then on south as far as Naples and Sorrento. There the trip would end, and with the view of Vesuvius to the right and across to Capri on the left, he would forget the torments of the world and just live for himself and his love. Yes, Sorrento! There was a splendid bay there too, just as here in Flensburg, and the stars shone down there too, but much brighter, and when the sun ushered in the new day, it was a real sun and a real day.

These were the images that arose for him, and as he saw them near enough to touch, the waters of the bay surged close by him, dark and sombre despite the streaks of light that fell on them.

It was late when he returned to the inn, and he spent the following day reading and chatting occasionally to Hillmann. But when evening came, he felt the need to go out and walk the town's streets and alleys, and whenever shutters were still open or not properly closed, he looked in, and outside more than one house, when he saw the happiness inside and the child on its mother's arm with the husband stretching out a hand to his wife, he was suddenly assailed by fear of what was to come, and what stood before him was all that he had lost, and not what he was about to gain.

What a Christmas Eve! But it passed, and now it was the first day of the holidays, and slowly as the hours dragged by, it finally turned seven and the ship's bell rang. Holk stood beside the old captain, and when they reached open water an hour later and he was free to spin a yarn, Iversen told old tales and new. It was a fine trip, the air was mild and, standing under the starry sky until after midnight, they calculated that they were likely to arrive in Copenhagen half an hour ahead of schedule. They congratulated themselves on this and soon afterwards the few passengers who were making the trip retired to their cabins. But then the weather outside changed, and when at five o'clock they were level with Møn, or presumed they were, the fog had become so thick that they had to let the fires under the boilers go out and drop anchor. The silence, as usual, woke the sleepers, and when they emerged on deck a quarter of an hour later to look out for the coast of Zealand, they heard from the helmsman that the ship was no longer underway.

'How long?'

'Well, we'll probably be moving again by midday.'

Midday had indeed passed when the fog finally lifted and the journey could be resumed. A day lost, and no longer any question of an audience at the Princess's palace. The lights were already burning all round the harbour when, shortly after five, they berthed at the steamer quay.

At his lodgings Holk was received this time by the elder Frau Hansen, and not by Brigitte as usual; she went upstairs ahead of him and lit the lamps, asking about nothing other than the weather and whether he had had a good trip. As to whether the Countess was well, or the Christmas festivities had been joyful and merry, not a word, and when Holk for his part asked after the two ladies of the house and then after the Princess, Widow Hansen replied in that peculiar tone of innocence in which she possibly even surpassed her daughter, 'The *Fräulein* is out of bed again.' The way it came out struck even Holk, but at that moment he was preoccupied with far too many other things to counter the comment, so he let it pass, asking only for the newspapers and a good cup of tea. 'I'm frozen from standing all that time on deck.' Frau Hansen brought both. Because of the holiday there were few papers; Holk scanned them quickly and then went to bed early. He did not fall asleep immediately, for the last few days had taken their toll on his nerves.

He was up early again. Frau Hansen (Brigitte once more failed to appear) brought breakfast, and because she perhaps felt she had gone too far the evening before, she blithely retailed the town gossip with such verve that Holk not only found himself rid of his irritation at the woman's earlier impertinence but, to his surprise, rid too in good measure of his dejected mood. The way the good Hansen told it, everything, even the most sensitive matters, became quite natural and thoroughly amusing, and when she had gone, it seemed to Holk that he had heard a sermon that, if not exactly moral, was full of wisdom about what life actually was. He summed up what he had just heard; its general drift was: yes, Count Holk, it has always been like that and it always will be. You can take everything seriously, but you can just as well take everything lightly. And those who have mastered the art of taking things lightly, they are *alive*, and those who take everything seriously are not, and are afraid of ghosts that don't exist. 'Yes,' Holk concluded his reflections on what he had just heard, 'the good Frau Hansen is right. Take it easy, take everything easy, that's the best way to travel, that's what people like best, and a laughing face is the first step to victory.'

Twelve had not yet finished striking when he stepped out of his lodgings into the Dronningens Tværgade and turned towards the Palace. It was the third day of the holiday, the weather had cleared up and the winter sun lay on the streets and squares. 'The Fräulein is out of bed again', those had been Frau Hansen's words the previous evening, and this was no doubt accurate information; but it still seemed highly unlikely that the Fräulein would be back on duty after such a serious bout of fever, and so, without previous enquiry at the Princess's apartments, he climbed up to the second floor where Ebba was accommodated. Karin opened the door. 'To see the Fräulein?' – 'Yes.' Karin went ahead while Holk followed.

The Fräulein was sitting in an armchair by the window, looking out at the square where there was not a trace of life; there were no longer even the autumn leaves dancing over it. When Holk entered, Ebba rose from her armchair and walked towards him, friendly, but subdued and sober. She gave him her hand and then took her seat on a sofa that stood further back, away from the window, pointing to a chair and inviting him to bring it closer.

'I'm expecting the doctor,' she began quietly, with an effort that was more feigned than real. 'But it's always soon enough for the doctor, so I'm sincerely pleased to see you. It's a chance to talk about something else for once. It's so boring always having to tell people about one's condition – it must be boring for the doctor, but for the patient too … you spent the holiday over there. I trust you found the Countess's health happily improved and that you had a pleasant holiday.'

'That I did *not*!' said Holk.

'In that case I must hope that you were not to blame. I have been hearing so much that is positive about the Countess; the Princess, who visited me yesterday, was full of praise. "A woman of character," she said.'

Holk forced a smile. '"A woman of character" – yes, the Princess is fond of that phrase, I know, and what she means by it is that not everybody has this kind of "character". She may be right. But it's easy for princesses to be keen on "character", because in their position they seldom meet it. People of character may have a hundred good qualities, and indeed they do, but they are hard to live with too, and that's the last thing princesses usually like.'

'The whole world sings the praises of your gallantry, my dear Holk, and I, because I have no reason to do so, am the last person to dispute that; but to your own wife you are ungallant. Why do you wish to diminish the Princess's praise? Princesses are not as a rule liberal with praise, and one may add to their praise but not detract from it. I feel exactly as the Princess does and am full of sympathy for the Countess, indeed I feel for her, if that's the right expression.'

Holk's patience snapped. 'The Countess will be grateful to you for that. But I think I may say, her astonishment will far outweigh her gratitude. Ebba, what kind of comedy is this? Countess this and Countess that, and then a woman of character, and sympathy and finally feelings for her. Do you expect me to believe all that? What's happened? What's caused the wind to change? Why suddenly so formal, so sober? I wanted to talk to you before I left, not to ascertain my good fortune, I was certain of that, or at least thought I could be certain, no, I simply wanted to see you, to be sure you were all right before I went over there, and in that frame of mind I did go and I experienced a day of strife, and uttered words … words which, to put it bluntly, you must know as if you had witnessed the whole scene.'

Ebba threw back her head. But Holk went on, 'You throw back your head arrogantly, Ebba, as if to say, I know what words were spoken, but I don't wish to know, and I disapprove of every one of those words.'

She nodded.

'Well, if I've got that right, I ask you again, what is all this about? You know how matters stand with me; you know I was in your net from the very first day, that I tried all I could, perhaps more than I should have, to possess you. And in all that you led me on, so that now I stand here before you as I do, guilty or not – deny it if you can. Your every word inscribed itself in my soul. And your looks said the same, and both words and looks told me that if I were to leave you,

you would all your days regret not having been carried away on that splintering ice-floe out to sea to your death. Deny it Ebba – those were your words.'

As Holk was speaking, Ebba had leant back and closed her eyes. Now that he was silent she sat up, took his hand and said, 'My friend, you are incorrigible. I recall telling you right at the beginning of our acquaintance and then again later, more than once at any rate, that you were in the wrong place. And I take none of that back, on the contrary. What I told you then, in a moment of high spirits, just to tease you and taunt you a little, I must repeat here in all earnestness and at least half in accusation. You want to be a courtier and a man of the world and you are neither. You're only half a man, and on both counts you break the basic rules that apply to everything, and particularly to what concerns us at the present moment. How can anyone cast up words to a lady which that lady was foolish or perhaps just kind enough to utter in an unguarded moment? All it needs now is for you to cast up what happened, and that's the end of the cavalier. Don't interrupt me, there's worse to come. Mother Nature has given you everything that it takes apart from constancy to make a good husband, and that's what you should have remained. Away from that, you're on terra incognita, blundering from one error to the next. In love, the moment rules; one experiences the moment and enjoys it, but anyone who tries to hold on to it, or derive rights from it, rights which if acknowledged would overturn all greater rights, all genuine rights, in a word all true legitimacy – anyone who does that, and at the very moment when his partner has the sense to take thought, solemnly insists on appearances as if they were a marriage certificate, that person is no champion of love, he's just its Don Quixote.'

Holk leapt to his feet. 'Enough, now I understand; it was all just a game then, all just a farce.'

'No, my dear Holk, only if, with your misplaced seriousness, you were to have taken literally what was meant to be taken lightly, only then, which Heaven forfend.'

Holk stared straight ahead in silence, confirming once more that she had struck home. 'I see,' Ebba continued. 'So the stupidest thing that could happen has happened! I refuse to take any responsibility for that. I have never made myself out to be better than I am, and no one can say of me that I ever seriously claimed to be anything I wasn't. Those words were words; even *you* must have known that much. Yes, Holk, court life is dull and boring, here as elsewhere, and because it's boring, one is either as pious as Schimmelmann, or ... how shall I put it ... as *non*-pious as Ebba. And now instead of plundering all the hothouses of the land and strewing flowers in my path or, like a troubadour, singing the praises of his lady and then moving on to try his luck elsewhere, you want to commit me to one word, or not much more than that, and turn a game into something deadly serious, all at the expense of a woman who is better than both of us, and whom you are wounding deeply just because you choose to play a role you're unfitted for. Once again, I refuse to take any responsibility. I'm young, which you no longer are, so it wasn't up to me, bored as I am here, to preach morality and tremble with apprehension and keep you on the straight and narrow – that was not my business, it was yours. I deny any guilt, and if there was any (perhaps there was), well, I've no desire to multiply it tenfold or a hundredfold, and to turn a mere peccadillo into what I myself would consider genuine guilt.'

Everything was going round and round in Holk's mind. So *that* was the happiness he had dreamt of! Preparing to embark on this path, he had been filled with a tormenting and uncertain feeling, with the question of what the world, the children who would inevitably be estranged, and what in the long run perhaps even his own heart might say. His soul had been confronted with that, but only that. And now he was being turned down, turned down flat, his proposal rejected, his love spurned, and all with a decisiveness that precluded any further attempt to win her over. If only he could at least have found a sense of outrage to act as a counterweight; but he was denied that too, so completely that he found her, as she stood there and destroyed him with her supercilious tone, more alluring than ever.

'So it all ends,' he continued after a short pause, 'in humiliation for me, and, with the curse of ridicule into the bargain – all just *pour passer le temps*. All just a triumph for your vanity. All I can do is accept it and submit to your new wishes. But with one thing, Ebba,

I can't comply; I can't accept that I was duty-bound to doubt the seriousness of your feelings; on the contrary, I believed that I was entitled to believe in them, and I still do. You've simply changed your mind and decided – for reasons it's not up to me to probe – to call it a game. Well, if it was a game and only that, if that's what you're saying, you played it supremely well.'

And with a bow to Ebba, he left the room. Karin, who had been listening, stood outside. Contrary to her usual practice she said not a word, but her manner as she took Holk down the long corridor clearly indicated that she disapproved of what her mistress had done. She was remaining true to the Count, on whose kindness and probably also weakness she had perhaps been building many a plan for the future.

31

Almost a year and a half had passed; it was the end of May and the London squares presented the same pretty picture as always at Whitsun. This was especially true of Tavistock Square; behind the railings the carefully watered lawn shone forth in the freshest green of spring, lilac bushes were in full bloom, and the yellow panicles of the laburnum hung far out over the railings into the street.

It was a delightful picture, and one also enjoyed by Holk who occupied the first-floor rooms in an old but very well conserved, double-fronted corner house with a balcony running round it. He still felt an attachment to this district from the time twenty years earlier, when, as a young attaché at the Danish Legation, he had lived in this same quarter, and in November of the previous year when he had arrived in London, he had taken it as a good sign that he managed to find lodgings that appealed to him in this very place.

Yes, Holk had been in London since November, after travelling the world and visiting all the famous beauty spots where, year in year out, many thousands seek diversion only to come to the realization in the end that home at its dullest is still better than the wide world and all its variety. He had taken his leave of the

Princess in writing, and had written a full and heartfelt letter to
Arne, appealing to him not to abandon him in these difficult days,
after which he had travelled first to Brussels and then to Paris, but
with so little satisfaction that by Easter he was already in Rome and
a few weeks later arrived in Sorrento, where he had once hoped to
spend happy days with Ebba. Happy days which had not of course
eventuated; but the strain he had been suffering all the while had
finally been dispelled by the company of a charming English family
with whom he shared an annexe at the Tramontana Hotel, and he
had once again learnt how to live, and more importantly how to
care about the lives of others. So the weeks had passed with coach
trips to Amalfi and boat trips across to Capri, with the boatmen in
full song; but the hot season soon set in and it drove him away from
this congenial idyll earlier than he would have wished, and up into
Switzerland, where, much as he usually liked it, nothing on this
occasion had been right for him: Lake Geneva was too dazzling, the
Rigi just a procession of hikers and Pfäffers too much of a sana-
torium. And so, because he felt drawn, if not back home, at least
further north to the Germanic world, he decided to try London, to
which he was linked by happy memories of his youth, and where
he had a pressing invitation from his friends who had left Sorrento
at the same time. So, on to London! He had now been there for six
months, and felt as much at home with the conditions and social
forms, akin as they were to those of Schleswig-Holstein, as a home-
less man had any right to expect. Yes, the social conditions had
satisfied him and there were other things besides to free him from
his growing sense of loneliness, at least for hours and days at a time.
His little passion for the theatre, which in former times had made
his days as an attaché so agreeable, was revived, and as the Princess's
Theatre was quite close to Tavistock Square, he could regularly
be seen in the stalls where Charles Kean was at this time staging
his epoch-making Shakespeare revivals, putting on productions
of hitherto unheard-of lavishness—*A Midsummer Night's Dream*
or *The Winter's Tale* one day, *The Tempest* or *Henry VIII* the next.
He also made the personal acquaintance of the selfsame Charles
Kean in the course of the winter, and when he had finally made the
acquaintance of Charles Dickens too, in the famous actor-manager's

much frequented house, he found himself, without neglecting his friends from Sorrento who were country gentry, drawn into all manner of theatrical and literary circles whose lively and high-spirited activities he found uncommonly attractive. Dickens himself, in particular, had become his great favourite, and on the occasion of a whitebait dinner at Greenwich, he had proposed a toast to his new friend the great storyteller, despite knowing only *David Copperfield* of all his works, though he regarded him, on the strength of that one novel, as without peer among living writers. When all present encouraged him amid laughter at the end of his toast to read more of the works, he claimed he must refuse, since even Dickens himself could hardly better *Copperfield*, for which reason further reading would really only serve to dilute his enthusiasm for the author.

Social events like this, regularly attended by celebrated ladies from the artistic world, such as the beautiful and much courted Miss Heath and above all Miss Atkinson, whose genius in the role of Lady Macbeth was undisputed, were more than mere diversion for Holk, and he might not only have been rid of his loneliness but had his spirits raised and restored as well if he had felt any degree of freedom. But this was just what he lacked; for that patch of earth to which he clove with his entire soul, on which he had been born and where he had been happy for decades, precisely *that* patch of earth was closed to him, and would presumably remain so, if he did not succeed in making his peace with society, a peace for which a reconciliation with Christine was an absolute precondition. But that, to judge from what he heard from home, was unthinkable: for however much the Countess insisted that the children should neglect none of their obligations towards him, and should for example respectfully reply to every one of their father's letters (he wrote often, because a sense of abandonment drove him to do so), all steps taken to effect a reconciliation had been in vain. With characteristic frankness Christine had enlarged on this question to her brother, this time abandoning her high moral tone. 'You have all,' she wrote, 'grown accustomed to consider me abstract and doctrinaire, and I may in past years have tended more in that direction than was right, at any rate more than men like. But I can assure you, I am first and foremost a woman. And because that is what I am, there remains one thing in all that lies behind us that troubles my vanity, or my self-respect. I don't want to put it any higher than that. Holk, to put it bluntly, is not properly cured. If he had married Fräulein Ebba over there, and in the long run realized that he had made a mistake, then I might have been able to come to terms with that. But that is not what happened. She simply didn't want him, and so, not to put too fine a point on it, for me the painful possibility still exists that if she *had* wanted him events would have taken an entirely different course. Then presumably my turn would never have come again. In this tragicomedy I play something of a *faute de mieux* role, and that is not pleasant.' Holk had been told the main burden of this letter of Christine's, and what was stated in it was permanently lodged in his consciousness, in spite of the concerted efforts of Petersen and Arne to revive his hopes of a happy ending. 'You must not surrender to this feeling of hopelessness,' Petersen wrote to Holk. 'I know Christine better than any of you, even better than her brother does, and I must tell you this, that besides her Christian love, which teaches forgiveness of the guilty, there is also in her a real and true woman's love, so much so that she labours under a certain amiable weakness with regard to you. I see this in the letters which reach me from time to time from Gnadenfrei. The whole situation is more favourable to you than you think, or deserve, and it would spoil my last hours if it were otherwise. In any case, at eighty one knows how things are going to turn out, and I guarantee, Helmuth, that I will place your hands in one another's again as I did once before, and that shall be my last holy act, and then I will lay down my office and wait for the call from God.'

It was at the beginning of April that Petersen wrote this, and if Holk for his part did not trust the more-than-half portion of certainty it expressed, there were often times when it served to raise his spirits. Today was such a time, and he was sitting replete with cheering images on the front balcony of his house under the branches of a fine plane tree which might have stood there more than a hundred years earlier when this entire district of the city was built. The high sash windows which reached down to the floorboards and were half-open at the bottom allowed him to move

freely between the room and the balcony, and the fire in his drawing
room, burning more for the look of it than for the heat, together
with his morning cigar, increased the sense of well-being that he
for the moment enjoyed. Beside him, on a light cane chair, lay *The
Times* which, because until that moment the delightful spring scene
before him had distracted him, had today, very exceptionally, been
laid aside. Now, however, he picked it up and, as was his wont,
began by reading the left-hand column of the large advertisements
section where, displayed in crisp small brevier, the family news
from London society was recorded: births, deaths and marriages.
Today, as ever, these three rubrics succeeded one another, and when
Holk reached marriages, he read: '*Miss Ebba Rosenberg, Lady of the
Bedchamber to Princess Mary Ellinor of Denmark, married to Lord
Randolph Ashingham, formerly 2nd Secretary of the British Legation
at Copenhagen.*'

'So it's true,' Holk said, paling but otherwise not particularly
moved, and he put down the paper. Perhaps it would have offended
him more deeply if he had suddenly come upon it as something
totally unexpected. This was not, however, the case. As early as the
end of the winter Pentz, whose correspondence kept him up to date,
had reported this marriage as something which would sooner or
later take place, concluding a lengthy letter with the following lines:
'And now, my dear Holk, a snippet of information that will interest
you more than all these stories from the Hansen abode – Ebba
Rosenberg yesterday apprised the Princess of her engagement
which, however, to facilitate the removal of certain impediments
that stand in its way, must for the moment remain secret. The
gentleman she proposes to favour with her hand is no less a person
than Lord Randolph Ashingham, whom you will remember, if not
from Vincent's then perhaps from a soirée at the Princess's. It was
right at the beginning of the '59 to '60 season. Lord Randolph, who
is said to own all the land in an entire London district (perhaps the
very one where you are currently living), as well a forest of fifteen
million fir trees in the county of Fife – this Lord Randolph, I am
able to tell you, has been considering this matter for a year, or more
accurately has been constrained to consider it, because all kinds of
misgivings were raised by an even wealthier uncle from whom he

stands to inherit. And in actual fact these misgivings persist. But Ebba wouldn't be Ebba if she didn't manage to provide the wildly eccentric uncle with proof of her virtues in the realm of the chic and high society, and so the engagement will be announced very soon. All just a matter of time. Incidentally they both, his lordship and Ebba, have nothing to reproach one another with; he, like so many of his kind, is said to have been burnt out at fourteen and is marrying Ebba to have someone to keep him amused with gossip, from which point of view he has made a good choice. She will say things every day, and later actually do things, that will astound his lordship; perhaps she will set the fifteen million firs ablaze and thus display herself and her beloved spouse in their true light. And now *tout à vous, beau Tristan*. Yours, Pentz.'

This had been the content of the letter earlier in the year, and the two lines in *The Times* had been no more than confirmation. 'It's all to the good,' Holk said after a while. 'That's an end of it. Her ghost was still haunting me and I couldn't quite banish it. Now she has done that herself; everything is gone, everything is blown away, and whether or not Christine remains lost to me, must perhaps remain lost to me, at least she will have her proper place in my heart again.'

In the course of this conversation with himself, he again picked up the paper he had laid aside, intending to get to grips with a report from Berlin which detailed fully, it seemed to him, the doubling of the strength of the armed forces and the formation of a party opposing it. But today he was not in the right frame of mind for this, and was soon looking out over the top of the paper. It was just striking nine from nearby St Pancras Church whose tower he had right before his eyes, and down Southampton Row, which ran along the square on the side facing him, rolled cabs and more cabs, coming from Euston Square Station and travelling to the city centre. He picked a plane tree leaf hanging near him and began to play with it, and only when he heard the sparrows chirping more and more loudly above him did he take some crumbs and strew them on the balcony in front of him. The sparrows instantly dropped out of the branches, pecking and fighting among themselves, but the next moment darted up again, for there was a quickly repeated knocking at the front door: the postman had come. Holk, whose birthday was the next day, listened attentively, and soon afterwards Jane came in and handed him four letters.

The four postmarks, Gnadenfrei, Bunzlau, Glücksburg and Arnewiek, left Holk not a moment's doubt as to whom the letters were from, and their content seemed to bring little that was new either. Asta and Axel had penned stiff and formal and rather brief congratulations, and Petersen, who was normally in the habit of writing at great length, limited himself today to offering his congratulations. This was not a pleasant experience for Holk, and his good humour was only restored when he opened Arne's letter too and found many affectionate and friendly words in the first lines. 'Yes,' said Holk, 'he is standing fast. Unchanging, just the same. And he would actually have had most cause to be angry with me. His dear sister's brother. And of course that's the reason and the explanation. He loves his sister, worships her almost. But he has lived long enough to realize very well, despite his bachelorhood, what it means to be married to a Saint Elisabeth. If only she were Saint Elisabeth! who was gentle and forbearing … But no more of that,' he interrupted himself, 'I'll just become bitter again, instead of staying calm and conciliatory. I'd better read what he says.'

Arnewiek, 27th May '61

Dear Holk,

Your birthday is just round the corner and you mustn't be without my good wishes. If they arrive a day too soon, as I suspect they may, then take it as a sign of how urgent my need is to wish you all the best. Need I spell out the wishes that I cherish for you? Today again they add up to but one thing, that your moment of reconciliation may be near. I am well aware that you have no confidence in this possibility and seek to justify this in Christine's character. And an inner voice that whispers 'she has a perfect right to her attitude' may of course confirm you in your lack of trust. But things look more favourable now. You have suffered from your wife's dogmatism and severity, and I gently warned Christine, before there was any thought of a serious rift, not to try to force you into a sectarianism designed for linen-weavers* or an asceticism that went completely against your nature. The charges against Christine that my warning contained were justified and, to repeat again what I have often said before, I have neither desire nor cause to take any of them back. But in her very confessional strictness, from which we have all suffered, we can also find the cure. Whether the love for you which is still alive, as she reveals in her letters, often against her will, might be strong enough for forgiveness and reconciliation, I can only leave an open question; I say neither yes nor no; but what her love is perhaps incapable of she may feel compelled to do because of her sense of duty, once everything is placed in the right hands. In the right hands, I say. A struggle is still going on inside her, and the ideas our good old Petersen, who incidentally still persists in his confidence, puts in his letters have borne little fruit to date, at any rate they have not overcome her misgivings. But what our old rationalist friend, whom she loves so much and about whom her only reservations are in church matters, what our old friend Petersen has been unable to achieve, should, I think, at the right moment, be a simple matter, or at least not overly difficult for Schwarzkoppen, who four weeks ago was appointed Superintendent General. I have turned to Schwarzkoppen, whom I have seen almost daily in the last week, with the pressing request to take the matter in hand before he leaves us and the district here, and since his religious convictions coincide with his personal wishes for you and Christine, I have no doubt that he will succeed where Petersen has until now failed. If Schwarzkoppen was always the decisive authority for Christine, how much more so now that the Arnewiek Seminary Director has become a true beacon of the church. He has been appointed to Stettin in his native province of Pomerania, and will leave us at the end of September to take up his new office there on 1st October. I don't want to add anything further to this letter, least of all to bring up business matters. That's for another time. I now see Countess Brockdorff frequently, sometimes in her house, sometimes at the Rantzaus', but occasionally

---

* Allusion to the first line of a German popular song: 'The linen-weavers have their own guild ...'.

here in Arnewiek too, when we have Mission sessions, at one of
which, as a very unworthy member, I recently had to preside.
Christine turned down my invitation for Whitsun, ostensibly
because Fräulein Dobschütz has been unwell since spring and
needs looking after. The real reason, I imagine, is that she has
no inclination to return to places and circles which only bring
back painful memories. In her eyes Gnadenfrei has so many
advantages, not least that she can hide from the world there.
But I comfort myself with the thought that her need to hide
herself away will fade, and we shall very soon see her return to
the world, and to her old happiness again, a happiness that was
interrupted only by a sudden delusion. A delusion that in the
end became a guilty act. What would I not have given to see you
both return this Whitsun, to see the whole portico at Holkenäs
in the green of May and the ancient coat of arms above the
entrance garlanded again with a wreath of roses. May the future
bring this about, the near future, and with this wish let me close.

Yours, Arne

Holk laid the letter aside and with a happy sigh of relief looked
across to the square, where everything was bursting into leaf and
bloom. The impression he was now left with was of purest joy;
possibilities which he had hardly believed would ever come to pass
were taking shape, buried hopes were resurrected and demanded
to be realized, and having drifted apart outwardly and inwardly for
years, the separated couple were moving once again into the 'Castle
by the Sea', and the happiness of old had returned.

32

And Holk's dream was fulfilled, or seemed about to be fulfilled.

It was St John's Day,* and there was a sunny blue sky over the
whole of Angeln, at its sunniest over Schloss Holkenäs. A long line

---

* 24th June, day dedicated to John the Baptist, closely associated with the rites and
festivities of midsummer.

of carriages was drawn up alongside the hothouses and conserva-
tories, and the Holk coat of arms above the portal bore an ivy wreath
with white and red roses woven into it. Arne had wanted myrtle, but
Christine had insisted on ivy.*

Twelve was now striking from Holkeby, and the twelve strokes
had hardly died away when the great bell, now pulled by two men,
gradually began to reverberate, proclaiming far into the land that
the ceremony, for which all friends and families from near and
far had gathered here, was beginning. Thus it was, and it was not
long before the high glass door leading out into the park opened
and those of the curious, and they were many, who had secured
good positions between the flowerbeds now saw everyone in the
room forming a procession, and Holk and Christine appeared at its
head, the Countess in white satin, in her hair a wreath of orange
blossom with a veil hanging from it. Behind the couple, who were
to receive the blessing of the Church for the renewal of their
marriage vows, walked Asta and Axel, Arne with the elder Countess
Brockdorff, and then Schwarzkoppen leading Fräulein Dobschütz,
many others behind them, and finally all those who had asked to
be present in the procession to the ceremony, and whose participation, because they were not close friends, had especially rejoiced
the hearts of the couple being reunited in marriage. Servants from
various households joined in, and when the procession which set
off towards Holkeby had gone beyond the gravel path between
the fir trees in the park, it walked through a guard of honour
formed by the farmers' daughters of Holkeby together with girls
from the neighbouring villages, who all held baskets in their hands
and strewed flowers in the couple's path, some, unable to resist the
flood of emotion, throwing their baskets aside and pressing forward
to Christine to kiss her hand or even just the hem of her dress.
'They're making a saint of me,' said the Countess, trying to smile;
but Holk, to whom she had whispered these words, could see all
of this was causing her more pain than joy, and that she was filled,
as was her nature, with fearful, painful thoughts, or was perhaps

---

* Myrtle is a symbol of fertility, chastity and purity, traditionally worn or carried by
brides in Germany; ivy is associated with marriage as a symbol of faithfulness and
with death as a symbol of eternal life.

even linking this excess of adulation with dark premonitions for the future. But the vibrant life around her dispelled this, and as she heard the bells multiplying loud and clear until it sounded as if all the churches in the lands of Angeln were determined to join the celebration of this rare festival of reconciliation, all her sadness fell away at least for a few moments and her heart was borne aloft by the sound as it rose to heaven.

And now they had reached the low churchyard wall, along which, just as when Asta and Elisabeth had sat there in the past, tall nettles again stood and layers of sawn-up tree trunks were stacked high, and when those at the front had passed by it, the procession moved through the gate and in between graves towards the church, whose doors were wide open, showing the brightly lit altar at the foot of the central aisle to full view.

There Petersen was standing.

He had long been poorly, and in addition to the burden of his years there was now that of serious illness. But when he had heard it said that 'if Petersen hadn't recovered by St John's Day, Schwarzkoppen was to deliver the marriage sermon', he had made a complete recovery and had insisted, in response to counsels of care and caution, that he had to be the one to lead his beloved Christine back to happiness again, and were it from his deathbed. This had touched everyone, but to him it had given back the strength of his best years, and now there he was standing as straight and upright as nineteen years earlier, when on a St John's Day too he had put the couple's hands in one another's.

The singing had begun the moment the procession entered the central aisle, and when it now stopped, Petersen briefly addressed the assembly, avoiding anything personal, especially any reference to the 'unjust man over whom there is more joy in heaven than over a hundred just persons'. In its place, in a prayer that was simple but deeply moving for all gathered there, he called down the grace of God on the reunited couple and then pronounced the blessing.

And now the organ joined in, and outside the bell began to ring again. The long procession of wedding guests took the path along the beach and, reaching the boardwalk that led to the landing-stage for the steamer, turned left up the terrace to Schloss Holkenäs.

There the wedding feast had been laid out in the front portico so that all the guests had an open view of the sea, and when the moment came, if not for a toast, at least for a short festive address, Arne rose and, bowing to his sister and brother-in-law, said, 'To the fortune and happiness of Holkenäs.'

All were strangely touched by these words, which sounded almost melancholy, and those sitting closest to the groom quietly clinked glasses with him.

But outright joy there was none, and all present had the anxious premonition that the 'happiness of Holkenäs' was to be, if at all, for that day only, perhaps to be buried again on the morrow.

33

The sense of mourning that had predominated at the beautiful ceremony seemed, however, to be proving unjustified, and the 'happiness of Holkenäs' really did appear to be renewing itself. At least this was the impression of all those who were outside the inner family circle. The couple lived for their love, entertained a good deal (more than usual) and paid visits in the neighbourhood, during which Holk for his part was unfailingly relaxed and in good spirits, yet anyone who looked closer could see quite clearly that there was no real life in all this. There was peace, not happiness, and before the autumn had arrived, Fräulein Dobschütz and Arne were no longer in any doubt that as far as Christine was concerned, there was only the will to happiness; and this was certainly strong. There was no longer any question of differences of opinion, and when Holk, as occasionally still happened, launched into a genealogical excursus or some model agricultural plan, the Countess showed not a trace of that superior smile that for Holk had so often been the cause of irritation and ill humour; but all the anxious avoidance of anything that might disturb the peace, breaking off conversations when chance brought up an awkward subject, the constant caution and vigilance, brought with it so much that was dispiriting that even the last years before the catastrophe, when the real happiness in their marriage already lay behind them, could seem by comparison like happy days.

Holk, with his spontaneous and sanguine nature, for a long time resisted this realization, choosing to overlook the reticence, almost timidity with which Christine met his well-meant approaches. At last he did become impatient and, by the end of September, in a frame of mind in which ill-temper alternated with deep concern, he decided to speak to Fräulein Dobschütz and sound out her opinion, and if possible her advice.

A clear, fresh autumn morning lay over Schloss and park, and here and there gossamer clung to already leafless bushes. Asta had come home from boarding school the previous evening and was dying to go down to Holkeby to visit her friend in the village straight after breakfast, which they had just sat down to. 'I'll come too,' said Holk, and since Fräulein Dobschütz had already agreed that she would accompany Asta, all three then descended the terrace to take the slightly shorter and more beautiful path along the shore. The wide expanse of water lay almost unmoving, and only now and then did the foam on the light swell slide up close to the dunes. Asta was happy to see the sea again, and would break off the account of her experiences at boarding school when some marvellous shimmer of light glided across the silent waters, or the seagulls dipped their wings; but all of a sudden her interest in the sea and the effects of light was gone – catching sight of Elisabeth Petersen who was step-ping down out of the dunes on to the shore, she rushed towards her friend and kissed and embraced her. Holk and Fräulein Dobschütz were left behind, which very well suited the two friends who were walking on ahead and naturally had a world of things to tell one another, but it pleased Holk too, because the rapidly increasing distance from the girls offered a fine opportunity to have the frank conversation about Christine with Fräulein Dobschütz that he had so long wished for.

'I'm glad, my dear Dobschütz,' he began, 'that we're alone for a moment. I've wanted to talk to you for some time. What's wrong with Christine? You know I'm not asking out of mere curiosity, far less to complain and less still to make accusations. There have been times when you've had to listen to that kind of thing, when you've had to be the peacemaker; but as you know, my dear friend, those times are in the past and won't return. All conflict is done with, and when I stroll through the park with Christine, as for example just this morning before breakfast, and a squirrel runs across our path and the swan swims across the pond, and Rustan, who is with us, doesn't make a move, perhaps not even if a flock of hens were to fly up – then a picture keeps occurring to me, a picture of Paradise that I once saw: all the creatures in that picture were walking together in peace, the lion beside the lamb, and the Lord God came and spoke to Adam and Eve. Yes, my dear Fräulein Dobschütz, that's what my life now reminds me of, and I could be content, should perhaps be so. But I'm not; in fact I'm anxious and depressed. If this were only about me, I wouldn't waste a word on it, I'd see the comfort and joy that, despite the present peace, is still lacking, simply as due penance for me, and I wouldn't complain, on the contrary I'd perhaps feel something like satisfaction. For atonement is not only something an injustice demands, atonement also satisfies us because it corresponds to our sense of justice. So, once again, in speaking now I'm speaking not for my own sake but for Christine's, and because each day shows me that she would like to forget but can't. And now please tell me what you think.'

'My dear Holk, you've already said it in your own words, I think – Christine wants to forget but she can't.'

'And has she said anything to you about this? Has she given you to understand that it's all in vain after all?'

'Nothing like that.'

'And yet you share my conviction?'

'Yes, my dear Holk, unfortunately. But you mustn't take anything more painful from this sense that is constantly with me, in particular not anything more definite than necessary, or permissible. I know nothing for certain. For if, as before, Christine still treats me as a friend – and how could it be otherwise, when every hour of the day shows her how much I love her – she's no longer frank and open with me. Just as she holds her peace with everyone, so she does with me. This is, of course, deeply saddening. She used to pour out her heart to me and when, on that unforgettably painful day, we walked out of the house to live through that difficult time together, first in the village and then in Arnewiek, and finally in Gnadenfrei, there was not one of her thoughts or one of her feelings that I didn't know. We were two people, but we lived *one* life, so complete was our understanding. But that was all over the day Christine moved back here. With her fine sensibility, she told herself that a new time of joy and happiness had dawned, or at least was due to dawn, and because–pardon me for saying this, my dear Holk–true joy failed to come, and because she found it unseemly to complain further, or perhaps even ungrateful towards God, she lapsed into silence, and to this day I can only guess what goes on in her mind.'

Holk stopped in his tracks and stared straight ahead. Then he said, 'My dear Fräulein Dobschutz, I came seeking solace and advice from you, but I can see I shall find none. If it is as you say, I don't know where help is to come from.'

'Time, my dear Holk, time. Time is mankind's good angel.'

'Ah, if only you were right. But I don't believe it; time won't have the time for anything. I'm not a doctor, and I've no inclination to peer into hearts and minds. All the same, this much is clear to me: we're drifting towards catastrophe. You can live happily, and you can live unhappily, and happiness or unhappiness can survive to a ripe old age. But this resignation, this smiling–that kind of thing doesn't last long. The light of our lives is joy, and if it goes out, night falls, and when it does it's best if that night is death.'

A week later there was a small celebration at Holkenäs, only close friends were invited, among them Arne and Schwarzkoppen, with Petersen and Elisabeth too. They sat outside until dusk, for despite the advanced season the air was mild, and it was only when the lights were lit inside that they left the area under the portico, first to take tea in the large garden room and then for a little music. For at boarding school Asta had developed into a little virtuoso on the piano, and since she had come home this had led to almost daily meetings and hours of practice with Elisabeth. Today some new pieces were to be played in honour of Schwarzkoppen who would be leaving his Arnewiek post in the next few days, and when the servants had stopped running to and fro and the clatter of tea things had finally ceased, the two girls began to search feverishly in the music case until they had found what they needed, two or three pieces only, because Holk viewed music-making as socially intrusive. The first to be performed was a song from Flotow's *Martha*, quickly followed by 'O, wert thou in the cauld blast' by Robert Burns, and when the last lines of this song had faded away to general applause, Asta announced to an audience that had become ever more attentive that now a real folksong was to follow; for Robert Burns's poems were not true folksongs.

Schwarzkoppen objected strenuously to this, and found support from Arne who, exercising his prerogative as uncle, added, 'It's just the latest boarding school taste', and having launched into the subject would certainly have gone a good deal further and made several more such provocative remarks had not Holk at that moment intervened, repeatedly asking what the folksong they were going to perform was actually called.

'This song isn't called anything,' replied Asta.

'Nonsense. Every song has to have a title.'

'That used to be the case. Now you take the first line as the title and put inverted commas round it.'

'Indeed,' laughed Holk, 'I can believe it.'

And with that the dispute was silenced, and after a few bars' introduction by Asta, Elisabeth began to sing, her beautiful voice doing equal justice to words and music:

> 'Are you thinking of times gone by, Mary,
> By the fire at the end of the day?
> Do you wish for those times to come back, Mary,
> When you were merry and gay?'

> 'I am thinking of days gone by, John,
> Of joy I had no lack,
> But my happiest days of all, John,
> I wouldn't wish them back ...'

At the end of this song and its accompaniment, everyone, Holk included, surrounded the piano with warm words for Elisabeth who received the compliments with embarrassment. 'Yes,' said

Asta, delighted at her friend's triumph, 'you've never sung it as beautifully as that before.' Everyone wanted to hear the last verse again, and there was only one person present who did not share this wish, because it had not escaped her in the midst of the general hubbub that Christine, just as two years earlier when the melancholy Waiblinger song had been sung, had quietly slipped out of the room.

The person who noticed this was naturally Fräulein Dobschütz, who was immediately beset by doubt as to whether she should follow her friend or not. In the end she decided to do so, and went upstairs to look for Christine in her bedroom. And there she was, sitting with her hands clasped, staring at the floor.

'What is it, Christine, what's the matter?'

And Fräulein Dobschütz knelt in front of her and took her hand, covering it with kisses and tears.

'What's the matter?' she repeated, looking up at her. But Christine, easing her hand out of her friend's hand, quietly said to herself,

'But my happiest days of all,
I wouldn't wish them back.'

34

A week had passed.

The air was mild, and if it had not been for the Virginia creeper with its red autumn leaves climbing up some of the columns at Schloss Holkenäs, one might have believed that it was St John's Day and midsummer again, and that the beautiful ceremony that the whole of Angeln had joined in celebrating three months earlier was being celebrated once more. For not only were house and park bathed in bright summer light, almost as they had been then for the Count and Countess's second wedding, but today, just as on that day, the long, majestic line of carriages was there again and had brought numerous guests. And once again the bells were ringing out into the countryside, and the girls of Holkeby were lining the village street and strewing flowers, just as before when the wedding procession had appeared. But today they were strewing white asters, and the person making her way down from the Schloss was a dead woman; ahead of her the singers, behind the coffin Holk and the children, and then, in a long procession, their relatives and friends. Petersen was standing at the church door, and he walked ahead of the mourners to the grave that was prepared beside the dilapidated old crypt. Here the singing stopped, all heads were bared, and then the coffin was lowered and the earth closed over Christine Holk. A heart that longed for peace had found peace.

From Julie von Dobschütz to Superintendent General Schwarzkoppen

Schloss Holkenäs, 14th October 1861

Reverend Father, you wished to hear about our friend whose death was the first news you had from here after taking up office in your old homeland. It is a pleasure for me to comply, for amid all the pain, it is always comforting and uplifting to be able to talk about the dear friend who has died.

On the day you last saw her, a thought was already ripening in her soul that she may have carried within her for some time. Perhaps you recall the elegiac, almost melancholy folksong which Elisabeth Petersen sang that evening – Christine left the room immediately afterwards, and I believe that from that moment her mind was made up. I found her deeply shaken, and I confess that fearful premonitions at once filled my heart, premonitions that I only managed to counter by reminding myself of our dear departed Christine's steadfast faith and Christian sentiments, the Christian sentiments that sustain life as long as God wills it.

The day that followed seemed to justify me in this confidence. Christine, as she told me, had not retired until a late hour, but her appearance bore no trace of lack of sleep, on the contrary, there was a freshness about her that I had not seen since the day of the renewed union. When she came down to breakfast she was more obliging and friendly than usual, almost cordial in her tone, and encouraged Holk to go out two days later on a shooting party to which he had just received an invitation from Count Baudissin. Then, oddly, they discussed matters of dress in quite some detail, only of course in respect of Asta, now turned seventeen and preparing to come out in society, at which words her eyes filled with tears.

The day passed in this fashion, and the sun was already low when she asked me to walk to the beach with her. 'But,' she added, 'we must hurry and be down there before it grows dark.'

Straight afterwards we went down the terrace. When we reached the bottom she decided against walking along the beach, the sand was so damp and her footwear so light, and so we went up on to the jetty, carrying on a conversation in which the Countess seemed intent on avoiding any at all serious subject. When we eventually reached the quay and the little flight of steps where the steamers berth, we sat down on a wooden bench which Holk has only recently had placed at this spot, and looked into the sun whose reflection on the virtually motionless sea was almost more beautiful than the colourful splendour of the clouds above it. 'How beautiful,' said Christine. 'Let's wait for the sunset here. It's turning chilly though, perhaps you could fetch our coats. But please, spare yourself the steps, just call up the terrace. Asta is sure to hear you.'

She said all this with a touch of embarrassment, because it was against her nature to say anything that was not true; but even if she hadn't shown this embarrassment, the whole thing would still have struck me as odd, because, with her almost excessive tenderness and kindness towards me, she was always anxious to avoid asking me to do little services for her. She could also see what direction my thoughts were taking, but I was unable to tell her outright what was troubling my mind, and so I went back along the jetty and up the terrace, for the business about 'calling up the terrace until Asta hears you' was not really meant.

When I came back to the end of the jetty, the Countess was nowhere to be seen, and I now knew what had happened. I hurried back to fetch help, although I was certain that all would be in vain. Holk seemed dazed and could not think what to do.

Finally, the village was alerted and they searched along the jetty and shore far into the night. Boats put out to sea and headed towards a sandbank, barely washed over by the waves, that lies diagonally across from the jetty. They searched for hours, but with no success, and it was only early the next morning that some Holkeby fishermen came up to the Schloss to report that they had found the Countess. We all then went down. The look of silent suffering that her face had worn for so long had given way to an expression of almost serene transfiguration, such had been her heart's need for peace. So as to avoid the climb up the terrace, a bier was fetched from the church, and she was borne through the dunes into the village, and then up the gentle slope of the drive through the park. Everyone crowded round, the poor people whom she had looked after lamented and bitter words were spoken which the Count did not hear, at least I hope not.

How the burial took place and how Petersen, as I myself can testify, was able on that day to satisfy the most orthodox of hearts, you will have read in the *Arnewiek Messenger*, which Baron Arne sent you, and perhaps in the *Flensburg News* too.

It only remains for me now to add a few things that may throw light on the Countess's state of mind and what made her take the ultimate step. Within the same hour that we had brought her up from the shore, we went to her room to see whether we might find a farewell message. In fact we found she had started letters to several people, which showed that she had been wanting to take leave of those closest to her, of Holk, Arne and of me as well. On the sheets addressed to Arne and myself there were phrases like 'with my thanks', and 'when you read these words', but it was all scored out again, and on the sheet starting 'Dear Holk' even they were missing. However, a crumpled and then carefully smoothed out piece of paper was folded together with the sheet intended for Holk, and on it was the song that Elisabeth Petersen sang just before Holk's departure for Copenhagen, when her singing, as with the folksong from the English I mentioned above, made such a profound impression on Christine. Reverend Father, you will certainly remember that song which we heard so recently, though the earlier one may well have escaped your memory, which is why, if I may, I will include the first verse here. It runs:

> The best in life is peace,
> Of Earth's enjoyments all;
> What lasts from that great feast?
> What never turns to gall?
> The rose that blooms soon fades,
> For all that Springtime laves,
> Pity him who hates,
> And almost more, who loves.

The last line was faintly, scarcely visibly underscored. A whole story lay in that shamefaced little marking.

Your office and your faith will give you the strength to face the death of your friend, but the dearest thing in my life has gone out of it, and what I am left with is poor and empty. Asta asks me to send you her greetings, as does Elisabeth Petersen.

Yours most sincerely
Julie von Dobschütz

Afterword

by HELEN CHAMBERS

Theodor Fontane's standing in Germany is comparable to Jane Austen's in the English-speaking world. He is supreme in dialogue, and his best work is an elegant and engaging blend of irony, penetration and compassion. His literary ancestors include Shakespeare, Scott and Heine; his writing often has a tragicomic edge and addresses the relationship between the old and the new. A distinctly modern sensibility to the challenges of reality in flux lies behind stories of human relationships which are at the same time readily recognizable and surprising.

Unwiederbringlich, written between 1887 and 1890, is the first novel that Fontane managed to place in the prestigious *Deutsche Rundschau* ('German Review'). It was serialized in the first half of 1891 and appeared in book form later that year. There were strongly favourable initial reactions. Fontane was particularly gratified by praise from the eminent Swiss writer Conrad Ferdinand Meyer, saying he had waited all his professional life for such appreciation of his artistry. The reviewer in the *Kölnische Zeitung* ('Cologne News') reported enthusiastically too on the novel's subtle delights: 'It is a quite delectable book, something of a literary Whitstable oyster', pointing up its refined brilliance, while recognizing that not all readers might have the discriminating palate to appreciate it fully, 'spearing it crudely like horsemeat', when it should be 'savoured as it slips over the tongue'. The review is worth quoting more extensively:

In this novel, as elsewhere in Fontane's works, we see the views of a mature connoisseur of life who does not moralize directly, nor launch complaints against the world order, but sees the most bitter disaster emerge from pardonable error, here and there indeed from the misguided application of good, a writer for whom good and evil are relative concepts and who recognizes as the worst evils of all the follies, weaknesses and mistakes that everyone is prone to and which bear within them the seed of catastrophe, but only to the extent that external conditions allow that seed to develop. But for all that, Fontane does not deal in pessimism, he does not paint grey on grey. 'Be wise, be on your guard!' that is what he says to us, shrugging his shoulders regretfully, as he tells the sad tale. He tells the story quietly, in a calm tone; it is seemingly unadorned, but his relaxed, flowing discourse is shot through with the fine points of the most delicate turns of phrase.[*]

Fontane is generally seen as the social chronicler of the life and times of Germany in the declining years of the Kaiserreich, and *No Way Back*, set in an earlier period, remains one of his lesser known works. It is now seen, however, as indisputably one of his greatest.

As with many of his narratives, the plot has its basis in fact. Prompted by reading Fontane's work, a Frau Brunnemann, a Privy Councillor's wife, sent him details of a case she knew of as a possible subject for literary treatment. In his novel Fontane retains the bare bones of the original situation which involved a triangular relationship at the Strelitz court in Mecklenburg in 1842. After many years of marriage, the good-natured, handsome Baron Karl von Maltzahn divorced his clever, pious and sickly wife because of his infatuation with a lady-in-waiting to the Grand Duchess. Rejected by the manipulative lady, who then made a brilliant marriage, he travelled in Europe. In 1851 there was a reconciliation between the couple who remarried in the spotlight of general rejoicing, but the Baroness became increasingly depressed and in 1855 took her own life, leaving a suicide note containing only one word – *Unwiederbringlich* ('Irretrievable'). Taking this as his title, Fontane transferred the story to Southern Schleswig and

---

[*] *Kölnische Zeitung*, 6 December 1891.

Denmark, setting it between 1859 and 1861. The transposition involved extensive research and careful groundwork, but allowed him to develop the symbolic texture of the narrative in relation to the sea and nature and the land and civilization, to play on 'Northern Romantic' associations and to structure it around shifts in location.

Reflecting on the purpose of the novel in general, Fontane's view was that it should tell us a story we believe in, making a fictional world momentarily seem real and leaving us with the impression that we have been living among real people – some of whom are kind and agreeable while others are interesting and full of character – and in whose company we have found pleasure and enlightenment.* A firmly realist project, focused on human psychology in a specific social context. *No Way Back* is one of a number of Fontane's novels which look at asymmetric and dysfunctional marriages. Marriages in crisis are often symptomatic of instabilities in society at large, and through the exploration of marital relations Fontane addresses two areas that remain central to his interest in the *comédie humaine*: the matter of contrasting personalities or perhaps more accurately attitudes, and whether such differences can be resolved; and secondly, the role of social pressures in determining relationships and behaviour. Gender relations within and outside marriage provided him with the ideal context for both. The use of contrasts in terms of character, origins, allegiances and affinities is at the heart of his work both thematically and structurally. He employs parallel and contrasting configurations to tease out and relativize individual stances, woven seamlessly into conversations that touch on paintings, poetry and historical anecdote. In order to provoke his readers into recognizing and acknowledging the existence of opposing positions, Fontane confronts them with the problem of resolution in narratives that suggest, without insisting, that acceptance, accommodation, resignation and not the eradication of difference may be the humane response. Seen on one level, Fontane's understated novels are about conflict management, but on another, by showing that any given character is not always on

---

* Review of Gustav Freytag's novel *Die Ahnen* ('The Ancestors'), *Vossische Zeitung*, 14 February 1875.

the same side of a particular opposition, the questionable validity of oppositional notions is revealed. Christine may be rational, unbending and hyper-articulate when it comes to running the house and criticizing her husband, but she is also emotional, unsure of herself and tongue-tied when it comes to dealing with her feelings.

Fontane's first social novel, *L'Adultera* (1880), which resolved a cultural and social misalliance by divorce and successful remarriage, was followed by *Cécile* (1886), *Irrungen, Wirrungen* (1887)*, and later *Effi Briest* (1895), where marriages of convenience spell psychological incompatibility and impose constraints on individual freedom. *No Way Back* (1891), by contrast, presents the anatomy of a marriage which has been a love match between social equals. Count and Countess Holk have been together for seventeen years, bringing up two well-adjusted children. In their forties, both are good-looking, well-liked in their local community, and supported by sympathetic friends and relatives. But already in the opening chapter a minor note is struck as we hear that Holk, against Christine's instincts, has built a new house, a neoclassical-style Schloss in the sand dunes, to replace the old crumbling ancestral building further inland. A jocular reference to its resemblance to the temple to Neptune at Paestum discreetly sounds a warning of sacrifice and irrational menace from the sea in an opening description that sets up a core opposition between land and sea, Schloss and water. The dichotomy of socialized habitation and the elemental domain is linked to Christine, predominantly associated with the house and social norms, and Holk and his Swedish mistress (of an hour) Ebba von Rosenberg, who are associated with water and instinctual desires.

The disintegration of the marriage is traced through the loss of the right tone between the partners, something that Fontane lets the reader hear in conversations and, after Holk departs to dance attendance on the Princess in Copenhagen and Frederiksborg, in letters. The narrative comments on the progressive loss of the right tone between them, most crucially in Holk's encounter with Christine in Chapter 29. Fontane shows how verbal communication

---

* English translation by Peter James Bowman entitled *On Tangled Paths* (Angel Classics, 2010).

can be eroded to such an extent over years by assumed familiarity with the partner's patterns of thought that the original closeness created by speech is replaced by unacknowledged mutual resentment and incomprehension, so that the scope for honest exchange is fatally undermined.* This is seen clearly in Christine's recourse to the preformulated words of poems and songs, culminating in the abortive suicide note in which her capacity for articulation of her feelings is reduced to the faint underlining of someone else's words. She has irrevocably lost her own voice, and so her self.

This is a novel about marriage and morality in which there is no straightforward moralizing. It has a steady forward dynamic. Though the central character is male, the range of strong and complex female figures tends to confirm Ebba's observation that 'the history of women is usually far more interesting.' The fundamental difference in outlook between the light-hearted, fun-loving Count Holk, an affable man of spontaneous, passing enthusiasms who enjoys life and avoids problems, and his serious and highly principled wife, whose cast of mind owes much to a strict religious upbringing in a boarding school run by the Moravian Brethren, may seem to indicate incompatibility, but as Christine observes, 'I think only the couples involved know what marriages are like, and sometimes even they don't know.' And when Holk seeks air, light, diversion and sensuality elsewhere, it is one of the ironies of the tale that he is in turn rejected for taking things too seriously, and is once more, as at home, subjected to mockery and sarcasm from a female tongue.

That the overall tone of the novel despite its tragic outcome remains remarkably bright over large stretches has to do with its narrative structure which affords the reader access to reality predominantly through the eyes of Holk whose cheerful egocentricity is tempered by moments of genuine concern and affection for his wife when she is there and absorption in the moment when she is not. Like Effi Briest, he is a charming, ebullient character, who slips into adulterous guilt without making a conscious choice. He is as surely seduced by the much younger Ebba as Effi will be in the later

---

* Alan Bance in *Theodor Fontane. The Major Novels* (Cambridge, 1982) sees *Unwiederbringlich* as a novel of marital crisis in middle age.

novel by the much older Major Crampas. As soon as he leaves home
in Holkenäs and crosses the water to Copenhagen, he is affected by
the urbane hedonism of the Danish capital, a new environment he
is ill-equipped to deal with.

More than half the novel is set at the Danish Princess's court,
facilitating Holk's gradual development to the point where adultery
and the breakdown of his marriage is possible. The court milieu
in Denmark represents a different set of values, an escape from
Christine's oppressive piety and strait-laced disapproval. Centring
on witty conversation, it affords the opportunity to reveal Holk's
character through his interaction with a range of individuals from
the maid Karin to the Princess. The excursions and visits leading
to discussions of Danish history and culture cast sidelights on
the personal situation in the present. Ironically, Holk who hoped
to escape from a demanding, mocking wife and the constrained,
monotonous life in an isolated coastal Schloss finds himself at court
in a not entirely dissimilar position. In Holkenäs where his more
intelligent wife ran the home and his brother-in-law the estate,
Holk seemed dispensable except as a decoration. His function
at the Danish court is also of second-order importance, dancing
attendance on a sickly old lady who does not rise till late in the day
and providing amusement for her lady-in-waiting. Fontane's close
knowledge of Danish dynastic history, fraught with tales of royal
mistresses, enriches the narrative.

No Way Back has the strongest undertow of sexuality of any
of Fontane's works, seen especially in Holk's encounters with his
landlady's alluring daughter. The description of Brigitte Hansen
as a Dutch beauty with gold ornaments in her hair is an echo of
Heinrich Heine's *Aus den Memoiren des Herren von Schnabelewopski*
('From the Memoirs of Herr Schnabelewopski'), written in the
1830s. In Heine's comic text we find not only the gold-plate
ornaments but numerous other elements of the later Copenhagen
scenario too. We are in a sea-washed land with beautiful daughters,
there's a landlady who teases erotically over tea drunk from fine
Chinese porcelain. When the elder Frau Hansen takes tea with
Holk, the cups are familiar signs, orientation in a disorientating
foreign environment. Brigitte carries the breakfast tray like a shield

before her shapely bosom, echoing the chivalric ironies of Heine's description of the landlady of the Red Cow Inn who is 'shielded by the Frisian gold plates' and 'enveloped in the armour of her damask skirts'. Heine describes her as a china doll, presenting token resistance to his advances. This is echoed in Fontane, indirectly, in Brigitte's posing and charade of stalwart respectability, and also in the descriptions of the courtiers Erichsen and Schimmelmann in the likeness of china ornaments, displaying a certain exotic artificiality.

There is a broader parallel here between the work of the German émigré in France and the novelist of French descent. In Heine's exuberant, explicit and earthy memoir which is packed with playful incongruities between higher and lower discourses, Schnabelewopski weighs up the relative merits of the cuisine and the female types in different countries, declaring in the end that it's all a matter of taste. *No Way Back*, in turn, finds Holk and Fontane contrasting types of women. Heine's frivolous exploration of the male response to female types underlies Fontane's more serious one. The scene in Chapter 15 with Brigitte serving Holk breakfast in his room involves outrageous, strongly sensual flirtation on his part, and although it is a far cry from Heine's comically exaggerated scenario, it nonetheless retains the quality of sensual immediacy and the dynamic of socialized sexuality.

This relaxed and playful scene, where Holk shows he is in control of the game of sexually charged manoeuvring, comes not long after his much tenser initial attempt at social intercourse with the attractive Ebba von Rosenberg. Here Ebba has been in control, while Holk's attempt to reach safe conversational ground by talking about her family name, since he is something of an amateur geneal- ogist, ends in the exposure of his snobbery. When Ebba dismisses his speculations about her links to Bohemian and Silesian nobility and tells him outright that she is the 'granddaughter of Meyer-Rosenberg, King Gustav III's favourite court Jew', Holk's discovery is a literary reprise of the last stanza of Heine's satirical poem 'Donna Clara'. Here the spoilt, beautiful, anti-Semitic daughter of Spanish nobility hears from the handsome knight she has chosen to dally with – to her he resembles St George – that contrary to her assumptions, he is 'the son of the great and widely praised scholar and Rabbi, Israel of Saragossa'. In both cases class assumptions have rendered the aristocrats incapable of recognizing or valuing otherness. Fontane uses the exchange to comment on Holk at some length, both critically, seeing him as 'a dyed-in-the-wool aristocrat', backward- and inward-looking, hidebound and elitist, and also to show that Holk judges the incident less on its substance than in terms of social form, that is, of how Ebba handled it. This can be read negatively as revealing a concern with form over substance, or more positively as illuminating one of the core concerns of the novel: in Alfred Arne's words to his sister Christine, 'It's not the viewpoint that matters; it's the way it's represented.'

The verse in *No Way Back* is highly significant in the narrative texture. Early on, Fontane uses two stanzas from Uhland's poem 'The Castle by the Sea' to encapsulate the temperamental difference between Holk and Christine. The Count knows the first verse only:

> Hast thou beheld the castle?
> The castle by the sea?
> Clouds of gold and crimson
> Glide over it silently.

His wife points out in a tone of long-suffering superiority that he does not know how the poem ends and quotes:

> The stormwinds and the waves
> In tranquil slumber slept;
> I heard within its chambers
> A funeral dirge, and wept.

This is actually the fifth of eight stanzas. The final stanza focuses on parental mourning for a dead child. In *No Way Back* the death of a child represents a traumatic loss from which the marriage never recovers. Christine is unable to let the child go, while Holk gets over the death with cheerful, relative indifference. Each finds the other's response inappropriately extreme. For the purposes of the surface of the novel, for the establishment of opposing positions, and the prefiguration of the end, Fontane uses fragments of existing poems which have intertextual links to the complete originals. Wilhelm Waiblinger's poem 'The Churchyard' is quoted in Chapters 6 and 34:

> The best in life is peace,
> Of Earth's enjoyments all;
> What lasts from that great feast?
> What never turns to gall?
> The rose that blooms soon fades,
> For all that Springtime laves,
> Pity him who hates,
> And almost more, who loves.

This is the first of eight stanzas. Fontane first read the poem when his young friend Bernhard von Lepel sent it to him from Italy in 1846. Its sentiments remained close to his heart and he cited its first line at intervals throughout his life.

The cemetery in question is the Cimitero acattòlica near the Cestius pyramid in Rome. The Swabian poet Waiblinger (1804–30) led a scandalous and latterly unchristian life – he left the Protestant church, spent the last years of his short life in Rome, and was buried in this cemetery where Keats and Shelley also lie. As far as the novel is concerned, apart from intensification and elaboration of the theme of longing for peace and release from the pain of love, the unquoted stanzas of the poem refer to pre-Christian, classical times. This links to the classical/romantic opposition embodied respectively in the architecture of Schloss Holkenäs and Schloss Frederiksborg. The return to classical harmony (such as Arne, the peace-maker, suggests in relation to the new Schloss, with its neoclassical design) is never open to Christine. However, it is perhaps also significant that the kind of death foreshadowed by the lyric I in Waiblinger's poem is not associated with orthodox Christianity: there is no direct mention of God, but of a quasi-religious framework linked to mythology, Elysium, nature, and fellow human beings. The emphasis in the poem as a whole is on solitude, pain, and the tentative hope of release from it. All these associations correspond to Christine's death, through her suicide also outside the framework of Christian orthodoxy, alone and seeking respite from pain in nature. Although Holk, when he hears the title of the poem, 'The Churchyard', rather snidely comments: so that's why it appeals – namely to Christine's morbid religiosity – the light, warmth and colour of Italy with which much of the poem is none-theless imbued finds its reflection in the description of Christine's sun-bathed funeral procession, and in the narrative perspective at the end of the novel which deliberately underplays potential morbidity.

Closer investigation of any of the historical figures mentioned or discussed in *No Way Back*, as well as references to and quota-tions from literary works and the visual arts, reveal hidden layers of meaning. When Holk in Chapter 6 tries to persuade Christine to accompany him to Copenhagen, he mentions among its attrac-tions for her its churches and the work of her favourite painter, Melbye. The context suggests religious paintings, but in fact Anton Melbye, like his brothers, is celebrated for marine subjects and the allusion links Christine to notions of freedom and escape into the wider world, more typically connected to Holk, or into the elemental realm of the sea, beyond the social and domestic milieu she inhabits. The comment on her taste in art conceals intimations of hidden desires and affinities. The historical allusions in the novel include a web of references to royal mistresses, and to the power of erotic desire and the role of sexual entanglement behind the scenes of public life. Christine Munk, positively portrayed as 'one of the most good-humoured but also one of the tenderest of women', subsequently left Christian IV for another man, a fact Pastor Schleppegrell chooses not to report. Christian VII, whose portrait Holk contemplates in the Princess's audience chamber as an image of the establishment, led a life marked by susceptibility to fashion and the influence of others, by debauchery, mental instability and court intrigue; he divorced his neglected wife amid recriminations over infidelity. Ebba Brahe (1596–1674), who provided Fontane with the given name for one of his central characters, was, like the latter, a Swedish royal favourite – in her case of King Gustavus

Adolphus II; she later married a general, details which tie in with the novel's concern with legitimacy. The surface bloom of the novel is bedded on rich layers of loam from which the meaning grows, in an organic and wholly integrated way. The reader does not need to be aware of all this to follow the novel, but the degree of infusion of the text with extra-textual material is remarkable.

Like all Fontane's mature works, *No Way Back* raises questions about whether things could have turned out differently, was there perhaps another way? The title in this case precludes this, but that is very much one character's view, Christine's. She acknowledges herself, 'Guilt is everywhere, and perhaps mine is the greater.' Why does Holk misjudge Ebba's feelings and intentions so disastrously? The answer comes, perhaps, in their final confrontation in Chapter 30. Ebba's harsh initial judgement is borne out: 'He's vague and half-hearted, and that half-heartedness will get him into trouble one day.' But it is not only Holk who is subject to the influence of the moment. Fontane repeatedly shows sudden shifts in mood in other characters too. Our control over impulse and circumstance is limited, and well-intentioned human beings can readily take the wrong path and have to make the best of the consequences. There is nothing black and white about this story. Ebba, who might in some ways be seen as the destructive principle – the way she is connected to the elements of fire and water suggest this – is a high-spirited, attractive and intelligent woman who clearly often has the author's sympathy, not least in Chapter 22, where she articulates views close to the heart of her creator. She highlights the importance of women's history as opposed to masculine narratives of battles and action and asserts that 'Grand style means bypassing everything that actually interests people'. In practical terms, she simply follows the line that a girl has to look after herself.

Fontane was an admirer of Thackeray's *Vanity Fair*, a novel with which *No Way Back* has family resemblances. It shares Thackeray's ambiguities of judgement, and in Ebba it presents a figure of a type similar to Becky Sharp, a charming, heartless adventurer, who sees through and manipulates other characters and often mediates the author's perspective. *No Way Back* has been seen as a sister novel of disillusionment to Flaubert's *Madame Bovary*, and Fontane's distanced, unsentimental and seamlessly crafted style does indeed have much in common with Flaubert's literary technique, though the French novelist, for all the ostensible neutrality of his narrator, is less tolerant of his characters' weaknesses and exposes them to a more glaring spotlight. Fontane was writing at the end of a century and as a latecomer to the tradition of the European realist novel, and his novel also partakes of the concerns of the new age. Holk can be seen as embodying a crisis of masculinity, while the prevalence of (nervous) illness in the female characters – Christine, the Princess and Ebba are all affected – is a common trope of fin de siècle decadence. A concern with gender and sexuality lies only just below the surface in Fontane's novel which appeared in the same year as Frank Wedekind's *Spring Awakening*, and whose heroine's problems have been read as Freudian repression. The reviewer in the *Kölnische Zeitung* highlights Fontane's modernity and observes sarcastically that at a time when Ibsen is being worshipped by German youth, Fontane is being dismissed as no more than a witty old buffer. A Berlin production of Ibsen's *The Lady from the Sea* was reviewed by Fontane in 1889, as he was completing the manuscript of the novel, and his main criticism of Ibsen, whom he admired, is that the play is too programmatic, not psychologically plausible in its insistence on an unconvincing notion of free will. This is not a trap that Fontane falls into as he portrays the psychological depth and complexity of his figures and their relationships.

Fontane is one of the great literary masters of conversation. The film director Michael Haneke turned to him as a model when he was preparing the film *The White Ribbon* (2009), set in a pre-1914 north German village. The conversations enacting Holk and Christine's deteriorating relationship anticipate the tragicomic tenor of the dialogue in canonical twentieth-century American domestic dramas, such as Tennessee Williams' *The Glass Menagerie* or Edward Albee's *Who's Afraid of Virginia Woolf*. There is no direct connection between these playwrights and Fontane, but Samuel Beckett, on the other hand, knew his Fontane well. His play *Krapp's Last Tape* not only makes clear reference to *Effi Briest*, but there is surely also an echo of *No Way Back*. Like the novel, *Krapp's Last Tape* is a text about the irretrievable past, here ironically preserved on tape recordings of the ancient and isolated figure Krapp. Its final words are 'Perhaps my best years are gone … No, I wouldn't want them back.' These hold the sting of the same disillusioned, modern sensibility that we find already adumbrated in the figure of Christine in *No Way Back* and articulated in similar words in the last lines of the folksong that move her and isolate her from the company in the penultimate chapter of the book: 'But my happiest days of all, John,/ I wouldn't wish them back.'

This novel displays a fresh and unconventional treatment of familiar themes. Marital infidelity here is the product of boredom and irritation rather than of grand passion. The remarriage would be far from a happy ending even without the heroine's suicide, which is relatively underplayed. In the course of the narrative, sympathy is subtly shifted around a cast of characters who are individually appealing but in the main, without intending it, make wrong moves and cause each other pain. The changing settings of the novel are a masterstroke. Each is deftly individualized, invested with a strong sense of place and times past. As each location in turn becomes stifling or otherwise uninhabitable for the protagonists, whether Holk or Christine, the plot moves on, progressively shutting down options. Taking a biographical view of the novel, one could say that Fontane has chosen to reflect the intractable incompatibility of his charming feckless father and his strict and disapproving mother while also, as he wrote the first draft, coming to terms with the death of his eldest son. It is a novel that speaks humanely of human problems of family and death. At the same time, through its Scandinavian maritime topography it is a novel with wide horizons. The seascapes of old battles, accounts of sea-crossings to and from Denmark and Sweden, to Baltic islands and latterly to Italy and England, voyages to Greenland, America, China and Siam determine the texture of this restless narrative. It finally comes to rest, provisionally at least, on a greeting from the young friends Asta and Elisabeth, the new generation who will succeed Christine. This is Fontane's characteristic forward-looking refusal to close the gaps and resolve life's ambiguities.

Translators' Note

The first translation of *Unwiederbringlich*, uniquely for Fontane, was into Russian, in the year of original publication, 1891; it was serialized in a St Petersburg journal under the title *Bez vozvrata* ('No Return'). The explanation lies in the keen Russian interest in Denmark at that time; Tsar Alexander III's wife was a former Danish Princess, Dagmar, daughter of Christian IX (on marrying in 1866 she converted to Russian Orthodoxy, changing her name to Maria Fyodorovna). A Danish translation followed in 1894, entitled *Grevinde Holk* ('Countess Holk'). The publication of this edition led Fontane to comment regretfully, 'My dear Englishmen, for whom I have done so much, still persist in leaving me in the lurch.'* He was referring to his many translations of English poetry and ballads, his original works on English and Scottish themes,† and the numerous references to English history, literature and commerce in his works – to the point, as the reader of this novel will have seen, of using English words and phrases in his fiction. An English translation of *Unwiederbringlich* was not to come until 1964, Douglas Parmée's version entitled *Beyond Recall*, published by Oxford University Press in the World's Classics series – the first complete English translation of any of Fontane's novels. Fontane was still left somewhat in the lurch, however, since Parmée did

---

* Letter to Wilhelm Hertz, 11 December 1894.
† These include *Ein Sommer in London* (1854), a collection of articles on London, and his fascinating and amusing 1858 Scottish travelogue, *Jenseit des Tweed* (English translation by Brian Battershaw, *Beyond the Tweed*, 1998, distributed by Angel Classics). There is also a translation of his reviews of London Shakespeare productions: Theodor Fontane, *Shakespeare in the London Theatre 1855–58*, translated and edited by Russell Jackson (London: Society of Theatre Research, 1999).

not see fit to translate the poems which are of signal importance for the novel, leaving them in German with prose translations in footnotes. A decade or so after Parmée, the first translations of *Unwiederbringlich* into other languages appeared, beginning with Romanian, Italian, French and Hungarian.

It has been the aim of the present translators to produce a version that conveys as much as possible of the force, freshness and subtlety of the original and remedies a range of deficits in the earlier translation. We have paid particular attention to descriptions of location and movement through space. The pioneering earlier version tended to lose the sense of movement, spatial relationships and dynamism of the original through an overall urbanity of style. It also displayed a general looseness with tense which undermined the pace and impact of the original, and there were a number of inaccuracies (French, not German, was the translator's specialist language), including social forms of address. These blemishes all matter; in Fontane's work precise spatial relationships and descriptions of location and indications of social status are always crucial, not least in this novel where they frequently carry symbolic significance.

A crucial passage in Chapter 19, for example, a description of Frederiksborg as the Princess and her entourage approach via the market square, is imbued in the original with a sense of Northern romantic mystery and of anticipation of events to come. It also signals the – as it will prove – dangerously close proximity of prosaic reality to the alluring appearance of fairytale romance. The earlier translation, by dropping two references to the view and visibility, loses the impact of the original's revelation in stages towards the full sight of the castle as Holk and Ebba see it for the first time. It also changes the spatial configuration of Fontane's description, which draws the eye down from a patch of high blue sky to the castle standing in the midst of a sunset – a glowing vision illuminated by changing light, whereas the climactic point of Parmée's version, 'against this glow were silhouetted the lofty towers of the castle of Frederiksborg', offers a more limited image of the castle as a two-dimensional dark shape against the sky. Finally in this passage, Fontane has the important detail of the small lake with its reflection of Frederiksborg 'entirely filling the narrow space between the little town and the castle'. Holk's problems derive in part from his inability to choose or indeed adequately distinguish between the poetic and the prosaic, between romantic notions and the exigencies of everyday reality, and the symbolic detail in descriptive passages such as that mentioned here is significant in conveying this. Translating the fine grain of a Fontane text, retaining its balance and careful nuances, is a constant challenge.

The text we have used is contained in Theodor Fontane, *Werke, Schriften und Briefe*, I, vol. 2, edited by Helmuth Nürnberger (Munich: Carl Hanser, 1971); other editions of *Unwiederbringlich* were consulted.

H.R. and H.C.

Historical Persons, Places and Events
Mentioned in *No Way Back**

Adalbert of Prague. Archbishop (956–97); murdered on a Christian mission to convert the Prussians.

Albrecht, Archduke of Austria, Duke of Teschen (1817–95). Austrian general, apparently confused in Chapter 3 with Archduke Ferdinand Maximilian (1832–67). Before he was briefly and disastrously Emperor of Mexico, Archduke Ferdinand began to develop Austrian seapower and to build the battle fleet with which Admiral Tegetthoff was to secure his victories. He was a keen scientific explorer (see also *Tegetthoff*).

Alhambra. Pleasure gardens in outlying Copenhagen.

Anckarström, Jakob Johan von. See *Gustav III*.

Atkinson, Miss. Actress seen by Fontane at the Sadler's Wells Theatre in the roles of Volumnia, Portia, Lady Macbeth and Ophelia.

Bagge, Jakob (1502–77). Swedish admiral, captured by the Danes at the Battle of Öland, 30 May 1864, in which the *Makalös* ('Matchless'), the largest warship in the Baltic, was destroyed. Fontane calls this ship the *Makellos* ('Immaculate').

Basedow, Johann Bernhard (1724–90). German educational reformer who propagated Enlightenment ideas.

Berling, Carl (1812–71). See *Danner, Baroness*.

Bernstorff. Aristocratic family from Mecklenburg. Fontane was personally acquainted with Count Albrecht von Bernstorff (1809–73), Prussian envoy in London in the 1850s, later minister of foreign affairs. Christian Günther Bernstorff was born in 1769 in Copenhagen and, like his father, served his country in Denmark.

Blixen-Fineke, Carl Frederik Axel von (1822–73). Minister of foreign affairs and minister for Schleswig in Rotwitt's cabinet, 1859–60. Married to a cousin of King Frederick VII.

---

* Further to information given in the footnotes.

'*Brave Little Tin Soldier, The*'. Tale by Hans Christian Andersen.

Bülow, Frederik Henrik von (1791–1858). Danish general, instrumental in lifting the siege of Fredericia (q.v.) on 6 July 1849.

Bunzlau. Town in Lower Silesia in the former Prussian administrative district of Liegnitz (Legnica), now Bolesławiec, Poland. The Moravian Brethren (Herrnhuter) settlement of Gnadenberg was nearby.

Christian IV (1577–1648). King of Denmark and Norway from 1588; an ambitious monarch, founder of the Danish navy, who for all his reverses won the lasting affection of his people.

Christian VII (1749–1808). King of Denmark and Norway from 1766. Married his cousin Caroline Matilda, sister of George III of Great Britain. He fell into debauchery and later mental illness, becoming unfit to rule by 1772 and remaining king in name only while his stepmother Juliane of Brunswick-Wolfenbüttel and her son took control until 1784 when a palace revolution effected the regency of his son Frederick VI.

Coligny, Gaspard de (1519–72). French admiral, converted to Calvinism in 1559. As leader of the Protestant Huguenots he was murdered in the Massacre of St Bartholomew.

Congress of Vienna. The nine-month congress (1814–15) that settled the shape of Europe after the Napoleonic Wars was a famously leisurely affair.

Cornelius, Peter (1783–1867). Painter of the Nazarene School. He was commissioned by Friedrich Wilhelm IV of Prussia to produce frescoes for a royal cemetery, but the plan was abandoned because of revolutionary disruption in 1848 and the king's subsequent terminal illness. Cornelius's cartoons for the project, exhibited in Berlin in 1859, bore witness to an outmoded classical idealism and found neither public nor official favour.

'*Dance of Death*'. Famous painting dating from 1463 which hung in the Church of Mary in Lübeck. It was destroyed in the Second World War.

Danebod, Thyra. Wife of King Gorm the Old (c.910–c.958, q.v.), traditionally regarded as the first king of Denmark. She is said to have been responsible for the building of the Dannevirke, a defensive earthwork in the south of the country.

Danner, Baroness (1815–74). Referred to in *No Way Back* as Countess Danner: Christine Louise Rasmussen, formerly a governess and dancer, and mistress to the king's private secretary Carl Berling, who helped her set up a hat shop (1844–47). Berling passed her on to the king, his boyhood friend. In 1848 she received the title of Baroness, and in 1850 her morganatic marriage to Frederick VII took place. She was avoided by the royal family and on the king's death retired to live in luxury in Cannes.

de Meza, Christian Julius (1792–1865). Danish general who played a key role in the Danish victory at Idstedt/Isted (1850, q.v.), after which he was a national hero until his controversial dismissal as commander of the Danish forces in the German-Danish War of 1864 (he was later exonerated).

Dronningens Tværgade. Literally 'Queen's Cross-street', a street in Copenhagen near the royal palaces and the harbour.

Du Barry. Jeanne Bécu, Comtesse du Barry (1743–93), mistress of Louis XV of France from 1769 (succeeding Madame de Pompadour), like Danner was previously a milliner.

Du Plat, Peter Henrik Claude (1809–64). Danish officer; as a major-general he fell at Dybbøl (Düppel) in the Schleswig War of 1848–50.

Dyveke ('Little Dove'). Dutch mistress of Christian II of Denmark (1481–1559). Her mother accompanied her to Denmark where the king's anti-nobility policies were attributed to the influence of these two commoners. An aristocrat whose hand she had refused was accused of causing her death by poison and executed. The story was the subject of numerous literary works including a novel in the style of Walter Scott by August von Tromlitz (1773–1839), which Fontane was reading in 1885.

Elisabeth, Saint (1207–31). Landgravine Elisabeth of Thuringia, also known as Elisabeth of Hungary, known for her piety and good works. The subject of numerous legends, she was canonized four years after her death.

English fleet ... on its way to Russia. During the Crimean War (1853–56) a Western allied fleet operated in the Baltic, undertaking an expedition in 1854 to blockade Russian ports.

Eric XIV. King of Sweden, 1560–68, a gifted musician and artist; married his mistress Karin Månsdotter. He was deposed in 1568 because of mental illness and died in prison, poisoned on his brother's orders.

Erik the Red (c.950–c.1007). A Norwegian banished from Iceland; he landed on Greenland first in 983, taking other settlers there a few years later. His son Leif sailed c.1000 to Labrador, and from then until the twelfth century sailors from Greenland and Iceland made crossings to North America.

Faaborg (1814–64). Danish lieutenant-colonel who fell in the German-Danish War of 1864.

'Farmers' Ministry'. The 'Farmers' Friends', a political group to the left of the national liberals who were briefly in government in Denmark from December 1859 to February 1860.

Ferdinand, Prince Frederik (1792–1863). From 1848 Hereditary Prince of Denmark, uncle of Frederick VII, whom he predeceased.

Fredensborg. A Danish royal castle built between 1719 and 1724, in north Italian style, by Johan Cornelius Krieger.

Fredericia. Location of a battle in the Schleswig War of 1848–50; a Danish victory.

Frederick VII (1808–63). King of Denmark, 1848–63.

Frederiksborg. From 1560 a Danish royal castle. Situated outside the town of Hillerød north of Copenhagen. The main building complex was completed in 1625 by Christian IV. It was a frequent residence of Frederick VII who installed his archaeological collection there; restored after the fire on 16/17 December 1859 and later turned into a museum.

Friedrich Wilhelm IV. King of Prussia, 1840–61, but replaced as ruler in 1857 owing to ill health by his younger brother (later Wilhelm I) as regent.

Glücksburg. Former seat of the Dukes of Holstein-Sonderburg-Glücksburg, from 1779 in Danish hands. Frederick VII died there in 1863.

Gnadau. A community of the Protestant, Pietist Moravian Brethren; founded in 1767 in the Prussian administrative district of Magdeburg.

Gnadenfrei. A Moravian Brethren community founded in Silesia in 1742. The Brethren set up their own educational establishments.

Gorbersdorf. Health resort in Lower Silesia, now Sokolowsko, Poland, sometimes known as the 'Davos of Silesia'.

Gorm the Old. The first internationally recognized king of Denmark, reigning from c.936 to c.958; father of Harald Bluetooth (q.v.).

Gøye, Brigitte (1511–74). Wife of the Danish naval hero Herluf Trolle, renowned for her piety and good works.

Groth, Klaus (1819–99). Low German dialect poet; attacked Fritz Reuter in 1858 for his allegedly coarse style of writing in Plattdeutsch.

Grundtvig, Nikolai Frederik Severin (1783–1872). Influential Danish theologian, historian, pastor and poet with an anti-rationalist outlook. He strove for a vibrant Christianity with priority given to the 'living word' and maximal independence of local congregations.

Gustav III. King of Sweden, 1771–92. Assassinated by Jakob Johan von Anckarström at a masked ball at the Stockholm Opera. Verdi's opera *The Masked Ball* is based on this incident.

Hall, Carl Christian (1812–88). Leader of the national liberals and the Eider Danes who sought to incorporate Schleswig into Denmark up to the River Eider. He was in power as minister president from 1857 to 1863, with a brief interruption in 1859–60. Hall had strong disagreements with the king, including that over Baroness Danner.

Halle. German university town which Christine prefers to Jena because of the influence in Halle of August Hermann Francke (1663–1727), one of the fathers of Pietism. The reputation of the University of Jena rests rather on the philosophers Fichte, Schelling and Hegel.

Harald Bluetooth. King of Denmark, c.958–85. Son of Gorm the Old. His reign saw Denmark's conversion to Christianity.

Heath, Miss. Actress seen by Fontane playing Anne Boleyn in Shakespeare's *Henry VIII* at the Princess's Theatre.

Hermitage, The. Grand hunting lodge with a large deer park near Klampenborg.

Humboldt, Alexander von (1769–1859). Naturalist and explorer.

Humboldt, Wilhelm von (1767–1835). Statesman, scholar of linguistics, history and philosophy, founder of the University of Berlin.

Husum. Home town of the writer Theodor Storm, on the west coast of Schleswig.

Hveen. Swedish island in the Sound of Øre, Danish until 1658. The island was given to the astronomer Tycho Brahe by Frederick II in 1576. The castle Uraniborg, with its observatory, was built there for Brahe's ground-breaking work on the planetary system. In 1597, however, he lost his patronage and was forced to leave Denmark.

Idstedt (Isted). Scene of an important Danish victory in the Schleswig War of 1848–50. The battle, in which the Danish general de Meza played a key part, was in its time the largest military encounter in Scandinavian history.

Jean Paul. Pseudonym of the German writer Johann Paul Friedrich Richter (1763–1825), influenced by Laurence Sterne and more concerned to represent inner developments in the soul than with outer action.

Jena. See *Halle*.

Josephina, Queen (1807–76). Wife of King Oscar I of Sweden and Norway (reigned 1844–59). Born Joséphine Maximilienne Eugénie Napoléone, daughter of Eugène de Beauharnais and granddaughter of the Empress Joséphine.

July Revolution. Uprising against Charles X of France, 27–29 July 1830.

Kean, Charles John (1811–68). Actor and manager of the Princess's Theatre, 1851–59, son of the great tragic actor Edmund Kean. Between 1855 and 1857 Fontane published a series of nine essays on productions he saw in London at the Princess's, Soho and Sadler's Wells Theatres.

'King of Thule, The'. Famous ballad by Goethe about a king whose dying mistress gives him a goblet symbolizing their love and his fidelity beyond the grave.

Klampenborg. Seaside resort north of Copenhagen.

Klopstock, Meta (1728–58). Wife of the German poet Friedrich Gottlieb Klopstock who was buried beside her in 1803.

Kongens Nytorv. Literally 'King's New Square', a large, elegant square in Copenhagen.

Krake, Rolf. Legendary Viking king, also the name of a Danish battleship which played a prominent role at Dybbøl in the German-Danish War of 1864.

La Rochelle. French port on the Atlantic, Huguenot stronghold from 1570. Fontane's forebears were among the Huguenots who emigrated to Prussia to avoid persecution after the Revocation of the Edict of Nantes in 1685.

Lille-Grimsby. Place-name invented by Fontane by analogy with Great Grimsby on the Humber Estuary.

Louis Napoleon (1808–73). Emperor of France as Napoleon III (1852–70). He was the object of Italian assassination attempts in 1855 and 1858.

Lundbye, Sigvart Urne Rosenvinge (1820–64). Danish officer; fell in close combat at Dybbøl in the German-Danish War of 1864.

Magenta. Village in Lombardy where France and Sardinia defeated Austria on 4 June 1859.

Malchin. Town in Mecklenburg.

Marson, Are. Icelandic chieftain who sailed from Greenland to Labrador c.980–1000.

Marstrand, Wilhelm (1810–73). Danish historical painter, who painted two great murals in the chapel in Roskilde Cathedral where Christian IV is buried.

Melbye, Anton (1818–75). Danish painter of marine subjects.

Moltke. Originally a Mecklenburg aristocratic family; from 1750 Danish counts. Adam Wilhelm von Moltke (1785–1864) was leader of the Danish cabinet in 1848 and president of the imperial council in 1854.

Møn: Island in south-eastern Denmark.

Monrad, Ditlev Gothard (1811–87). Danish bishop of Laaland Falster, minister of culture, 1859–63, then minister president; resigned 1864.

Munk, Christine (1598–1658). Mistress of Christian IV, with whom he had a morganatic marriage (1615–29). She left him for another man and departed from Frederiksborg in 1630. The stone mentioned in Chapter 22 is still in place.

Oehlenschläger, Adam Gottlob (1779–1850). Acknowledged from his lifetime as the Danish national poet; internationally known for his lyric poetry and ballads.

Olaf Cross. Ancient gold cross with the inscription 'Olaf' found in 1849 on the island of Ourø.

Ottensen. Formerly a village near Altona, now part of Hamburg.

Rachel, Élisa. Elisabeth Rachel Félix (1821–58): French actress who relaunched public taste for classical tragedy.

Ragnar Lodbrok. Legendary king of the Normans, who ruled in the Baltic coastal regions c.850. His name means 'rough trousers'. He met his death when he was cast into a snake pit by King Ælla of Northumbria.

Rainville's. High-class restaurant with a garden on the Elbe, in business from 1799 to 1867.

Rantzau. Well known aristocratic family from Holstein, dating back to the eleventh century, with numerous branches in Germany and Denmark.

Rassmussen, Frau. See *Danner, Baroness.*

Reuter, Fritz (1810–74). Low German dialect writer and poet; rebuffed Klaus Groth's critical attacks in 1864, defending his use of language.

Roeskilde (today Roskilde). Town in Zealand, seat of the Danish monarchy and a bishopric from the fifth to the tenth century.

Rönnow, Joachim (c.1495–1544). Diplomat and chancellor, appointed bishop in 1529 by the king and cathedral chapter but not recognized by the pope. With the advent of the Reformation in Denmark in 1536 he was imprisoned by Christian III.

Rottwitt, Carl Eduard (1812–60), leader of the 'Farmers' Friends.' See *'Farmers' Ministry'*.

Rud, Otto (1520–65). Succeeded Herluf Trolle as commander of the Danish fleet; died in Swedish captivity.

Scheele, Ludvig Nicolaus von (1796–1874): From 1854 Danish minister for foreign affairs and for Holstein and Lauenburg.

Schnepfental. Non-confessional boys' school founded by philanthropist Christian Gotthilf Salzmann (1744–1811).

Semnoni. Germanic tribe, originally from between the Elbe and the Oder.

Snorri Sturluson (1179–1241). Icelandic poet, historian and collector of Old Norse sagas and poems; the major source for knowledge of Norse mythology and Old Norse poetry.

Sorel, Agnes (c.1422–50). Mistress of Charles VII of France.

Streit's Hotel. The best hotel in Hamburg at the time depicted.

Süderbrarup. Archaeological site of major excavations during Frederick VII's reign. The king's collection of Bronze and Iron Age finds was largely destroyed in the 1859 fire at Frederiksborg.

Tavistock Square. Square in Bloomsbury, London, where Charles Dickens lived for a time. Fontane lodged there in 1852 but lacked the self-confidence to visit the celebrated novelist.

Tegetthoff, Admiral Wilhelm von (1827–71). Austrian admiral. In 1859, while still of junior rank, he accompanied Archduke Ferdinand Maximilian of Austria (see *Albrecht, Archduke of Austria*) on a botanical expedition to Brazil; he distinguished himself in the German-Danish War of 1864 and as commander of the Austrian navy defeated the Italian fleet at Lissa in 1866.

Tersling, Cornelius Georg (1812–98). Major in 1859, Lieutenant-Colonel, commander of the 9th Danish Regiment, in 1864.

Thomsen, Christian Jürgensen (1788–1865). Archaeologist, director of the Old Norse Museum, Copenhagen.

Thompsen-Oldensworth, Adolf Theodor (1814–91). Schleswig-Holstein politician with German sympathies.

Thorvaldsen, Bertel (1768 or 1770–1844). Famous Danish sculptor. He made a statue of Hope for the von Humboldt family grave at Schloss Tegel near Berlin.

Thott. Probably Baron Otto Reedtz-Thott (1785–1862), gentleman-in-waiting at the Danish court.

Thuringia, Landgrave of. Wilhelm von Hessen-Kassel, married to Louise Charlotte, sister of King Christian VIII of Denmark, 1839-48. Their daughter Louise was married to Prince Christian of Glücksburg, later King Christian IX (reigned 1863-1906).

Tivoli Theatre. Open-air theatre for *commedia dell'arte*-style pantomime in the celebrated pleasure gardens in Copenhagen.

Trolle, Herluf (1516–65). Danish admiral and statesman, commander of the fleet victorious over the Swedes at Öland in 1564 in the costly and inconclusive Nordic Seven Years' War (1563–70) in which Sweden fought against Denmark, Lübeck and the Polish-Lithuanian Commonwealth.

Uhland, Ludwig (1787–1862). German late Romantic poet, author of internationally celebrated ballads. Longfellow translated 'The Castle by the Sea' and 'The Luck of Edenhall'; Mrs Gaskell chose a stanza from another poem as an epigraph to her first novel, *Mary Barton* (1848).

Uhlenhorst. District of Hamburg much visited in the mid-nineteenth century because of its picturesque situation on the Outer Alster.

Valdemar the Conqueror. Valdemar II (1170–1241), under whose leadership the Danes conquered many lands on the Baltic, subjecting North Germans to Danish rule.

Vasa, House of. Royal House of Sweden from 1523 to 1654.

Vincent's. Well-known Copenhagen restaurant at 5 Kongens Nytorv; succeeded by the high-class Hôtel d'Angleterre. Fontane stayed there in 1864.

Waiblinger, Wilhelm Friedrich (1804–30). Swabian poet influenced by Hölderlin, whom he befriended when the latter was mentally ill. Fontane changes the third and fourth lines of the stanza quoted from the poem 'The Churchyard' at the end of chapter 6 and again at the end of the novel, removing the extremism of the sentiment.

War in Italy. In 1859 Austria fought against France allied with Sardinia. Austria's defeat helped prepare the ground for the unification of Italy.

Worsaae, Jens Jacob Asmussen (1821–85). Danish archaeologist and Inspector of Monuments.

Wrangel. Aristocratic family with its origins in Estonia, of particular importance in Swedish history. Karl Gustav, Count Wrangel (1613–76) was a noted Swedish commander in the Thirty Years' War; one of the principal characters in Schiller's play *Wallensteins Tod* (*The Death of Wallenstein*).